The Lunar Saga of Samhain

Written by Azhorg

edited and promoted by: TeaTime

Art by swishgirl

Chapter 1: The Draugr Burial Mound. (Southern Ulster province)

**"Who is that shrill one,
who rides a hard road,
has fared that way before.
He kisses hard
who has two mouths
and goes only on gold?
Heidrek King,
think on that." (Riddle of Odin)**

Connacht was knee deep in the peat bog and already the Draugr (some describe them as undead norsemen) were crawling from their burial mound in swarms. Connacht had to dodge yet another clumsy swing of a battle ax from these rotting bastards. Thankfully his thick armored long-coat, known as a Brigantine Coat, provided good protection, a combination of a thick leather jacket, wool gambeson, chain-mail, and segmented plates that were sewed all together in a flexible yet durable coat.

Connacht was a middle aged man, strong, tall and fierce but having grown somewhat portly from excessive drinking and feasting over the years. He had a wild beard and mane of Auburn-red and gray hair but wore a tall, pointed, iron helmet which deflected many of the draugrs' axe strikes. . He was a handsome man, high cheekbones, full round face that had an easy smile and brown eyes tinged with green though life was hard and he had a few missing teeth from brawls and battles.

For Connacht was an elite mercenary warrior called a Gallowgalas, a seasoned veteran of many wars, battles and skirmishes who could afford heavy armor and great steel weapons in service to the Clan Lords of the isles of Samhain. He was also honor-bound as a Gallowgalas of Clan Gunnar to clear out these cursed burial mounds of his ancestors… the Draugr!

The Gallowgalas rolled with his shoulders to deflect another axe blow from one of those undead bastards. The draugr that swung at him was tall, muscular and somewhat lanky. It's axe was rusted but heavy, almost like a large hog-splitter cleaver, it could easily split his helmet in half if it struck the helmet at the right spot with enough force. Our Warrior, deflected another overhead attack with his great sword, he caught the handle of the axe with the parrying hooks on his sword and then twisted the axe to his left side and then counter-attacked by smashing the crossguard of the sword right into the Draugr's mouth, it's teeth exploded with black gore from it's face. The undead norse was stunned.. for just a few seconds to give Connacht the opening he needed!

Connacht swiftly recovered from using the defensive half-swording technique to the offensive Strike-of-Wrath stance, he shifted his left hand back onto the handle of the sword from the upper riccaso and swung his blade up in the air high and then brought it crashing down, chopping right through the shoulder of the Draugr and splitting it in half. The Great Blade made a dull chopping noise like a cleaver to a ham hock accompanied by the sound of ribs and vertebrae popping from getting split in half by the full force of the sword. The Black blood exploded out of it's back and half of it's body came crashing to the ground with a heavy thud.

Connacht then kicked the rest of the monstrosity right in the gut and it crashed into the peat bog's rancid waters with a thud... rotting organs and black blood spilling everywhere! hah! Even that didn't kill the undead terror as it slowly began to pull itself back up!

“Damnation! These undead are tough! I heard tales that these Nordic walking dead has to be hacked to pieces and then burned in a fire to put them to true death!” Snarled Connacht as he deflected another axe strike, using a half swording technique with his Great-sword (known locally as a Claymore) and catching the axe’s handle on the sword’s parrying-hooks from another attacking Draugr (“parrying-hooks” effectively are a smaller set of cross-guards located above both the larger cross-guard and the secondary leather handle known as a Ricasso, this unique design allowed the blade to be used like a quarterstaff when fighting defensively and easily catch and deflect the weapons of the wielder's enemies mid-strike.). He swiftly retaliated with a sweeping slash that chopped off the terror's arm and the blade crashed into its stubborn spine with a sickening crunch.

“By Crom's hairy balls! You have fought these abominations before? That must describe the large scar across your skull!” laughed Lachlann, Connacht's nephew and his squire (called a Kern in the local tongue) serving under Connacht's tutelage. Lachlann was a Kern, a young man and nephew of Connacht, he also had curly auburn hair, green eyes like Connacht, he was tall and lithe of build, almost as tall as his mentor.

"Back! Back you bastard! I hack at thee!" Lachlann caught a broad-ax right into his shield, the axe bit deep and splinters exploded out of the shield as they showered everyone nearby. He then swiftly counter-attacked with his broad sword by hacking the Draugr's axe-handle directly in half, the axe's head still lodged deep into his shield.

Lachlan swiftly retaliated by driving his arming sword right through the draugr's eye with a sickening schlorp! The blade exploded out the back of it's skull, ebony gore burst out, ripping a jagged hole through the monster's iron helmet... This temporarily paralyzed it. Lachlann then swiftly followed with a decapitating strike, cutting the Damned's head right off...this still didn't kill the creature but now it wandered around almost comically swinging it's axe with a frenzy. Lachlann swiftly jumped behind the headless creature and kicked it square in the back... sending it right in the direction of it's kindred, wildly hacking at them as they also hacked at it's carcass to pieces. It's ax got caught right in the ribcage of another draugr with a sickening crunch before it was chopped into inky giblets

"Ach! Lachlann yee talk too much and you should focus on fighting!" roared Finlay, the blonde Kern, as he swiftly dodged a clumsy spiked-mace swing by leaping back, the heavy, crude mace slammed into the thick clay of the bog, wet earth exploded from the impact and got stuck in the ground. Finlay had wild, dirty blonde hair and blue eyes. He was somewhat shorter than both of them, and somewhat fatter though he was almost as strong as Connacht.

The Draugr tried to pull the mace free but Finlay already leapt right behind the monster in range and with a mighty overhead strike, split the monsters head right in half with his own battle-axe, cutting right through it's rusted helmet and splitting it's blue face open with a loud crack of shattered bones! The Draugr roared in agony as the creature's head split wide open like a rotten pumpkin, dark gore sprayed everywhere.

Finlay spun around quickly and smashed the axe's pommel in the monstrosity's face, it's rotten teeth exploded in a bloody shower of decayed yellow ivory and noir gore, sending the terror reeling backwards into the bog.

"Alright lads! Let's pull a feigned retreat up the hillside, let them follow us up the hillside in a line and then we will hit them with the tar bombs and fire whiskey!" Connacht smiled in a feral way to his Kern

They smiled back and nodded their heads.

The Draugr began to crawl up from the wet bog and onto the clay hillside, these draugr still shambled forward and attacked but were hacked to pieces when they got to close to our heroes.

"Don't underestimate these bastards lads! They already killed the Gallowgalas Angus Mac-Lear and his kerns who came before us! Don't let them surround yee! Remember these are not yer regular walking dead, they were fierce veteran warriors in life and they still remember how to strike swiftly, with power and kill thee with one blow!" Snarled Connacht after dodging another ax attack but intercepting the ax handle with his sword's cross-guard and then...

...chopped the weapon right in half with a loud crack! The Draugr looked confused as it's weapon crumbled into two pieces right onto the hillside. Connacht recovered his great sword swiftly with a wild twirling strike, that whistled loudly and the blade chimed gently as he brought the sword smashing into the monster's flank and hacked it's legs out from under it with a loud crack of split bones.

Black blood and blue flesh spilled out everywhere as it's dismembered legs crashed onto the slick hillside. Though not dead the creature was severely stunned from the splitting strike. The Zombie was sent tumbling back into the undead horde, which sent many of them crashing onto the ground from the powerful impact.

"Now lads! Hit them with the bombs!" Roared Connacht.

Finlay and Lachlann swiftly grabbed their tar bombs from their wastes and hurled these clay pots right into the downed horde of undead. Crack! Crack! Crack! Went the clay jars as they burst upon impact on the cursed Creatures who were then covered in sticky, black tar.

Connacht lifted up a glass bottle of what looked like a very strong, amber colored, grain whiskey... flecks of red pepper, sulfur and iron powder could be seen within... he held the flask up to a silver ring on his left index finger and screamed "Kuanan!" the ring began to glow a golden-orange bright light that formed a glowing "K" like symbol.

The Bottle with the grain-whiskey began to glow bright amber-red in color and shake violently, it was hissing and white smoke was steaming from it's cork-stop... Connacht counted to three, he could feel the bottle violently shaking and boiling in his hand as the magic began to do it's work, he then flung the glass bottle directly at the horde of walking dead, who were slowly picking themselves up.

Kaboom! The bottle of Fire-whiskey exploded violently as fire enveloped the horde and sent them flying in all directions! The Tar on their bodies kept them burning as the fire began to make their rotten flesh fall apart and even melt.

Connacht, Lachlann and Finlay roared in defiance and charged down the hillside to attack the fallen undead. The three of them flew into a berserk rage or **Raistrad,** for they knew that only entering into such a wild fury would allow them to defeat such a swarm of foes. Wildly hacking with their swords, axes and maces... rotten skulls were smashed, heads hacked from shoulders and limbs were chopped off from cadaverous bodies! The burning body parts fell into the brackish bog water and the flames were extinguished as dirty black smoke polluted the air.

The battle appeared to be done, the horde was literally hacked to pieces...but suddenly the tough bastards were still moving about and crawling in the foul peat water. Fingers, hands and arms crawled about like undulating worms, decaying heads were trying to bite the three heroes.

"Careful lads! The hands can still claw and the heads can still leave a terribly diseased bite! Come, we must build a large funeral pyre and burn these damnable wretches completely to make sure they are permanently dead!" Connacht warned.

"Aye Dad!" Lachlann replied sarcastically.

"Call me "Dad" again and I will swiftly kick yee in yer plums!" Laughed Connacht. They all began to go to work, using shovels to scoop the writhing and rotting body parts of the draugr, then hurling them into a bonfire pile.

"What does "Kuanan" mean?" Finlay inquired.

"Lad, that means "Fire" in dwarven runic-form. The tale goes that the first ancestors of the mountain dwarves were ruled by a Mountain King named "Durin" who named the first generation of dwarves with these runic names, and since they were the first ancestors of the dwarven race, their magic still empowers these runes to this day. The Dwarves worship their ancestors and it was rumored that these powerful spirits hatched from large maggots that crawled out of the very soil itself in the dawn age." Connacht replied.

Lachlann and Finlay looked amazed, kinda like children hearing stories around the campfire for the first

."By the Way, move out of the way!" Connacht warned and the kerns swiftly leaped out of the way from the pyre.

"Kuanan!" The Gallowgalas roared and flung another Fire-Whiskey bottle directly at the pyre, it exploded in amber flames as the writhing body parts began to burn red hot.

They could hear the muted, monstrous cries of the undead in agony as the fire torched their flesh to ash and charred their blackened bones to dust.

The screaming eventually died down... hilariously Connacht pulled a slab of jerked beef from his satchel with a flat stone and began to cook some meat on one of the burning draugr. This one wasn't burnt to ash yet and tried to bite Connacht but Connacht quickly placed a chunk of the sizzling meat in it's mouth instead...ironically the draugr began chewing on the meat!

Lachlann and Finlay looked at him in disgust. "What lads, yee wanting some, yee jealous of our house guest?"

Connacht laughed as he pulled out a knife, cut the roasting meat into ribbons and began eating it while pouring himself a spiced, red wine into his drinking horn. The burning zombie still seemed to enjoy eating the meat it was offered.

Connacht then pulled a glass vial or what looked like an amber liquor mixed with chunks of mushrooms and even a strange azure blue, glowing liquid which seemed to float atop the dark amber liquor...like how oil doesn't mix with water. He popped the cork and drank the strange elixir...almost painfully by his expression.

Finlay looked at Connacht with an astounded expression "What in ye gods are ye drinking, Uncle?" He smiled in bewilderment.

"Ach! Lads! This is a tonic some of us rune user consumes... its mostly Wormwood Absinthe which tastes like wood alcohol, then mixed with Fly Amanita, Psicobilin mushrooms and finally the very blue blood of the fae folk!" Connacht answered "It fuels my Runic Magicks but by yee gods it tastes vile, like fire alcohol mixed with coppery blood but by gods will it get ya good and proper high. This state of altered thinking allows one to harness the magic in the memorized runes."

"How can you drink and eat with the stench of this bog? It stanks of shyte!" Finlay laughed.

"Las a seasoned Gallowgalas mercenary... you just drown it out with more wine and or liquor!" laughed Connacht.

"Ahh Alcoholism! If the monsters don't kill yee then drinking will by taking yer liver! Speaking of drinking the pain away, pass me a wine-skin will yee!" Implored Lachlann.

"Now that lad, sounds like a future drunkard Gallowgalas! Here's one on the house!" Connacht flung two wine-skins at both Lachlann and Finlay who quickly began drinking the spiced wine without abandon.

"In the morning, we will raid the burial mound, defile it and steal whatever accursed silver or gold coin can be found within... who knows maybe yee might find an enchanted weapon like a flying spear or a singing sword! maybe even a lusty battle-ax!" Connacht roared in laughter.

The three of them made their way back to the forest road and slept surprisingly peacefully through the rest of the night in the Shelta wagon-circle. Connacht rode with the *Grai* Shelta tribe or *Horse Tribe* in their tongue, from the northern realm of Clan Gunnar down to the central lands of Clan Lennox and Clan Calhoun. They were almost at the rugged lowlands of Clan Lennox. The Shelta had various tribes of wandering nomads, some served as farmhands and tinkerers, others were fishermen and boat wrights, The *Grai* tribe generally performed as musicians, entertainers, fortune tellers in their grand carnival, there were tribes who specialized as merchants of exotic and antique goods, Some tribes specialized in gambling especially when it applied to horse races, there were tribes that had no shame in legalized prostitution while a few tribes were notorious for thievery. Tragically the Shelta as a whole suffered frequently from local bigots due to prejudice from the actions of a few infamous tribes or when it was convenient to rob them of their wagons and horses.

It was rumored that the Shelta tribes who specialized in carnivals had wondrous beasts and monsters kept caged up in silver-leaf wagons like the man-eating harpies, the fearsome manticore, talking seals known as Selkies and even the legendary unicorn…others gossiped that illusions were placed on old animals to make them look fierce.

Connacht respected them since his youth and promised to protect the Grai Caravan on it's journey.

Connacht snuggled next to his mistress, a busty, plump woman of middle age… Bonnie, a lusty lass with a small army of children who didn't know their fathers but were raised lovingly by the tribe nonetheless. Connacht thought to himself of how unusual the Shelta were as a peoples, how they used hedge magic so commonly, were they distant relatives of the wild men from the other side of the Samhain Isle? Were they a tribe of changelings?

Bonnie rolled over to Connacht in the wagon bed and whispered "Well well, the big Ostramann warrior has returned to his Shelta big mama for a little fun." She smiled, her wild auburn hair billowing with the light autumn wind. She gave him a passionate kiss on the lips but then drew herself up "My my, you are a tad bit musky ye big lummox." she smiled "maybe wash yerself in the nearby stream with this lard soap, to make the night of passion a bit more bearable?" She giggled

Connacht laughed to himself and walked out of the wagon, already the Shelta elders were heating up a cauldron of water and began using huge ladles to the steaming water into a portable, wooden tub that probably was a large oaken wine barrel that was sawed in half. This barrel must have been big, big as a hogs-head, tonne or a butte barrel by the look of it. The Elders began pouring the hot water from the cauldron into the wooden tub while other elders poured some of the colder creek water to cool down the scalding bathwater. Connacht took off his armor and accouterments, covered in necrotic blood, bog mud and rotting vegetation then gave these items to the Elders, so they might wash them.

He also bribed the three elderly Shelta with a few silver coins for their service. He then entered the barrel-now-bathing tub and began to bask in the water. Tragically it was only big enough for him. Suddenly Bonnie, his plump mistress, waltzed over to him and began to scrub and bathe him with a large block of hogs-lard soap and a wooden brush...she wasn't shy, she scrubbed every nook and cranny, especially the lower extremities.

Connacht enjoyed her lathered hands rubbing his phallus, buttocks and plums so softly but with a little force, he groaned and he could feel his erection rising...growing...lengthening from Bonnie's plump fingers.

9

Suddenly he was fully erect, beyond his navel and Bonnie smiled. "let's take this pervy business into the wagon yee frisky silver fox!" she smiled.

Connacht wrapped himself with a quilted blanket to dry himself, gleefully leaving the tub as he entered into her luxurious wagon of oak.

"We are both large, mayhaps we should reinforce the wagon as to not snap it in half!?!" Implored Connacht.

Bonnie Smiled "I already beat ya to it! I placed several large pine logs directly underneath the wagon! Come!" she smiled and gently grabbed his hand and escorted him into the wagon. Connacht lay down on a freshly made bed of hay, thick wool and linen blankets. "My darling, I am exhausted, mayhaps you crawl on top and ride me like I am a mighty stallion!" he winked and smiled at her.

"Oh I love riding a wild horse!" she laughed as she lifted up her dress, her plump thighs and backside quivering with each heavy footfall, she turned around with her huge, pink buttocks and she easily engulfed Connacht's throbbing manhood. She was rather roomy deep inside but so silky... she began to bounce up and down, slightly, then harder and with furious force...Connacht could feel his entire phallus getting sucked deep inside her, even his testicles were getting pulled inside those silky, warm and wet walls.

He looked up and he could see his long phallus gently getting sucked in and then pushed out with each movement of her hips. Suddenly she began to breath in a ragged manner and start to moan, the muscles in her walls got tighter and tighter as she slammed her massive buttocks down on his hips...thank the gods he was strong! The Wagon creaked and groaned with their combined weight...suddenly Connacht could feel the seed rising from his plums filling up his shaft...his manhood became thicker, longer and he could now few the wall of her uterus, so soft but still giving him a firm resistance...his head kept poking her cervix, but she was a tough, mature woman who loved it...like an explosion of orgasmic essence, he erupted inside her and her thick labia wrapped around his manhood so tightly...so much cum, so deep inside such a curvaceous woman...she slowly pulled her self-off his lap, groaning lowly, he could see his long and limp penis sliding out of her as white milky seed poured out all over their legs and messy nether regions.

"Oh Bonnie! that was amazing." Connacht moaned.

Bonnie turned around and said "I always aim to please me darling, do yee want me to take those two Kern and teach them how to be men?" she smiled devilishly.

"Aye they're good lads and of twenty something summers. They are probably a bit sexually frustrated, go forth and give them that sweet Bonnie lovin!" Connacht smiled. He was happy that the Shelta women were not picky or fussy, they were very focused on mixing blood with the local Caledonian tribes and clans, this basically kept them safe, for many warriors knew that their wild children rode with the Shelta... hence they were hard pressed to massacre them no matter what their lords and jarls command of them.

Bonnie sneaked off like a plump, fleshy cat and as she prowled the night, she found Lachlann and Finlay near the fire, frustrated that their amorous advances towards the witches' coven was denied that night.

She whispered into their ears pleasant and delicious promises and the young men shot up like excited horses, laughing and running off into the night to fill Bonnie absolutely full of their love seed.

Bonnie had a ravenous sexual appetite and many men knew that it was impossible for one man to satisfy them, even if he was hung like a stallion. Lachlann and Finlay topped and bottomed her, take turn to absolutely stuff her like a holiday goose...and she absolutely loved it.

The three sisters quietly eavesdropped on the orgy. These sisters' kingship was not by blood but by magic pact.

Llewellyn said "by the gods they are really giving it to big Bonnie! Oh I like that thick cock on Finlay..." she was lightly drooling in her harlequin suit of red, purple and blue patches.

Claidogna smiled "I kind prefer that long dicked Lachlann, he is not so fat and more handsome. But I would also dream of being stuffed by both of them." Llewellyn smiled "me too"

Claidogna laughed "Silly, you have a penis too, yee prancing femboy!" She smiled

Llewellyn looked visibly saddened "I know, I wish I had one like yee but you know I am a woman deep inside." a small tear dripped down her eye.

Claidogna looked remorseful "I am sorry beautiful, it's true yee are a lovely woman and it's not the end of the world sweet sister...you have an amazing lady penis that most men would envy. Mayhaps one day we shall find a way to give you the uterus and labia you always wished." Claidogna smiled.

Llewellyn smiled "well for now I truly love my phallus, it's almost as big as Connacht's, the fooking horse!" she laughed.

Derdre waltzed into their hushed conversation and said "Oh my, I understand you lasses, I grow jealous of so much love making, so many partners but alas I just want to find true love." she bemoaned.

Llewellyn and Claidogna hugged their beloved sister but then Bonnie groaned, another massive climax as those two rough, tough and handsome Kern warriors gave her yet another screaming orgasm.

The three witches looked again and smiled "honestly, right now I envy that big woman." Dredre quietly laughed and the other two said "same".

"Well sisters, could you use my body for tonight." Llewellyn smiled and the two of them grinned, gently grasped her hands and led the Harlequin femboy off to a night of pleasure.

They thought they were safe but this was not entirely true...Something or many things were watching from the nearby sycamore forests.

As the three heroes embraced their mistresses near the camp fire, warm in their wagon beds, as The Shelta people played up the lute and fiddle, drank cider and ate salted pork.

Suddenly several glowing eyes emerged from the forest to stare at the fire and it's encampment.

They were small, diminutive fae folk, with a mouth of exaggerated size and razor-sharp teeth, their wings were a dull purple, their skin a pale blue and their eyes shined a hot yellow in the fire light... they gathered in the various sycamore and oak trees of the lowlands to watch.

quickly one flew forward, it gently flew into each wagon to take a quick look and then darted past the rest of the swarm hiding in the oak and sycamore forest.

This small fae creature flew up to a much taller being standing atop a colossal cedar tree, it was of incredible beauty but very cruel of face, his skin a dark purple, his hair a shock of white, he wielded a terrible spear and he towered taller than most men but with a extremely lithe and swift body.

The greater fae being could see through the darkness and by the gods was he aroused at seeing so much passionate thrusting, groaning, kissing, love making and the volumes of seed spilled all over the campsite.

"Lord Arawan! Lord Arawan!" the blue faerie spoke.

"Gah!" shouted Lord Arawan "Shut your loud-mouth you banal fool! You will break the glamour we share in this wasteland the human clans call their

Homeland!" he paused for a moment. The Blue fairy looked at lord Arawan and could see that he was biting his lip, and his tunic barely hid his massive erection leaning towards his left leg. The Fairy playfully smiled

"This Gallowgalas…He wields both silver and cold iron in equal measure! These things are anathema to our kind." Said the blue fae..

Lord Arawann sighed "Yes Mog...yes sweet Mog...The large, older Gallowgalas fascinates me! I have never seen such a mighty warrior also be able to harness the powers of magic, to harness the glamour, to break through the banality of reality and harness the crude powers of Runic script!" He said in fascination.

"Correct Sirah! Correct!" gasped blue little Mog "He has potential! He might even have power equivalent of our dear beloved Aunties and Hags... wonder if he could break Aunty Oonah's curses? Or the Ben-Nighes which dwell upon the highland roads?" wondered Mog.

"Mog! Send your Slaugh swarm beyond the highlands! Inform the Puca's three and the Kork Brothers! I will also need swarms of Boggarts, a pack of Cu-Sith, bloodthirsty Redcaps, even my arrogant kinsfolk the Leanan Sidhe, maybe even a accursed Black Annis or a monstrous Fachan! And just in case all else comes to ruin…we might need to awaken the terrible Dullahan! This Gallowgalas named "Connacht" is remarkably deadly like nothing I have seen before..." Growled Lord Arawann in fear.

"Yes! Yes! Your Majesty!" stuttered Mog "My kinfolk, the Slaugh, live to Obey!" and with that he gently whistled to the swarm of Slaugh. Suddenly, a swarm broke free from the trees and flew high in the atmosphere towards the moon.

Even the Shelta nomads gasped in terror witnessing such a massive flock of dark fae. Lord Arawann smiled, flapping his immense gossamer wings with a slow pulse... "well well, Connacht! Even you and your retainers couldn't survive what lays before you!" Monologued Lord Arawann.

………………………...The Next Day.....................................

Connacht and his men awoke, they ate a humble breakfast of porridge with dried apricots, raisins, chopped figs, goats milk and bog butter...the wheat porridge was surprisingly gentle, creamy and mildly sweet. After the meal, they fetched mauls, two-headed axes, digging bars and other tools then they went back to the burial mound in the peat bog and walked within it's stone walls... each sarcophagus was opened, a humble assortment of silver coins, copper brooches and amber baubles... was their reward. It was slim pickings at best.

"Well lads, this assortment of baubles, ambers and silver coins will be able to pay for beds, drinks and meals for a week, maybe a fortnight. Connacht casually stated. "To think the others that came before us died for a few months of coin for drinking and feasting? Let's pay our Shelta lovers and then make our climb to Clan Calhoun's Stronghold."

They all laughed heartily yet shook their heads grimly.

Connacht took a long pause and a sudden memory seemed to stir inside him "But maybe, just maybe the treasure stash of our wicked ancestors might just be buried near the burial mound and not directly in it...let me use my runic rings to help me find it." Wondered Connacht

As Connacht scanned the smoldering ruins and chunks of carcasses he wondered aloud "This cannot possibly be? There must be more treasure! The Ostramann ancestors were known for being insanely greedy and hiding loot they pilfered!"

Connacht looked about and then whispered "FEHU!" to his rings and suddenly the runic symbol materialized on his rings, glowing a dark amber, golden hue and his hand leapt out like it was a magnet and pulled him going north west towards the sea. He could feel the fae-blood liquor burning in his blood as activated the Rune of wealth's magick!

He kept following his ring as it dragged him past this tree and that knoll until it finally guided him to a black mound of wet earth. The ring vibrated aggressively at the mound.

"Lachlann! Finlay! Make yerselves useful and fetch some shovels from the Shelta Tinkerer's!" with that the two Kern ran back to the wagonburg and retrieved two shovels, The Shelta didn't stop them nor ask because they knew that treasure was in this peat bog, but only if your fearsome enough to fight the accursed dead that dwell there.

They brought the wrought iron utensils to Connacht and he started digging with Finlay's help. The dug down several feet and the ring started vibrating and chiming so aggressively that Connacht said "looks like we found treasure my lads!" and they all released a wry wolfish grin as they quickly kept digging faster and faster to shovel out more of the black compost which filled covered their awaiting cache. Chunks of darkened soil came flying out easily, some pale roots or burrowing insects released with each shoveful but otherwise nothing spectacular. Soon they quickly cleared four feet of soil, Connacht was breathing heavily as were the other lads when Lachlann's shovel finally hit something hard with a discerning **Clink! Clink! Clink!** Of something metallic!

Soon they careful began brushing the black soil around the glinting object which made such a noise and lo and behold! They discovered something quite astounding, a giant silver ring on a gargantuan finger, decorated with various tourmaline gems, truly amazing! As they dug aggressively around it they found more silver rings bedecked with semiprecious gemstones like agate, onyx, turquoise, amethyst, ivory and so on... suddenly as they dug and brushed more and more soil around these rings, they discovered a massive hand with five of these gigantic silver rings, each ring was big enough to fit snugly around their thigh!

This massive hand was long dead and was quite cadaverous, the peat bogs tannins must have preserved this pale, almost translucent hand, which intricately one could see a multitude of black veins in the otherwise alabaster flesh.

Connacht rested his gauntleted fists on his armored coat where his hips would be and pondered "Must of been one of those frost giants our ancestors spoke of...Jotnar or something like that? Well he is long dead whatever he was...now how do we get these bastard rings off his long dead fingers?" he pondered. "Boyz what if we grease the rings off his hands with the bog butter from the burial mound?" but he was rudely interrupted by Lachlann.

"By the giant floppy cock of The Dagdha, let's just chop these fingers off and take a ring each!" Lachlann then reached for his two headed splitting axe and stuck the ring finger of the dead giant. He cut it off with one massive blow and picked it up for closer examination...black blood was slowly leaking out from the severed finger; it was almost as thick as cooking oil. Lachlann quickly held the dismembered finger aloft and victoriously laughed

"Haha!" "Finders keepers lads!" he guffawed in mocking victory....

Finlay Sneered "Ya Greedy Bastard! How do ye know if that corpse was truly dead?!?" Suddenly a muffled screaming could be heard from somewhere nearby...

"Hush ye foolish Knaves!" roared Connacht, suddenly the earth shook violently "What was that?"

This time the earth shook once again and far more violently, it was such an intense earthquake that the wet mud split asunder with a massive chasm! The stagnate waters of the peat bog rushed inside this newly formed rift in the earth with a violent churning.

Lachlann suddenly realized the finger and ring he was holding up in the air, started wriggling and squirming like a decapitated serpent. He screamed in terror as he flung the spasming finger to the wet earth of the bog.

Time seemed to stop for our three heroes as they stood there in shock looking at the earth being violently split open from what must have been a local earthquake.

Then, out of nowhere the earth ceased shaking. Connacht looked at Finlay and Lachlann and smiled "Guess that'll be over!" he laughed...but he was interrupted because the earth exploded out from underneath them as they were violently flung into the air to come crashing down unceremoniously in the foul bog water!

A ferocious behemoth came erupting out of the putrid bog! The blackened peat, mud and green-scum came raining down in all directions like a hail of filth! The stench of rot, offal and carrion assaulted the senses!

The Necrotic Titan was screaming in rage and agony! One of the giant's fingers was cut off!

"Þú skera af mér fingurinn! Þú mjólkurdrykkjandi drengur!" screamed the zombified giant in the ancient Johtun language.

Connacht could still speak the Volsungg tongue of his Ostramann ancestors and he looked at Lachlann in panic and translated "You cut off my fooking finger! You milk drinking whoreson!"

Lachlann looked furious "I haven't drunk fooking milk in ages! I'm a man and a proud alcoholic like anyother Ostramann or Caledonian in the Samhain Isles!" with that he furiously drew his razor-sharp broadsword and round shield, ready for battle!

The rotting giant leered in close, his putrid breath hit the three like a wind of decaying flesh, as his mouth and lips spoke, they could see the massive bursting pustules in his maw and the pale white maggots pouring out from between his teeth like a vile rain of decay.

"Ég mun éta þig upp og skíta þig svo út! Hálfkyn!" Snarled the draugr giant with a vicious sneer that streaked across the blackened, rotten flesh of his face.

In stark contrast to his putrid frost bitten and pallid flesh he still had a massive red beard, weaved into great braids and decorated with bronze and bejeweled brooches.

Lachlann looked back at Connacht anxiously and said "what did that bastard behemoth say now?"

Connacht looked back in terror and said "He said he is gonna eat you up and shit you out, half breed!"

Finlay was not so foolhardy as Lachlann and screamed "We should run as fast as we can!" he screamed in hysteria.

Connacht shook his head "Nay lad, even for an undead giant his legs are four meters long and he can quickly outrun us. If we don't kill this enraged monster he will probably go on a murderous rampage, slaughtering our Shelta allies nearby!"

Connacht turned to Finlay and spoke, staring him right in the eye and said "Besides lad, we have a sworn duty to protec..ugh!" Connacht screamed as he was interrupted by a massive rotting hand that swiftly grabbed him and hefted the Gallowgalas into eye level of the hulking corpse.

Then with a quick flick of its cadaverous hand it flung the warrior into its putrid, rot filled, gaping maw!

"Uncle!" shouted Lachlann and Finlay in unison as Connacht disappeared into the monster's foul mouth.

The Zombified colossus slowly picked itself up from the bog water, laughing manically and then spoke it it's deep rasping voice. Each mighty hand leaving a massive, muddy pit as hit hefted itself up from the filthy mire.

"Yes! You two should have listened to your uncle! Yer definitely fooked." The Draugr giant chortled menacingly.

"He Spoke in Caledonian?" Finlay gasped to Lachlann.

"Of course I do! We Jotnar still speak our slaves' languages! Now Die in terror while I...*gryahhhh!" The Giant screamed as it doubled over in agony while clutching its large stomach.

"By the Sagging teats of The Morrigan! What is that bastard doing?" screamed Lachlann.

Suddenly the tip of a mighty sword burst through the pallid and rotting flesh of the Giant's belly...this sword tip sawed back and forth rapidly and opened a massive wound on the behemoth...it's rotting, gray intestines and pitch-black blood came pouring out of the ragged wound on its stomach...and with all the rotting shit, blood and organs came freedom...freedom for Connacht who was still alive but completely covered in disgusting ichor!

Connacht landed on the bog water with a mighty splash and it was rather humiliating to be covered in the feces of a long dead Jotnar but he was still alive! He turned to Lachlann and Finlay and roared "Well yee milk drinking cowards are thou goin to stand there with thine cockels in yer hands or ye going to help me slay this abomination!" Connacht's teeth gritted in rage.

Connacht Roared "Uruz! Tiwaz!" two nordic runes at once and suddenly the trio's muscles began to swell while their skin grew small yet hard scales of stone. The three of them roared in fury and flew into a *Raistrad,* a type of divine rage that only giants, the kin of giants and the gods could fly into.

It was said that the gods themselves, especially the Aesir, The Johtuns, the Vanir and Tuatha de Denaan could only fly into these berserk rages of divine wrath that gave them the power to slay scores of enemies or slaughter foes far more massive than themselves.

"Uruz and Tiwaz" represented two gods, Vidar the lord of strength and vengeance and then Tyr the god of honorable warfare and justice.

The giant corpse struck first and punched Connacht with a mighty strike. Wham! Connacht lifted up his Claymore defensively putting one hand on the Ricasso-handle and the other on the greater handle, counterstriking the massive incoming fist...with a sickening crack he partially split the behemoth's fist asunder! Though he was sent skidding back across the putrid and slick soil of the bog...leaving a massive skid mark across the ground from the sheer impact of the fist.

The Giant roared in agony and hefted his rotten fist into the air, easily lifting the stubborn Connacht into the sky and flung him about like a wild dog death-rolls a rabbit in its savage jaws but Connacht was empowered and enraged and would not be flung from the rampaging colossus.

Finlay suddenly furious with rage, grabbed a massive maul he was using earlier at the burial mound. He charged the Draugr Giant, his heavy footfalls thundered across the mud, his heart racing with a almost manic, electrical frenzy. Hefting the brutish two-handed tool high into the air he used all his might to swing wildly down with a strike of wrath so powerful that when he connected with the Undead titan's knees it released a massive thunderclap and shards of bone exploded out in every direction like a lightning bolt striking an oak in a storm. The giant screamed in agony; his deep bass baritone voice suddenly jumped an octave or two to match the horrific pain.

The Monstrosity crashed face first! Boom! And fell upon both both Finlay and Connacht. The Impact was so massive it showered bog water and clay everywhere!

Lachlann now furious, he hefted his great two headed splitting axe into the air. The fury in his heart made him feel like a massive current of lightning was surging through his heart and into his swollen muscles. He now charged towards the giant and struck the behemoth with such force that the heavy axe actually made a crack through the horned, ridged part of the Giant's skull...which was an act of immense strength for the front area of a giant's skull is thick and stalwart like that of a full-grown Ram but of immense size!

The giant swiftly picked himself with his left arm and slapped Lachlann with his right, back hand with a thunderclap! Connacht was still tenaciously hanging onto that hand with his sword. This sent Connacht and Lachlann flying into the Bog and skipping across it's foul waters like skipping stones to slam into the nearby weeping willows with a thud.

Finlay was furious to see his kindred flung so dishonorably across such sickening, shit covered ooze and knew that the giant just needed to pick himself up to get his full revenge...he ran, faster than he ever ran, his bulging legs pumped with fury, his footfalls slammed on the mud and he leapt...

.… realizing this is the first time he has ever ran so fast with such power and leapt so high with such incredible potence! The wind whistling past his ears and the wake of his charge rippling across the bog waters.

He could see the rotten giant and the undead horror turned its head to see Finlay quick approaching like a furious plump meteorite!... He brought down his Maul, the blunt hammer side of the tool, with such fury on the embedded axe that axe was permanently warped by the potence of the blow! Sparks exploded out from the colossal strike and the axe was forced all the way past the skull and deep into the rotting brain matter of the cadaverous Gargantua...the blow was so furious it split the giants rotten head wide open and pustulant brain matter and black blood rained down in foul chunks of corruption...shattering and spraying the entire peat bog with the monsters vile ichors and organ meats.

The Draugr Jotun was slain, probably the chieftain of the tribe of warriors buried in that Cairn that they cleared out.

Finlay hefted the mighty Maul onto his meaty shoulders and walked over to both Lachlann and Connacht who were totally dazed and slowly lifting themselves from the putrid bog water. Dropping the heavy weapon with a thud he offered a hand to both and he helped pull them up, bracing himself with his new strength and stout weight.

"Look at all these Silver Rings that giant Bastard left behind" Smiled Finlay "Ye can thank me for getting the killin blow!" he smiled.

"Shut it yee Clot-Drippy Bungler! My magic and Lachlann's axe helped yee get that killing blow!" Connacht burst in laughter as Finlay's arrogant smile suddenly disappeared.

"I jest yee Clype-Dreep-Baichle! Thou art amazing my boy! I think yee might be a bastard child of mine! Incredible! We all did an amazing act!

Connacht then turned to Lachlann and with a furious bark "Lachlann ya Blearthering Gomeril! You only get one pinky ring for waking up that monstrosity! Use yer brains or die young! Now help me set the hairy-arsed bastard alight so he might narry rise from the dead again!" Connacht then began hurling buckets of tar and dry logs of pine with Lachlann into the cracked skull of the Jotnar. Connacht screamed the fire rune "Kuanan!" and he spat a great gout of fire into the giant's skull which set the still screaming Jotnar's head aflame in a raging inferno.

"Two Silver Rings for me, Two for Finlay and only one for Lachlann! We give the rest to the Shelta and they will forever be in our debt!" Connacht commanded and the two Kerns nodded in agreement.

"Besides now we can pay the Shelta Folk to simply hold a carnival for free with all this silver. We already were sworn to protect this caravan as we escorted them to the stronghold of Calhoun Dun, The Fortress of Clan Calhoun. Apparently, our paymaster, Lord Hjalmar Gunnarson has spent quite a gold coin organizing the feast and festivities for the Dowry of Lady Rhona! This will surely impress her elderly noble father, Lord Duncan Calhoun" Connacht smiled.

"Aye, this also relieves us of the grinding poverty and fighting-off of anything that tries to pillage across our dirt-poor clan; the lands of Clan Knox." groaned Finlay.

"Aye lad, the great clan war ravaged our homelands and the neighboring lands of MacIvar." Sighed Connacht bitterly.

"Connacht isn't your father the lord of those lands?" Lachlann inquired.

"I am the last surviving son of Lord Falkirk Knox, but he is estranged to me." Connacht sighed in sorrow.

"What would you do if yee ever become lord of those lands?" Finlay asked, smiling like a fox.

"Lads, I would grant sanctuary for tribes of Shelta folk, woads and picts trying to survive as long as they respected our laws of generosity. I wouldn't allow any bigotry towards the fae folk of the Seelie Court." Connacht looked dreamy eyed at the idea of a sanctuary homeland for exiled of the Caledonian lands.

Finlay and Lachlann both rubbed their chins impressed.

Chapter 2: From Lowlands to the Highlands (Ulster province to Knox lands)

**"I carry a greater load dead than alive. While I lie, serving
many men; if I were to stand, I should serve a few. If my
entrails are torn out to lie open out of doors, I bring life to
all, and I give sustenance to many. A lifeless creature which
bites nothing, when loaded down I run on my way yet never
show my feet.
What am I?"**

Connacht, Finlay and Lachlan wandered across the well worn dirt roads of the Forested Lowlands also known as the Dun-na-Ri Forest of Clan Knox. They traveled with the Shelta Wagon people across the well worn dirt roads of the lowlands.

Connacht also hefted a mighty ancestral greatsword, known as a Claymore, sheated in a fine leather hilt upon his left shoulder. Lachlann and Finlay now bedecked fine armored coats of Chain and scalemail after acquiring so many Silver rings from the dead giant.

The land was speckled with great, ancient oaks bearing fat, bronzed acorns on their boughs. The Knox Clan farmers could be seen with their herds of swine, they where using the humble billhook to strike the boughs of the trees to knock the fat acorns from the oaks, the swine would wait and then devour the acorns greedily. This oak forest was truly ancient and tended to by the members of Clan Knox but other trees grew among the oak like the golden leafed sycamores, pine and fir trees in the higher latitudes. Various other trees grew along the ravines, glens, river beds and lowlands such as crab apples, wild cherries, chestnuts and the flowering dogwoods. The trees had various lovely rust colored lichens growing on their boughs, especially on the oaks... strangely enough many of the oaks where shattered or split in twain with great scorch marks in the areas they split.

Lachlan turned to Connacht "what split these oaks? Witchcraft?"

Connacht smirked "Nay lad, though there is magic in the isles of Samhain, honest to gods natural events split these mighty oaks... lightning from the storms that emanate in the solstice seas or even from the deep Ginnungagap ocean.

These Storms come in the cool spring or cold winter as massive cyclones with one great-eye-of-the-storm and generate so much power and energy, then something within the oaks draws their thunderous might and they get split in twain. I have seen it since a wee lad."

Finlay looked in surprise "aye, sirrah but looketh. Saporlings yet spring again from the felled giants (oaks)!" and he pointed at bushes and saporlings growing from a shattered stump.

Connacht nodded his head "Aye lad, for ye see that Oaks do not just live above ground but much of them lives underneath... when burned by fire or split asunder by lightning they can regrow their top half once again deep from the starchy reserves in their massive tap roots.

Their roots grow so deep they can tap into nearby creeks several feet away or even underground pools of water! Also, their roots are also incredibly mighty and can crush large boulders into narry but fine powder... of course over quite some time."

Connacht continued "when a foul blight struck down the fields of potatoes and barley of Clan Gunnar and Clan Knox, during the long years of the Clan Civil War, our people talked to the ancient druids and they taught us a way of boiling acorns, hurling out their poisons and then grinding the boiled nuts into a fine flour to make bread! This acorn bread literally saved our people from what would have been a terrible famine! Plus acorns fatten up hogs incredibly quick. The Oak is truly a sacred tree that deserves much respect."

"It is said that in the deep forests certain giant Oaks are labeled *Biles,* and that druids write on the trunks of these mighty trees in their ancient language of Oghma. The word druid comes from two ancient Caledonian root words, *Dru-* meaning oak and *Vid-* meaning truth or wisdom. Some rumors even say the mightiest of Oaks and other trees are actually a race of sleeping giants known as the Firbolg. But alas there are so many myths throughout all of Caledonia that it's hard to determine what is truth and what is merely a convenient story to confuse inquisitive children!"
Connacht smiled.

The Dirt road followed a creek in as it winded it's way through the ancient Oaken forest. Connacht noticed an elderly woman with a crooked back, wearing a long green dress, who sat on the side of the road on a large slate boulder. Her baskets had various ground vegetables like radishes, potatoes, carrots, sun-chokes, dandelions, stinging nettle, turnips, onions, cabbage, beets and kale. Several small children gathered around her, their faces masked with rags and their bodies heavily covered. Many of them peeled potatoes.

"Oy Auntie! How much for some potatoes and sun-chokes?" inquired Lachlan.

"The name is Aunty Oona, and the potatoes are 1 copper a pound, the sunchokes are 1 copper per two pounds." Aunty Oona said. Her face was heavily wrinkled and she lifted herself up on a oaken shillelagh.

"Alright, might as well buy four pounds of potato and four pounds of sunchoke." Lachlan gave Aunty Oona 8 coppers.

"Not only are ye a brave Kern but a generous lad as well, bless ye." Aunty Oona smiled, her eyes sparkling.

Connacht chuckled "can I pay ye in cold-iron coins for some radishes?" he pulled forth four coins of iron with the symbol of a king with a crown of horns.

"Nay, take that accursed iron money and hurl it into a Loch of Lennox!" Aunty Oona screamed.

Connacht guffawed. "A jest Aunty, a Jest. I shall give thee four coppers for some raddishs."

Aunty Oona gave him a dirty look "listen here yee Gallowgalas, you know and I know that kind of humor could get you killed or bewitched!" with that she snatched his copper coins and gave him just two radishes.

27

"Don't worry Aunty, yer secret and your "children's" secret is safe with me!" Connacht laughed. Aunty and all her children stopped what they were doing and scowled at Connacht.

Aunty Oona approached Connacht and looked him dead in the eyes "Listen brute, if you find a cauldron of silver coin in the wilderness of the Calhoon highlands, just remember it's mine, but I shall reward ye half once it's delivered to me. I have a corn dolly of lughnasa said to protect a person from any fell magicks."

"sounds like ye old tale of the clurican who steals pots of silver and gold from sweet old crones that dwell in villages." Connacht chortled.

Aunty Oona scowled at him "be respectful lad, honor our glamour and silence, the banal ones don't need to have the veil lifted upon their dreaming." she said

"Just remember lord Connacht, Never forget a Debt and Death before Dishonor for beauty is life and love shall conquer all." Aunty Onna looked directly into Connacht's eyes and her eyes seemed to almost glow a faint azure blue.

"Aye Aunty, I know these ancient tenets and respect the Glamour. Pardon my mischief." Said Connacht.

"Ah, syrrah, I forgive thee, trickery is always appreciated as is a good jest." Smiled Aunty.

Connacht, Lachlan and Finlay waved good bye to Aunty Oona and her strange children and continued their journey with the Shelta across the lowlands on a dirt road. They came to a fork in the road with one path going uphill into a landscape of scrub oak, heather, sage and occasional glens of great pine trees... thick milky mist covered the higher elevations from eye sight, and only the occasional fir tree or great hill top peaked from the misty low flying clouds.

Lachlan turned to Connacht "Something was strange about Aunty and her children..."

Connacht smiled "Between the three of us... they were not human."

Finlay turned about and gasped "are you saying they were fae folk?"

Connacht nodded in agreement "True, they were relatively harmless fae folk, either neutral hearth-fae or even possibly Seelie fae. Show them respect and honor your debts and they will leave thee be or protect ye. Be careful of them when dealing with the Unseelie Fae though, for they are savage and only wish vengeance against humanity from times before history was even recorded. Thankfully they seem to live either beneath the earth or in the dark lands beyond the borders of the Twelve Duns."

Lachlan looked puzzled "when Aunty Oona said "Never forget a Debt and Death before Dishonor for beauty is life and love shall conquer all." what did she mean by that?"

Connacht turned to Lachlan with a serious look "That is how she revealed herself in a subtle way, to never forget a debt is important to they fae, especially the Seelie. Debts and Oaths empower their magic, which they call Glamour. The Seelie fae actually might have created Chivalry and hence their oaths are so powerful that they would choose Death before dishonoring it, though they are very shrewd as to when they give an oath. It is currency to them.

They also believe in beauty in all things and that love of the beautiful shall conquer all, even if that means loving someone who can be beautiful with in their heart. For the Seelie are said to be beautiful of heart but the Unseelie are only beautiful of body."

(Several hours later as Twilight approached)

The Shelta Wagons were leaving the river valleys and grass vales of the lowlands but they haven't quite reached the flowering heather covered hills and pine forests of the highlands just yet. They traversed these borderlands as the sun was already waning in twilight.

As evening set in, the Shelta Wagon village stopped and camped nearby a village known as Kirk Yetholm, The Village was right on the shores of a large Loch or Lake. This Loch was called Loch Rannoch and it was more known for being very long but not very wide. For the Villagers of Kirk Yetholm could see across the body of water to the forested hills of the other-side of Loch Rannoch, and a strong swimmer could swim across it in an hour. Though small this village was well defended, each bastile house formed from great boulders of granite, slate and mortar and all centered around a large bonfire, the whole village was surrounded by a thick wooden wall of stout pine logs and towers for archers.

At night the sheep and swine were herded through a wooden gate into the inner courtyard of the village. The houses and walls were already decorated for the upcoming Samhain festival with several carved turnips, squash and pumpkins carved into ghoulish Jack-o-lanterns. The tallow candles alight and glowing a dark, eerie orange, especially the candlelight was almost dancing about hauntingly during the night.

The Villagers also constructed a humble Wicker-man, similar to a scarecrow but much larger and far more robust, from the pine and fir wood which grew on the hillside. Much of the wood and brush was already dead and dried. This effigy would be burned during the night of Samhain, said to drive away the wicked fae and spirits of the dead. The Village, though humble also seemed mysterious yet welcoming with the orange light of the jack-o-lantern and the green eery light of the fire flies.

The forests nearby were an interesting combination of Oaks and Pines, the ground cover also had an interesting mix of the heather brush and wild grass. This region was truly a fusion of both Highland and lowlands.

The Loch itself is a famous landmark of the colder, alpine highlands but just further east and south were various marshes where many waterfowl rested in the weeping willows and sycamores that surrounded the marsh, this being a clear sign of the environment of the lowlands.

Connacht looked out to bonnie's wagon to the other-side of the Loch Rannoch as the sun finally set. He could hear the long, mournful cries of loons and the chorus of frogs croaking in the tall grass near the lake. Throngs of fireflies began dancing in the moonlight as the full moon appeared in the horizon.

"Ahhh, sweet Bonnie lass, nights like this are truly enchanting." he sighed in amazement. Bonnie smiled "enchanting is putting it mildly" she wrapped her plump, soft arm around his dense, powerful arm and held him close. Connacht smiled "I am excited for this great wedding between lord Hjalmar and Lady Rhona, we are only a few days before arriving to the Calhoun Stronghold. I am friends with Lord Duncan."

Bonnie's smile faded a bit "you know Lord Duncan personally executed a whole tribe of Shelta-folk during the Clan Wars?" Connacht's smile soured. "Yea, he slayed the entire *An Lucht Gé* , The Goose Tribe, we had to incorporate the survivors in your Knox lands into our tribe."

"Bonnie Lass." Connacht frowned, "That war was truly horrible. And Duncan was an ally of our clan and the *Lucht Ge* were simply bringing in food rations to feed the army of pikemen from Ivar lands. They got caught up by a furious warband from Clan Calhoun, enraged from MacIvar raids that ravaged the highlands of that realm." Connacht had tears of guilt gently pouring down his cheecks.

"Sweet Bonnie, when I become lord of my impoverished highlands, I swear unto thee that the Shelta people and the many exiles across the Samhain Isles will be able to find sanctuary in our lands." Connacht smiled and Bonnie smiled back teary eyed, never before offered sanctuary for her people. She was never offered so much generosity from the local people of Samhain and felt something skip a beat in her heart like magic.

As Bonnie's Wagon approached the Shelta-folk called out *"Greys Grissed!"* and their horses came to an abrupt halt. They camp outside of the village in a nearby fallow fields, the Shelta tinkerer's began to take out their anvils and hammers, pounding out tin and or cutting the giant's multiple silver rings in smaller chunks which they began to fashion in Torqs, coins, brooches, rings and other forms of jewelry.

The local villagers wandered by and started buying the jewelry, selling smoked meats, small barrels of cider, flirting with the seductive Shelta women, teasing the handsome, swarthy lads and even dancing with the exotic femboys who were all of twenty summers or more. They began drinking, dancing around a campfire and eventually paying for a passionate night of love. The ouds and lutes, the tambourines and harps played wild songs of passion and mystery.

As the weekend of revelry wore on, Connacht, Lachlann, Finlay and a flirtatious Shelta Harlequinn named Llewllyn, were sitting near a campfire next to the local peasantry of Kirk Yetholm. They shared some champagne and the irony flavored Blood-sausage with rye bread. Hearty food, mixed well with the sour yet sweet local jam made from local marsh cranberries.

One of the villagers began to speak "damn shame, the marsh has become, gods damned Bog Leapers have crawled into the place, it was already a treacherous place with the Basket Weaver that lurked there but he mostly stayed sedentary in the southern most pond of the marsh." he bemoaned.

Connacht Raised his eyebrow "Hear that lads? Sounds like some dark Fae plague these fine folk. I want you to tackle this problem by yerselves! Just watch out for Bog-Leapers, their jaws are powerful enough to rip an arm off! They hide in shallow waters then ambush sheep, hogs, children, hounds and even drunken fishermen!"

Llewellyn, a lithe, long haired and extremely pretty harlequin slid next to Finlay and whispered in his ear "listen handsome, let's help these humble farmers, for they can in turn honor a debt they owe us and this village could be a sanctuary for the Shelta. I have an excellent idea for thee, we can slay this whole pack of monsters with a clever trap."

Finlay smiled and turned to the villagers, "If we kill these Bog-Leapers will you in turn give sanctuary to this tribe of wandering Shelta peoples?"

The gathered farmers looked at each other, weary from the threat of the nearby bog, nodded their heads in agreement. One farmer spoke up "If you kill the lot of them I shall give you a whole wagon filled with smoked sausages, cheeses as well as several barrels of Cider!"

Connacht looked at Finlay, Lachlann and Llewellyn and he smiled. "Sounds like a good deal lads and lasse!" he said as he smiled then playfully winked at Llewellyn.

"Here is a secret of Bog-leapers, they are very aggressive when they smell fish-oil or tallow that they unthinkingly pounce right out of the pond...if there are hidden spears in brambles or brush you can impale the lot of them as they fling themselves at their prey." Connacht said sagely.

"Silver fox you are wise as you are strong!" smiled Llewellyn and she led Finlay and Lachlann off towards the southern marshes.

"Finlay, don't forget this!" and gently threw his locked and sheathed Claymore, towards Finlay who caught it easily with one hand. "Impaling doesn't always kill them, they can regenerate surprisingly fast! Also don't forget that speaking to a Basket-Weaver is generally better than trying to fight them, they are surprisingly deadly enemies when roused!"

"Just remember that this sword thirsts for blood! It was rumored to have been the very sword of the famous Berserker of the early Bronze age, CuChalainn as he was tied to a massive stone during his death. Do not draw it in vain!" Warned Connacht.

Connacht then closed his eyes and cleared his throat, Finlay looked at him oddly as if Connacht was about to theatrically perform song and dance.

"Lugaid mac Con Roi flung three deadly spears,
Each one struck true, robbing three kings of their years,
Cuchulainn roared in pain, his stomach split asunder, ,
His body warped, his bones broke like thunder,
Reformed he did but now a rampaging giant,
He fought furiously to his death, always Defiant,
He tied himself to a boulder to die standing,
His Death was soon this is what he was understanding,
Queen Medb's army attacked but our Hero slayed many,
Three days and nights he fought at Kilkenny,
Until the raven of Morrigan landed on his shoulder,
and then his corpse fell from that accursed boulder."

Connacht recited.

"There lads, that poem should silence the blood thirsty spirit of CuChalainn, who died after standing and fighting for three days!" Finlay looked shocked, the power of the poem moved him greatly.

The Full moon was rising in the night sky, the grass fields and Oaken Glens were illuminated by silvery and azure moonlight. Wild grass as tall as a man surrounded many of the glades and fields that led to the marsh. Finlay, Llewellyn and Lachlann marched through the well worn dirt road on the way there. Schools of green glowing fireflies danced along the wooden posts separating one farmers field from another.

As they could see the great soggy area of ponds, marshes and bogs before them one tree in the marsh suddenly stood much higher than the rest, and was far more massive...of all the trees, this was truly unusual, it was a titanic Sycamore, possibly a hundred feet tall! Llewellyn gasped "Oh, a *Biles* Tree! We must get closer so I can read it's script" she smiled, performed a cartwheel and playfully skipped and pranced her way to the behemoth tree.

They cleared the marsh, leaping from large river stone to river stone to get to the massive tree. Finlay and Lachlann could hear the large toads croaking and the tiny frogs chirping as they neared in, brushing back the loose leaves of several weeping willows to approach to the dark, shady undergrowth of this Behemoth Sycamore.

Llewellyn reached out in her multicolored, checkered coat, with her white linen gloves she touched the tree and she closed her eyes...she could feel the throbbing between her eyes and opened her minds eyes chanting "Sham"...once the third eye was open she could see the trees magnificent aura of radiating blue and green, peaceful, calm, happy, spiritual colors...she then whispered "yam! Yam!" repeatedly until her heart chakra opened and she could feel it!...the powerful snoring and pulsing heart beat of something mighty...something huge, peacefully sleeping, both below the tree but also being one with the tree.

Suddenly she willed, she asked firmly but politely for the swarming fireflies to surround the tree and illuminate it... at first they heard her plea... but she kept begging them, over and over within in her mind and more and more began to approach her and the mighty tree she touched.

Suddenly they began to slowly swarm the tree, gently flying about the cottonwood colossus and illuminating areas of stripped bark with a strange system of writing, a series of long and short scratch marks which intercepted each other. The orange and green glowing insects illuminated the azure blue of the moonlight.

She opened her eyes and she smiled "look at all the Ogham written upon this sacred tree! Let me fetch some coal and parchment from my satchel!" she beamed at Finlay.

Finlay was stunned with the beauty of the whole thing...so many lovely little fireflies dancing around these epic and majestic trees but the tree itself was etched, scarred with so much of this bizarre writing. Long scars intersected with little scars, the little scars starting from the top but leaning down to the left or right...and this was in know as the secret language among druids...or as the Nordics called them...Witches.

Llewllyn quickly placed pages of parchment atop these etchings and swiftly rubbed charcoal on the the paper...suddenly much of these strange writings were quickly transcribed onto the parchment pages that she used, she finished and quickly rolled the pages and placed them back in her satchels. "Bonnie and my fellow coven of sisters would love reading these incantations and stories written upon such a sacred and ancient tree! Many of them first planted in the earliest of eras by the Firbolg themselves or around the battles of Maig Tuired...as the rumors go anyways." She smiled

Finlay whispered "How will we get these Bog-leapers by the way? What do they enjoy eating?" he inquired.

"Connacht was right, they do love sheep and lamb but they go crazy for

35

mouflon or the wild highland sheep! That very gamy scent and rich tallow drives them wild! Let's head back to village, I remember they had some domesticated ones." Llewellyn beamed.

Finlay smiled and they turned around to enter the village once again, hopefully the farmers were still awake. He thought. It was already 2 past midnight.

Llewellyn, Finlay and Lachlann approached the village, right to the gypsy campfire were many of the locals were dancing and kissing the Shelta peoples. The Shelta were a poly-amorous people who made quite a few coins from selling their love for a night. Both the Shelta and locals of village were already drunk and passionately kissing, some even making love, for the lose flowing clothes of the Shelta could easily be parted, they didn't even notice the trio sneak back in.

Llewellyn whispered in Finlay's ear. "our kind make love to repopulate from the last war, we mix blood with the different ethnic peoples of the Caleonian isles because if we carry their blood they would be much more hesitant to persecute us." Llewellyn smiled but her eyes darted into Finlay's with most seriousness.

Luckily they found one villager asleep next to a barrel of smoked and salted muflon meat, most of it was cut into legs and back cuts, but there was also fatty cuts of belly-fat. Llewellyn snagged a few pieces and a leather pouch from one of the sleeping villagers, but in turn placed a small handful of silver coins, freshly made from the giant's rings, into his pocket.

"Hope he forgives us for the intrusion and I think he will enjoy that handful of silvers!" she smiled. Shelta learned how to pickpocket since they were youths but some tribes only used such arts when desperately needed.

As she snuck out of the encampment she quickly darted to a large oak tree where Finlay and Lachlann was waiting. she quietly chuckled to herself

but then she suddenly noticed that Finlay and Lachlann were standing
there in terror.

"what's wrong? Yee see a Banshee or something?" she quietly laughed as
she ran up to give Finlay a playful smooch, she closed her eyes and gave
him a gentle peck on the cheek.... but was rudely hoisted into the air! She
hung there dangling, a strong, long arm held her aloft. It was Connacht
and he appeared before her, face to face. The furious look on his face was
rather intimidating.

"lass did you just steal from that farmer?" he whisper snarled, barely able
to contain his anger. "I am trying to protect your Shelta people from
getting butchered! You were too young to remember when the clan civil
war broke out and many of your kind were burned alive on wooden
bonfires for being witches!" he growled.

"Yes! Yes! Ya cantankerous old Gallowgalas! My elders tell me this
constantly, unhand me ya big brute!" She quietly snarled. Connacht
dropped her unceremoniously and she hit the grass with a thud.

"Besides! I paid him with a few silver coins!" She whispered.

Connacht looked at her, groaned and rolled his eyes. "Fine lass, but don't
make a habit of it! I love you lot, I don't want to butcher a horde of angry
highland peasants for yer Shenanigans!" he quietly groaned.

She quickly got up, playfully punched him in the shoulder, leapt in the air
and farted on him. She then pranced as she sauntered away with Lachlann
and Finlay, the three of them giggling the whole time.

Connacht laughed to himself. "Fooken Harlequins!"

It was already 3 at night and they approached the bog once again. Finlay
took his axe and chopped down several branches from a dead oak, he then
made a fire using dry heather brush, the branches of the dead oak and his
knife. To start the fire he used the same seax-knife and brushed it roughly

against a flint stone, This quickly started a fire and he took turns with Lachlann and Llewellyn, sharpening sticks that were as tall as a man, burning the tips and gathering them into bundles. They then quickly cooked the cold Muflon meat to heat it up and used the gamy scent of it to perfume the air. "This will drive them crazy" she whispered.

Llewellyn helped guide them to a spot in the pond where she could hear a mixture of deep croaking like massive toads with a high pitched and faint chirping like that of wild bats. She could see them in the water, their auras aggressively glowing red as they swam with purpose, hunger and anger in the bog water. The water of the pond gently, but with power, had a wake left behind as they strange creatures patrolled the waters.

She beckoned for to Finlay to crawl up first, he had the bundle of sharpened wooden spears and she pointed to various locations where Finlay crammed these makeshift spears into the earth, hidden within the foliage of ivy and various mulberry bushes.

Finlay and Llewellyn couldn't help themselves and gathered a few of the overtly ripened mulberries, By Lugos, they were the sweet, red grapes and black berry notes as well as rich flavors. Some even had a tad bit of a fermented aftertaste but enjoyable nonetheless,

Llewellyn then slapped Finlay to stop gorging himself "stop, yee gluttonous little piglet, bring Lachlann hear with the sizzling Muflon hammocks!" she aggressively whispered into Finlay's ear.

Finlay walked back and turned to where Lachlann was hiding, he beckoned to him silently and Lachlann now snuck over to Llewellyn's hiding place... she gently grabbed the Wild Sheep skewers and hung them directly over the wooden pikes.

"Allright yee handsome devils" she whispered " let's fling some stones into the nearby water to provoke them into fury!" and the three of them gathered some flat, river stones, then with both experience and strength, flung the stones who skipped across the pond water.

Suddenly the water began to burble in fury, mud and clumps of grass were flung into the air. Llewellyn could see their terrible forms... They had wings like massive bats, but bodies of toads as large as the giant mastiff hounds, their strange tails looked like lizards but tipped with vicious barbs.

Suddenly they burst out of the water, gnashing and biting furiously with their rows of spiked teeth. Llewellyn quickly opened her arms and whispered "Falaichte!". Suddenly a swarm of these furious aberrations leapt into the air and soared directly at the ropes with mutton hammocks, each one of them snapped their massive jaws around the legs ripped them right off the tree only to directly impale themselves on the wooden pikes below...wooden spear tips quickly plunged right through their wings, legs and even stomachs with ease.

"Now Lads! Take those silver weapons and hack them to pieces!" Lachlann and Finlay quickly charged out from cover. Finlay hefted Connacht's claymore from it's sheath and hacked furiously with the greatsword, until he watched the wretched monsters wings and midsections already healing from the impaled wound.

Lachlann ran right past shouting "stop gawking or they will regenerate! Hack them to shreds already!" and he was wielding his sword and Finlay's broad sword in two different hands, wildly hacking and slashing at the impaled Bog-Leapers, chopping legs, wings, tails and heads off with each strike and slash.

As the Bog leapers attacked Finlay would not be outdone and used the longsword to split the monstrosities directly in half. Like lighting, more began to surge from the swap and fly directly at them, Lachlann and Finlay were not caught off guard and used their blades to Block the incoming beasts... the monsters charged into those razor-sharp swords so aggressively they cut themselves into bloody pieces.

The fighting was swift and furious, the sharp blades hacking, slashing, gutting and disemboweling the beasts...thankfully their swords were etched with silver runes in the style of the Ostramann clans or with silver knotwork across the blades in the style of the Caledonians.

The silver leaf on the blades made the wounds fatal, It was said that simple iron weapons actually could only temporarily cut these Bog

39

Leapers into pieces before their parts would wriggle themselves together again. But Silver burned them badly, the wounds stopped regenerating as the terrors bled their azure blue blood all over the marsh.

Lachlann and Finlay looked about, their wild, wool like hair was covered in the blue blood of fae as was their proud clan tartans. This was but a minor setback for a whole village was liberated from these beasts.

All of them quickly grabbed glass and porcelain vials and gathered the blue blood of the fae... for it harnessed the very power of magic incarnate. Llewellyn knew this stuff could power the magic of the coven or empower the low magick of Connacht into devastating explosions of devastating sorcery.

Dierdre and Claidoghna, Llewellyn's coven sisters, would love to have this stuff around in spirits like absinthe, especially in times of desperate need for, life was harsh, unexpected and short in the Samhain Isles.

Suddenly she could hear something in the wind "alas fair changeling child" she could more sense it in her mind "feed me those bog leapers and I shall give yee a gift." the voice psychically transmitted into her mind.

"Did you hear that lads?" She said

Lachlann and Finlay looked at her strange, "heard what? Ya little fool ya. I heard nothing!" Lachlann sneered.

"There!" she pointed at a small mud island filled with sticks and reeds jutting out. She quickly grabbed two dead bog-leapers, she marched up to the mud island and flung the corpses into the center of the island.

The island quickly slammed shut, as a massive set of snapping jaws clamped around the cadavers of the fae beasts. Suddenly the monster reared it's head out of the water and said "how kind of you to feed me. Give me the rest of these irritating bog beasts and I might give you an very special gift!" in a gravely voice.

The beast was long, like a giant eel but with a huge and wide mouth like that of a gargantuan catfish...but it's teeth was truly terrifying...for they were serrated into spikes like backwards facing tridents! Llewellyn shook with fear thinking about how if that bit someone it could simply roll and saw their entire limb right off!

"Who are you? What is your name?" she implored.
The Monster only replied "I am the basket weaver and I am enemy to the bog leapers!"

They finished hurling the dead Bog-leapers into the Basket-Weaver's maw... Suddenly the creature rose to it's full height, like some horrific snake of monstrous proportions. It spoke with a deep and cruel voice "come children, check my maw, I believe a splint of bone is digging within my tooth and it hurts so painfully!" He said as he opened his giant mouth open, his gums had blotches of blackened flesh and other areas of pinked flesh.

Llewellyn smiled and said "Alright mighty fish beasty, I shall easily do it but in a mere moment's notice!" she smiled and she waltzed right into the monsters maw to inspect the wound in the monsters mouth.

The Basket-Weaver smiled as she walked in..... and quickly snapped it's mouth shut! Lachlann and Finlay were furious at the deception and the monster laughed as it began to pull itself deep in the deeper parts of the nearby pond...intending to drowned the sweet Llewellyn in the deep, murky waters below.

The beast stopped it's laughing and started to scream in agony, it's eyes wild and wide open as it trashed about...finally it hefted itself up into the canopy of the trees and sneezed furiously...Llewellyn came flying out of the monster's mouth, covered in mucus as she was laughing maniacally.

The Basket weaver screamed in agony, "what have you done, Harlot! Oh by the Tuatha De Denaan! I am in agony!" it screamed horrifically.

Llewellyn simply laughed and said "this is some of the strongest chili powder and horse radish sauce from all of Vyzantia! No monster in these frigid northern lands has ever developed a taste for such fiery spice!" she smiled.

41

"Now Monster, fetch me my gift before my two brutish friends here hack yer guts open and cut yee into wee pieces!" she mockingly laughed.

The Basket Weaver looked terrified and coughed up a strange item from it's gullet, an amber colored flute made from the tusk of a long dead Mammoth from the steppes of the eastern Altai.

Llewellyn smiled. "Such a lovely flute of nature! Here beast, drink this rich milk-butter from my satchel, it should cure you of the burning spice!"

With that she flung a small jug of the thickest cream into the poor Basket Weaver's maw for which gave the monster a sudden level of respite.

"Thank the Tuatha!" the Basket Weaver replied. "I must return to my bog" and with that he sunk below the dark waters to form his basket trap once again.

(Later on that Night)

Llewellyn returned to camp, playing the most somber of dirges from this ancient flute and she was hailed a heroine. It was early in the morning, somewhere around 4am. Connacht smiled for the lads returned from their first adventure and already cleared out the bog from these man eating beasts. "I am proud of ye lads!" he beamed.

As the Caledonian villagers, Shelta nomads and Ostramann mercenaries cheered and danced. Their wagons getting packed with meats, drinks, trenches and smoked cheeses for such a heroic act. Somebody was watching them, she hunched over but would otherwise be tall, her claws scratched the willow trees bark in anticipation and hatred...her warped "children" also took their other monstrous forms, like mastiff dog's in face with sagging folds of skin but strong and heavy of body. They watched from the shadows of the marsh as the foolish humans celebrated their victory over the monsters of the marsh... who were their beloved, monstrous pets...

Chapter 3: The Celebration of Sahwin at Castle Calhoun.

"An eater lacking mouth and even maw; yet trees and beasts to it are daily bread. Well-fed it thrives and shows a lively life, but give it water and you do it dead.

What am I?"

Connacht's Claymore impaled two young highland pikemen with one swift charge, The blade plunged through the chest, heart and ribcage of the first and then right through his back while impaling the second soldier in the same manner with a horrifying cracking noise as the blade pierced right through their sternums. He twisted the blade to his left side and ripped a massive gash through both militiamen as they screamed in agony. Crimson red blood erupted from their jagged wounds and they fell to the emerald green grass of the highlands. They bled out like slaughtered swine and then collapsed onto the grassy valley as they died.

Connacht was furious, He hefted his greatsword high into the heavens and brought it crashing down into the flank of the enemy pike formation, he cut the arm off one soldier with a brutal hack and then grabbed the sword in a half-swording stance. He then proceeded to smash the Crossguard into the teeth of another spear-bearer! The blow knocked out the man's front teeth with a violent shower of crimson gore and ivory bone. The soldier was in agony and was knocked back, stunned from so much pain. Connacht quickly smashed a pike aside with one parry of the mighty sword and then brought the pointed pommel crashing down on the temple of another young warrior. The temple of his skull was shattered with a loud crack and the militiamen screamed, then fell over in severe agony, blood leaking from his eyes, nostrils and mouth.

Connacht spun his sword in great arcs when fighting offensively or grabbed the blade's ricasso (the secondary handle above the crossguard) and used the sword like a staff when fighting defensively. The Clan Ivar pikemen were stuck in a mountain pass and could not move effectively, packed into the pass like salted hams in a box.

His Claymore Impaled, Hacked, Slashed, Chopped, Parried, Blocked, Bashed and Crushed with the Pommel, each dismemberment, each brutal death made Connacht feel more and more furious…it was as if the blade wanted to the drink blood of these soldiers! The pikemen were getting cut to bloody shreds from the wild, sweeping arcs of his Greatsword for they had only leather armor.

They were chopped in half, their legs and arms hacked off, their stomachs were ripped wide open from the sawing motion of the blade! They counterattacked in full force but Connacht would use his sword like a staff and block their clumsy spears, bash them in the teeth with the Crossguard or crush their eye sockets with the Pommel. The Pikes themselves were hacked in half or easily deflected when they struck his heavily armored coat of plates.

 Many of them drew their Messer Swords, broad swords built for hacking and slashing, but against his defensive half-swording style and his thick armored coat, their stabs were easily deflected and countered. Connacht simply chose to ignored many of their attacks which harmlessly bounced off his heavily armored coat. In many ways he wanted them to strike him, for they were wide open to get cut to ribbons by his brutal blade!

Connacht tore a bloody hole right through the Ivar clansmen's pike-formation but eventually he was surrounded by hundreds of pikes and broadswords. He fought fiercely the whole time but chunks of his armor began to get torn off, his helmet was getting dented from their furious onslaught. They started wearing him down, thankfully the ward of Tyr, granted him hardened scales on his skin, but the Rune of Tiwaz would soon fade.

Connacht still fought furiously, ripping open soldiers' bodies with his blade, chopping them in half at the shoulder, with one expert strike he decapitated three Clan Ivar pikemen at once! Then with another sweeping arc from his blade several Ivar men had their legs hacked off which many horrified soldiers tumbling down the mountain still screaming, arcs of crimson blood left trails of gore in their wake. Deliving such a devastating flurry of attacks exhausted him badly, he was gasping for air. He could feel his lungs pounding and his lungs thundering, he was about to faint!

From the distance a loud, familiar ram's horn could be heard, it's clarion call ringing across the mountains! Suddenly a horde of pikes rushed forwards, the bloodied soldiers determined to impale Connacht in unison. He grabbed his blade at the ricasso handle and caught the most of the pikes on the flate of his blade! Hefting them up in the air with his incredible strength but lo! Other pikes came in, striking him all over his torso, most were deflected but several pierced through his armor and bit deeply into his flesh underneath.

Connacht could hear a voice in his mind "Butcher them! Slaughter them! Drink their blood and never retreat!" his sword seemed to gently vibrate each time he heard this ghostly whisper in his mind.

In an instance war-horns could be heard from behind Connacht! Reinforcements! A swarm of furious, allied Halberdiers led by the swift, one eyed Duncan, lord of the Calhoun Clan! He Came charging down the mountain with his furious Axebearing warriors.

Connacht's Knox highlanders also joined ranks with Duncan. They came surging down the mountain pass with their heavy footfalls. Their shorter, Lochaber-Axes were perfect for the environment, the weapon's thick spear-heads easily pierced through the Pikemen's leather armor while the heavy Axe-Heads chopped both pikes and pikemen to bloody pieces with a sickening hack!. They surged like a furious stampede of rampaging bison that swept the stubborn soldiers aside like a flood washes away a spider web.

The Pikemen fled in terror and their fleeing men crashed into other pike formations who were marching up the mountain, this in turn shattered their well-organized ranks. Duncan-the-one-eyed ran up to Connacht and said "yer bleeding heavily lad! Rest for now, we got this!" he smiled. Connacht shook his head and roared "Berkano!" the rune of life and rebirth, his ragged wounds began to slowly knit themselves shut. He felt revitalized and his second wind gave him Heart! He furiously stormed down the mountain, his heavy footfalls thundering against the rocky road and his Great-sword cleaving, hacking, and butchering any Ivar warrior who stood defiantly in his wake!

The Ivar pike formations shattered, they fled in terror and any of them who were bold enough to stand and fight where surrounded by a swarm of furious axe-bearers who cut them to Gorey shreds! Duncan turned to Connacht "Stop! We have won, the bastards flee back to their homelands of the Fjords of Orkney!" Duncan smiled, slapping his hand on Connacht's blood-soaked shoulder.

Victory! His men cheered, lifting their poleaxes in the air! *Honor! Vigilance!* They cheered. Connacht hefted the Clan Knox banner high, his family clan! It's tartan patterns and colors waving wildly, red, blue, azure, green, yellow and in pattern only recognizable to his Clan. The Clan Coat of Arms was flown high, a symbol of a great helm, a shield with a eagle and the motto "We will defend this!" Bagpipes wailed in celebration and Boudhrain drums thundered. One hundred men smashing a two-thousand-man army! Victory! Heroism! Wake up! Hooray! The men began screaming and cheering. Victory! Wake-up! Honor!

But then he realized that all these fine young men, now dead on the field, they could have been his bastard sons?! Tears began streaming down his face! How many sons did he murder that wouldn't see their loving wives and parents again? Wake-up! They could have been his distant kin! Fookin Wake-up! They could have been Ostramann cousins, children born from Nordic men and Caledonian women! Just like him!

Wake-up ye Pig Fookin arsehole!

Suddenly Connacht awoke from his dream. Covered in a cold sweat, grabbing himself all over for bloody wounds...just old scars. He sighed in relief. The Battle of Dun Lennox, Where the Knox Clan rallied from the mountain strongholds and smashed the greater Ivar army was now long gone! Truly an amazing battle in his prime but tragically so many youths perished in that brutal Clan War.

 He realized that if it wasn't for him and his men, the allies of the Gunnars would have stormed through the mountain pass and ravaged Clan Calhoun's lands. Thank the Denann they were defeated there.

 So much blood though, so many fine young lads and lasses butchered, violated, crippled and mutilated during that horrible war two decades prior. He was a young lad back then, naive and filled with hope. Until he witnessed the horrors of the Clan civil war and the barbaric acts committed.

Bonnie laughed gently "Victory! Honor! Heroism! "WE Will Defend This!" Buwahahahaha!" she guffawed.

Connacht frowned "listen here yee silly heifer, that was an important battle and many of my friends died in that war...besides it was our Clan that gave sanctuary to the Shelta when it was all those other High and Great clans that butchered your people like cattle! Don't mock me!" he snarled.

"Allright my love. Goodness! We Grai Shelta have nothing but respect for yer Knox Clan... you just sounded so incredibly odd with yer muffled screaming and your weakened punching of the sides of the Wagon, you were in such a deep sleep but that dream must have been so potent."

Connacht laughed, he realized she didn't mean anything by it and chuckled. Still, he felt a twinge of sadness as tears came running down his eyes. He remembered the horrible war... children cut to pieces, women torn open, innocent farmers impaled on pikes and Shelta Gypsies hanging from trees on the roads... Clan civil wars were horrific events that many of the people of Samhain feared more than the plague itself... and the Unseelie fae came flooding down from the mountains to devour the dead and raid their cattle, sheep and even children from abandoned farms...Connacht could never forgive them for that...

The journey across the highlands to the great stronghold of Clan Calhoun was hard and even treacherous. The mist was thick like milk, the wind howled like bane-sidhe (banshees), cold rain and hail pelted them, dampening their wool gambesons beneath their Armored coats. Finally, when Connacht, Lachlann and Finlay arrived to the granite-walled stronghold, they were met with the loud clarion call of horns, drums and dancing Calhoun folk. Connacht could feel his ears, cheeks, forearms and chest get incredibly hot to counteract the wet, freezing rains.

They entered through the wide-open, oaken gates of the stronghold, crudely built but strong and sturdy. The vast open courtyard was filled with revelers and cooks, merchants and clan warriors. Their Clan Tartans and coat of arms were hanging from the castle wall, a red stag with a black X behind him. Their tartan was dark blue, green, yellow and azure in it's own plaid pattern.

The Grai-tribe Shelta left their wagons and horses outside the castle walls in a circular formation and they all disembarked, giving their animals feedbags full of oats. Their guard dogs followed with the Shelta Houndmaster who sat at his own table and fed them tallow and scraps of meat.

Connacht rested against a large cairn as he witnessed the lighting of the Great Fire of Sahwin Eve. The festival fairing goodbye to the Summer Season and coming of the winter.

A large bull was slaughtered, roasted and Clan Calhoon feasted on the rich marbled flesh of this mighty beast as it was roasted on pikes surrounding the epic fire of the wicker man. Generous portions were given to their guests; loaves of potato bread complimented the beef. Lord Duncan, head of Clan Calhoun cheered and welcomed his guests but lady Rhona, his daughter, seemed bored or listless. She was wearing a fine green dress with her red hair combed to her shoulders, her breasts were pushed up through a bodice as well as her lips full, plump and with a rogue lipstick.

 Connacht was impressed of how ravishingly Lady Rhona had grown, truly she was a full woman but he remembered his place...she was going to be wed to the mighty lord of the Gunnar Clan, his ancient clan enemies who now became tenuous allies...thankfully this marriage was believed to unite the Clans of the Highlands with the Clans of the Northern Isles in a strong peace treaty.

Clan Gunnar was already there, their banner with their coat of arms flying high, crimson red background, a symbol of a mighty fist bearing a hefty axe aloft. They sat at the northern side of the courtyard at their own feasting tables while lord Calhoun, his men and his guests sat at the southern end of the courtyard at theirs. Gunnar clansmen were large, stout, strong and many of them looked unfriendly and simply uncaring as they devoured generous portions of meat, bread, ale and their own mead (honey wine).

As Connacht and his kerns walked through the castle gates he was suddenly approached by the massive Jarl Hjalmar, lord of the Gunnar Clan. This man towered over many other men; he was powerful of build, wide of shoulder but somewhat portly. He had a great round head atop a massive thick neck, his beard was a dark mahogany brown and tied into various thick braids. He turned to Connacht with a frown "Yer a wee bit late!" He snarled.

"My apologies lord, there were savage Draugr on the road, I am honor-bound to cleanse their burial mounds!" Connacht respectfully implored.

"Slaying Draugr? Allright ye Milk-drinking cheese-faced shilpit, Mim-

49

moothed, sniveling worm-eyed hotten blaugh! Yer lucky I am feeling generous!" With that Hjalmar hurled three small bags to Connacht. He caught all of them. When they opened the bags it was filled with a handful of scintillating golden coins. Hjalmar turned around, walked off and avoided contact with them throughout the night.

Connacht snarled "Milk Drinker? That arsehole, I would impale that fat nord like a roasting pig if it wasn't for his generosity!" he quietly snarled. "Still, damn, these golden coins should last us for months!" Finlay exclaimed and Lachlann simply replied "Aye! We could exchange that for so much silver!"

But he quickly turned his eyes to the festivities inside the castle walls and smiled, forgetting about that loud mouth asshole. The feasting, the drinking of spiced ale and cider, the dancing around the burning wicker man, the parading with masks of various fae, goblins, bogarts and ghosts. Connacht loved the previous holiday celebrations of Sahwin, were summer ends and the winter begins, when the Seelie court fades in power and the Unseelie reign. A Dark and dangerous time of year but incredibly exciting nonetheless.

After feasting, dancing and drinking, gifts, pastries and candied fruit were given to children. The fruits were apples, berries and nuts, lightly baked and covered in honey. Soon the revelers grew tired and they retreated to their fortified bastel houses, the stronghold of Lord Duncan and even back to the wagonburg of the Shelta...some lucky Calhoun locals sneaked into the loving arms and warm beds of lovely Shelta men and women to have a night of passion.

(On the Day of Sahwin.)

 Connacht awoke to the day of Sahwin proper and he had eaten well that morning, the clans sat around great tables and cooked up several cauldrons of the creamiest porridge. Connacht added the slightly musky goats' milk with various local tart and sweet berries like cranberries and blueberries.

Honey and rich butter were there to complement their humble gruel that was served on plain bread trenchers. This breakfast was in turn served with a fine, warm, honeyed pine-needle tea

As the day passed, he witnessed the lads and lasses assemble their costumes and masks, they hid various treats of honeyed nuts and pastries across the stronghold's interior. The cattle were released on the fields, the barley, wheat and rye where already harvested so the beasts simply ate the hay and weeds which grew around the Clan's walls. They all slept peacefully for the next day of Sahwin proper.

As Twilight settled upon Sahwin Proper, the assorted clans and tribes once again united in mirth for feasting, dancing, gift giving and celebration. This time a colossal moose was paraded into the castle grounds and Lord Duncan gave Jarl Hjalmar a gargantuan axe, etched with silvered knot-work patterns. Truly a glorious gift, Hjalmar bowed in respect, hefting the mighty axe in the Air and with one titanic strike, cut the thick, muscled neck of the moose in one massive strike! Blood flooded all over the castle courtyard floor while the assembled host roared in excitement for the sacrificial feast to begin!

 This time Clan Gunnar was given the honor to roast the sacrifice before the gods of the west and the north. The moose was skinned, gutted and its best organs were placed in pots or pikes, the offal was fed to the dogs. Fatty gooses, piglets and lambs, all slaughtered, skinned and gutted, were placed within the moose's empty stomach cavity and then the opening was sewn shut... a great wooden skewer, more log than spear was driven through its mouth and out it's backside by the Ostramann butchers and cooks.

The epic carcass of the moose was placed over a small mountain of red coals and roasted from midday towards twilight. Various herbs like Juniper twigs, rosemary, basil leaves and sage were stuffed into the moose's nostrils, throat, anus and sliced openings in its meaty flanks between the ribs. Finally, strong red wines were poured into the openings of the beast to soften the meat.

51

Connacht, accompanied by his kerns Finlay and Lachlann, turned to lord Duncan and said "By the Gods these fooken nords always have to have the biggest cockel in the entire room! What a bunch of show-offs bringing in a whole Moose...what next? Are they going to roast a fooken Dragon? Mayhaps a whale?"

The all covered their mouths laughing at the sheer bombastic nature of the Nordic roast. Lord Duncan, while laughing, shushed them "let's not enrage these Ostramann berserkers while they cook us a meal, at least they are being generous!"

Lady Rhona could barely contain her laughter, slamming her fist repeatedly against the oaken table while trying to hide her chortles.

 A local bard known as Finnigan; who was short, plump and feminine amn, had long pointed ears and curly chestnut hair crowneing his head. The hair dropped down to his shoulders in lovely locks. Some said he was a changeling or half-elf for his beautiful features and lovely voice but that was wild rumor. He hailed from the distant island of Beltaine; said to be a place of the Summer Palace of the Seelie Fae.

He came sliding dramatically in on well-oiled boots across the cobblestone courtyard and began singing a lovely song of the origin of the holiday of Sahwin. This song was named "in honor of the island of Samhain, for this was where Fionn Mac Cumhail defeated the king of the Unseelie, Aillen, at the great castle of Dun Tara." he versed. Though this is but one of many tails of how Sahwin started and how the island of Samhain became named.

"This was where the great Prince Nuada was slain, king of elvenkind and replaced by Lugos, Half-elven, the Sun God. Where the the Dark Tyrant, Balor the Destroyer and his rampaging army of Formorians Giants, Orcneas, Sea Serpents and other terrors were smashed in battle at the Second battle of Maig Tuired." he lauded

"Samhain was home to the ancient race of mountain-Giant's known as the Firbolg, who were said to sleep deep under the earth, Imprisoned beneath mighty trees in the mountains. It was said they taught the wild peoples, the Woads, the art of magic." he recanted.

The assembled host suddenly grew quiet as Finnlay gently hammered the dulcimer and began to sing in a crescendo, hitting both high octaves, middle octaves and low ones while his Dulcimer harmonized with his voice. Llewellyn suddenly broke free from the crowd and played her mammoth tusk flute, the airy and subtle notes gave the melody an almost ethereal and otherworldly note to Finnigan's rhyming verses and elegant dulcimers chords that harmonized in the darkness.

 Finnigan sang as he played upon his fine dulcimer of steel strings on oaken frame.

"When the Summer leaves and the Winter comes.

The Veil grows thin and ancestors return.

The parade of faeries and play of Drums.

The beasts are sacrificed and the pyres burn.

 The Harvest are done; the gourds will be carved.

The lanterns of Jack will hold the red-hot burning coals

Cider sweet and roasted beef is served

The sagas are sung and the praising of goals

 For Fionn held the spear and waited for the Night

In came the Cruel King of the Unseelie

Playing a cursed harp and spat a fiery sight

Fionn then flung his spear and it struck readily

 Victory even though Dun Kara burned heavily

The Fianna sung Fionn's name victoriously

A burning man built in great mockery

A feast of flesh, sweet treats eaten greedily.”

 He then paused theatrically and catching the audiences' attention.

(Finnigan then suddenly jumped right back into song, startling the audience.(

 “Hail Fionn Mac Cumhail slayer of the dark King!

Hail Lughasa slayer of the giant and terrible Balor!

Hail the dance of fire where Dead and Living Sings!

Hail the Autumn feast for Samhain's Songs of Valor!”

Finnigan stopped singing as the assembled clansmen and women cheered in appreciation of his performance. Suddenly the Bodhran drums thundered with the Uilleann pipes and fiddles.

 A mirthful jig it was with the participants danced in circles and burning torches around the great burning wickerman in celebration.

Connacht smiled, Finnigan's poem was short but sweet. Connacht sat down on the great oaken blank with the Clan Calhoon chieftain known as Duncan the one eyed. Our Warrior was happy to have traveled to Clan Calhoon lands, for he was hired to protect the Shelta Carnival who was paid to bring great mirth to the wedding alliance between Clan Gunnar and Clan Calhoun. Tragically he felt a wince of pain for Lady Rhona for she was offered as a token of appeasement between the former enemy clans and he could see the sorrow in her lovely eyes.

 But something irritated Connacht, for being a formidable mercenary guard, he knew that Clan Calhoun lived very close to the mountainous border of the dark side of the Island... the side of the island where the savage, mad and cursed fae dwelled ... they were known as the Unseelie and they hated the men of the north and looked in disgust even at the local tribes of men who predated his own Knox clan.

54

Those fickle beings generally stayed on their side, the dark eastern and northern side of the Island but they were not shy to lead raids past the twelve duns to pillage the cattle of men and steal their grain.

Did they even eat what they stole or did they do this simply for a malicious form of humor to watch the clans people starve? Nobody knows, but Connacht knew their weaknesses... cold iron and silver. For he was not a simple minded Gallowgalas warrior, he also knew secrets of alchemy which he learned from an apothecary that immigrated to Dun Kara all the way from the far western lands of the Vyzantine Empire.

Connacht turned to Duncan "Good Chief Duncan, what beverage in your opinion, would help wash down this magnificent roast of beef?"

Duncan one eye, turned with his good eye to Connacht, he was crowned with violet flowers from the highland heather and spoke "aye, lad I would say the spiced cider from your Clan Knox or your lord's boysenberry mead from Clan Gunnar, your clan still has the talent from your mixed galeo-nordic ancestors to make a fine cider infused with wild berries." Smiled Duncan the one eyed.

In walked the bride, Rhona, she also wore a multicolored crown made from wild mountain flowers in a white and green flowing gown. She wasn't willowy thin like the princesses of so many fairy-tales but quite stout though in a very effeminate way. Her legs were like thick oak boughs and corpulent, her rear was pendulous and she was somewhat portly but her face was round like a baby and sweet. She smiled at the assembled audience and walked before her massive groom Hjalmar. Rhona handed her hand to Hjalmar and he gently kissed it, she blushed... but Connacht could see that some tears were running down her cheeks as she held them back.

It was too painful for Connacht to dwell on this arranged marriage so he simply turned his attention to the fine dinner feast before him. The boysenberry mead was rich and delicious and it complemented the fatty, marbled and bloody chunks of moose. This rich meat was served with the earthy potato-bread and dumplings, and the roasted assortment of beets, radish, cabbage and buttered carrots. Connacht ate well but watched the groom and bride quietly from the side of his eye... he could quickly sheath and strike with his arming sword or his mighty claymore so swiftly the human eye couldn't keep up... great lochaber-axes were hoisted on hooks directly on the walls behind him.

 He must always be watching and on guard lest a rival clan member attempt an assassination.

Thankfully the bride-to-be and the groom-to-be went their separate ways to their own clan bedrooms.

Clan Calhoon had a grand Bastle-House, damn near a castle or fortress for a humble clan of cattle farmers and ale brewers. Their slate and granite walls were stout as was their mighty oaken gate portcullis.

The bon-fire that of the burning man, a defiling ritual and monument was burning extra hot on this Sahwin night... both clans danced furiously around the fire, in a great masquerade performance and celebration, many of the highlanders wore the masks of various dead spirits or of mischievous fae.

Connacht smiled as he witnessed his squires (called Kerns in the Samhain Highlands); Finlay and Lachlan, danced with several of the plump womenfolk of Clan Calhoun. Mixing of Clan blood was good, the children were generally born healthy and it strengthened alliances between clans.

As Connacht made way to his humble quarters and pulled off of his brigantine armor and wool gambeson coat, he quickly slid into his hay bed and pulled the heavy bear fur blankets. He took a jack-o-lantern and filled it with smoldering coals back to his hearth, he then flung the coals into the fire pit and it helped him start a new fire to warm up his sleeping quarters. The nights in the highlands are both cold and damp, hence the hearth fires helped drive out both and keep the lungs of the sleepers healthy and free of the cold fungal rot.

As he pulled into his bed for sleep, suddenly both Finlay and Lachlann snuck into the sleeping quarters near their master Connacht.

"My, you Lads are rather quick!" Connacht laughed.

 "Syrrah, taking time to pleasure womenfolk is something only the most wretchedly of poor men worry about! Besides we gifted them generously, they were paid for their 'labor"!" laughed Finlay.

Connacht laughed "Alright lads, just remember when doth find thou truest love... let her have hers before thou art have thine. Not all women should be made love to in the fashion of a common whore,"

Finlay laughed "alright man, thou art ruin such a night of pleasure and festivities with moralizing? Celebrate in our victory!"

Connacht roared in laughter "Aye, you lusty two stallions! The two of you have a point. The life of a mercenary is hard and sometimes too quick... it's good for the both of thee to enjoy as much debauchery as possible."

Connacht poured himself and the lads tall horns of spiced ale... the drink was magnificently flavored with honey and hazelnut... heady, warming and intoxicating. From his bed chambers he could hear the bard Finningan playing the exotic, Vyzantinian, two headed flute known as the *duduk*. It's haunting melody allowed this battle-scarred warrior to fall into a warm, mirthful sleep of pleasure devoid of nightmares and the terrible nostalgia which afflicted men of war.

As Connacht drifted into his slumber, he could hear the soothing yet haunting melody play, moving through the bastelhouse stronghold towards the northern wing...wasn't that where the bride to be was housed? No matter, the clan guards should keep her chastity safe from any lascivious or lusty bards of possible changeling persuasion.

Connacht drifted swiftly into a deep sleep and dreamed of a terrible battle between two giants, a green mother of the forest battling a terrible giant of the northern seas. The two battled, fighting over the lands of what looked like the northernmost orkney islands. One represented the freezing northern seas and the sea giant hurled chunks of glaciers at the forest mother... in turn she summoned a powerful southern wind which melted these icy boulders in place. The mother of the forest slowly began losing the battle and she screamed, screamed in terror and looked directly at Connacht and screamed "why?!"Why!?!

Chapter 4: The midnight raid of the Unseelie.

**"Who is that great one
who grasps the earth,
swallowing wood and water.
Bad weather he dreads,
wind, but no man,
and picks a fight with the sun.
King Heidrek,
guess my riddle?"**

Connacht awoke from his slumber to the screaming of women! they were under attack! The nearby Calhoun barn's were set aflame and became raging infernos! Horses and cattle were screaming in agony and terror. How did the enemies get in the stronghold though? This rustic clan fortress was built quite sturdy... Connacht wondered .

He realized he had no time to wonder and He ran out of his bedroom with Finlay and Lachlan came surging out with shields, javelins and broad swords. Thankfully his brigantine coat was easy to don in short time. As they ran outside Connacht noticed something strange, a heavy fog descended upon the stronghold and many of the Clan warriors fell into a deep sleep, even though there was screaming, fighting and a barn set aflame!

Suddenly the thick fog released great Swarms of ravenous, winged fae creatures, known as slaugh, warped and monstrous relatives of the playful sprites. They attacked like a swarm of ravenous, bloodthirsty bats... flying in swarms, biting bloody chunks out of the Calhoun peoples. These miniature flying monsters picked up a screaming goat in the air and flew around it like an angry swarm of bees...they quickly ripped the screaming goat to bloody shreds as chunks of bone, viscera and bloodied bones fell to the ground. They then sadistically laughed in their high-pitched voices about what they had just done!

Connacht grabbed a satchel of powdered iron dust and flung it at the ravenous swarm of maddened sprites... the powdered cold iron exploded, which instantly caused the ravenous swarm to scream in unison, they were in great agony for the unseelie hated the touch of cold iron or silver...bane of all fae kind.

The screaming slaugh clawed at their wings, fanged maws and multifaceted eyes many of them flew away in misery while the other half plummeted to the ground and died in screeching agony as they melted into bloody gore on the rocky earth.

"Come lad!" screamed Connacht and looked at Finlay. He ran over to the burning barn, the roof a raging inferno and the animals screamed and roared interror. He clasped his hands together and nodded at Finlay.

Finlay nodded his blonde head and jumped onto Connacht's folded hands to parkour over the barn window. Finlay crashed down on the hay bed with his hob-nailed boots and quickly rolled toward the barn door and with one swift kick, kicked off the wooded bar that held the door firmly closed...

The barn doors swung open and the horses and cattle stampeded in terror out of the burning barn.

Lord Duncan the one eyed ran out with his sons, daughters and farm-hands in fear from the great gate of their Keep.

"Connacht, great Gallowgalas, don't worry about me, we will fight this fire with the well-water! Go fetch the cattle and horses... keep them safe from the ravenous Unseelie! The Cu-sith and Bogarts will slaughter the majority of them if you don't get to them with haste! I will pay thee handsomely in silver coins if you save those animals!" cried Duncan Calhoun.

"Aye, syrah, I shall fetch these beasties and protect them from the ravenous fae!" Connacht roared and with a wave of his hand "Finlay! Lachlan! Come to me lads, we got cattle and horses to protect!"

Connacht leapt upon a galloping horse and chased after the terrified animals... Finlay and Lachlan were so swift of foot they could easily follow behind the horse. Many of the Calhoun and Gunnar warriors followed Connacht, grabbing their mail-coats, Lochaber-axes, swords, spears and various other weapons.

The cattle and horses stormed out to the fallow fields outside of the castle and formed into a defensive circle. Connacht realized they were surrounded by darkness... he quickly pulled forth a potion made of a glowing sea algae called Noctiluca Scintillans, or some other fancy and pedantic terms the alchemists of Ravenna have named it. He drank the potion swiftly and the almost pitch-black darkness of night became illuminated with a blue green glow! His eyes emanated this potent bio-luminescent light and it revealed a swarm of savage and bestial fae in the grain fields, The cattle formed a defensive circle to fight off these terrors.

Connacht leapt off the wild horse and surged towards the pack of brutish boggarts... the bestial fae were squat and stout but built powerfully, their maws were similar to the mastiff hounds being able to crush a man's shin bones with one bite. What was truly deadly was the heavy pole-arms these stout brutes deftly wielded.

These raven-beaked halberds which the locals called Bill-hooks were both farming instruments but also hefty weapons with good reach and could punch through helmets, shields even skulls with a well-placed strike.

He flung another cold-iron powder bomb at these brutish fae and it stung and burned them, but they were made of sterner stuff than the slaugh. They roared in agony and pain and the powder burned their eyes and noses making them bleed... but they had the fortitude to bear with the pain and fight on... never the less it dazed them and gave Connacht enough time to charge past their bill-hook formation and attack them with his claymore with merciless sweeps, chops and overhead strikes.

Connacht and his kerns attacked the stunned Boggarts, Connacht's great sword struck true and hacked off the limbs and heads of these brutes, each blow sounded like a cleaver hacking apart a pig's hammock.

The boggarts struck clumsily but did occasionally strike Connacht, thankfully his stalwart armored-coat deflected these blows from the bill-hooks... the bill-hooks that struck true did pierce his thick coat of iron and mail, thankfully the thick woolen gambeson underneath robbed the piercing blades of much of their momentum, still though, the blows that did pierce even the gambeson they bit into his flesh and he was bleeding in many places.

Every blow the boggarts landed on the berserk Connacht, he then retaliated tenfold; arms were chopped off, heads decapitated, pole-arms split in twain, stomachs ripped open with the great sword to leave the screaming boggarts disemboweled and holding their innards in their slick, bloody hands.

The surviving Boggarts fled in terror to the rocky homes beyond the Twelve Duns mountains! The borderlands between the human clans and the unseelie fae.

Suddenly a terrifying and deep howl could be heard... the cu-sith have arrived! These pitch-dark wolves from the dark moors from beyond, posed a formidable threat to even some of the most formidable fae-beasts that a gallowgalas could battle.

Quickly Connacht reached into his bandolier and drank a potion made of tea tree honey and aloe-vera, for these were some of the finest potions made by the famous alchemist of Vyzantia known as Naram-Sin. He could already feel his wounds stop bleeding and begin to slowly knit itself together.

He heard Lachlann in agony, a halberd blade bit into his thigh "Finlay, lad, fetch another of the panacea potions, use the propolis to close this man's wounds and feed him the potion to heal and staunch his bleeding!" Finlay quickly caught the potion of panacea that Connacht threw his way and poured the vibrant green elixir into Lachlann's mouth, he then procured the resinous propolis into the bloody wounds of Lachlann and closed the ragged wound with the potent adhesive substance.

The boggarts could be heard screaming in terror as they fled uphill to their highland homes... they were almost distant now, Connacht slowly turned his back and began to prod the cattle along with the butt of his Claymore... some of the older cattle, exhausted now, slowly hung back as they followed the herd back to the fortified Clan Stronghold.

Suddenly one of the animals screamed in bloody terror and Connacht spun around in horror... the oldest of the cattle was viciously getting torn to shreds as it screamed in agony... bloody chunks of gore and viscera was flung into the air around the cow as it thrashed about it torment. Great bloody claw marks ripped bloody gashes all over the cows hide on all sides... as if some invisible monster was tearing the poor beast to shreds.

Connacht quickly reached for his potent wormwood spirit; The hallucinogenic drink that fueled his hedge magic. This potion was potent and the average man would hallucinate but those trained in the mysterious arts of alchemy could reverse the phenomena to see the unseen.

Only then Connacht saw the terror before his eyes, two vicious Cu-Sith, giant wolf or houndlike beasts with massive fanged maws, one large finger-claw on each front foot... thick, corded muscles running down their shoulders and neck, their thick neck hair hackled high in rage. The beasts had glowing azure eyes with slits... and they can now see that Connacht could see them in the savage act of slaughter!

These beasts were quite strange though... their bodies were more like apes in many ways; they could stand up and walk like men at times or climb up trees... but they could easily descend on all fours and in turn gallop across the highland heather when pursuing prey... and they could become invisible when they wished it.

There were two of them, one was a silvery color, the other an almost midnight black, but there auras of dark red with black veins illuminated them to Connacht.

The obsidian Cu-sith looked like a male and it stepped in front of the silver one, guarding her for she was pregnant and her teats were swollen. As Connacht approached, the Dark Cu-sith released a terrifying howl so horrific that many of the Calhoun clansmen fled in terror!

Only Connacht endured, having fought dark fae on numerous occasions and knowing of the nightmarish abilities. Connacht had his silver-etched claymore drawn, He could see the Cu-sith violently tearing bloody chunks of meat from the dying cow, the poor beast breathed in ragged agony as the predatory fae tore bloody chunks out of it's body, the look of paralyzing terror was struck across its face.

The Black Cu-sith suddenly spoke "Gallowgalas I see"... it growled "I have slain several brave clansmen and quite a few nords in skirmishes in the forest but a Gallowgalas, no less skilled in alchemy." it chuckled in a sinister fashion through its fanged lips "that would be quite the battle no less!"

Connacht looked the beast in its glowing blue eyes "I fear no man, beast, walking dead nor fae and your howl has no effect upon me!"

Connacht and the Cu-sith circled each other Connacht called to the his kerns and the assembled warriors of Calhoon.

"Listen lads and lasses, best ye seek solace in the Bastle Houses and stronghold walls, the thick oak beams and solid granite should give yee protection for thine and thy cattle!" he commanded.

The Dark Cu-sith quickly turned to his beloved "Run my love, tell lord Arawann that there is a deadly Gallowgalas upon the borderlands!" and he roared in rage. The female Cu-sith quickly ran away from the oncoming battle, descending onto four legs and running as swiftly as she could through the highland grass, scrub oaks and mossy stones that littered the land. She looked like a silver blur as she sped through the rugged terrain towards the borders of the Twelve Dun mountains.

The beast stood up on it's hind legs, it was clearly two feet taller than Connacht and it charged at him like a blur, the beast was fast, damn fast as it closed the distance, faster than an eye blink! A flurry of claws and bites struck out at Connacht, he knew that he was neither as fast nor as strong as the beast so he had to take a more defensive and humble method of combat, the art of half-swording.

He grabbed the ricasso handle with his left hand and deflected the slashing claws and found a sweet moment in time to smash the pommel of his sword in the face of the monster, shattering one of it's front teeth with the blow and knocked the monster back. The beast was in agony but it swiftly retaliated, slashing Connacht's face with it's large dew claw and bloodying him badly. Connacht knew this was coming and rolled with the vicious attack in a twirl to quickly recover using the inertia and adjusting his left hand to the handle once again to deliver a devastating counter attack that slashed through the beast's throat...too bad the beast exploded in a cloud of dark shadow where the blade would have struck the Cu-Sith's throat.

Connacht smiled and quickly spun around twirling his Claymore in swift circles and he struck true. For he knew that the Cu-Sith loved striking their enemies right from the back and lo and behold the beast reappeared in it's solid form behind Connacht and was aiming to bite through the back of his nape and delivered a paralyzing blow. The arrogant beast did not see that counter attack coming and clutched as Connacht's drove his sword into it's throat, blood came gushing out from the ragged wound.

The Monster quickly looked up in it's death throes and bit down on Connacht's left shoulder, it's fangs bit deep right through the brigantine armor and agonizingly pierced deep into his flesh!

Connacht knew he was badly wounded and gasped in pain, he grabbed the sword on the ricasso-handle and he then rammed the sword's tip right through the monster's open neck and deep into its skull! The tip of the claymore violently bursting out of the top of the monster's head as the Cu-sith's eyes rolled backwards, dying instantaneously...

From across the distance Connacht could hear the terrifying howl of the other Cu-sith... she knew that the father of her children died! The silvered claymore glowing with Argentine light, slowly burning into the flesh of the dying beast. He could feel the sword whispering "More Blood!"

Connacht groaned "Finlay, Lachlann, gather up the dead slaugh and grind them up lads, we will need their pixie dust for future potions. Also cut off the toes of the boggarts and the eyes and tongue of that Cu-sith." he gasped as he made his way to the Calhoon stronghold. The ragged bite wounds were bad... Connacht made his way to the hearth fire of the keep and took a short dagger then heated it near the flames…until the blade was orange hot!

The great warrior also took a wineskin of heather-whiskey and he sprinkled in the dust of blood poppy and one vial of bee venom and another vial of cobra venom... he poured this elixir into a silver goblet from his bandoleer and uttered a word "Rollo" and then drank the potion. By the gods it was awful but the black infection around the wound stopped spreading so rapidly.

Connacht slept very poorly that night and had terrible fever dreams of horrible fae spirits attacking, slaughtering humble farmers and ripping apart their livestock. He slept near the hearth fire and could barely breath, it was agonizing. He awoke in the morning and finally his fever broke, drenched in sweat, he vomited the contents of his stomach into the fire and it seemed to soothe him slightly of his affliction.

Connacht sat around the fire and Calhoon's daughter Rhona served him porridge mixed with blue berries and honey. He slowly ate and his health began to recover; the morsels of porridge mixed with butter and sweet berries was tantalizing to the taste buds.

Connacht wiped the beads of sweat from his forehead and leaned back and groaned, he finished this fine porridge and could hear his vertebrae pop into place.

Duncan Calhoon, sat next to Connacht, the smaller children gathered around and looked at him. Connacht smiled at the children wearily and the children smiled back at him.

A snaggle toothed lad of eight summers smiled and looked right into Connacht's eyes and said "can you tell us lads and lasses a story?"

The other children, womenfolk and young warriors looked terrified from the ordeal of suffering from the Unseelie raid in Sahwin, a Holiday said to appease both humanity and the Unseelie fae that lived on this island.

Duncan leaned close with his heavily scarred and wrinkled face, Connacht could smell the well-oiled eye patch on his face. "Aye Connacht, many have heard that you can tell quite a tail...mayhaps you tell a tale related to Sahwin to get their spirits up." he whispered in Connacht's ear.

Connacht smiled "sure" he coughed and began

"Long ago...before the Nords, the Woads, Shelta and Caledonians, before man and Fae clashed ...There was a heroic race of gods, allied to an ancient race of men...who fought an epicbattle on this day...against savage giants who came from the deep ocean... the second battle of Mag Tuired...The forces of the Tuatha De Denann assembled at the great battlefield of *Mag Tuired* for the second time during the great age of the Tuatha. This time the Tuatha De Denaan, their allied human tribes of picts, their elven children the Aos Sidhe and even the mighty, subjugated race of Firbolg giants formed an alliance to Overthrow their Tyrannical masters, The Formorians!" he paused

"The Formorians were a race of sea giants, descended from the horrible titan known as Orcus. Tho they began their advance from the sea shore, the violent northern oceans of Ginnungagap crashed furiously in the wake of a mighty storm but this didn't bother the great sea giants and their stout orcneas slaves. Balor, the one-eyed destroyer, The Tyrannical grandfather of Lugh the radiant, led his titanic army from the frigid waters to crush this revolution of elf, god, firbolg giant and men, who he despised and perceived them as upstart slaves."

"The Ruler of the Tuatha De Denann, Prince <u>Nuada Airgetlám</u>, who led a mighty charge of his fey knights, made up of the finest Aos-Sidhe, called the Fianna, across the battle field riding mighty unicorns, their bronze lances piercing through both the savage orcneas warriors and even their titanic Formorian overseers in scores., Their unicorn steeds crushed the orcneas skulls and bodies underneath their thunderous charge."

"The unicorns themselves released the stunning brilliance of the full moonlight that blinded the enemy forces, weakening and shattering their formations of formidable pikes and pole-arms."

"Prince Nuada, held his silver arm high into the heavens, wielding a terrible spear known as *Gae Assail*, a barbed spear said to slay any foe instantaneously and even a nick on the most formidable foe would leave a mortal wound. Prince Nuada remembered the first battle of Mag Tuired against the Firbolg Giants and their pict allies."

"The Mightiest Firbolg Giant, Sreng, the champion, who towered as tall as the greatest of fir trees which grow upon the mountains, struck Nuada with a monstrous axe that split his shield in twain and ripped Nuada's arm asunder! Nuada roared in agony but retaliated and flung mighty Gae Assail right through the heart of Sreng, piercing his heart and killing him instantly."

The Tuatha De Denaan and their Aos Sidhe allies won a terrible victory. The first battle of Mag Tuired lasted for four days, The Firbolg king **Eochaid** was slain by the Morrigan, the death goddess, herself. . The Firbolg queen sued for peace and took prince Nuada as a lover, who impregnated her with the future Dagda (The great god). When Dagda was born, he became the new king of the Firbolg giants and ultimately forged a revolutionary alliance with the Tuatha. After the victory of the Tuatha, the God **Goibniu** forged Nuada a fine silver arm for battle.

Tragically a few years after this alliance was formed between Tuatha, Firbolg, Pict and Aos Sidhe a massive army of Formorians and their orcneas slaves invaded the solstice isles from the sea, their leader was the tyrant Balor, son of Orcus, who was said to be invincible in battle and his army was far too massive for both the Tuatha and the Firbolg to fight alone. Both factions immediately sued for peace.

For Several decades the Tautha, the Firbolg, the Picts, The Gauls and the Aos Sidhe were enslaved by the Formorians. The Dagda himself was king of the Firbolg but was enslaved with his kin, forced to till the fields to feed the ravenous armies of the Formorians... The Tautha and their Aos Sidhe servants forged fine bronze arms and armor for the Formorians armies.

Strangely enough in a few years the Formorians would retreat from the solstice isles to return to their ocean homelands of Ginnungagap to celebrate their victory and offer their sacrifices to their dead ancestor, Orcus, vengeance against all oath-breakers. King Nuada was still recovering during this time so he was replaced by Bres, son of Balor who forced himself on the Tuatha goddess Brigid, Nuada's Wife. Bres at first was compassionate but became more and more tyrannical like his father during his long reign. When Bres became an adult Balor allowed him to rule over the solstice isles and pay him tribute as he retired deep into the northern seas.

King Bres forced the Firbolg and Dagda to build a mighty fortress of granite boulders, called "Dun Bres" where he held lavish feasts and drank deeply of ale and cider, but only his formorian allies were invited to these feasts, the feasting halls guarded by their strongest orcneas warriors.

"During this period of the Formorian Tyranny, the God Cain snuck into Balor's mountain castle and gave a big kiss to Balor's daughter Enya! Whoosh! Out pooped a baby! (Connacht winks at Lachlann and Finlay and they cover their mouths, quietly laughing.). Lo and behold this baby becomes the Mighty Sun God, Lugos, the spear lord."

"Lugos aka Lugh made his way to Dun Bres and worked as a servant under King Bres, to learn several crafts and arts that made the Formorian Empire mighty indeed."

"Lugh helped Goibniu, the god of fire, forge the silver arm and reattach it to King Nuada, Lugh and Goibniu helped crafted the mighty spear Gae Assail and gifted the former king Nuada with such a mighty weapon."

Eventually Lugos and the Dagda would no longer tolerate the the reign of King Bres and they mustered the Morrigan, Oghma the lord of magic, Nuada and many other Tuatha together with an secret Alliance with the Fir Bolg giants and they quickly besieged the mighty fortress of Dun Bres. Bres and his Formorians awoke with hangovers to see their orcneas honorguard getting slaughtered on the fortress walls. They fled in terror from the mighty slave army that knocked down their stout oaken gates and stone walls.

Bres and the surviving Formorian guards fled to the ocean and swum down to the deep northern seas to inform the mighty Balor of the betrayal.

70

Balor awoke from a deep slumber in a great rage, killed half of Bres's Formorian honorguard for being cowards and summoned a mighty army in the deep seas then marched up the dark sandy shores, through bleak continental shelves to emerge on the northern shores of the island of Samhain.

Which brings us back to the second battle of Mag Tuired, which took place in my home province of Connacht!

The Dagda, the great god, as he was called, king of the now allied Firbolg Giants, joined the battle with the second wave of pict warriors, a race of men loyal to the Firbolg giant's, covered in blue woad paint, weilding bronze swords, spears, maces and shields but charging into battle naked. They were accompanied by the mighty Firbolg Giants, who were corpulent of body but mighty. They were fierce, incredibly brave, swift and numerous... Dagda lead their charge right into the unlimited tide of pallid and eyeless orcneas... The Dagda was a giant of a god, His beard was thick, his gut was large, his tunic barely covered his pendulous buttocks or his massive sagging phallus. Rotund and fat, but also incredibly powerful, he hefted house size boulders and flung them at the swarms of the orcneas and shattered their formations with ease. When both armies of mortals clashed, shields, axes, swords and mace shattered skulls, disemboweled stomachs and hacked arms from their sockets.

The Dagda himself swung his mighty oaken *Lorc* club with such fury that he paved in the skulls of any Formorian overseer that challenged him in battle, numerous orcneas arrows were stuck in his corpulent body, making him look as if he was a porcupine, this hardly bothered him. The Firbolg Giants smashed into the Formorian adversaries and the beach of Mag Tuired shook with the thunderous footfalls as the opposing giants wrestled and struck each other with colossal oaken clubs.

The Dagda would take Lorc, his mighty magical club, and slam it in the earth when too many of his Pict warriors or Firblolg allies died, this act would send magical glowing green roots and vines to heal his allies from certain death. Being badly outnumbered by the countless hordes of

71

orcneas and Formorian Giants, who surfaced from the shores. The Dagda's magical club gave the outnumbered Tautha and their Pict allies a strong advantage as fallen warriors rose from the dead to battle once again. For the Dagda's power of life and death was personified in his mighty oak club, the Lorc. This would at least give the defenders an even footing over the near unlimited horde of Balor's armies.

It was said that one of the many reasons for the second battle of Mag Tuired and the broken peace treaty was that the Dagda himself marched right into the greatest war camp of the Formorians and challenged them to an eating contest...

The Dagda himself met the armies of the Formorians before the second battle of Mag Tuired...The porridge was prepared in a great cauldron, and held 20 measures of bog-butter, 20 tons of goats milk, and 20 tons of flour. Into this mix they added all manner of ingredients – honey, apples, dried cranberries, figs, cheese and whole honey combs. The Orcneas built massive troughs from oak that were miles long and then poured the mixture into these troughs (This breakfast of Dagda is still celebrated on Sahwin day! Connacht exclaimed to the amazed children) and the Formorians demanded that the Dagda eat it or they would slay him on the spot. The Formorains began to laugh at his fat stomach and bragged of how easy of a kill this would be...until they witnessed the Dagda begin to eat...and eat...and eat... for the Dagda seemed to never grow tired of eating or ever be finally full.

Trough after trough of porridge was poured into his mouth and then casually hurled away when finished... he feasted for an entire day and he finished the last trough. He then released a monster belch and incredible flatulence which made half of the enemy army vomit in disgust. Wiping his hands on his gargantuan belly he picked his teeth and looked at the shocked Formorian host, smiled and said "thank yee, I believe I finally feel full!" with that he had a deep belly laugh and walked back to the Tuatha warcamp. (The children laughed when Connacht broke character and belched loudly in the style of Dagda)

"But the Dagda played a trick for he devoured most of their food supplies and his Woad-warriors stole the rest...When King Balor discovered this, the day after he personally executed ten Formorians who fell for this trick and ripped their stomachs out and wrapped their intestines around 10 great cairns.

"Anyways, enough of that glutton Dagda! Let's get back to the second battle!" Connacht chortled and everyone had a good laugh.

"As the battle progressed the Morrigan herself and her two sisters appeared; Bridgette and Rhiannon. The three-sister goddess represented three different aspects of fate and life itself. Death, Life and Rebirth, Past, Present and Future. The Morrigan was a powerful goddess of witchcraft, war and death and she was followed by great swarms of crows.

She oversaw a high altitude upon a tall mountain near the battlefield and witnessed everything below. The goddess trinity raised their hands into the high heavens and a storm of raining fire fell upon the formorian host. Scores of orcneas, their entire formations crumbled from the magical onslaught as the Fianna Knights tore through the fleeing formations of orcneas... the Formorians cracked their savage scourges upon their warriors but to no avail as the orcneas fled in terror."

The first wave of Formorians, who were led by the former King Bres was completely shattered in battle, Prince Nuada cheered in victory with his Fianna knights, Lugh, his most loyal servant and flag bearer, played a mighty conch to symbolize their victory. The Dagda cheered with the Picts and their Firbolg allies; their mighty roars echoed across the cliffs that faced the shore. The Morrigan and her sisters raised their arms to the heavens in praise.

But lo, a terrible horn played from the seas itself. A Formorian giant so mighty he towered over the Dagda, as tall as a mountain, emerged from the sea like a glacier of fury. Balor, the one eyed, pointed his finger and a mighty wave from the ocean rose up and simply brushed away the Fianna

Knights and Pict warriors as the furious onslaught of the wave pushed them aside like a hand brushes away a spider web. As the wave pulled back, The Armies of Balor rallied and surged onwards, renewed with courage.

Connach continued.

"The Pitched battle was terrible, the Aos-Sidhe, Fianna, Picts, Gual warriors all fought savagely in the fields of mire. The Dagda was surrounded by fierce Formorians who wailed on him with great clubs.

Many dismounted Fianna drew their silvered great swords and cleaved their way through the Orcneas, Formorians and various other horrors brought to the battlefield as Prince Nuada himself led the charge to Balor.

Balor roared in Rage and unleashed a mighty fiery blast of burning hot fire from his one terrible eye... in an instant the shining host of Fianna knights was annihilated and Prince Nauda of the silver arm had a massive hole burned through his torso...

Prince Nuada lay dying on the sand as the dark thunderclouds opened up and thick rain fell upon the once valiant, silver haired king of the Aos Sidhe and the Tautha De Danann. Lugh ran to him and held him in his strong and heavily tattooed arms. Lugh weeped bitter tears for Nuada was like a father to him and now he watched him dying before his eyes.

"Finish this, slay him!" gasped Nauda and his last breath left him. Lugh closed the first king's eyes and placed his hand on his spear, the Gae Assail, the slayer's-lance.

Grabbing his mighty silver spear, Lugh roared in Rage to the thunder storm above. His muscles flexed and he entered into a mighty burning rage known as the *Ríastrad* , a horrible rage that gave him incredible agony. His bones snapped in multiple places, his muscles grew so quickly it literally ripped his skin open, he vomited blood and his body caught on fire. Lugh arose as a giant, as tall as the Dagda himself, but a horrible visage of war! (The Children gasped in shock, but Connacht winked at them with a smile and they quickly giggled as he broke character).

Lugh was now a giant like the Formorians and the Firbolg and he charged in battle. He stomped on the formations of orcneas, shattering them under his mighty boots. He drove his deadly spear through the stomach of one Formorian, ripped it out and impaled another, then tore the spear out and charged a Formorian protecting Balor...impaling the weapon through the stomach of the giant, lifting him into the heavens and flinging his carcass over his own head.

Lugh could now see Balor, and Balor was wildly using his powerful beam of fire and carving lines of burning destruction through the battlefield killing allies and enemies alike in his bloodthirsty rage.

Lugh hefted the mighty silver spear of spoke his oath of Vengeance to Gae Assail.

*""**Gae Assail***!" said Lugh, the sun god. "Storm Spear! I have taken thee from the first king Nuada. You have never failed him and he has always recovered you from war. I now have you from the Silver Prince and he from the Firbolg before him. If ever you came from the forges of the Aos Sidhe, go now and speed well! Bring Down Balor the Tyrant, my accursed grandfather!""*

Lugh roared in such rage and flung the mighty Storm Spear with incredible power! It flew through the heavens with such violent force and struck Balor in his great burning eye, the spear then exploded out of the back of Balor's skull, showering the battle field with black blood and gore.

This did not outright kill the horrible king of the Formorians but he did scream such a horrible roar of agony... that even his own army stopped in their tracks.

"Return to me, Gae Assail!" Screamed Lugos and the spear turned around and flew through the heavens with such force that it impaled itself into Balor's back and exploded out of his chest, having completely savaged the heart of the giant king. The Spear flew true and swift and Lugh caught it with great expertise... still ringing and vibrating in his hand.

Balor looked in the high heavens with his now shattered eye with the swirling thunderstorm and gasped...He slowly collapsed and struck the shore with such force that both armies tumbled... even the white cliffs suffered nearby rock-slides from such a monstrous earthquake... the surviving armies of Formorians and orcneas screamed in terror and fled back into the ocean or deep into the caverns of the sea cliffs in absolute horror. Their god king was slain.

King Bres wept in rage and sorrow, screaming "Father!" to the raining heavens as he embraced the dying Balor. As he screamed in impotent rage and gnashed his teeth in despair, he did not see the mighty Dagda walking up behind him until it was too late.

The Dagda smiled, his face battered and blood leaking down his eyes and nose. Bres turned around and noticed the mighty Dagda now hovering over him with the great Lorc club, hefted on his shoulder. "Ah, ya miss your monstrous da? Well, let me send you to meet him."

Bres last words was "No!" but the Dagda was not only incredibly strong but surprisingly swift of sword arm and smashed Lorc down on Bres... all that was left was a bloody stain of the former king!. "

"The Samhain isles were saved; the honorable dead were buried in twelve great Duns across the high mountains. Prince Nauda was buried in his own Dun with his loyal Fionna knights. It was said that prince Nuada might not be dead but actually sleeping deeply under the earth and he became the god of the underworld as we know now." Connacht said to the amazed children.

"For several months there was great festivals of feasting, drinking, men and women getting to know each other well, burning wicker men to represent Balor and his Formorians, sacrificing of cattle, swine and sheep for feasting and to represent the sacrifices the Aio-Sidhe, the giant Firbolgs, the godlike Fianna and the humble picts made to save their island home. The Dagda impregnated so many women it was said that the next generation basically repopulated the isles from the devastating losses suffered during the Formorian Invasions. The Formorians were beaten so badly they were never seen again." Connacht smiled and finished his story.

The Children gasped and awed in wonderment. "But what happened to the Gods, the Fianna and their elf like Aos-Sidhe knights? What happened to the Picts?" said one red headed child.

"Nobody really knows, many druids say the Godlike Tuatha De Danann fell into a deep sleep in their crystal and stone palaces deep under the earth. The Firbolg were said to have merged with great oaks and pine trees across the Caledonian Islands. The Picts are said to still live in the twelve duns as the wild men of borderlands, it is said the picts can turn into beasts. Maybe they became the fierce guardians of the deep forests known as Faoladh...or the Selkies? Kelpies and various other strange beast-men of the highlands, lochs and lowlands. The Aos Sidhe? Maybe they turned into the Seelie and Unseelie fae that we know today?" Connacht wondcrcd.

"Remember children, we feast to honor the Dagda's victory over the Formorians! We burn the wicker-man to honor Lugos's victory over Balor! The Jack-o-lanterns are made because they are so ugly it scares the orcneas! We wear the costumes of ghosts and fae to represent the Aos Sidhe being reborn as the fae! Just remember that even the kindest of gods can have a horrible wrath!"

The Children gazed in wonderment and stared at each other in disbelief.

Suddenly a terrified loyal maid ran in the feasting halls where the children gathered. Duncan swiftly turned to look at the frenzied maid in bewilderment.

"Lord, lord! The bride-to-be has vanished and we believe Finnigan was the culprit! He also cannot be found." she screamed.

"Connacht, I need ye now more than ever! Find her or there will be a clan war between Clan Calhoun and Clan Gunnar!" snarled Duncan the one eyed.

"My Lord, we never meant to betray thee!" Replied Connacht "But on my word I shall retrieve thy daughter Rhona."

In stormed the Clan Gunnar Groom, Hjalmar Gunnarson. "Gallowgalas, don't fail me! I will have you and your kerns gutted unless you rescue my bride!" The children ran away in terror to hide under the tables from witnessing Hjalmar's rage.

"Hjalmar it will be on my honor to retrieve her but next time you threaten me don't do in front of the terrified children!" Connacht snarled.

Hjalmar scoffed "get it done!" and he stormed off.

Chapter 5: The trail to the Twelve Duns and the Pucas.

**"Truly no one is outstanding without me, nor fortunate; I embrace all those whose hearts ask for me. He who goes without me goes about in the company of death; and he who bears me will remain lucky for ever. But I stand lower than earth and higher than heaven.
What am I?"**

Connacht, Lachlann and Finlay stormed out of the oaken gates of the Calhoun Stronghold. Connacht felt somewhat recovered but at times he could still feel nausea from the alchemical medications attacking the curse that ravaged his body from the Cu-Sith's bite.

Three horses were arrayed right outside of the castle walls. Connacht turned his gaze back to Duncan, now standing on the stronghold walls and said "I thank yee for lending us these fine horses, this will help us ascend the highland roads and rescue yer beloved daughter!"

Duncan waved and said "fair thee well, hopefully those stallions should get yee there in good order! Remember time is of the essence and speed well!" Duncan's tone began to soften, realizing that the Knox Clan Gallowgalas was not responsible for such an affront.

Our heroes swiftly rode off into the distance through the light mist of the early dawn hours. Lord Duncan waved goodbye and turned around to face his kinsmen but then he suddenly witnessed the same three stallions! They were being groomed by his retainers and clan warriors. "Wait a moment! whose horses were those?" He wondered aloud but Connacht and his kerns were riding swiftly to the horizon.

"Dammit lads! We need to get to them! They have been set up by the Unseelie! Fetch our horses!" Roared Duncan-the-one-eyed and his soldiers did as they were told. Within moments he was riding out of Dun Calhoun's oaken gates, in hot pursuit after Connacht and his kerns.

Duncan-the-one-eyed rode with six of his swiftest scouts, known as Border Horse Reivers and they moved as swiftly as they could, they already lost sight of Connacht but noticed the hoof prints on the dirt roads going into the eastern highlands.

Suddenly they came to a old women on a fork on the road, the axel of her wagon was stuck in a ditch.

"Help me! Help!" She cried. Duncan and his riders swiftly came to a stop and helped lift her wagon from the ditch and back onto solid ground.

Duncan-the-one-eyed looked at her and said "tell me madam, have yee seen three horsemen? One middle aged Gallowgalas and two of his younger kerns, two redheads the other a blonde?"

"Ah Sirrah! Of course I have! They have ridden west!" And she pointed her finger to the western road going into the western lowlands of Ulster.

As Duncan turned his head to look west he noticed fresh hoof tracks going down the hill.

"Mayhaps a detour?" he snorted in wild disbelief. "Come lads, lets go get him at Kirk Yethholme!" and swiftly he jumped back on his horse and they galloped swiftly to the setting sun of the west...to Loch Rannoch.

Aunty Oona gently laughed to herself, *the fools fell for the most simple form of illusions!* Her Ox simply walked up to her and began speaking "Quickly Aunty we need to inform Lord Arawann that Connacht is coming!" the ox form quickly dissolved into the tall, powerful body of a wolf-like humanoid with silver fur.

"Well then ride like your life depends on it ya fool Cu-Sith! Airgid yer mate Oidhche didn't die in vain!" Oona snarled.

The Silver Cu-sith Airgid growled in anger, she remembered how Connacht killed her sable mate so brutally.

She quickly changed her shape to a giant wolf. "Come Aunty, jump on my back for I can run up cliffs and mountains and will swiftly get to Dun Aos Sidhe before Connacht!" she spat his name on the dirt road.

Oona leapt upon Airgid's back and Airgid swiftly galloped across the highlands, fast like a blur of silver lightning streaking across the brush.

Meanwhile

Connacht and his Kerns rode higher and higher up the elevation of the highlands. The cold, damp, mist slowly receded as the sun climbed higher and higher during the day. The Wind was cold and harsh, their lips cracked and their bodies chaffed under that constant bombardment of harsh gales. Connacht could feel his nose, face and chest became smoldering hot to combat this freezing wind.

The scrub oaks, the sage, the heather and wild grass gave way to great pine forests which were covered with snow. The roads were less maintained and they had to move over both fallen logs and areas where great avalanches and landslides destroyed the road. The journey was very rough, large boulders made the way rugged and slow going but the horses were surprisingly sure footed and covered some of the most harsh terrain.

Suddenly a great snow capped mountain appeared before them on the horizon.

"Is that one of the twelve duns? Is that Dun Cerrunous?" Implored Finlay.

Lachlann looked at Finlay "Bretheren that has to be Dun Nuada, where Prince Nuada and his Fianna knights were buried"

"Nay Lads, that is Dun Aos Sidhe, the burial of both men and Sidhe after the second battle of Maig Tuired. Dun Cerrunos has many skulls, horns and antlers placed upon it, Dun Nuada has silver coins placed on string that criss-crossed several wooden poles. Dun Aos Sidhe simply has a great rock mound placed upon it with various bronze spears and flags to cover it, flapping in the wind."

"And the Three of you Tossers shall never get there alive!" a nasally voice suddenly emerged near them but they looked in shock and confusion.

"Show yourself fae! We don't wish to kill you but if you force our hands we will!" Connacht roared.

"Fat chance that, yee ragamuffin! Thou wilt drowned in freezing lake-water before yee shall knowst who betrayed ye!" said another high pitched voice that was very close.

Suddenly one of the horses screamed in rage and the others followed suit, they ran as swift as possible through the dark and frozen forest.

Connacht roared "lads, leap off yer horses for they have gone mad!" All three of them tried to leap off their crazed horses but it was as if they were being held in place by the saddles.

Finlay's horse, turned it's head completely around like an owl! Then it began speak with a crazed look upon it's face, "You lads will be drowned or flung into a jagged ravine before you ever get the chance to get off our backs!" The monstrous horse laughed maniacally.

Finlay screamed "Connacht! We have been tricked! These are no horses!"

Connacht quickly grabbed into his Bandoleer, looking for a satchel of either iron or silver but wasn't able to find anything as his horse began to violently kick and leap as it charged faster and faster through the forest.

His horse began laughing "What are yee looking fer, Gallowgalas?!? Ya can't find yer magic powders aye?" suddenly he could see a frozen lake emerge ahead of him in the distance, the forest clearing was approaching fast.

Faster and faster the horses charged, purposely leaping towards low lying branches and boughs so the tree limbs could comically slap their riders right in the face and stop them from getting off.

Suddenly Finlay's horse went speeding out before them! It surged through the trees deftly and adroitly. The horse leapt with incredible power across the forest into the clearing, laughing manically as it sailed across the sky and landed through the ice with a thunderous Krak! The ice shattered violently as Finlay was in tow screaming and crying all the way into the freezing cold water.

Connacht snarled in rage, but luckily he found his pouch of silvered powder bombs, he lit them then flung them before himself and it exploded in the air before both his and Lachlann's "horses".

Boom! The bombs burst in the frigid air and the shimmering silver powder covered everything around them! The "Horses" screamed in agony and changed in both size and shape. Connacht and Lachlann unceremoniously crashed into the forest floor and tumbled hard across the snow and rocks.

Connacht groaned, he was tough but he hit the forest floor hard and slammed into a log, shattering it under his bulk. He touched his ribs and arms, phew! Thankfully nothing was broken.

"lad, are ye all right?" Connacht said as he looked around, he could now see that Lachlann was completely knocked out. He ran over quickly and checked his body... "still breathing! no broken ribs, no cracked arms or snapped neck!.nor shattered back... thank Lugos the Sun God!"

"Filty half-norse pig!" ***Cough cough*** "You have no right to praise their names!" growled an agonized voice on the forest floor.

Connacht looked around and witnessed two dazed creatures, their bodies were like humanoid cats, with paws and claws, sharp fangs and slit eyes. One's hide had gray and black stripes, the other was a bright orange with various spots of light brown. Their ears though, were long and floppy like rabbits and their faces were humanoid, with high cheekbones, chins and pronounced jawlines, human like eyebrows and so forth... yet also catlike. One suffered a broken arm and the other suffered a broken leg, Connacht could see their broken bones jutting out of their skin.

"*Pa-Toua!*" Connacht spat at them with disgust "Ploughing, whorsesons, Wankers, Sods, goat fookers and milk drinkers!!!" Connacht cursed. "Fecking Pucas! Who paid ye? Answer me swiftly or
I will slit yer throats and make blankets from your mongrel hides!" With

that Connacht pulled forth his arming sword, etched with silver inlay.

"Sirrah, fine-northern Gunnar lord!" The Gray Puca Implored "We were paid by a Clurican that stole the silver coins from an Aunty of the lowlands who calls herself Oona. In turn he is a servant of a Bane-Sidhe lord who lives on Dun Aos Sidhe!"

Connacht looked bewildered, "Tell me Puca! Can this Ban-Sidhe warlord change form? Does he fancy himself a human woman?"

The Puca look terrified and kept silent, until Connacht held the silver sword up to his throat... the Puca could hear the humming of the excited silvered blade... the burning effect against his skin. Knowing that a silvered blade could inflict a final death he hesitated until he felt the burning agony of the blade being pressed down on his neck! He yelped and spoke up "Yes! Yes! Lord Arawan? Fancies a bride to be and he resides on Dun Aos Sidhe!"Connacht released.

Meanwhile Finlay's horse smashed into the ice of the river and the ice violently shattered. **Ka'doosh!** He was flung into the freezing waters and his body suffered a great shock!

It was almost as if his heart stopped in his chest. Finlay was terrified that this would be his death, here in this frozen, highland loch. Suddenly something caught his eye in the freezing water, as his vision grew black, shining and brilliant, silver coins in mounds within a great bronze cauldron, shimmering with the cold winter sunlight which was shining in the freezing waters... *wasn't that the pot of Oona?* He wondered.

His mind began to drift into shock and unconsciousness, when something bite him in his shirt and pulled him up out of the water.

He was soaking wet and barely conscious, Finlay came riding out of the water on the fae horse which plunged him in the water! He was almost pale blue with freeing shock. The Horse was dragging him with it's teeth, biting down on his mail coat. The Animal dragged him towards Connacht and Lachlann then dropped him in front of Connacht.

The horse quickly changed shape into a pale-white Puca. "Please don't kill

Lukka!" The puca said with a feminine voice "He is the father of my kittens! Please don't slay him!" She wailed. "See here is your young friend, I was just joking!" The white feline smiled.

"Oh Draga, do anything this Gallowgalas says!" cried Lukka.

"First! Make a fire and you better help me keep both Finlay and Lachlann alive or I will slowly skin you alive!" Snarled Connacht.

Draga quickly gathered wood into sizable mounds and using a tad pit of magic and hot breath to quickly breath fire onto the dry twigs, kindling, grass and logs this quickly produced a fire which began producing smoke.

"Heal my friends and make them warm!" Connacht growled and Draga quickly followed suit. She pulled both Finlay and Lachlann towards the fire and she snuggled next to them as she licked them clean of the cold water.

Finlay and Lachlann started to awaken but crawled back in terror when they witnessed a cat humanoid caressing and licking them back awake! Mind you this wasn't a lustful embrace but more like a mother kitten warming and cleaning her kittens.

"Calm yerselves lads! She is giving you warmth the same way she would give warmth to her own kittens! They are our prisoners for now, we have broken their illusion and if they want to live freely and run through the forest and play pranks upon the unwary they better listen to our orders!" He gave them a steely eyed stare.

Connacht kept his eyes on the three Pucas and swiftly placed his hand in his leather bandoleer. Quickly he drew three silver runic rings and a vial of blue ichor.

"The Three of you, place these rings on your index fingers of your right hands!" Connacht commanded and the puca hesitantly did as he ordered and immediately their flesh began to burn slightly. White, slow moving smoke emanated from their fingers into the air as the silver burned them.

Connacht drank the blue Ichor from the vial, the blood of fae and gagged, for the fluid was foul tasting but potent."ANSUZ! HAGALAZ! EHWAZ!" he shouted and in an instant each silver ring shined brightly with a golden glowing rune! Hot fiery sparks erupted from each rune, showering the snow with burning hot sparks like that emitted from a forge.

"I punish you puca, by the laws of the Dwarven Rune-Ancestors and the All Father, I curse you to serve me! Reform to Horse!" He shouted

The Puca screamed in agony as their bones and bodies twisted, cracked, healed and reformed into the three magnificent horses!

"First he was a journeyman of Alchemy and now he is a journeyman of Runic Seider? I am jealous!" Finlay Scoffed.

"Live as long as me lads and you too will learn the arts of the common-folks hedge-magic!" Smiled Connacht "Now shut yer gobs! Ye need to drink this potent fire whiskey... peppers, ten times distilled rye-whiskey, smokey oaken barrels and sulfur! This should infuse your bones with fire!" He Smiled

Connacht pulled three tall flasks, filled with a very potent whiskey... the stench was intense and potent.   "Kuanan!" Connacht roared at the tall whiskey flasks, infusing the spirits with fire magicks.

Suddenly the potions began to glow a hot orange-amber color and He smiled. "Bottoms up!" he laughed and poured some of the fiery concoction down his throat. He then handed the other two bottles to both Lachlann and Finlay. Finlay swiftly pulled the bottle from Connacht's hand and said, "Whatever hedge magic or witchcraft this might be, I damn near froze to death and Pneumonia won't take me now!"

He downed another third of the fiery concoction but he doubled over in pain as the fire hit his stomach and he loudly belched. What emanated from his mouth was golden fire! By the firery-balls of Lugos! It was disgusting, he almost wanted to vomit... but he felt nice and hot, the snow literally melting around him. He felt amazing! Lachlann was stunned from what he just witnessed but he shrugged swiftly and downed his flask of fire whiskey.

Lachlann almost vomited but Finlay slammed his hand around his mouth and did not allow it. By the gods it burns going down! It was like agony or torture! But then Lachlann also quickly recovered and was smoldering hot! Sweating in this freezing cold air. His sizzling sweat dripped down on the snow and instantly melted the ice particles.

The Puca horses spoke "Truly sirrah you are not just a mere dumb brute or materialistic mercenary! You can actually harness the lesser hedge magic, pray how did you learn such powers?"

Connacht turned to the talking horses and said "My Ostramann kin taught me the art of Rune-Smithing, but alchemy? I learned that from being a Varangian Guard in Vyzantina and from devouring the blue blood of fae!" Connacht laughed but the Puca-Horses looked in terror.

"Uncle my do these Unseelie fae hate us and the Nords so much?" Finlay asked innocently.
"That's a long story but I will give yee the short version now, Lord Arawann will not be atop Dun Aos-Sidhe for too long." Connacht replied.

Connacht began "Hundreds or maybe a thousand years ago a tribe of Nordic peoples came invading from the Yule Islands. It was said they already conquered the dwarven kingdom of Yule and turned their once glorious King, known as Weyland and his people into slaves, breaking their left legs to keep them from fleeing, they were forced to work the forges and mined the mountains. The greatest dishonor was the nords torturing them and stealing their magic, the Elder Runes. Weyland and his people made excellent tools, jewels, arms and armor for King Nithudir and the Skjoldung tribe, sons of the half-giant Skjoldur."

"Weyland went insane, he led a small revolution killing the sons and daughters of King Nithudir for enslaving his people and maiming them. King Nithudir was gone, he went whaling with his greatest Huskarl-warriors on an epic hunt to slay a deadly white whale, said to be the largest and most ferocious of it's kind." He continued.

"Weyland, king of the dwarves of Yule, seized the longships of Nithudir and with his subjects sailed to the island of Samhain. He landed in the eastern regions of the Samhain Isles. He spoke with the Aos-Sidhe King;

Ith Og-Briganthia, who granted protection to him and his followers in the kingdom of the Autumn Elves or the kingdom of An-Fhomar, in their tongue."

"The Skjoldung King, Nithudir, lost many men but finally slayed the mighty whale and returned to his conquered kingdom of Yule. When he arrived at his palace he was shocked, his queen, sons and daughters...his royal servants all butchered. He roared in fury and sent emissaries to all the Norse tribes and even a tribe of Johtuns from the Isenvald, the great polar wall of ice."

"Three Great warlords answered his call; Cuill the bear father, Cecht the Raven lord and the giant Gréine, the slaughteror. Long story short the Nord armies smashed the Autumn Kingdom and burned their glorious palace of Dun Tara. The Aos-Sidhe and their seelie followers fled underground or were slain. The Tuatha gods were so saddened they left to the spiritual dreaming realm known as Tri-Na-Nog and fell into a deep sleep."

King Ith Og Brigantia of the Aos-Sidhe and King Weyland of the Dwarves vowed allegiance to the ancient Crones Three. They were cursed but their bodies warped in monstrous forms as they changed, they became the first Unseelie! Forever bound to an oath to seek bloody vengeance on all Nords who invaded the Samhain Isles. The Unseelie armies rose from the earth during the night and attacked the Nordic armies who overran the palace of Dun Tara. The Nords fought furiously but were either slain to a man or driven past the borderlands of the Twelve Duns.

"The Nords who sued for peace were transformed into Dullahan while the nords who fought on were cursed to be the Draugr or the flayed Nukalvee. So now we are cursed to fight our damned ancestors or the maddened fae for as long as we dwell here." Connacht sighed.

Finlay and Lachlann were mortified to hear about the horrific crimes their ancestors commited.

"Anyways lads, I will tell yee more about that sad story another time, yer alive and warm! If I tell yer mothers about this they will surely make passionate love to me and yee will be Uncles to my little bastard afterwards!" he jested, chuckling wildly.

Connacht was impressed with himself, his nephews mood changed and they laughing hysterically having recovered from what could have been death by exposure. As they laughed something heavy could be heard in the forest, The laughter died down and Connacht whispered "did yee hear that lads?" One of the Puca horses smiled and turned to Finlay, whispering "yer fooked now ya goat defilers!"

Thoom! Thoom! Thoom! Went the heavy sounds as the sound grew closer and closer...

He heard the thundering and heavy footfalls behind him. "Damn!" he muttered "I was so busy with the admiration from these Pucas... We have been ambushed!" Connacht shouted.

From the forests emerged three giant, red-furred ogres! Thoom! Thoom! Thoom! Their heavy footfalls thundered across the forest floor! They had the heads of boars with razor sharp tusks jutting from their roaring maws. Each one of them wielded one large oaken club that could easily pave in the great helm of a knight or gallowgalas from their mighty blows.

Connacht snarled "Come on lads! Here we go again!" with that he grabbed his mighty claymore and charged into battle against the oncoming Hogsmen!

Chapter 6: Pursuit of the Banshee Lord.

"I am a gallery without wood or stones,
or any other form of earthly matter;
no one destroys me, yet I disappear;
no one erects me, yet I rise again.
What am I?"

Lady Rhona, bride to be, could see the handsome Bard Finningan, said to be half-elven or a changeling child from the temperate island of Beltaine. His teeth were perfect and white, his eyes a lovely deep green, his ears slightly tipped and his face both round yet handsome. He had dirty blonde hair with a well trimmed looping mustache that hugged his handsome jawline. She knew that he might be somewhat too handsome for her but tonight before she was forced to join the Brutish Hjalmar from the Galeo-Nordics also known as the Ostarmanns clan from the far north... she might enjoy the embrace of such a handsome specimen. She was tall and her body was voluptuous but she covered her smile for she knew that her teeth were quite crooked and misplaced... even missing a few teeth. People speculated that maybe her father and mother where slightly too related or that she ate too many sweets like honey nut pastries when she was a youth.

Both of them wore their masks from the great dance around the effigy of the burning man... she had the mask of a mare, painted brown and white with a horse mane made from actual horse tail fur... and Finningan had the mask of a sly looking fox.

She was a tall lady and stood as tall as many of the Nordic Ostarmann warriors, and they seemed to lust for a strong and homely woman. She was a little bit on the older side for clan marriage, she was now in her thirties. She knew that she wasn't the prettiest woman but her body was that of an amazon, thick yet soft thighs, wide hips and a plump backside... and of course two great pendulous breasts with large silky, pink nipples which tapered down... the handmaidens teased her for having utters like a cow. She knew that the other lasses were jealous for many of the greatest warriors swooned for her, wanting to bed a giantess and have her mighty children.

She secretly had two children for she was lusty like any man and she quietly gave her children born out of wedlock to infertile married couples in the nearby lands to raise. After her second child she became much more selective about the men she bedded, she wanted to get married and not just find another night of intense pleasure. She wanted to raise her future children in peace without gossip.

Finnigan was a handsome lad, though somewhat short for her taste and a little plump, his fine facial features, lovely eyes and hair, and his silky smooth and ivory skin made her mad with desire. Many of the lusty handmaidens told her that he was also surprisingly gifted in the loins.

She invited him into her quarter and she poured him a few drinks of spiced wine and berry mead. Their eyes connected, he looked deeply into her eyes... the wine and his sexy eyes were intoxicating and she leaned in close...she closed her eyes and pursed her lips... and she could feel him embrace and firmly yet softly kiss her lips... she wasn't technically proud of her thin lips but his lips were truly fat and juicy, pink and plump...so silky as they kissed more and more passionately.

She quickly unlaced her bodice and gown as he quickly pulled his trousers off... they were both impressed and gawked at each others naked bodies...her great sagging breasts unfurled unceremoniously and slapped against her belly button and his phallus and heavy pendulous testicles hung down damn near to his knee caps. Her labia lips were quite large and hung down, like two great slabs of beef, she was unshaved and her ginger pubic hair was quite wild on her pelvis.

“My apologies Finnegan, I had two children...” but he cut her off “Oh lady Rhona, a wild and lusty giantess like yerrself doesn't have to apologize, I like a seasoned matriarch who is fertile like a river valley. Don't apologize for yer curvaceous and rubenesque form.”

She gently yet forcefully pushed him to the bed, he was already erect from her lusty and forceful advances. She hovered over him and gently pried her lower lips wide open and pulled his large member inside of her...they both groaned, he was thick and long and she could even feel his head gently kiss her cervix.

She rode him hard and long, she could feel his thickness and she could feel her large lips grip his shaft...they bit their hands at the same time and came together...gods she loved it, she could feel all his warm seed dribbling down from inside her.

She smiled, touching his warm body and rubbing her hands on his chest, though it was a little hairy he trimmed most of it down and the hair felt smooth. She didn't like hairless men or men who are too hairy...but a tad bit of moss on her man drove her crazy.

"Finningan, the tales are surely true, yee are quite the lover and I wonder if yerr part horse..." she smiled

"If I am a horse my love then yee might be part cow." he said playfully as he played with heavy breasts she quietly chuckled. "anyways my love, let us sleep peacefully, I shall play my Vyzantinian *Duduk* to help yee sleep." With that he pulled out his two headed Duduk.

The Samhain festival was dying down. The revelers retreated to their beds and chambers, Lady Rhona herself felt exhausted and her eyes easily drifted to sleep, she crashed onto her hay bed and wrapped herself in thick wool blankets to keep herself warm during these cold autumn nights in the Samhain highland nights.

She slept in her warm bed as Finningan played his melancholic duduk flute, she had pleasant dreams of making love to the bard like a wild beast.

Suddenly those pleasant dreams seemed to end, she dreamed of the roof of her quarters being violently ripped open and swarms of small, black, midnight blue and purple fae creatures descened upon her, their iridescent and gossamer wings beat rapidly.

Her lover Finningan began to change in this dream, his skin became a dark blue and he grew suddenly taller and more muscular, great white antlers and a mane of black hair sprung from his head and he wrapped his mighty arms around her and hefted her into the night sky upon his beating wings like that of a purple moth from the deep forest.

From below she could see the stronghold of her family, Clan Duncan, in flames... a mighty older warrior, possibly Connacht, with his two squires, ran out fighting savagely against these fierce fae invaders. Strange dark hounds and hordes of portly, pig faced humanoids came surging forwards to the stone walls and barley fields of her ancestral stronghold but she was whisked away into the high heavens by this swarm of flying creatures.

She rode across the night sky, witnessing the small hamlets and villages, the sleeping herds of cattle and sheep within these bastille houses, she could see the twelve duns mountains and then as the swarm flew down in this horrible nightmare she could see a great dark pine forest in the mountains.
This nightmare swarm flew between the trees and swarms of great spiders emerged from the pine needles to shoot strands of silk around her body

Suddenly Lady Rhona awoke from such a strange nightmare...only to realize that this dream was no dream at all! She awoke in a bed made of spider webs between the mighty pine trees of this hilly forest. She was a prisoner in this web in this strange and dark pine forest. Yet strangely enough she was still covered with thick wool blankets and sheepskin rugs... this kept her safe from the harsh cold winds. A Tall, strong and handsome fae lord stood hovering before her on his rapidly fluttering insectoid wings.

"Dont yee recognize me my sweet fertile cow", he smiled "This is the real me, the, "Finningan" who seduced yee at the Samhain party, listen my lusty and busty damsel in despair, you're my prisoner now and you better behave. Besides the real Finningan was waylaid and abducted, taken to Gunnarholme!" he mocked.

She was both shocked, disgusted and yet strangely aroused. She thought to herself *"If he impregnates me now, then I can simply paint him off as a terrible brute who ravaged me."* She smiled

"You're not going to kill me are yee?" She inquired,

He beamed "I hope not, I just want to impregnate yee, would yee allow me this honor to have my baby?"

She twinkled "yes but yee know that I will have to tell everyone that yee abducted me and ravaged me like a savage. Besides I am so glad that Aunty Oona arranged for a terrible brute like you to kidnap me from such an accursed wedding to that oaf Hjalmar!" she bit her lip and winked.

He responded "Well, my lady, I shall lower yee from the web and then lets get to more ravaging! Thank the dark gods the Aunty set this whole thing up." he winked and blew her a kiss.

Lady Rhona looked somewhat worried "When will yee let me go? I cannot live in the Unseelie side of the island forever."

Lord Arawann looked at her with lusty eyes "I want to impregnate yee with child and then we shall secretly take you back to your castle...I have a hag's potion yee should drink to hide this pregnancy from your future "Husband" Hjalmar, he will think this child is his own."

Lady Rhona looked puzzeled "so we are going to effectively make love in this strange forest for days? How will I bath? Eat? Drink? And who will I talk to?"

Lord Arawann smiled "don't worry my love, the aunties shall take care of yee, especially aunty Oona."

An Elderly and diminutive woman approached, but she walked through the forest floor with horse hooves "My dear, lets get yee a comfortable bed made from a giant toad stool!" Oona smiled.

Lord Arawann laughed and looked to Aunty Oona +**This fool Lady Rhona has no idea the war that will be unleashed from her changeling.**+ Arawann psychically signaled Oona, they both had a knowing smile.

(Two days later in the Twelve Duns)

From the forest emerged three Korks or boar-men, similar to ogres but covered in thick boar fur, tusks and running on procine trotters. Each one of them wielded a large oaken club that could easily pave in the great helm of a knight or Gallowgalas if they were too slow to avoid their mighty blows.

Connacht snarled, "Come on lads! Here we go again!" With that he grabbed his mighty claymore and charged into battle against the oncoming Hogsmen!

The mighty Kork warriors surged forward and slammed their mighty clubs at the three heroes who charged them, but Connacht and his kerns were too quick for them and quickly dodged the clumsy attacks of the boar-ogres.

One Kork swung down on Connacht and he leapt to the left dodging the clumsy brute who was incoming from his right hand side. He quickly stepped counterclockwise while swinging his great sword with his hips and slamming the blade into the Kork's meaty shoulder. The greatsword bit deep, it's silvered knot-work patterns glowed blue-white and burned the giant beast, the Kork bellowing from the dolorous blow! Connacht smiled in savage victory but his victory was rudely interrupted, a meaty fist struck him right in the chest and sent him flying through the snow covered forest floor!

Connacht was sent tumbling through the snow but aggressively grabbed a large log and righted himself from being prone. Quickly he turned his eyes and witnessed Finlay screaming in pain, being bear-hugged by a mighty Kork.! If he didn't act fast the brute would make the poor youth's ribs explode and kill him instantly. Connacht swiftly hurled his claymore into the snow and flung three silvered dirks at the Kork brute! The blades pierced deep into the fleshy hide of the beast, their silvered knot-work etchings glowed with azure moon-fire and the beast released Finlay as it screamed in agony.

The monster writhed in utter pain as it ripped out the glowing, bloody blades from it's body.

Lachlann leapt on the back of the last Kork and began stabbing with his silvered broadsword right into the monster's thick and muscular back, it roared in horror as the silvered blade bit deep into it's shoulder.

The muscular Kork was in a maddened frenzy as the glowing silver-blade tore bloody chunks into his stout back and shoulders! Quickly he grabbed Lachlann by his ginger hair and flung him at a nearby tree, Lachlann slammed into the tree with a thud that snapped a sizable branch in half with a crack!

Connacht realized that this battle was going to be a fierce and pitched battle, he slammed his runic rings together and screamed "Kuanan! Kuanan! Kuanan!" and angry red fire began to erupt from the bodies of himself, Lachlann and Finlay...Strangely enough the flames neither burned nor consumed the flesh of all three. The Gallowgalas called forth the magic within the fire whiskey they consumed earlier unleashed it's power!

Finlay remembered the legend that the Nordic peoples learned the magic of Runes from the Dwarves they enslaved. These dwarves lived in the arctic isles of Yule, each Runic word or letter was the name of one of their ancestors who descended from Durin and Modsognir, the first dwarves.

"It was said the 1st dwarves crawled from the earth, sleeping inside the bodies of massive maggots. Durin and Modsognir first awoke and helped their kin awaken, the 2nd generation was given Runic names. It was said that Odin, the sky father named the twins first and gave them their respectful Runic names, hence why the dwarves are eternally grateful to the one eyed sky father." Finlay remembered Connacht's lectures.

Lachlann, Finlay and Connacht flew into a wild *Riastrad* rage once again, the magic of the fire Rune Kuanan formed a cloak of magic fire around themselves and this magical fire burned as hot as a bonfire! They leapt at their respective Kork enemies and wrestled them to the ground. Their fiery bodies seared and burned the roaring hogsmen brutes, Lachlann vomited a cone of furious fire from his stomach onto one of the Kork Brutes and the beast started squealing like a suffering and terror!

Connacht was somewhat surprised but suddenly he felt the urge to spew a great deluge of hellfire at the Kork he was facing and the flames engulfed the poor bastard, burning off all it's coarse black hair and making the beast drop to the floor, wailing and flailing in agony.

Finlay smiled, he leapt on his rival Kork and bear hugged the monster this time! Fat popped and skin was searing off the hogsmen as it desperately tried to claw Finlay off his body! The beast finally freed itself by throwing Finlay off! It ran like a crazy, still on fire and it leapt into the nearby freezing lake **"Kra-doosh!"** went the freezing water! Grate plus of steam erupted off it's hide as it plunged into the freezing waters.

"Hold! Fierce Ostramann warriors! Please!" screamed one of the Kork Brutes. "Spare us...mercy...we are the sons of Cromm Cruagh! we were only sent here to capture you!" Said the beast in a harsh and guttural voice.

"Hold lads! Don't kill them yet!" shouted Connacht "We can bind them to a Geas and we will have them in debt to us for saving them." smiled Connacht in a sly fashion. Finlay and Lachlann sheathed their swords but kept an eye on their wounded porcine opponents.

"Alright beasts, where has Lady Rhona been taken to in these gods awful Seelie lands?" implored Connacht.

"Lord Arawann has taken her to Dun Aos Sidhe, just a half days journey north and east of here!" said the great Kork.

"What are your names, beasts?" Snarled Finlay, Connacht nodded his head, for knowing the names of Fae Folk is to have power over them whether friendly Seelie or hostile Unseelie.

"Alright I am Gronk...he is Borkk...and he is Uguk..." said he defeated Kork leader in a guttural deep voice.

"Well Gronk, Borkk and Uguk you will escort us and our fae steeds to Dun Aos Sidhe and we will have need of your protection, expect I alone will fight Lord Arawann and save lady Rhona." Connacht exclaimed.

Connacht pulled forth a vial of blue liquid, mixed with colorful mushrooms "Alas lads, witness my alchemy, for I barely have any magic power myself... I must consume either fae blood or hallucinogenic substances like mushrooms or wormwood liquor to fuel my powers!”

He pulled forth two fairy-wings with a “M” symbol, placed them on his fingers and shouted “Ehwaz!” he then turned to the three hogsmen. “You shall guide us to Dun Aos Sidhe and protect us when we are in these Seelie lands! Ehwaz!” (Ehwaz was the nordic rune of partnership and trust) violet and green sparks exploded from his rings and covered the Kork in multicolored light.

The defeated Kork warriors picked themselves up and limped north-east “Follow us...we accept your geas” Groaned Gronk in a defeated yet smoldering tone.

(Several hours later, Climbing up the summit of Dun Aos Sidhe)

The Borderlands between men and Unseelie fae was brutal and was an eternally cast in autumn. Only a few days after the glorious Sahwin festival butsnow and ice were already assailing these mountainous peaks and vales.

Low hanging clouds easily brushed over the landscape of the twelve duns and gently sailed past the mighty fir and pine trees, eternally evergreen no matter the weather, that dotted this alpine landscape. How this landscape of mostly evergreens contrasted from the lowland forests and glens. Their leaves were changing to gold, dark reds and brown to match the mood of autumn and the hibernation of the sun.

This thing didn't change though, it was the eerie and whimsical jack-o-lanterns or Ignis Fatuus that were left through the roads, bastille houses and strongholds across the landscape. They were carved by the locals from various gourds such as pumpkins and turnips with candles were placed in their mouths for illumination.

Connacht always loved the jack-o-lanterns hung along the roads and hamlets of his Island home of Samhain. Long before the Ostramann or “Galeo-Nordics” of the north thought of these traditions as simple minded superstitions that only the pictish tribes from beyond the duns or the "woad warriors" practiced. . Even the Shelta nomads or "wagon peoples" who wandered like gypsies across the solstice isles frequently used Jack-o-lanterns to drive away or appease the cruel and mercurial fae.

But something was strange, this region was said to be barely habitable. Strangely though these number of lanterns seemed to be quite substantial. Connacht then noticed, in the woods, a host of blue men who appeared from the pine needles and heather bush.

Lachlann whispered "there is a small army of them...Connacht what do we do?" he said in fear.

Connacht cleared his throat and said "listen lads, put down your weapons, don't attack them, these are men known simply as the "Woads"! They are the only tribe of humanity accepted by the Unseelie Fae. Put your weapons down and your hands up, show signs you don't want a fight..."

Lachlann put his shield and broadsword down, Finlay placed his twin war-axes down and all three lifted their hands into the heavens.

What might have been a hundred or more warriors emerged from the brush, some were bare chested, others walked in in tartan pajamas or kilts with fur trimmed boots. Many had spiked hair and looping mustaches, many of them bore broad-leaf spears, axes and falx sabers all made from a very durable bronze. Some bore armor but it was strange, it seemed crafted of hard wood like oak.

These warriors were tattooed or painted blue, possibly from the Woad plant that grew like weeds in the Samhain Isles and nearby Caledonian Islands. The whole tribe seemed to be there, men and women, youths and elderly, all warriors, all lithe yet strong. All incredibly silent, far too silent.

Among them was one elderly woman, probably the druid healer, surrounded by four mighty Faoladht, similar to werewolves or Vukodvlak, but guardians of sacred land.

"You...have...crippled...our friends." uttered an elderly woman, almost completely covered in the blue Woad paint. "Why...you...hurt...them?"

said the Elder as she placed a hand on the kork, Gronk.

"Self Defense." Said Connacht "We won't kill them. We will only place a Geas on them." he stated. "Ahh, we thank you." Said the Elder. "Careful, Gallowgalas" She said "Dullahan riders on the mountain roads".

Connacht looked at Finlay and Lachlann in alarm.

"Take this torc," said the Elder, "For it only speaks the truth on those who bear it."

Connacht reached out to take the bronze torc but suddenly the four guardian Faoladht werewolves snarled, they were protecting the tribe's druid.

She shushed them into silent obedience, "Quiet you beasts...this is no enemy!" she barked and the four wolf men went silent, Connacht reached out again and the druid handed him the Torc "You will need this to find the truth!"

"We must leave now...but take this Salve, made of white honey and aloe vera (She placed a crude clay pot in Connacht's gloved hands)...placed it on the hands of the Kork guardians. "That should heal those wounds" she said and with that the werebeast guardians and her blue tribe of Woads simply turned around and simply walked away into the forest.

"Vukodvlak are their guardians?" gasped Lachlann "aren't these beasts impervious to iron weapons?"

"Listen lad, those are not Vukodvlak though distantly related, they are known as Faoladht, the guardian-wolves of the druids." Replied Connacht. "They are fearsome guardians of the twelve duns, the standing stones, the dark forests beyond and all the strange, mysterious peoples who inhabit these forbidden lands."

The three of them looked as the strange blue Woads disappearing into the snow covered pine forests.

"I have heard of the blue people known as Woads and Picts, but I have never seen them. Lord knows why the Unseelie fae leave them unharmed?" Inquired Lachlann

"Because they were loyal to them and they were here even before the Sidhe and their Tuatha De Denann gods arrived...they were the first peoples and they worshiped the ancient giants known as the Firbolg... who once wandered these lands openly in ancient times...but now are said to be cursed into a deep slumber, imprisoned inside the *Biles* by the Tuatha De Denann." Replied Finlay.

Connacht sneered "Or mayhaps they pay a "tithe of blood?" There are grim stories from the dark forests of the Kingdoms of Saxony and Thurgundia. Peasants who live on fertile farmland in cursed forests, for they pay a tithing to the powerful crones who control those enchanted woods. It is said they pay a blood-tithing, which is they give one child per family to the Crones. What happens to the children? Nobody really knows but stories say that the crones either devour these children whole or turn these children into horrible monstrosities."

Everyone went silent, the concept of being forced to play a blood tithe to crones was far to horrible to even comprehend.

Chapter 7; Battle at the mountain pass of Dun Aos Sidhe:

"While yet you hold me, I escape your grasp;
You watch me flee and cannot keep me back;
However hard you squeeze me in your palm,
I will escape your hand and leave it empty.
Who Am I?"

Connacht, Lachlann and Finlay were guided up the mountain by the three Kork Warriors and rode upon the backs of their Puca-horses. The trail was steep and the journey was freezing cold as the mountain winds ushered in the winter chill. They were nearing the top of Dun-Aos-Sidhe, the burial place of many loyal Aos-Sidhe warriors after the second battle of Maig Tuired, many Fionna knights and Sidhe warriors were slain by Balor and his forces and they in turn were buried in this sacred mountain which was littered with great burial mounds in homage of these loyalists.

As the day came to an end, Gronk and his fellow Kork warriors went out to hunt and lo did they come back from their foray. Two dead sheep, one dead dear and the last one brought back several dry pine cones.

Connacht quickly used his runic magic to invoke fire through Kuanan and started a hearty hearth-fire while Finlay and Lachlann used their daggers to gut the game, skin their hides and remove most of the bones. To prepare the meat they rubbed salt, sage, star anise, brown sugar and chili powder to the meat.

Thankfully, trade with the cosmopolitan eastern empire of Vyzantia blessed the sea fairing Ostramann with an assortment of refined spices over the decades. What was once considered the most dull and insufferable of food across the Solstice Isles quickly gained respect as gourmet cuisine due to the spice trade.

Half an hour passed and the smell was so rich, that even the accursed horses' mouths were watering. The meat was shared evenly among Kork, The Trio and their Puca-horses.

Connacht laughed "bizarre seeing horses with fangs tearing through meat like voracious wolves, at least pretend to look like horses around human company will ya!" he chortled.

Dragga and Lukka replied through their queer horse mouths "alas we cannot eat grass! It tastes horrific, don't you know we mostly eat meat? Sirrah, please, mayhaps you have a feed bag you can place jerked meat or salted bacon within? Or even some fried biscuits or hearty potato-bread? Ya know we also love the taste of cider!"

Connacht laughed to himself "Great, talking horses with the appetites of ravenous teenage boys!" they all laughed. "Don't worry lads, after I encounter this lord Arawann and rescue lady Rhona you will be set free but you better not turn on his after you have been given freedom. Don't you dare turn on us though or may Orcus deliver his most potent curse upon yee oath-breakers!"

Dragga and Lukka looked at each other and smiled or attempted to smile with their horse mouths. Zazu, the third puca joined in with them and began to nibble on Lukka's mane looking for ticks to eat.

"We...rest...here...found cave!" snorted Gronk in his deep, grumbling voice.

Gronk guided them inwards to the cavern but the cavern was hewn by hand. Inside was various great stone mounds with statues of fine elven warriors, almost watching over the mounds that were crafted there.

"Oh no Gronk! These are the burial mounds of Aos Sidhe warriors... this must have been the loyal Fianna knights that were slain in the battle against the Formorians!" Finlay trailed off. Uguk and Bronkk look concerned. "It is said that Dullahan were born from Sidhe burial mounds or was it the turncoat Nordic Thanes?" Wondered Finlay but Bronkk simply snorted, found a warm place, laid down and slept.

"Ach! That is mere rumor! I believe they were born when the Autumn palace was sacked by the great frost Giant Taran and his army of Draugr!" Replied Lachlann "Besides we are not raiding their tombs for silvered coins or bronze armor! We will be fine!" he scoffed.

Connacht looked about and replied,"Listen lads I love the fact that you are so cocksure in your knowledge of Solstice Isle lore...but we better make circular wards of silver dust to protect us from any hateful spirits of vengeance that might lurk these halls." With that Connacht drew a great circle around the camping party and then unfurled his rucksack blanket, drank his cinnamon spiced ale and retired for the night. Finlay and Lachlann also pulled forth their blankets from their respective rucksacks and slept for the night as well.

But the Korks and Pucas stayed awake, while resting. Oh how they wished to kill the Ostramann Gallowgalas and his related Kerns but they could not bring themselves to it. The Korks repeatedly reached for their clubs with murderous intent but the geas were such powerful enchantments, placed upon them that their hands would immediately drop their clubs or move away from paving their skulls in. Those who broke a Geas or Oath could invite the Hellish wrath of Orcus, father of Orcneas and Formorians, slayer of oath-breakers, cannibal god of the dead.

At some point the Geas forced the cursed fae to fall into a deep, dark slumber. They dreamed strange dreams of dark knights riding upon nightmare mounts, riding down their enemies and hacking them to pieces with the gigantic executioner's axes. They made a camp fire and slept around the crackling flames.

Several hours later it was Dawn and the sun shined it's frigid rays of light across the freezing sky...what was a raging fire was nothing more than humble smoldering coals.

Connacht, Finlay and Lachlann poured themselves a serving of spiced ale in their drinking horns, followed by apple cider to wash down the after taste... this cleared their pounding headaches from the dry and cold atmosphere of the Twelve dun mountains.

Connacht placed a thumb on the left side of his nostril and fired the phlegm from the right, though gross it seemed to completely clear a pounding sinus headache after drinking pepper infused ale in the mornings. He then grabbed a glob of pine tar and placed it in his mouth...he started chewing on the pine tar and the acrid yet refreshing taste both cleared his bad breath and seemed to clean his teeth from last nights meal of lamb and venison.

"Just a few more miles," Connacht whispered to himself. "We can do this!" he exclaimed.

They started their journey up the mountain once again. The same harsh cold wind beat on their face and cracked their lips, it was even able to cut through their thick armored coats and chill their bodies beneath. Lachlann coughed fiercely as he marched up the mountains, somehow the cold winds seemed to irritate his lungs further.

At some point they cleared several turns and bends in the road when the party finally arrived to a monolithic mountain pass, two mighty granite boulders, one to the left and the other the right, possibly deposited there from an ancient Ice Age long before recorded history, said to have been left when the frost giants ruled over much of the northern world at the dawn of recorded time. Their giant runes where carved upon these Cyclopean Menhirs that flanked both sides of the stone road that lead to the summit of Dun Aos-Sidhe. In this boreal fir-forest there was various burial mounds that was sprinkled all over the forest floor, covered in snow and dry pine needles. Various worn statues of warriors could be seen in this forest and all were etched with Oghmic script from the ancient druids of the pict peoples.

Suddenly from the mountain pass appeared a Dark Horseman, the local tribes of Samhain had only one terrible word they shared for such a dark rider, such a herald of doom. They called this being a Dullahan, known as the Dark Knights of the Unseelie.

A mighty rider, clad in dark iron armor, covered in jutting spikes at all angels. His helmet was one monolithic great helm of almost obsidian black with two burning green eyes that seemed to burn through his facial slit. Wielding a colossal Lochaber-axe (like a primitive Halberd, it is a pole weapon with a cleaver head, a spear tip and a hook on the back), resting upon his shoulder and being held by a brutal gauntlet that seemed to grind in violent anticipation. Many believe that these brutal fae knights were once the elegant Fianna riders, elven cavalry who rode giant foxes and lynxes into battle. Others argued they were the elite Nordic Thanes who turned on their own armies.

Everyone agreed that they were deadly, especially mounted on their ebony stallions known as Nightmares, which dripped crimson burning blood as they charged across the battlefields to allow their dread masters decapitate their foes with one strike!

Surrounding him was a brutal host of Redcaps, cursed dwarves with sharp fangs and tusks, covered in thick armored jackets, they dyed their hair and braided beards scarlet red from the blood of either fae or human who foolishly wandered into their ruined towers and haunted mines. They were one of only a small number of fae who could utilize iron as armor and weapons. The Redcaps were impatient and slammed their spiked morning-stars against their iron shields in anticipation of slaughter.

This host of unseelie warriors led by the mighty Dullahan upon his burning nightmare mount was rare indeed. These creatures were only summoned during an event known as the "Wild Hunt" when a powerful Fae Lord beseeched the terrible power of the cursed unseelie warriors of the land to destroy a clan stronghold or assassinate a foolish clan warlord.

Connacht quickly turned to the three Kork warriors, Gronk, Bronkk and Ugluk. "I will break my Geas and give you freedom if you help us defeat this warband assembled before us!" Connacht pleaded.

Gronk scratched his chin with a cunning smile "Freedom meh? Me know just the thing...Bronkk and Ugluk, lads, fetch dem dead trees and fallen logs...cuz we iz going kaper tossing!" He grunted in his low speech.

With that, Gronk, Bronkk and Ugluk swiftly found two dead trees and one fallen log, they then ripped them out of the earth followed by loud popping noises. The pig-men hoisted up these make-shift weapons like shields, roared into the heavens and charged at the band of furious red-caps! The

vicious red-caps roared and counter-charged down the mountain pass!
Both sides smashed into each other with a deafening crack!

The Dullahan came charging down the mountain pass at full gallop, his
hellish stallion's hooves struck with such fury, stones shattered, sparks
exploded outwards, snow was furiously kicked up from the thunderous
advance of each furious clack of hooves upon the rocky road!

Gronk met his Nemesis full on and just as the Lochaber-axe was about to
Impale him through the eye he smashed the rotten log into the ground,
deep into the earth and intercepted the weapon's spear tip! The burning
nightmare smashed into this mighty log and went flying into the air with
it's rider.
It was as if time stopped, as they hurtled and cartwheeled through the sky
from such a fearsome impact. Flaming hooves flailing, the horses fanged
mouth roaring, the Lochabre-Axe being splintering the log in half!
splinters flying everywhere! A Thunderous crack of wood!

The host of bloodthirsty dwarves crashed into Bronkk and Ugluk's tree
trunks, their vicious and heavy maces and cleavers hacked gouges out of
the soft pine logs, their spiked shields drove into the wooden barrier as
they slammed their heavy hobnailed boots into the rocky soil and furiously
pushed both Korks downhill...like a vicious tug of war between fanged
dwarves against giant boar-men.

Gronk turned to Connacht with a sly grin and roared, "The Dullahan is
yours! Me help my brothers!"

Connacht nodded and surged towards the Dullahan, the Dullahan swiftly
leapt from a prone position and landed on his feat standing up! Standing
with his Lochaber-axe ready to strike.

Connacht looked at Finnlay and Lachlann "Go yee ginger-devils, Yee
Rambunctious hooligans and warlike Sirrahs! Hurl yer bombs at those
wretched redcaps and help the Kork drive them back up the mountain
pass!" He roared.

Lachlann and Finlay looked at each other with devilish grins, nodding
their heads in unison and said "Alright old man, he is all yours!" as they

surged past the duel, broadswords drawn with fire bombs ready. They lit them and as they surged up the mountain pass to the brutal tug-of-war between boarmen and blood dwarves.

Connacht switched his stance from that of his left leg forwards and his great sword held above his head.The offensive Uberhander, a perfectly offensive stance to deliver devastating counterattacks deadly overhead strikes, to something much more unorthodox. He now held his sword completely backwards, both hands gribbing the blade and the pommel and crossguard now facing his enemy! To any untrained eye this looked absolutely backwards and insane but swordsmen knew this was a desperate style, known as the Mordenhau! Used only against enemies covered in heavy armor, the sword now functioned like a warhammer agains their thick armored plates!

Basically he held his sword entirely backwards in the style of "Mordhau" or "the murder stroke". He realized the sharp blade of his claymore and it's pointed tip would do almost nothing against the thick, dark-iron plate of this undead knight. The only thing that would work is to smash his pommel and crossguard on his enemy like a hammer and hopefully crack those plates apart...enough to ram his sword tip inside!

The Dullahan, The massive Dark-Knight charged with his brutal Halberd directly in front of him, ready to Impale our Gallowgalas with the spear-tip! Laughing in a deep, bass voice with sheer malice! Such fancy footwork and technique seemed utterly futile against this massive enemy with sheer otherworldly fortitude. The Armored Colossus surged onwards ready to drive through Connacht's flesh! The Dullahan lunged forwards but Connacht swiftly side stepped and parried the axehead with the Ricasso-handle then quickly counterattacked by smashing the heavy pommel into the side of the Dullahan's great helm with a loud **CRACK!** The knight was dazed and sent tumbiling forwards, but shook his head and quickly recovered. He turned around, now weilding his pole-arm like a quarter-staff and slammed the shaft of the weapon into the flate side of Connacht's blade.

Now Gallowgalas and Dullahan clashed blades, gripping their weapons with both hands and pushing back and forth in a furious tug-of-war. Connacht retaliated by half-swording his weapon and ramming the tip into the visor of the Dark-Knight and with such furious force, screaming in full rage! With a metallic screech the visor was ripped free from the helmet and was sent flying down the mountain side! Thrack! Thrack! Thrack! Went the face-guard.

He then Quickly followed up with a circular step, using his powerful hip-muscles he whipped the pommel around and smashed it right into the Dullahan's great-helm with a thunderous crack! He could feel the violence of the impact vibrating up his sword arms like jelly! The impact left a brutal crater on the back of the helmet! Any mortal man would have been stunned by such a monstrous blow!

But no! The Dullahan laughed in defiance and twisted around with such relentless force, Connacht was viciously struck with the cleaving axehead! The strike rendered a vicious, bloody gash right through Connacht's brigantine coat! The cut was nasty! Blood was gushing down his torso. Connacht swiftly leapt back to touch his chest and noticed blood was all over his hand!

The Dullahan laughed deeply, his voice sinister and mocking. He wrenched his shattered helmet from wide shoulders and flung it down the mountain! The helmet clanked unceremoniously as it struck boulder after boulder as it tumbled downwards!

The head of the Dark Knight was invisible except for the burning green eyes, literal bale fire leapt up from those ghastly orbs and they looked directly at Connacht!

The Dullahan laughed "Fool Gallowgalas, idiot mercenary! Wandering whore-monger and gypsy breeder! I am your Doom and will be the butcher of your squires! I shall split you asunder, rending you as morsels of meat, cleaving you from crotch to crown with my axe! After that I shall feed your defiled corpses to those animalistic boggarts and keep your head Impaled on the speartip of my weapon!" The Dark-knight mocked.

"Lord Arawann awoke me from my tomb in Dun Tara and I answered his call! Filthy nord man-thing, I shall butcher you now like how your people slaughter hogs! Did you not think that wandering into the Twelve Duns would not invite our wrath!?!" growled the Dullahan.

With that the massive Juggernaut charged forth once again with his gargantuan polearm and struck swiftly, right for Connacht's neck but he once again caught the shaft of the blade on his handle, spun around, redirected the force, knelt down and slammed his back into the Behemoth's chest!.The Lochaber-axe swung wildly as it was deflected into the thick ice with a sickening crunch!

But the Dullahan was also crafty in combat and brought the weapon around and impaled the spear tip right through Connachts armored boot and pinned his to the ice!

Connacht bit his lip in agony and then screamed "Iza!" (the rune of ice)... Frost quickly formed up the weapon's shaft...he could hear the Dullahan knight grunt with rage trying to pull his frozen Pole-axe free! Tragically this also meant that Connacht's foot was frozen to the impaling weapon!

He quickly freed his blade from the Axe's frozen shaft and turned to faced the Dark Rider! Our Gallowgalas pivoted the tip of the sword upwards and rammed it through the invisible head of his foe! Though the head was not able to be seen he could feel the steel bite deep into something there.

The Dullahan, herald of doom, laughed once again in his ghastly voice, "No mundane sword can smite me! Even if wrought of silver and cold iron! Only magic can return me to my eternal slumber!"

Connacht smiled and screamed "Thurisaz!" the (Thor's rune of Storms), suddenly bolts of violet and azure lightning leapt down from the heavens and struck him and his greatsword at the pommel! The electricity harmlessly passed through his body but coursed down from his blade and surged between the burning eyes of the doom knight. The surge went down, down, down into his armored body!

The rider began to violently scream and seizure as the electricity coursed through his armor. The Dark Knight was being electrocuted. Connacht quickly hefted his enchanted sword into the cloudy heavens, roared to the Aesir sky gods and brought the weapon down furiously again with one mighty strike! This blow would have decapitated the stoutest of men but the burning green eyes of the Dullahan leapt into the heaven's like two malicious hellfire-sprites and quickly raced away to the east, to the forbidden lands of the Unseelie!

His mighty armor shook violently and suddenly fell apart, the chunks of plate crashed loudly to the ground...but there was no body to be seen!? Connacht gasped, that fight was intense, he took his Pommel and smashed the ice around his foot...especially fighting such a cursed foe...he turned his head to see the Kork warriors and two kerns locked in a epic "tug of war" against the red caps. Gronk joined his kin and slammed his log into their ranks but the dwarves returned their attacks, wildly hacking at the Kork's legs or arms in retaliation and the three were covered in bloody gashes!

Lachlann and Finlay hurled bombs of silver powder and burning tar grenades at the Red Caps! **Boom! Pow!** The bombs exploded, this caused quite few casualties as the tusked dwarves roared in rage and agony, their skin welting and blistering from the onslaught!

Connacht roared "Uruz!", slamming his runic rings together. This rune represented the mighty Auroch, the sacred animal of Magni, son of Thor and god of strength. With that he could suddenly feel his shoulders, arms and legs bulging with potent strength! He ripped the impaling halberd out of his foot and charged up the mountain, snorting furiously and slammed into Gronk's back! Gronk gasped as the wind got knocked out of him but the Red Caps pushing against him were knocked back several feet from the impact!

Gronk gasped "Me am fine! We go!" and Lachlann with Finlay slammed right into Bronkk and Ugluk's back pushing them forward with determined ferocity. Connacht roared once again "Uruz! Auroch of the north! Fearsome cow of the giants!" and suddenly the kork's and the kerns grew massive and mighty!

Their legs and backs bulged with power and they surged fiercely, with relentless determination. Their enemies were driven back more and more, yard by yard our heroes tenaciously advanced until they shoved the red-caps back to the top of the mountain pass! With great effort our fearsome heroes flung them off a cliff and they hurtled down into steep ravine, screaming in fury the whole way down!

"Alright Pig-men! Yer free as long as you don't betray us!" Snarled Connacht and just like that the Geas was broken but with a condition.

Gronk whipped around and said "Ye never made such a promise with a caveat...you should know that the sons of Gromm and Kromm will find a way to punish oath-breakers like yee! But for now, we will at least keep our end of the bargain and leave...know this, that Lord Arawann is just beyond that bend...in a palace of ancient pine trees with a gossamer canopy of spider webs and glowing mushrooms. He is far faster than anything you have ever battled in your life...so keep your wits about yee."

With that the three massive pig men stomped down the mountain pass to vanish in the forests below.

Connacht Smiled and turned to his horses "Yee Puca are not free until we leave the borders of the Twelve Duns!" The angry Puca-horses only sighed in frustration. They knew that a Geas was a potent spell and breaking the sworn oath would cause a very serious curse to fall upon them.

One of the Puca-horses snorted and said "Ironic to witness an Ostramann use the dwarven Rune magic against the cursed dwarves who created it in the first place!"

"Well lads!" Connacht shouted excitedly, "Just beyond this bend of the mountain we will encounter a deadly foe! Prepare yeeselves, we will be fighting Bane-Sidhe, whose screams can stun the most hardy of warriors or even kill the elderly. Their iridescent wings make them extremely swift and deadly, darting in to impale foes with their silvered Glaives."
Finlay and Lachlann looked at each other with grim determination.

(Elsewhere on the fated mountain of Dun Aos-Sidhe)
Lord Arawann hefted lady Rhona's legs high above her head, she could feel him deep inside her and he thrust very deeply one last time! She could feel his powerful hips and even the tip of his manhood gently kiss deep inside her warm cervix and then he roared in pleasure! He quickly orgasmed so deep inside her she could feel the warm cum flowing all hot and wet within her womb.

They were making a baby and she loved it, she told him to breed her and breed her he did. She was being bred like a cow and she wanted more of it. Two other Leanan-Sidhe (lesser dark elves, like Bane-Sidhe but without wings) were sucking deeply on Lady Rhona's pendolous breasts and she received her tenth screaming orgasm as Lord Arawann exploded deep inside her large, silky vagina.

He was exhausted and pulled out, her meaty labia lips seemed to almost hug his great shaft as he slowly pulled out, penis limp from such a massive load. *"Gods these witches are total whores, oh how she could live on the wild side of the island and be bred like a mare in heat by these tall woads and Bane-sidhe warriors."* She fantasized.

Even the wandering gypsies known as Shelta arrived, disembarking from their wagons to join in the lascivious festivities of feasting, orgies, drinking and performing magic ceremonies. Though this was not the Grai tribe, they were unfamiliar.

High atop Dun Aos Sidhe the congregation of Lord Arawann's wild hunt was all around feasting and drinking from drinking horns. The Bane-Sidhe elites where breeding amongst themselves and even with the strange blue woads from the deep forests. This mountain should be freezing but some strange magick made this place an eternal spring, cool wind and a warm hearth fire.

During the full moon after Sahwin they wanted to have many Changeling babies so they might grow up to infiltrate the Caledonians, the Shelta, Picts, Nords and even the unwary Ostramann tribes. This island once named An-Fhomar changed it's name in homage to Sahwin now was called the Isles of Samhain after Lugos's great victory against Balor and his Formorians.

A very corpulent and fleshy witch approached Lady Rhona and laid a warm but wizened hand upon her, then looked up at her and smiled. "lass, mi name is Lady Oona and you are lucky today, for you have become swollen with a child, I can feel new life deep within your womb forming! Come deary, follow me to the crystal cavern and eat porridge, we have an especially fine and smooth porridge made with goats milk, honey, nuts and an assortment of berries.

"You will need this as your child grows inside you during the blood moon sabbath or as Hjalmar might call it, Zer Walpurgisnacht! The night of the witches orgy!" With that she snapped her plump fingers and a host of child sized men followed her and immediately started cooking a porridge, stirring the pout, fetching various ingredients and sweeping the floor.

The Blood Moon was out in all it's crimson glory, Lady Rhona could see the blood red moon illuminating the night sky...some say its the burning of the scare-crows at small farms, the giant wicker men at clan strongholds and or possibly even jack-o-lanterns... Who knows but the air was polluted with smog during this time of year and it gave the full moon a blood red tint, quite haunting and ominous to everyone who could witness it.

Otherwise the air was pristine with fresh skies for most of the year on Samhain. Only late fall caused this event of a Crimson full-moon to arise. Others say it was the blood of the ancient gods that gave birth to the Tautha De Denaan before they fled Johtunhiem, fleeing from the fierce Aesir sky gods in the dawn of time also known as Ymir's Ice Age. This was an era were the gods of the world battled against the monstrous hordes of Ymir's children, tribes of warlike giants who avowed vengeance for the death's of Ymir and his son Orcus.

"Meh, Who Knows?" She thought, *"these mythological stories are great and all but we are so long divorced from those eras they could all be myth."* She pondered.

A large, porous stone bowl was served to her, filled with glorious, steaming, white and creamy porridge made from the smoothest of wheat. She was given a bronze spoon, for she knew the fae folk, the hag born and even the Woads suffered at the mere touch of iron.

She took one spoonful and it was so gentle, sweet and amazing. She could smell the nutmeg and cinnamon, the rich creamy taste of goat milk contrasted nicely with the tart cranberries and apples which in turn was complimented by the warm, sweetness of honey and butter.

She gave the great, stone bowl back to the hag and the hag smiled from ear

114

to ear. Lady Rhona felt so good, her stomach was satisfied with such an aristocratic porridge. There was a warm fire in the cave, it's orange light shimmering gently from the various iridescent crystals in the great cavern. She could see the various massive stone mounds that were crafted within. Some kind of burial mounds for these ancient fae and human warriors and nobility no less.

Chapter 8: Lady Rhona's dream.

"My mother I bring forth, she brings forth me: I'm sometimes greater, sometimes less than she. What am I?"

Lady Rhona felt warm, full of food and full of Arawann's seed. She walked into the crystal caverns, the gems growing from the wall refracted and scintillated light in various kaleidoscopic lights of dazzling prismatic color. The glamour of fae magic radiated gently in this wondrous cavern.

She crawled into a warm bear-skin bed within what was once a large, stone sarcophagus chiseled from the bedrock itself during some ancient, long forgotten age of heroism. She quickly feel into a deep sleep, a small hearth-fire nearby kept her pleasantly warm. *"What an amazing night,"* she thought, *"amazing passionate sex with one of the most handsome fae beings I have ever encountered, an epic meal of the finest porridge and incredible sights to be seen during this blood-moon."*

Images of magic, lore, myths told around the fire, wild men and unseelie fae dancing about a great inferno. Her eyes grew weary and she drifted into the warmest and most pleasant of sleep mere mortals could only dream about.

(Lady Rhona dreamed, a strange dream. A sweet, childlike, voice narrated to her during this potent vision. As the invisible spirit's voice spoke her soul seemed to fly to location to location during a series of ancient battles and events that the gods known as the Tautha De Denaan experienced.)

A Vast battlefield of emerald grass in a great valley, somehow mostly devoid of trees aside from the occasional cluster of pine trees or a few groves of golden-leafed birch with it's brilliant virgin-white bark. Down from the hilltops came a massive army of men and giants, white of skin and covered in tribal-tattoos of red and black with one central eye painted on their chests.

Suddenly a truly massive giant, with one great and terrible eye emerged behind his horde! So colossal was he, that he had to walk upon his gargantuan arms and legs, he was so big he could not even stand upright as he moved forward one could hear the thunderous footsteps shook the very earth itself. The Army chanted, "Orcus! Orcus! Orcus!" as their leader plodded forward with each earth-quaking step.

"Was this an army of frost giants and their human slaves they forced into battle?" She wondered as she dreamed. Even the men were tall and powerful of build, possibly the sons of giants.

The giants leading them looked feral, wild curved horns, great sharp tusks and tufts of white fur on their mighty bodies.

The warband was almost like a sea of flesh, like an avalanche of muscle they poured down the hillside, trampling the grass while roaring "oath-breakers! Kin-slayers! We have come to avenge father!" The man-folk banged their maces and axes against their rounded shields, many warriors bore various barbed javelins on leather backpacks. The feral giants roared in rage and down the hillside with their elephantine legs.

Did this army hail from mountainous Johtunhiem, the freezing ocean of Ginnulgagap or even from the polar realm of the Isenvald? One could only speculate.

From the southern end of this great valley another army emerged in opposition to them, a host of deer-men and horse-folks appeared from the forested glens which dotted the southern hill-tops. Before them stepped two beautiful godlike beings, Epona, the mother of horses and centaurs while Cerunnos, the horned god, father of satyrs and hamadyrads, accompanied her to battle. Their animalistic children who wielded spears and longbows, cheered to the high heavens as they looked up.

On the eastern end were two giants who looked as brothers, one bore a mighty hammer the other had a glowing great Axe, they came with their armies...

These Giants led hordes of their giant-kin into battle. They were the famous twin sons of Orcus who rebelled against his reign, Crom, the mountain god and Grom, the cave lord. Though they were the sons of Orcus they betrayed him and his horde and eagerly joined forces with the gods of nature, the children of Danu, the long hated enemies of Orcus. Orcus swore vengeance against both the Aesir and Vanir (the Tautha De Denaan) for slaying his father Ymir during the birth of the world.

Epona and Cerunnos knew that Orcus wanted to slaughter all the gods born of Ymir's loins. He would slaughter both tribes, the nature loving Vanir and the Sky dwelling Aesir. Orcus was enraged for the tribes of gods betrayed Ymir as he slept and slew him.

Ymir's body was turned into a massive mountain range while his blood filled the valleys of Ginnulgagap and much of the great oceans were born from this event. In turn these oceans flooded various kingdoms and tribal lands of the frost giants or Johtun.

The Vanir and Aesir broke their oath to Ymir because he in turn murdered their mother, Danu. He then turned her corpse into several islands in the western seas, which probably became the Caledonian isles that are inhabited now." The narrating voice explained.

"The alliance were accompanied by an ancient female giant, dressed as an elderly crone, they could see her heavily wrinkled face and body of white skin and blue-woad tattoos. Ice and freezing winds whipped about this ancient witch, for this was none other than the grandmother of winter itself, Callieach the first crone." Rhona could actually see the massive crone towering over the fae army.

This voice seemed familiar to lady Rhona, who ever was narrating the history and lore of this event and the major figures of the battle sounded like a sweet, childlike voice in her mind's eye but she never heard this voice before. *"How strange"*, she thought.

Lady Rhona turned her mind to this dream vision and she noticed that the battle already started! The hordes of Orcus, almost uncountable in their multitudes surged across the grass plains... as they advanced Cerunnos blared his conch to the high heavens and his satyr and hamadyrad kin fired a hail of arrows that rained upon the hordes of their enemies like a stinging

118

hail from the high heavens.

Scores of these warriors fell to the arrows as they were killed by the hundreds, the battlefield was slick with pools of blood and mounds of warriors but yet this didn't even slow the advance. More and more came to die or kill but it mattered not.

The giants were barely phased though their bodies were pin cushioned with arrows, they moved within distance and grabbed the nearest logs or strewn boulders and flung them at the Satyr archers! Crash! Crack! Went the massive boulders. The Archers who were unlucky enough were crushed to gorey paste. The rest were quick enough to retreat behind the hill tops or into the forest of birch on the other to find cover. Cerunnos and Epona Roared, lifting their mighty ironwood pikes to the heavens, they charged forth with their contingents of unicorns and centaurs in triangular formations. The Hamadyrads cavalry-archers screened ahead and behind, firing scores of arrows and screening the advancing charge.

The Wild-Hunt surged faster and faster towards the hated foes, their hooves struck the earth harder and harder as they pushed their bodies harder and harder. The first wild hunt ever formed in history was assembled at this fated battle, and they crossed the land like a rampaging tidalwave.

Like an avalanch they crashed into enemy lines! Bam! The human warriors were driven through with lances and horns, their shields shattered from the colossal impact and their bodies were impaled. Their bleeding corpses were driven into other unlucky foes. Even the thick hides of giants, damn near impervious to arrows was not impervious to the driving force of the centaurs' lances which bit deep and tore through them. Not only was the lesser swarms of human warriors being overran but even frost giants were being brought down by the multitudes of impaling pikes.

Orcus roared in defiance because the battle was almost stopped! His roar summoned another wave of fierce warriors who came surging down from the northern hilltops! They were led by his two loyal sons, Balor the one eyed and Taran the father of winter. Balor used his one cyclopean eye to shoot beams of fire and annihilate scores of centaurs and hamadyrads. Taran opened his fanged maw and spat out brutal storms of freezing rain and hail at the fae armies, their arrows ricocheting and bouncing harmlessly off the giant's storm breath. These loyal brothers looked similar to Orcus, so mighty, even for frost giants they galloped on their knuckles almost like great apes, if great apes were the size of the tallest trees in the forest.

From the east and west two other great war horns blared into the heavens... in Lady Rhona's vision she could see that Tanaris was playing a horn made of silver and ivory, and the writing on it was not written in the native Caledonian Ogma script, no, this was written in what could only be the writings of the Ostraman, the Eldar Futhark Runic alphabet... But why would the gods of Caledonia be using an instrument of a long untrusted foe? This looked as if it was an Aesir instrument of war...the Gallarhorn?
The Horn only used by the Nordic gods Heimdar and Mimir?

Now the battle seemed lost, Epona and Cerunnos looked on in terror at the advance of Orcus and his monstrous twins. Epona and Cerunnos quickly retreated back to their lines, swiftly outrunning the giant horde, their forces quickly reforming and surging back to safety.

Lo from the western horizon, flying above the Solstice seas came a storm guard followed by his army! Tanaris and his Giant Eagles came riding in from the west, many bearing Aos Sidhe or elves, as the nords would call them. From the East Crom and Grom came charging out with their loyal human warriors and frost giants, They bore their mighty axes and hammers in battle as they charged across the battlefield!

Lady Rhona was impressed, both of these reinforcements smashed into Orcus's flanks at exactly the same time. Killing scores of humans and felling several dozens of frost giants simultaneously. Though this was not a one sided slaughter, Orcus's hordes were utterly fearless and fought to the death, soon mounds of corpses formed as small, bloody hills dotted the landscape literally everywhere. The fighting was so fierce that literal arms, heads and legs were strewn across the bloody sea that was a battlefield.

Orcus, went berserk with Rage, foam coming out of his gnashing, fanged jaws, his rock-like fists slammed into the earth! Wham! Crack! Two great waves of his army was butchered but two new waves came charging down the hills! He turned his fury on the forces of Grom and Crom, His mighty fists and hoofed feet struck the earth and caused the very earth itself to shudder as he galloped on his knuckles like a primeval ape.

Grom and Crom, both as tall as a mountain, counter-charged valiantly as Orcus smashed into their armies of giants and their kin.

Orcus flung him self into the air and slammed down on the armies of fierce warriors, Crom the Mountain god was smacked so hard they crashed into the literal hillside with a loud Thud! Orcus grabbed Grom and picked him up into the air then slammed with such force that earth exploded around him formed a massive crater! Tanar and Balor now renewed with hope and fury began to rampage through the fae armies...flattening men, picking up and ripping apart centaurs and crushing satyrs with boulders!.

The fae armies were getting slaughtered to a tee and many of their forces began to flee to the southern hillside, the Satyrs swiftly climbed up the trees to rain arrows down on fierce warbands of humans and their giant slave-masters. Even fearsome Grom turned to stalwart Crom and screamed "we need to leave, out armies are getting slaughtered!" but Crom kept fighting "Crom you fool! Your loyal followers will be butchered like lambs unless we leave!" scream Grom.

Lady Rhona could now see Crom grabbing his silver and ivory horn, covered strangely enough in Nordic runes but this was no mere runed horn, this was the mighty runic horn of Gjallarhorn! He blew upon it and released a mighty undulating note, that reverberated throughout the heavens.

From the Western sea clouds emerged first small silver specks but to the trained eyes this was no mere host of flying warriors. This was the Aesir, the sky-gods of the far north had come to battle! Crom scream "Nuada! Epona! Cerunnos! Tanaris! Callieach! You epic deities have arrived to save us from hordes of Orcus'! They brought an Aesir warhost with them!"

Off in the distance swarms of flying horses bearing stoic female warriors came raining down from the storm clouds of the northern seas! A Potent sky-god was flying high, riding a chariot pulled by two giant Rams across the Heavens. He was wielding a great two headed Axe with lightning leaping from it's blades. It was Thor, the storm lord and he brought the mighty flock of Valkries with him, and they flew towards the battlefield with incredible force. They joined force with the Fianna and charged into battle from the heavens, Impaling enemies with their lances and decapitating foes with their shimmer broadswords and battle axes.

The Nature loving Vanir, before they renamed themselves the Tautha De Denaan were now fighting besides their long hated rivals the Aesir! Following closely behind were other ancient Vanir deities. Prince Nuada the king of the elves was followed by a special contingent of eagle riding Sidhe known as the Fiannu and they dived downwards to impale any foe foolish enough to stand in the way!

The Great Crone, mother of all witches, Callieach was now joined by the Morrigan, the goddes of death, Brigid the Healer and Rhiannon the fae dreamer. She was the one to teach the divine trinity of Vanir goddesses true magic and yet she was also said to have taught three daughters of Orcus himself, masters of pulling the strings of fate. This second generation of fates aided her in battle bringing down bolts of chainlight to smite the foe and clouds of freezing mist to blind them.

Behind the Aesir gods came swarms of stalwart longships, furiously rowing past choppy seas.
These ships were a gift from Odin himself to the struggling Vanir and they were full of fierce Einherjar-warriors, who came directly from Asgard, the sky-god's homeland. These brave men and women were slain in battle honorably, then Valkries brought them back from using runic magic to serve once again as an immortal warband of the gods.

Thor and Tanaris Chariots hit the earth and they immediately plowed through formations of mighty warriors like they were mere stalks of wheat... the blades on their chariots decapitated, dismembered and crushed any foolish warriors who were not fast enough to evade the trampling rampage of both chariots. Tanaris would fling his mighty battleaxe while Thor flung his magical hammer Mjolnir, splitting the skulls of the fiercest frost giants or crushing their skulls into pieces of gore and bone! In turn the hosts of Valkyres and Fiannu crashed into enemy lines with their impaling lances, driving their spears right through the eyes and necks of their enemies. When the Cavalry lances cracked from the sheer number of impaled bodies weighing down on the weapons, they unleashed their scintillating broadswords and battle-axes, hacking off heads and arms on their trampling onslaught across the battlefield.

The Forces of Danu had a resurgence in courage, Epona and Cerunnos bellowed upon their horns to the high heavens! The fleeing fae stopped their route, Grom and Crom roared in fury to stop their routing warriors, who then savagely counterattacked with such fury it pushed the horde of Orcus towards the sea. Both armies met at a standstill and no quarter was taken until.

That is, until the armada of Asgard smashed onto the shore and the longships disembarked scores of elite Einherjar-warriors onto the shore. They came spilling in untold numbers behind the horde of Orcus, slamming right into the rear of the massive army. Einherjar were fierce warriors in life who gave no quarter and they were even greater after death! Their brigantine armor shimmered like glinting silver in the daylight, their strong square-like shields formed into thick-walls and their spears formed into dense phalanxes. The formations appeared like great, iron porcupines of death.

Waves and waves of the enemy crashed into their shield-walls, dying in heaps, being driven into impaling pikes while piercing javelins rained down on them from above. Heavy broadswords and battles-axes counterattacked enemies who got too close and arms, legs and heads were chopped off with a sickening Hack!

This well-ordered, wall of armor and death killed scores of Orcus's swarm, even mighty Ice Giants who crashed into the formations were impaled with so many pikes and spears that it took a toll upon the behemoths, though admittedly only the Ice Giants were strong enough to shatter the formations of Einherjar.

After the Johtun broke through their formations they would be gasping for air and bleeding heavily from pulling a multitude of bloody spears out of their bodies. In turn furious berserkers with great-axes would charge the bloodied giants and hack them to gory pieces, chopping off fingers, toes, Achilles heels even climbing up the giants, ramming their greatswords into their stomachs and ripping them open with massive gouges!

The Einherjar and their supporting Berserkers kept pouring out of the armada of longships, reinforcing those who were slain on the battlefield...but even they were slowly losing ground to the incoming hordes of Orcus. The Fierce Valkyres and Gods slayed Frost giant after frost giant but more kept coming. Mountains of the enemies corpses kept pilling up.

Crom Turned to Grom and said "Brother, it is as if our accursed father's war-host is truly without end! We must slay him, together we can crush his skull and split him asunder!"

Grom offered his hand to Crom and they both shook hands "Today, our oath is already broke, there is not point to honoring a foul oath! We shall slay our father and shatter his Horde! For Earth-Mother Danu!" Crom bellowed and Grom nodded his head in agreement.

Prince Nuada, king of the elves flew down on his mighty Eagle before them, quickly followed by two other great eagles. He was bedecked in the most brilliant of silver-leaf armor bearing a twisting lance in his hand.

"Great Warlords! It is a pleasure! Let us slay Orcus together, we must fly in the heavens and fall upon him like meteorites of doom so we may avoid his savage sons, Balor, of the burning eyes and Tanar, of the Freezing Maw!" Prince Nuada sweeped his hand out at the two other giant Eagles and both Grom and Crom mounted them.

"You see milady Rhona! This is the hour of fate, witness Crom and Grom mount these majestic Eagles and ride them into the heavens!" said the disembodied voice.

They swiftly mounted their mounts and flew into the high heavens with such speed. Higher and higher they rose until they flew above the storm clouds they could see far below, witnessing the massive battle unfurl.

Then Nuada, king of the Elves spoke "If we dive down from this position directly above we shall smite your father with thunderous force! I should be able to Impale him fully with my lance, Crom you can easily shattered his skull with a mighty blow from your hammer and you Grom, should be able to Slit his throat open with a strike from your giant Axe. I will leap first, then you Crom and finally you Grom!" they all looked at each other in fierce determination and nodded their approval.

Lo! They did as they vowed, first Nuada leapt and flew down from his eagle mount, his brilliant white flag flapped in the whipping winds as he dived downward faster and faster. Swiftly following him was Crom wielding his mighty warhammer, covered in blunt spikes for shattering armored foes with relative ease, the wind also whipped around him and was almost deafending as it whistled about him. Finally Grom followed suit with his savage cleaver, it's serrated blade hungry to butcher his tyrant father.

Nuada Struck first and drove his silver lance through Orcus with such power that it impaled the titan's shoulder with a massive crack and drove him right into the earth, pinning him there! Then Orcus screamed in horrible pain, his one eye witnessed Crom screaming and flying right at him so swiftly he barely had time to defend himself, he lifted a hand to defend his head but it was to late, Crom smashed right into Orcus's massive heavily ridged forehead with such incredible force that it released a monstrous thunder-crack! THWAK! His head violently whipped around away from the dolorous impact. The Thunderous blow shattered Orcus's left-horn into chunks of gory bone which erupted outwards, flying everywhere!

Finally Grom came thundering down like a ballista bolt from the high heavens and Struck with his giant cleaving axe, right through the neck of the Titan Orcus! This split his thick hide and flesh wide open and the blade bit deep.

Orcus roared a mighty scream as Grom viciously ripped the serrated axe out with such force that it's jagged teeth sawed right through neck muscles, his throat was torn wide open Orcus's jugular was split in twain. Orcus could no longer scream, as black blood came burbling out of his ragged neck wound and he gurgled in his death throes.

Orcus was slain, Taran and Balor, his last remaining loyal sons turned around in horror and ripped their impaling spears out of their bodies to witness their father dying on the western shore. They ran up to Orcus and covered his corpse with their monstrous bodies, arrows, lances and axes bit into them but they cared not, their thick hides and walls of muscles protected them from these annoying gnats. The Two sons wept in despair, their father loved them no matter how monstrous they appeared and protected them from other Johtun who wished to beat them to death for their deformities.

If it wasn't for the death of Orcus, the horde of Orcus would have eventually won, their numbers almost limitless. His host wailed and screamed, the vast majority of them fled away from the battle, up the slopes of the northern hill country and vanished into the mountainous landscape from where they once formed.

Orcus, pointed to the heavens and through his ripped open throat screamed "cowards! Oath breakers! All of you! You promised me you would fight to the death by my side! You promised you would not leave me!" and he snapped his trembling finger. His armies and the army of Crom and Grom began to scream in agony, for they broke a sacred geas.

Both giants grew bloody fangs and horns that erupted from their bodies, or vicious claws and spikes and as Orcus lay dying his sons, giants and human tribes writhed and warped in mutation!

So was born the first Orcs and their Formorian Masters! Grom, Crom, Balor, Taran and all their giant tribal kin grabbed themselves in agony and writhed on the grasslands screaming. Their skin turned gray-green, tusks and fangs jutted out of their misshapen mouths, their arms grew long and muscular but their legs became stunted and bow legged, their jaws became heavy and angular while their noses sunk in their faces, almost resembling the snouts of boars or great apes.

Many of them looked in horror at their bodies warped, they ran to lakes to see their reflections and to their horror they witnessed badly deformed faces and bodies. Hating their new bodies and warped faces they cried in rage and ran far away, many hid in deep caverns under the earth to never see their bestial features again! Here they formed into fierce tribes of humanoids who forever waged war with the people of the surface, they became known as the Orcneas.

Such was born the cursed Orcs and Balor became their new lord. The Orcneas poured forth at times like tidal waves to wage war upon the lands of the fae, men and even the gods themselves.

The Battle was horrific, bloody, and many were slain. The bodies of men and fae were placed in their proper burial mounds in the lands of Hravenholme. The Aesir gods demanded a temporary truce with their Vanir relatives but for a cost. Two gods, lovers, now must bind themselves to Odin and his Aesir court. So Epona and Cerunnos bowed their mighty horned heads to the King of the Sky Gods and he gave them two golden enchanted Torcs, which they placed around their necks to show respect and servitude.

The potent runes carved into these ornamental necklaces glowed azure blue and Epona and Cerunnos screamed in agony as their animalistic bodies warped. Bones cracked and their large bodies shrank, they violently morphed into a naked man and a naked woman of incredible beauty.

Odin gave them the names Freyr for Cerunnos and Freya for Epona, their transformation left them shocked and saddened but they gladly gave their immortal services to the King of the Sky Gods themselves and served him gracefully.

Odin now turned to the assembly of Vanir forest gods and their Fae host and asked "now one last god must volunteer to serve my court in Asgard!" So the ancient sea god, Lear, Father of Manaan, rose up and offered himself in service to the victorious sky gods

Odin also gave him a gold torc and the same ceremony was performed and the same agonizing metamorphosis happened. The ancient sea-god, king of the merfolk, morphed into a more human-like deity, Njord.

Prince Nuada and Callieach looked at their enslaved kin and spoke, "No longer shall we name ourselves the Vanir, we no longer see the warlike sky gods as our kin, we shall speak a new language written by Ogios himself and we shall name ourselves in honor to our giant mother...Danu...We will call ourselves the people of Danu or the Tuatha De Danaan!"

He lifted his deadly spear, Gae Bolg, into the high heavens and the fae host, the liberated giants and the tribes of men who could became to be known as the Caledonians cheered in victory.

The great longships of the Aesir and their Einherjar servants were left behind as a gift to the former Vanir who became the newly named Tuatha De Denaan. They entered these empty warships and sailed them west to their future island homes that would first be named Caledonia and or Trin na Nog. Each Island in turn received the names after great battles and or holidays to praise the Tuatha De Denaan for victories against the Formorians, siring the second generation of gods and so forth.

"You see lady Rhona" said the disembodied voice "The name of the Islands now are generally in honor to a god or goddess of the second generation."

"Sahwin of course is in homage to the great heroic gods who fought at the second battle of Maig Tuired, and the island's name came from this holiday." The voice said

"The island of spring, Imbolc is named after the holiday of the goddess of spring and healing, Brigid, when she healed a high king of the Caledonians and a holiday to celebrate spring. It will also be celebrated on her island and in her homage, great fire were lit, animals are encouraged to breed as are the people. People also meditate and perform rituals of cleansing, even spring cleaning for this festival. It is said that there are many Aos Sidhe kingdoms of fae folk hidden in its deep forests of that land."

"The Beltaine Isles of spring going to summer is the southern most isles right next to Lughanasa Isles, these islands are also the most fertile and a great number of grains, fruits various other foodstuffs grow frequently there. The holiday also represents fertility and the people of Beltaine are known to dance around giant maypoles, some say that these maypoles repersent the Dagda's mighty phallus as he impregnates the divine trinity of Brigid, the Morrigan and even Rhiannon. Aengus, the love god is said to reside in the Beltaine isles and many of the first generation gods are invoked during this holiday such as Cerunnos, Epona, Tanaris and even the ancient earth mother Danu." Droned the familiar voice

"The Isle of Lughnasadh is in a nearby isle to Samhain, named Lugnasadh in honor of Lugos for avenging Nuada and winning the second battle of Maig Tuired. This is the Island of Summer approaching Fall and this is the holiday of autumns first harvest and it takes place at the very end of summer as it approaches autumn. Also a breadbasket province." The voice stated.

"These four major isles have their respective holidays and each island has it's own Fire Festival to pay homage to the Tautha De Denaan. Strangely enough nobody has heard from the gods in centuries and even their subjects, the Aos Sidhe, the fae folk and the Seelie court has remained very elusive and hidden. But the Unseelie fae, the dark ones seem to have risen from the burial mounds of where the fae folk were slain during the human invasions."

"Be aware, mother, that Grom came to Samhain and left his Axe in the caverns below the Orkney Pensula but alas it was said he either abandoned his cursed children or they slayed him in battle. All that is left is his mighty axe at an Atlar. When the eternal winter comes you must tell Connacht of this legendary Weapon."

"It is time you awaken for I have given you the origins of these strange isles, when you dream again I shall tell you of more tales of these strange islands." The disembodied voice finished

(Lady Rhona Calhoun awoke.)

The Wild Antler Flutes bellowed wildly, the ram horns trumpeted and the Bodhran-drums thundered... this was a bad omen, Lord Arawann summoned his Unseelie host. The Wild hunt was called across the pine forests of the twelve duns. She knew what that meant, Connacht and his companions have arrived to rescue her and to bring her back to the drunkard giant they called Jarl Hjalmar.

Lord Arawann ran deep into the Grotto, as tall, muscular and handsome as ever, his brilliant crown of ivory antlers seemed to contrast so nicely with his dark violet skin. He looked at her with his dreamy magenta eyes and grabbed her waist, gently but firmly. "My love, it is time you flee from here" he said with his silky baritone voice. "My love, I shall defend your honor but if I am defeated in battle know this, you carry our love child, if Connacht wins go with him without struggle for at least our child will live in the lap of luxury." He then leaned in closely and kissed her passionately.

"Wow" She thought, *"those kisses are sheer magic... I feel like I am almost flying on my feet from such a kiss"*. Lady Rhona looked into his gorgeous, purple eyes and nodded her head in agreement.

Chapter 9: The Battle of Dun Aos Sidhe.

**"A wingless bird, fleeting to heaven from earth.
Each eye that meets me weeps, but not from grief,
And in thin air I vanish at my birth.
What am I?"**

(Dawn approached the next day, on the trail to Dun Aos-Sidhe.)
Connacht put out his fire after cooking up several links of blood sausage stir fried with red potatoes, fried barely and wild leeks. A hearty breakfast that he ate with the lads, it was flavored with a small amount of mountain dill to give it a slightly pickled flavor. They washed this meal down with some some pine needle tea flavored with a tad bit of honey.

He rolled up his sleeping cots and marched up the winding mountain pass, still bearing his sheathed greatsword on his shoulder and Lachlann now carrying the Lochaber-axe of the defeated Dullahan. Lachlann and Finlay flipped a silver coin three times to determine who would gain the right to carry such a mighty weapon and strangely enough fortune was on Lachlann's side. Connacht did not pick favorites and loved these two wild lads like his own sons. Today Lachlann won the coin toss, mayhaps tomorrow Finlay would win the toss and have the honor to bear such a mighty weapon.

"Only a handful of hours before we reach the top" Connacht exclaimed to his Kerns
"Aye Sirr" said Finlay

"Brace yourselves for a battle, take these fire whiskeys and silver powder bombs, yee will need them against the Arch-fae and his court that holds council on Dun Aos Sidhe mountain." Connacht then handed both Finlay and Lachlann a few alchemical flasks. The lads could see that these flasks glowed with a dim light, harboring the potent magic within them.

Finlay suddenly noticed a truly massive Fir Tree growing from the forest floor, towering well above the rest of the other evergreen trees in the snowy forest. Large part's of it's scaly bark was pealed back in large square swaths where the unusual writing of Ogham was written, the scars of the long lines either went directly down or pointed directly up and were intersected with the smaller lines.

Finlay looked at a bewildered Connacht and Lachlann who were beckoning him to leave the strange Biles tree and continue on their journey.

Finlay spoke "Give me some parchment and charcoal, for I must use charcoal to transcribe these ancient Druidic writings onto the papyrus parchment. The Three Sisters of the Shelta asked me to complete this task."
Lachlann sighed and casually threw Finlay him his satchel.

Finlay easily caught the items and began transcribing the ancient Oghamic text on the blank parchment. After a few minutes he was done, he rolled the paper tightly and wound some hemp rope around it, knotting the rope and putting the documents within his satchel bag.

"Llewellyn and Deidre will be able to transcribe these mysterious texts." he said cryptically.

"Oooh, so mysterious! Come lad, we all know yer too stupid to read these ancient writings like the rest of us Ostromann warriors! We need to head up the mountain before Lord Arawann assembles a Wild-Hunt mighty enough to take all us down!" Snarled Lachlann

(Meanwhile on Dun Aos Sidhe)
Lord Arawann could see the magnificent sun cresting above the Twelve-Duns and he smiled, Caledonia aka "the isles of Samhain" was a wild place filled with fierce fae and manfolk, he loved his fierce and beautiful home, though the cold wind of winter was blowing down from the north isles of Yule. he could feel it but he feared not the cold's embrace for Grandmother Callieach of Beara, the ancient queen of winter, was even on the Unseelie faefolk's side.

The Crone of winter was powerful indeed and could swallow the lands of the Ostramann and Yule isles in a brutal winter that would bring an extinction to these barbaric manfolk from Johtunhiem!. He smiled at the idea of watching the Norsemen slowly freeze to death, sent into rabid cannibalism feasting upon their cats, dogs and beloved children. *"The Bastards deserve that for burning Dun-Tara and slaying high king Ith-Og-Briganthia!"* he thought.

(Finally Connacht and his Kerns reach the mountain summit)
Connacht finally reached the mountain top with Finlay and Lachlann riding atop their enchanted horses. It was dawn and the sun shined through the clouds and mist which dotted the mountain tops of the Twelve Duns. The sunlight was a red orange and danced around the pine trees and snow which speckled the landscape.

Connacht reached for his last potion of fae-blood, having been harvested from the vicious Slaugh that he slaughtered at Dun-Calhoun. It tasted oily, vile and very bitter, but he forced it down and he could already feel the lightning like magic of the azure blood coursing through his veins and his veins glowed with a bright blue with the magic in his bloodstream.

He could see lord Arawann before him guarding a cavern of shimmering crystals, surrounding him where a host of redcaps bearing halberds, these burly dwarves, cursed by the three crones like the rest of the Unseelie host, stood almost as tall as a man and much more broad, they hefted their iron billhooks and formed a defensive schiltrom formation around Lord Arawann.

Lord Arawann stood almost two heads taller than his personal honorguard. Standing next to Lord Arawann where to other Leanan-Sidhe, the cursed descendants of the Aos Sidhe...they each bared a silvered and bronze glaive like their lord. Behind lord Arawann was the Silver Cusith and strangely enough a familiar elder Aunty...Aunty Oona!

Connacht still wielded his Claymore and now Lachlann bore the Pole-Axe of the defeated Dullahan while Finlay simply had his shield and broadsword.

Connacht bellowed "Lord Arawann yer actions could cause a potential civil war between Ostramann and Caledonian Clans on Samhain. Give up Lady Rhona or on my honor I will slay yer warriors to a man and take yer head as a trophy!"

133

Lord Arawann laughed contemptuously "Let us settle this in a duel, you win you get Rhona and If I win I turn you and your Kerns into my slaves!" mock Lord Arawann.

Finlay and Lachlans' heads whipped around and they looked at each other in alarm "Connacht I never agreed to..." Finlay groaned but was quickly interrupted "Shut it! I know what I am doing!" he snarled.

"And you! Aunty Oona, in league with that beast?" He pointed his finger at the snarling Cu-Sith "We trusted you all along and you betrayed us!" roared Connacht.

"Fool half-nord!" she snarled "You barbaric filth torched our kingdom of An-Fhomar ages ago! Lord Arawann will make a thousand changeling children and usher in an age where all Fae kind becomes Unseelie and they will hurl humanity back into the dark ages...where they belong!" She laughed.

"So yee were the one who planned this!" Snarled Connacht.

"She wasn't the only one...I wanted to be abducted by this handsome Fae-lord...not be bred to some violent alcoholic like Hjalmar!" shouted Lady Rhona.

Connacht was absolutely shocked from hearing Lady Rhona speak up about this affair and sabotaging her marriage.

"Lady Rhona if you abscond from yee marriage this will cause an immediate civil war between Jarl Hjalmar and Lord Duncan, another clan war means the Shelta wagonfolk would suffer genocide once again!" implored Connacht. Lady Rhona realized the horror that would befall her beloved Shelta peoples in terror...her mouth wide open.

"Silence my love, no need to speak, who cares for those filthy wanders anyways? Humanity breeds like rabbits!" mocked Lord Arawann, his laughter sarcastic and utterly mocking, she stared at him with disbelief...tears running down her emerald green eyes. *I absolutely love the Shelta...* She realized that Connacht wasn't joking in the slightest.

"That was personal Arawann! Aye, elf-lord! I agree to your terms, a duel between you and me!" Connacht seethed in agreement. He was crimson red in fury, for not only did Connacht love a Shelta woman but many of his lost children where born from a Shelta maiden.

Connacht and Lord Arawann squared off, Arawann stepped forward from his fierce honor-guard, his glaive vibrating and ringing in anticipation. Connacht walked forward with his claymore hefted on his shoulder he could hear the cursed sword whispering to him "Blood! Give me the blood of the wicked!"

They begin to circle each other and looking for a weakness...any weakness, weak legs, top heavy, being over weight, arrogance, impatience etc...Connacht was already fifty but quite strong for his age, though somewhat unbalanced...Arawann was physically perfect, lean, strong and light on his feet. Arawann though was arrogant and impatient, Connacht could see the smirk on his face and haughty demeanor. Arawann could barely get a read on Connacht, he looked intense, as if he respected how deadly Arawann could be and respected that prowess.

Arawann laughed at Connacht "surely old man, you think you can defeat an Unseelie lord in battle? I hail from a long line of fae lords...all the way to king Ith-Og-Briganthia and even lord Lugos themselves. Our kind is fast like lightning and with these enchanted glaives I can pierce your armor with ease!" Arawann scoffed

Connacht smiled "Have at it then **Sirrah**!", knowing the elf lord would hate the usage of the disrespectful term. "Ehwaz!" he screamed and he could feel power of a herd of horses coursing through him.

Arawann's smile faded and like a flash of lightning he screamed, a horrific, high pitched warbling wail which stunned allies and enemies alike as the redcaps clutched their ears in agony, blood seeping from their eyes and noses...the quivering roar of a deathly screamed warped the air itself around Arawann and moved as a wall of tortured wind towards Connacht.

Connacht was fast and screamed "Thurisaz!" the Rune of Thor's Thunder,

135

the roar was so mighty that it struck Arawann's scream head on and the opposing forces of roaring air smashed into each other and wrapped around each other so violently that they formed a small tornado of snow and pine needles! These opposing screams canceled each other with a potent burst of wind.

Connacht smiled and Arawann roared in fury and flew at Connacht full speed, his giant gossamer wings beating like a furious dragonfly! Roaring in fury, the fae lord surged forward to impale his prey with one fatal stroke. Like a lightning bolt Arawann darted forth, with murderous intent to slay our Ostramann Gallowgalas with one swift and overwhelming blow.

Connacht was magically enhanced now, he was lighting fast and quickly changed his swording stance from overhead strike to the Ox-stance, with the sword pointed directly at Arawann and held high and straight. The Fae Lord charged in, Glaive held in both hands, swinging in with a high strike! Our Gallowgalas grabbed his Ricasso-handle with his left hand and smashed his sword into the glaive quickly deflected the incoming weapon with the parrying hooks, inches away from impaling his eye! The impact was so furious it made the blade ring aggressively, he could feel the vibrations travel through his muscles his arms directly into his shoulders! The glaive was deflected harmlessly to his left and this forced Lord Arawann to over commit. With expert timing he slammed the crossguard directly into the bridge of Arawann's nose, shattering it with a loud crack! Azure blood poured out from his nostrils, his head was violently whipped back, eyes wide with agony as he roared in pain.

Arawann was furious, *"how did he miss his mark! How dare this mongrel defile my perfect face!"* With quick thinking he slammed his his left knee into Connacht's stomach.

Even through the armored jacket of plates was durable, it hit Connacht square in his sternum like a battering ram and knocked the wind out of him with such force it was almost like Connacht vomited air from his gut! Damnation though! it felt like driving his knee into a rock and hurt like all hells.

136

Lord Arawann quickly glanced with his right eye and noticed something strange, it was as if Connacht's skin was gray, tan and had miniature cracks all over it...like he was made of stone..Bam! Connacht's Pommel smashed into Arawann's jaw with an explosion of white sparks of pain and darkness... sending the fierce Bane-Sidhe tumbling across the mountain top violently and crashed into a pine tree unceremoniously! **Krak!** His silvered glaive slamming onto the ground skipping and **singing** as it bounced across the slate stones.

Lord Arawann wiped his face and his azure blue blood was all over his mouth, never has he ever been so sullied in battle against a man, let alone the soft men from the other side of the Twelve Duns.

He spat his glowing blood out, gasped for air and looked in rage as Connacht now smiled with a cocky smirk across his face. "Ostramann pig! I shall impale thee yet you pink faced sow!" and Arawann, snapped his fingers and his Enchanted glaive literally leapt into his hands vibrating with it's metallic song. They circled once again, Arawann now respecting the cunning old Nordic-wolf before him.

Arawann grew enraged just looking at Connacht's smug, pig face and he leapt forward, Glaive tip pointed directly at Connacht. He pounced like a fierce tiger, so swiftly an average man would have been impaled right through like a fish.

Connacht was waiting for this, he quickly changed stances to the Roof stance, his sword now hefted above his head. The same type of charging attack was followed by the same type of counter but something was wrong, Connacht noticed that Arawann was smiling this time! As their blades connected and he quickly deflected the swift moving blade over his head simply using his crossguard and pushing the weapon up, it felt too easy... But before he could smash his crossguard into Arawann's teeth, the fae lord didn't fall for it this time, instead Arawann swiftly leapt back and punched Connacht square in the face with his right fist! **Boom!** The blow sent Connacht reeling back in pain, seeing stars.

Arawann took the offensive Ox stance, his glaive pointed directly at Connacht's face and he began twisting his hips to the left and the right with great power, the glaive swiftly began flying in horizontal attacks directly at Connacht's face. If the blows were to land on Connacht they would either slash his face, temple or neck wide open! Killing or crippling him in an instance! The Elf Lord began to perform these deadly Zwerchau strikes; high, horizontal slashing cross-strikes coming at both the right and left side of Connacht's head. **Swoosh! Swoosh!** The blade went, as it spun faster and faster and Connacht countered the Glaive attacks by taking up the Balanced Pflug (or plow) stance with the Sword held directly in front of him vertically! **Tang!** The Gallowgalas counter-struck the horizontal attack from his right with a powerful overhead vertical blow! **Tong!** He quickly deflected another incoming horizontal strike this time to his left by hitting the weapon hard with another overhead blow! **Chang!** Sparks flew furiously from the exchange as violent impacts and vibrations surged up his arms, making his muscles feel like jelly.

Connacht had to block each strike with his supernatural speed. Deflecting each incoming strike with the Ricasso handle or the crossguard from his left or right side! **Tang! Tong!** Went the clashing blades as fiery sparks exploded from their violent impacts! But the Fae-lord's assault kept coming in...faster and faster! Harder and harder! The Elven lord looked like a whirlwind of death and each horizontal strike that was parried sent sparks flying or ripped chunks metal out of the Gallowgalas's armored coat! Connacht could feel the violence of the blows travel through his greatsword and into his torso, staggering him with each strike.

Each strike deflected was so forceful it knocked Connacht back from the impact, driving him further back with each furious spinning blow! One blow was so powerful it knocked Connacht directly into a mighty Fir Tree with a loud crash. **Krak!**

Arawann leapt into the air, spun-around furiously with his weapon and then brought down a powerful over-head chop that struck like lightning but Connacht swiftly half sworded his weapon, wrenching his arms up furiously and smashing his ricasso-handle into the oncoming glaive with great force! **Zang!** Our Gallowgalas was dropped on his back from the impact! Connacht felt the air knocked out of his lungs as he hit the ground with a heavy thud, thankfully that deflection saved his life, if he didn't deflect Arawann's glaive would have split his helmet and skull underneath in half! Arawann's incoming blade was violently deflected and sent into the nearby tree, the tip of the weapon impaled itself deeply into the wood there. **Krack!** Connacht swiftly recovered, placing both hands on the Claymore's handle and swung the sword over his head and then brought the blade crashing down on one off Arawann's muscular arms! **Hack!** The Blade violently chopped off Arawann's exposed arm with one mighty blow! A Shower of dark blue blood arced across the cold air as the dismembered arm flew across the sky.

Arawann's violet arm crashed to the earth and azure blue blood spilt out everywhere like a waterfall of gore! The Azure blood poured onto Connacht, lying directly below Arawann he opened his mouth and he could feel the potent magical, sanguinous ichor flooding into his blood stream as the glowing blue essence flooded down his throat! As Arawann screamed in agony and rage Connacht suddenly felt revitalized, his wounds slowly healed as his fury gave him a second wind.

This blood was potent! He could hear voices speaking throughout the forests, some voices deep, others in falsetto. Colored auras danced about all the trees! This fae lord'ss lifeblood was far stronger than any other fae's that Connacht has consumed before! He could hear CuChulain screaming in rage from inside his greatsword, ***Slaughtersong***.

Connacht leapt up from the ground and landed on his feet aggressively, balanced himself and fired a monster right-hand punch directly into the Arawann's jaw. **Krak!** Connacht heard the jawbone snap And the blow sent the elf lord hurtling with such force it sent him crashing into his Redcaps. The Nordic Gallowgalas then grabbed the stubbornly stuck glaive and then screamed "Uruz!" His muscles violently bulged larger and ripped the Glaive out of the tree with a loud **Rakk!**

"Finlay, here lad! It's yours! I still love my ancestor's claymore more than any fae-damned weapon! Don't ever say that I wasn't generous" Connacht gently threw the weapon at Finlay who watched as the glowing, humming weapon bounced and skidded towards his feet. Slowly but with sheer determination he bent down and grabbed the weapon with both hands, unceremoniously hurling his iron broadsword and shield into the snow.

Lachlann looked at Finlay in disgust "Well now I am just jealous, I also want an evil, pansexual elf-lord's singing weapon! I never get the good weapons!” In Finlay's strong hands he could hear the mighty weapon singing it's deadly blade song, humming or vibrating in anticipation.

“Don't look a gift horse in the mouth ye jackass!” laughed Connacht.

Connacht simply sauntered up to the Redcap warriors and said “MOVE! If ye want to be seeing yer precious fairy lord live, let me do my work!” and with that he unceremoniously lifted up the bleeding fae lord, grabbed his Claymore by the blade and whispered KUANAN! The fire rune awakened and made the sword orange hot, the air simmering around the sword in fury.

“Do yee want to live Banshee? What say ye, elf lord?” Connacht snarled
“ye...yes! Please!” gasped Arawann.
“Am I victorious?” growled Connacht “Say it!”
Lord Arawann wept, the tears running down his violet face “ye...yes...”

Connacht held the burning hot and glowing orange blade to Arawann's bleeding wound and placed the blade on Arawann's exposed flesh. Arawann howled in Agony but knew that Connacht was saving his life...for the burning hot sword cauterized his flesh and without that he would have bled to death.

“Now Bring that floozy for an aristocrat here, I want to see Lady Rhona!” Connacht roared... even the otherwise fearsome redcaps leapt in terror and quickly ran into the cavern and brought her forth... with Aunty Oona and her strange children following quickly after.

Connacht was in shock “Aunty Oona! What in the devils? What brings ye here! Answer me woman!” barked Connacht.

Aunty Oona sneered at Connacht “Listen you half blooded invader! Blood drinking nordic brute! This woman is pregnant with a fae-blooded child and the child is extremely important to our kind and yours!” She growled.

Connacht raised his two fingers in Aunty Oona's direction and simply stated “Yee are no helpful green-lady-of-the-forest, reveal yerself, Deceiver! MANNAZ!” the potent fae blood coursing through his veins empowered his Runic spell which banished whatever illusions that disguised this fae as the image of an older, plump women began to melt, ripple and peel apart like split end fabric.

She suddenly grew taller, a head taller than even Connacht, yet hunched over, her legs long and with clawed toes. Her hands had long, outstretched, filthy, black clawed fingers, each as long as a butcher's flensing-knives. Her skin was a pallid blue, she looked like she drowned in a lake as she was a pallid with greasy grey hair covering her cursed and fanged maw.

"A Bane-Nighe, of course, pretending to be a benevolent fairy-godmother, well well, the facade is now over ye marrow-sucking hellion!" Connacht snarled. "You'll give me lady Rhona at once or I will split your head from your neck to yer crotch!" Connacht roared.

The Bane-Nighe, towering over lady Rhona, smiled at her and patted her on the head, Lady Rhona looked drugged and dazed, she grinned at the monstrosity like it was her sweet and loving aunty. The Hag whispered in her ear and pointed at Connacht and then swiftly pushed Rhona in his directions.

"Ach! She is all yers deary! Keep her and her sweet little baby safe in these harsh lands, I am counting on it..." she then began to cackle in a sinister manner.

Lord Arawann stood up with the aid of his fellow Bane-Sidhe and said "yes, we promise you no harm will overcome you or my sweet lover! For she is bearing my child and we don't want anything to happen to that darling." Lord Arawann smilcd but almost fell over, The Bane-Nighe quickly grabbed him and balanced him against her considerable bulk. "Thank you my love." Arawann said and they kissed passionately on the lips.

"I will send my honorguard to guide you back to the borders of the Twelve Duns. Take her immediately back to the Clan Calhoun Stronghold and speak nothing of her pregnancy to Jarl Hjalmar unless his kin perform the infamous blood eagle on you for failing them or Lord Duncan would have you flung from his Castle wall's onto rows of wooden pikes! Let's just say a wee bit of fae trickery shall keep her pregnancy a secret from both Ostramann and Caledonian!" Laughed Arawann.

"Ye Better keep yer promise fae lord! If you break your own Geas I hope Orcus's curse fall upon yee and you turn into a eyeless orcneas! Bastard Elf!" Snarled Connacht and with that he gently grabbed lady Rhona and places her on his Puca-now-horse.

"Alright lads! Ya heard these fae bastards! It's time we head back to Clan Calhoun and not keep Lord Duncan and Hjalmar waiting! Don't want to get skinned alive and then flung onto wooden pikes... I mean that would already ad insult to injury!" they laughed grimly

The Unseelie host also laughed. "Shut yer Haggis holes!" snarled Connacht and the dark fae suddenly grew silent, having never encountered such a fierce human warrior like Connacht.

Suddenly Zazu, the horse puca spoke "yee gods this woman is fat! She is heavy with child!" as she leapt upon his back.
"Shut it horse! Less I feed ye silver powder!" growled Connacht.
"My apologies yer lordship!" stifled Zazu.
Suddenly Dragga and Lukka chimed in "Connacht please, we grow hungry! Do ye have any meaty rations we could devour?"
Connacht turned to his talking Puca-turned-horses that Finlay and Lachlann were riding atop.
"By the gods ye gluttons won't keep yapping about food! How about this you take us beyond the border and I'll feed you some Seal Jerked-meat. Sounds appetizing?" groaned Connacht.
"Deal!" said the trio of talking horses.

Lady Rhona, wobbling back and forth spoke in a warbling voice "oh how quaint, like a fairy-tale, talking horses! I feel like a princess!" She said in her drunken stupor.
Connacht sighed and shook his head "For a princess yer drunk like a harlot and ye smell like a sow" he whispered.
Lachlann and Finlay, laughed with their mouths closed, barely containing their laughter.
Several hours passed until the sun was setting and they reached the borderlands between the Lennox Highlands and the Unseelie Wildlands.

Before them was a Shelta wagon village and lo and behold Connacht's big boned lover herself. The strong but voluptuous mistress, Bonnie and she brought Lachlann and Finlay's two lovers.

"I missed ye my lusty bovine!" laughed Connacht and Bonnie replied "I missed ye my drunken pig!" they laughed.

"Oh by the way! We found a pot of Silver! Right here at a frozen lake near Dun Aos-Sidhe, give me your map of the Twelve Duns and I'll mark it!" Connacht insisted.
Bonnie gave him a cartographer's map of the Twelve Duns and he marked the area with an X with charcoal in the middle, near the Aos-Sidhe mountain. "Send out some of your stealthiest and bravest scouts, have them dress as Woads to not attract the ire of the Unseelie fae."

Chapter 10: Return to Clan Calhoun.

"One wind there is: ten sailors row amain
Two vessels, and one steersman steers the twain.
Who or what am I?"
The Satyr's Riddle.

Connacht, Lachlann, Bonnie, Finlay and lady Rhona had a wild night of dancing and frolicking especially with the Shelta wagonfolk. The Grai were a festive and wild tribe who had no qualms or prudishness when it came to drinking, fornicating and revelry. The gypsies of Caledonia strangely enough where not related to the wandering gypsies of the Vyzantine Empire in blood but very similar in life style, cultures, costumes and nomadic existence. Hence another term for these folk were false gypsies and tragically they suffered discrimination like the nomadic gypsies of the great empire to the East. But they sheer knew how to celebrate and happily mixed blood with friendly outsiders. Everyone easily found themselves a lover, even the scandalous lady Rhona.

As the wagonfolk and our heroes crawled into their wagons to make love and fall asleep. Llewellyn, Diedre and Claidogha snuck off with the map of the pot of silver. They traversed the snow covered forests of the twelve duns, occasionally having their journey interrupted by large owls gently gliding across the winter landscape or elk sprinting through the forest floor.

Finally they came to the site with their wagon, Llewellyn held out her lantern illuminating the dark, frozen landscape and finding the shattered ice and hoof prints on the nearby lake. As she looked deeper she could see the silvery, glinting glimmer in the water.

"Claidognha, dear! Fetch me a bill-hook why don't ye?" Llewellyn winked. Claidogna, dressed in a flowing, dark-green dress polled the long pole-arm from the wagon and moved towards the lake. They both grabbed the hooked weapon and reached deep into the cold water, hooking the cauldron with the hook of the weapon on the handle with a **Clank!**

They strained! They Pulled! They groaned! The pot barely moved. Deidre leapt down from the wagon and offered her strength. Once again they pulled and groaned and pulled! **Pop!** The Cauldron was pulled loose from the stubborn clay bed and dragged onto the shore.

Hah! It was theirs, the pot of Silver from Aunty Oona! And this cauldron was filled to the brim with glorious, thick, silver coins! The Three sisters began to dance and laugh playfully.

A gentle cough interrupted their joyfully exuberance. The Three of them hugged each other in fear as they turned to the large pine tree from where the noise emanated from. Suddenly a small, drunken little man in plum-red clothing stepped out from behind the tree. He wore a tall green hat and he bowed in an boisterous manner bordering on the facetious.

"Miladys!" said the small bearded man "How Fortuitous that yee have found our pot of silver!" as the strange little man began to scratch his bearded neck. He began to drunkenly prance towards the sisters but suddenly tripped over a rock and fell, face first into a pile of snow. Suddenly a pile of cards spill out from his fine, magenta coat and fell everywhere in the snow.

One of these tarot cards fell before Llewellyn's leather shoes and she looked down at this strange tarot set. The image on the card was that of a busty female leperchaun, in a busty dress and serving beer at a festival of fae folk. One of her nipples popped out her bustier in this painted card.

The small man, quickly picked himself up and started quickly collecting the tarot cards, all of them had salacious imagery of sexy elves, sidhe, pucas, brownies, hamadyrads and even sexy, bearded redcaps! Strangely enough the cards were gold-leafed.

"Ew, its a perverted fae!" said Llewellyn angrily, "let's leave this lascivious, pervy, gentleman to his nasty cards!" She said in disgust.

The small man shouted out "Wait, lasses, gentle ladies I have an offer fer yee! By the way, the name is Shamus the whimsical!" he said playfully.

"Allright Shamus! Ya dirty old man! What do yee want from us?" Said Claidogna wearily.

"Sweet ladies, lovely bonnie lasses!" Said Shamus "The pot of silver belongs to my employer, Aunty Oona but ye found it so now I must make an offer to yee to get my silver back! I shall only grant thee one wish for the pot!" He smiled drunkenly.

"We could use that silver..." Implied Deidre cautiously.
"Wait sweet sister...maybe I can finally have my metamorphosis?" said Llewellyn in desperation.

The sisters smiled, gentle tears trickled down their eyes. Claidogna nodded her head "Meh, silver comes and goes... but yer happiness matters more."

"Can yee change me into something else?" Llewellyn asked in desperation.

Shamus looked at her with a sad smile "Alas sweet lassy I cannot....but I know that Aunty Oona could...you must ready yerself for the ritual of metamorphosis my darling Llewellyn."

Llewellyn looked at Shamus in determination and nodded her head, a single tear dripping down her eye. "Aye, I am ready for this, take your silver back to Oona and let her know that I am ready for her transformation..."

Llewellyn and the sisters handed the pot over to Shamus, he nodded his head, tipped his ostentatious hat and sauntered over to the cauldron. He placed his hand on the pot of silver coins and said "Alas ladies, Aunty Oona shall grant yee audience for this silver. I fare thee a fair journey and bless yee on yer travels!" With the Shamus snapped his fingers and disappeared in a cloud of smoke.

(The Next Morning)

Everyone awoke and they started cooking breakfast; blood-sausage, porridge and haggis was being cooked over the fire, the organ smell of the intestinal haggis was strong, strange but also tantalizing. The Blood sausage was cooked with eggs and a stew made of wild stinging fennel, onion grass harvested from the mountains and several stewed potatoes was served. The men brought back pine nuts, wild strawberries, blue berries and an assortment of mushrooms, mints and exotic herbs.

"A Fine meal indeed" thought lady Rhona, she smiled as she consumed her meal, sitting on a wooden stump around the camp fire and warming herself with a thick woolen blanket. It was rather cold and quite damp this morning, away from the snow covered pine forests of the Twelve Duns but still chilly enough to leave dew all over the heather and grass that grew in the Calhoun highlands. The haggis was served on trencher plates; stale bread shaped like plates and generally used to serve gruel and stew. She used a two headed fork and knife to cut into her meal and that taste was awfully gamy yet filling. They were all served a pine needle and goat milk tea to wash down their breakfast.

Lady Rhona sighed, a deep sigh of despair. Bonnie heard her lament and quickly sat besides her comforting her.

"Alas wild princess, what bothers ye?" inquired Bonnie.
"Oh...I don't know, I love that fae lord Arawann but I know he is trouble...I don't know if I want to be a lady of a castle to a man I don't love." Lady Rhona lamented. "This life of being a mother and an aristocrat is boring and there are so much expectations to live by, don't lose face here and don't say the wrong thing there...if you do this it might cause a clan war that...I grow so weary of that lifestyle. I would rather be a lusty and wild Shelta woman like yourself, drinking as much cider and ale as I want and having a new lover each night, dancing wildly whenever I wish, spitting on the road and bathing whenever I wish, naked in wild mountain streams! Only the poverty is the thing that gets me..."

Bonnie scratched her plump chin, feeling Lady Rhona's plight and she whispered gently..."mayhaps, What if ye suddenly died after child-birth but the death is a false one? Being Caledonian those Ostraman will not burn yer corpse on a longship but instead will send you back on a wagon to be buried in a Cairn with yer Calhoun clansmen. You will then be

147

placed within a stone sarcaphogus in a cairn and ye can awaken in yer tomb opened and then ye can run free with us, be a green-witch like me!" She smiled.

Lady Rhona gasped with a smile "then I can be a wild-drinking woman, living my life with you fine Shelta folk wandering between the lands of man and the domain of fae, making alchemical potions and using lesser magicks as we wander from clan stronghold to clan stronghold. I will drink in the morning, make abortive potions for the womenfolk and sleep with anyone I wish!" She laughed.

Bonnie smiled "I advise you return to Hjalmar and give birth to the changeling baby and the changeling in turn will produce a twin from his seed. Once they are born the Ostramann of Clan Gunnar will be pleased as will Clan Calhoun. Trade will flourish and a strong alliance between your peoples will strengthen ties, protecting yerselves from any nordic sea raiders or woad forest tribes. Other nearby clans will keep to their borders and not engage in the time old cattle raids which plague the human tribes of this land."

Rhona replied "True, we don't want another century of Clan wars, those wars devastated the people and country side for decades. I don't blame Connacht, Finlay nor Lachlann for "rescuing" me, they probably were forced by Hjalmar to do this task or he would have probably burnt Clan Calhoun's stronghold and murdered every peasant on the mountain trail from here to Clan Gunnar's stronghold." Rhona's eyes began to tear up

Bonnie turned with heavy eyes to Rhona "Thank yee lady, you're one of the few aristocrats who understands the plight of the peasantry, the shelta and the wild folk of the hills. The last Clan civil war that took place was hard on our people...my mother told me terrible tales of the common folk having to slaughter their own dogs and eat them because the Clan raiders torched their wheat fields and slaughtered all their sheep and hogs. My mother told me that she had to hide in the forest and devour stinging nettle, red squirrels, rodents, mountain hares, aspen bark, rock moss and the roots of dandelions simply to survive... and many of us Shelta were blamed for the famine. We were burned as witches or driven into the hill country of the Twelve Duns were we swore fealty to the Dark and Mercurcial Fae folk. There were even stories that we had to pay a tithing of the first blood to the ancient Crones who are said to rule those dark woods like tyrannical gods...some speculated that the children were devoured, others believe that the Crones became pregnant after devouring the children and gave birth to all manner of Sinister Fae...whatever happened in those primeval mountains and woods are rarely spoken about among us Shelta." whispered Bonnie.

Lady Rhona nodded her head in agreement "So...Hjalmar, would he care about my death?" She asked.

"Nay, seems like he himself has a full figured Nordic wench who he truly lusts for, the greedy warlord seems to want the wild lands between him and Calhoun domains. Also the tariff free agreement on meat, fish and trade goods for his merchants would benefit both clans immensely. More money for Clan Gunnar and more rich meat from the sea for the heartlands."

"Besides, he needs noble children to allow him to claim dominion over his lands and clan Calhoun and lord Duncan only wishes to see noble grandchildren." Bonnie sighed.

"Yeah, father seems to only be focused on grand children of noble stalk, he doesn't seem to care much for anything else." Rhona replied as tears slowly dripped down her face. Lady Rhona began to weep bitter tears at the mockery that is arraigned clan-weddings, how it defiled the very sanctity of true, romantic love and instead the whole process was more focused on power, politics, greed and domination. "What a curse it is to be born a noble   where love is a trifling thing to be sacrificed to power and a strong defense..." Lady Rhona trailed as she wiped bitter tears from her flush cheeks.

"There there lass, I have a potion I can make, we named it the White-Snow potion ironically as a parody of an all too cliche story of a princess who fell into a deep sleep by an evil witch!" Bonnie chuckled. Lady Rhona realized the irony and began laughing, wiping away her bitter tears, hell even guffawing at such a clever joke. "But deary you must be careful for this potion will put you in a death like torpor which will have you flirting with the gates of the underworld itself. Mayhaps you take it on your first anniversary especially have false love's kiss from Hjalmar himself, so everyone would gasp in horror as you fall over "dead" from a mere kiss!"

They both laughed at such a warped joke of falling dead to False Love's first kiss.

Connacht smiled, he heard the ladies conspiring and chuckled to himself from the other wagon nearby. Honestly he felt bad for kidnapping the wild lady Rhona from her real love but alas...he knew that without having her wed to Jarl Hjalmar that this would provoke a civil war between clans. The Samhain Isles could not afford another Clan Civil war... it would weaken all the clans involved and possibly invite invasions from Saxony or Jotunhiem with even more vicious and blood thirsty tribes of manfolk, or hell the Unseelie fae themselves could rise up from across the mountains borders and go on a genocidal spree...wiping out the Ostramann tribes and forcing the Caledonians into indentured servitude while stealing all their cattle and sheep.

"Did the Ends always justify the Means?" He wondered. How he wished to not live in such an active war zone with such rich valleys and glens hotly contested over by bloodthirsty jarls, lords and even distant kings to the east of the solstice isles.

The isles of Yule are a good warning to any of those who become too complacent. His own ancestors damn near slaughtered the dwarves while many others retreated under the mountains or fled to An Fhomar to become cursed Unseelie. Alas, he sighed, he realized there was nothing he could do to correct the wrongs of history but he could at least prevent further bloodshed in the future with sacrifice and vigilance in this era but still, his mind nagged him, Do the ends always justify the means? This idea plagued him. How much needs to be sacrificed to ensure safety? He wondered as he rode on the on wagon gently bobbed on the mountain path.

As Connacht, his Kerns and the Shelta people wrapped up their wagon camp and made their way down the mountain, they traversed slowly but seriously for the road was rugged.

Strangely enough a rather soft yet melodic flute could be heard, similar to

150

the pan pipe or duduk played in imperial caravansary in the deserts of Cappodicia and Anatolia.

"Strange", though Connacht, *"I didn't think I heard such a instrument in my homelands"*, he wondered. Suddenly this strange flue could be heard harmonizing a with a gentle bagpipe in the distance.

As they approached a bend in the mountain road he could see two humanoids playing their instruments in the distance. They appeared as men standing on legs, but they looked as if crossed with deer and a human. One was male with antlers and the other was female and speckled like a doe. They danced as they played their instruments, the male playing the gently, droning bag pipes, made from hide of some long dead beast and reeds, while the female played the high pitched and shrill pipes made from antlers.

"What are these deerfolk called again?" whispered Lachlann.

"Spriggans of Hamadyrads, Children of Cerunnos" whispered Connacht

Suddenly one of the deer-folk deftly jumped down from the strewn boulders, it was the female doe. She played her antler pipes but also held one finger up to her lips, imitating to the Shelta to remain silent. She then pointed to a massive pile of rocks in the distance.

Connacht looked closer and then realized that something was strange about these rocks, they seemed to slowly move up and down...and between the notes of the wild mountain music being played he could faintly hear the sound of deep snoring.

"Oh lads..." he whispered in dread "they are performing their wild fae music to keep a massive beast asleep. You see those rocks snoring and moving up and down? That is no mere stone, that is a sleeping Trow! Subterranean relatives to the Nordic Troll. This heavy stone fists can smash plate armor and turn the warrior within to pulp." he implored.

The female spriggan once again lifted a finger to her mouth, this time more earnestly and with conviction, right at Connacht. The moving pile of stones near the mountain began to groan and cough...something was disturbing it's sleep.

Connacht nodded his head, and quietly waved to the Shelta folk to slowly ride down another path away which looped back onto the path. Suddenly, far-off behind him he could hear the faint sound of horns trumpeting in the distance. He looked back in terror, now he could see it! A whole host of Boggarts! Running down from the twelve duns, led by three Korks! He recognized those Bastards and they broke their geas!

The two deer folk quickly looked in the direction of the of the oncoming horde of goblins led by a trio of boar men still miles away but quickly surging down the mountains in a berserk rampage.

They turned to Connacht in shock and he shrugged his shoulders but then an idea came to him! He pointed at the sleeping Trow and then at the approaching unseelie horde and banged his fists together.

The Spriggans realized what he was implying and followed the Shelta Caravan to the other side of the road, still playing their wild yet soothing antler flutes and bag pipe while traversing the golden grass and red leafed heather.

Finally, when they crossed the road and the Trow was behind them the spriggans still played...but the rampaging horde of Boggarts were now gaining on them and getting closer and closer to the snoring Trow.

As they charged down the mountain screaming, their bulldog faces gnashing with their meat maws and snapping fangs the Boggarts didn't realize that it was too late.

Connacht waved his hand over his neck, symbolizing to end the flute and pipe music and the spriggans stopped immediately. Connacht then grabbed a large stone and flung it at the sleeping Trow, it hit hard enough to split a sizable rock on his hide and suddenly the beast roared in agony...

The pile of stones was furious and rose up from the earth, clearly a misshappen giant and it was made, fangs like daggers, tusks like spears and two massive hands with only three large clawed fingers, each finger ending in a massive curved talon like a Khazar war saber.

The Trow screamed in confused rage at the boggarts and the boggarts had the horrified look of terror seeing what looked like a pile of rocks rise up in the shape of some bloodthirsty giant.

Lo! The battle commenced, the Trow was furious and began to swing it's mighty arms at the bulldog faced boggarts, ripping into them with it's massive claws and bisecting the burly goblins in half. Swarms of them surrounded the enraged beast and began to strike it's rocky hide with their crude billhooks and lochaber axes, the blades clanged harmlessly of the rocky-hide or bit deep into the enraged monster's exposed flesh.

The Trow took some damage but the boggarts were getting slaughtered, even the fearsome kork warriors kept their distance and flung rocks at the beast to crack it's rugged hide. The Kork looked at one each other and nodded their heads in agreement, they rushed the rampaging Trow monster with great force and with determined effort bowled the furious monster over. BOOM! It hit the ground with an enormous shudder that even the Shelta wagons shook. The remaining boggarts and korks grabbed large stones and started smashing them on the beasts hide with several loud cracks! The Trow was still on a rampage and furiously bit, slashed and ripped apart it's enemies, crimson arcs of gore sprayed everywhere as dismembered body parts trailed everywhere.

The battle started to turn on the Trow, his rocky scales and boney growths cracked open to reveal the thick and raw flesh below but suddenly with great effort he swept his stout arms wide open and hugged all three of the kork and many of the boggarts in his powerful embrace! He then pushed against the mountainside and tumbled down the sea-cliffs like a humanoid boulder that tumbled and bounced down the mountain killing scores of the unseelie fae.

He finally rolled towards the sea-cliffs, lovely white with limestone and plummeted below with his enemies in tow to crash on the rocky shore with a massive **RAKKK!**

Lachlann rode his horse to look over the white sea cliffs and see the carnage for himself...by the gods of Danu! The murderous Trow was alive, he used the korks and boggarts to break his fall. When he smashed into the

153

rocky shore, crushing his enemies to pulp, he pushed himself up on his mighty arms and started feasting on their corpses.

Lachlann rode back to Connacht, Finlay with the rest of the Shelta, relayed the news and they all laughed. "Better to let a sleeping Trows lie!"Conacht roared and everyone guffawed hysterically.

Connacht quickly turned to Lachlann and Finlay, their wild ginger and blonde curly hair billowing gently in the shore's wind. He looked at them with a steely glance "I am proud yee boys aren't that foolish nor impulsive anymore! Remember when yee charged in to take that giant's silver rings at Ulster?" Connacht reminded them.

They collectively groaned "Gods above, yee know he will never drop that story!" Finlay sneered and Lachlann agreed "Of Course the curmudgeon will remember this to the grave..."

"Stop yer bellyaching lads! Just learn from this event, not every monster or fae needs to be fought directly, sometimes let yer enemies can fight each other to annihilation!" Connacht winked. They then raised their eyebrows in realization and nodded to the wisdom their uncle was spouting.

Several hours passed as they journeyed down the highlands and they were leaving the wild highlands of the impoverished Knox Clan and back to the fertile midlands of Clan Calhoun. The snow-covered pine glens of the mountainous borderlands disappeared them as they approached the heather covered pastures with herds of sheep, goats gave and cattle. The sun was setting on the woodsy ravines and scrub-covered highlands.

The three warriors were feeling lustful as was their Shelta Mistresses...or in Finlay's case he found himself his darling Llewellyn, so lovely of face and lithe with a catlike body. But all of them stunk like pigs, the long wagon rides, the rich meaty stews, the heavy sweating and no real change of clothes added up and on the best days they could be described as being even more musky than a goat.

154

They were close to the Calhoun Stronghold when they arrived at the what was called the Cauldron of the Dagda aka "the Springs of Brigid." The water was incredibly clean and must have sprung from some underground source like an artisan well, gently bubbling up from the side of the hills and possibly underground.

So clean and pristine this water was that one could look through it like it was a blue tinted glass. The Shelta found various dry wood nearby, they even cut down a dead oak and torched its remains in a circular fire-pit nearby. They made sure that the fire's bed was surrounded with large smooth stones.

The Shelta suddenly brought forth various wooden masks of animals. Finlay noticed them wearing these masks and they began dancing while other members of their tribe played Bodhran drums, bagpipes and fiddles. Finlay, Connacht and Lachlann were given beast masks as well. Finlay stood up and began to dance but the others were either too shy or exhausted.. He noticed that the three green witches might have been there, fitting he was given the mask of a hound for he found a tall and slender fox who so closely resembled Llewylln and she danced in a playful and flirtatious manner around him.

As night approached and the fire started to die down, many of the Shelta retrieved their iron shovels and dug up the smoldering, hot stones from the fire and flung them into the pristine spring! The water itself began to boil and hiss from the bombardment of hot stones for a few moments but then the stones cracked into fragments from such extreme temperatures. The boiling-hot water surged to the top and was then swept down the stream to be cooled, the pond water was now hot but pleasant.

The Shelta retrieved their lard-soap, made from hog's lard they gathered and cooked with hardwood ash. They then fashioned the raw soap that was crafted into squares, blobs, spheres and blocks using wooden blocks or other containers to then save them for events like this. Connacht and his squires were the guests of honor for being great defenders and generous gentlemen. Connacht and his Kerns still wore their painted, wooden animal masks.

The three warriors walked into the now hot springs with their masked mistress completely naked, who carried great squares of soap, and they proceeded to wash each others crevices in turns. The stench quickly faded as the elderly women and men of the tribes took their musky clothes and washed it in wooden basins with this crude globs of soaps. After they finished washing, they began eating apples and celery to wash their teeth, rinsing their mouths with the hot spring waters and spitting the contents into the grass.

Then the fun began! They then proceeded to guzzle down spiced mead and wine. They gently touched, caressed and even rubbed each other in salacious ways. Finally they could no longer resist such teasing and the orgy began. Connacht simply bent a large masked woman over, who was probably Bonnie and entered her from behind, she was deep, wet and welcoming as her womanhood completely swallowed his rock-hard phallus.

Finlay with a hound mask, grabbed a tall, blonde, long haired femboy and placed her on a large, smooth river-stone. He used his tongue to aggressively give her anilingus, she groaned, her naturally deep voice started hitting high notes as she was reaching climax. Finlay was erect,his penis thick but somewhat short. He plunged deep inside her and she groaned, he was obviously hitting the right spot within her anus and she screamed in pleasure, ejaculating her semen all over the stone or as the Shelta always joked with the femboys that he was "milking the elf"!

Finally, Lachlann's mistress pushed Lachlann to the side of the springs, resting him on sandy bank and she mounted him and rode him like a horse. He was rather long in the nether regions but not as thick as Finlay, he could feel his head gently poking against her cervix but it mattered little, the suctioning force of her deep yet tight vaginal walls was too much for him, her long breasts bounced aggressively as she rode, flopping around and clapping.

He roared in ecstasy as he came deep within her womb, she fell atop him as she always had a massive orgasm and they slept on the bank... gently pulled into warm wool blankets so they would drowned in the warm waters.

Connacht thrust deeper and deeper, His lover was roomy but she could

156

take his powerful thrusts and large phallus with ease. He preferred her, no whining about pain afterwards. At first he didn't feel much but as she came closer and closer to climax, her wet, wet walls began to clasp around his mighty phallus and he could feel the gripping now! It was as if she was greedily devouring his manhood.

Pulling him deeper into her lusty-abyss of pleasure, her large vaginal lips gripped his thick shaft as she roared so loudly during his climax. In turn she quickly tightened around him and he groaned as a massive load of his seed poured deep into her pink vortex. He felt like he came several times, deep inside such a mighty, meaty vagina and he grabbed both of her wide, silky checks and pulled out... limp and dripping, her large labia flopping out as his milky-white essence poured out of her and pooled on the pool's shore in a lake of white love.

That was amazing! Though Connacht, *by god this big woman completely emptied my scrotum*! Exhausted, Connacht and Bonnie crawled into woolen blankets and held each other for the entire night as they feel into a deep sleep. As Connacht's eyes drifted into sleep her could see other Shelta, males and females slink into the hot springs to wash and make love...strangely enough even the wild spriggans seemed to pick two gypsie lovers to fornicate with, seems like they were aiming to make changelings!

Connacht and his squires awoke in the warm, silky and loving arms of their respective masked mistresses. They gently kissed their loved ones awake as the crones and elders of the Shelta tribe simply began cooking a unique Nordic breakfast that quickly became popular over all Caledonia. The Shelta slaughtered a piglet that morning and drained it's blood into their flour, mixing the wheat flour with barley grain and this blood they began to mash into a mixture like flatbread cakes, then cook them on hot flat-stones near the new fire. The blood-bread was quickly cooked, mixed with some salt and other spices.

The Shelta and the Three Warriors ate their fill, adding the ancient bog butter to this crimson bread and having it served a stew made from chunks of piglet, dandelions, de-thorned stinging-nettle and green-seaweed all boiled into a stew in a vast iron cauldron. In turn this stew was served with pine-needle tea.

This excellent meal was served to the lovers who were adorned in clean, new clothes and watched the sun rise over the silvery solstice seas, from the distance a small pod of whales could be seen migrating south to give birth in warm waters.

The Shelta's livestock seemed to always wander with them so sheep and pigs migrated with the wagon tribes while the boat Shelta had geese, ducks and trained fishing Cormorant's who migrated with them on the rivers and lakes. The Shelta were gifted with music and their animals seemed to always find their way back to them as they played their antler flutes, drums, bagpipes and fiddles. In turn the tribes had large, fierce guard-dogs, covered with spiked armored coats and they had powerful bites that killed many foxes, hawks, wolves, boggarts and even bandits who came to close.

Finally after all this wandering; they arrived to the Valley of Calhoun and they could see the great stronghold before them but it was surrounded with tents! This was the work of Jarl Hjalmar and his whole army of Huskarl-warriors having surrounded the fortress. Thankfully it wasn't a siege just yet as farmers and merchants left the stronghold's gates with ease only to be leered at or verbally harassed by the throng of burly Ostramann barbarians.

Connacht noticed the royal tent of Hjalmar, colored a dark, burgundy red with a bronze colored fabric on the edges and turned to Bonnie then spoke "Stay behind me my love, tell your people to stay in the neighboring valley from which we left, hell, return to the Cauldron of Dagda! Something very foreboding is going on here and I know my kin, they can be angry bigots and would be happy to take their rage out on you fine folk. Hjalmar most be furious the lady Rhona has not arrived to his wedding yet, he wants to acquire all that land of Clan Knox, my family clan, between Calhoun and Gunnar as a dowry from Duncan. Stay back for we will have to bring him lady Rhona to appease his wrath." Bonnie nodded her head in agreement.

Connacht then looked at Rhona and tilted his head, she leapt on his horse and sat behind him, they then rode towards the royal tent of Hjalmar. "Forgive me Rhona, you know Hjalmar and Duncan would slaughter a million peasants to appease their besmirched honor. Tragically your prince charming is more like a prince of blood-thirsting." whispered Connacht.

"Aye, I know, some say his mother is a fierce bear." She whispered.

Connacht laughed "don't let him hear yee say that and it might not be entirely false, he flies into berserk rages sometimes where he almost become bestial. This is good in battle against other fierce Nordic tribes and their savage Berserkers but not so when in a noble palace. Of course he can be soothed with fine mead, laced with the most potent of mushrooms, but doing so makes him appear foolish and slow witted." Connacht whispered.

As Connacht, Lady Rhona and his squires approached the top of the valley, facing the Calhoun stronghold and Gunnar camping army, he shouted loudly "Tribe Gunnar, fellow Ostramann! Put down your arms, we freed Lady Rhona from the cruel fae lord known as Arawann and she is safe!" cried Connacht.

Hjalmar quickly exited out of his tent, snorting in rage, his great two headed axe in hand, covered in head to toe with his thick coat of shimmering, scale -armor. "Alas! Is that truly her?" he roared.

"Yes your lordship, we shall bring her to yee! She is unscathed!" shouted Connacht.

"Thank Odin's beard! Thank Thor's Hammer!" Roared Hjalmar Gunnarson as he hefted his mighty axe to the heavens and cheered. His army of fierce but loyal Berserkers, Huskarls, Thanes and Varnagjars rank and file lifted their assortment of brutish weapons to the heavens and also cheered. The Calhoun defenders applauded, thanking the Tuatha Dc Dcnaan for stopping such potential bloodshed.

Lord Duncan raised his clan flag high of two fighting stags behind a green and blue tartan and waved it regally to the heavens. Clan Gunnar raised their war flags high of a thor's mighty hammer, Mjonir clenched in a mighty fist and waved their banner, not to be outdone!

Though the lords did not wish to butcher each other, they knew that war was something that could have erupted due to vengeance especially of any

159

clan which broke an oath against the other. Thankfully a crafty, fierce and mixed-blooded Gallowgalas had love for both his peoples and stopped the bloodshed from happening.

Chapter 11: The Marriage of Jarl Hjalmar and Lady Rhona

**"From home I went,
from home I made my way,
I saw a road of roads,
and a road under them,
and a road over them,
and a road on all sides.
King Heidrek,
guess my riddle."** Odin

The Marriage of Lady Rhona to Jarl Hjalmar happened immediately that night, It was a bombastic affair, several fat cattle where marched into the castle courtyard and butchered, gutted, flayed, cut into great pieces and then the beasts where impaled on mighty wooden pikes and roasted over hot coals. Flagons of heather infused ale, some were black stouts, others golden hefenwizens, red marzens and brown lagers all served to the assembled host. Hjalmar brought his finest honey meads, infused with tart lingonberries, sweet blue-berries and exotic cinnamon was brought forth to drink. Wild, red haired Caledonian clansmen sat across from burly, blond Ostram. Various fine breads were served, covered in honey and nuts or mixed with soured potatoes and rosemary. Rich meat stews, steaming bags of haggis, sizzling links of blood sausage etc etc and so forth. A truly mighty feast where warriors, peasants and even the Shelta were invited into the clan walls to gorge themselves like wolves on the finest foods the highlands have to offer.

After the feasting the warriors danced with the local peasantry, silver coins where exchanged for nights of pleasure, contests of arm wrestling were encouraged to see whose tribes was the strongest and other sports such as caber tossing and even horse racing. The Shelta cheered and performed wild dances of fire-breathing to all those who attended. The combined tribal audiences were amazed and wowed who were as giddy as children from such an epic wedding festival.

At the Heart of the festival was the sisters three and Llewellyn the Harlequin did not cease to wow and amaze the audience before her. Her attire was fantastic, a riot of crimson red, dark blue and rich violet diamonds in borders of golden colored cloth. She wore a fine alabaster mask of Vyzantine-origin with a large, floppy, midnight-blue hat known as a *Chaperon*, famously worn by Harlequin who attached two bells, hung from each end which made a festive jingling noise as she leapt about.

She Danced, pranced, wind-milled and somersaulted, leaping from maypole to maypole in the court yard and performing spinning pirouette and finally spewing a potent liquor into a torch and exhaling a mighty gout of fire towards the amazed audience. Everyone present was amazed to see such a performance, they cheered, applauded and roared while showering her with silver coins.

Little did they know that it was subtly empowered with the very fabric of magicks which saturated this strange land of Samhain. Finlay cheered for his beloved and she locked eyes with him and playfully bumped into him saying "looks like the lecherous hound has caught his prey, the trickster fox!" she said jokingly and then comically kissed him on the cheek, then lightly slapped on the same cheek as she gallivanted and somersaulted off to disappear for the night.

Finlay knew that his feisty femboy harlequinn was delightfully playful especially after a bit of drinking and whimsical performances.

Deirdre used an assortment of Tarot cards and crystals to divine the future for many of the peasants lasses and lads who looked for true love. She sat upon a driftwood table with glimmering lanterns which flickered upon the satin cloth she placed the crystals and cards upon. She was no mere soothsayer who made predictions from the randomness of the card, that was mostly theater, she actually was truly gifted in the art of the seer and being able to awaken her third eye deep in her mind so she could see a potent kaleidoscope of future destiny.

She could also gaze upon the present and see the whirling colors of a person's aura, reading their moods and possibly finding spiritual parasites which orbited around their souls. Red was passion and conviction, Orange was lust and determination, yellow was happiness and optimism, green was harmony and compassion, blue was calmness and peace, purple was deep spirituality and intuition and whiteness was purity while Gray, Black and Brown were generally considered negative.

Those who had the restless dead feeding on them had to immediately go through a cleansing ceremony while Deirdre banished whatever cruel spirits that clung to them. This required using a circle of salt and reciting the names of the gods of light like Lugos and Bridgitte to cleanse their soul and the gods of darkness like the Morrigan and the dead Nuada to claim the troublesome spirit.
Tragically the white-witch Dierdre did not have a lover, she was asexual and dedicated to her craft, but there was one giant woman who lived in castle Gunnar which she fancied.

Outside of the Stronghold there was the final sister Claidona, the green witch, speaker of beasts. She had wild and wavy auburn hair and she spoke in a strange tongue, barking orders at horses and dogs. She was in the outer campgrounds of the Nordic Ostramann army and they were amazed as their horses danced in circles, stood up on their back legs and walked like humans, whined in different notes and fetched her items with their mouths to return them to her outstretched hand.

She was a fascinating women, able to give a simple command and have animals perform the most amazing of feats, she could also craft almost any type of potion or salve from herbs, animal fats, seed oils and a strange assortment of miscellany. Many that night purchased a potion or salve from her to cure impotence, baldness, infertility and various other ailments. Lachlann stood their, lanky as a pole, amazed at watching his beloved mistress use her craft upon the stunned throng of warriors before her.

Finally there was Lady Rhona, her face was tired and her eyes saddened at the concept of being wed to such a brute as Hjalmar. He towered over her by a foot and she was tall, he must have been twice her weight and she was already a large woman by Caeldonian standards. She could see the way he drank horn after horn of ale and mead that he was a glutton and a

163

drunkard.

Hjalmar alone ate an entire lamb by himself, with several loaves of thick potato bread to soak up the grease. Hjalmar did not wash his beard for it was covered in chunks of roasted meat and bread. Hjalmar had bad teeth and they stunk like rotting flesh when he spoke...but by the gods he was strong. He looked like he was Thor's slow-son out of wedlock; he had many of Thor's strengths, nearly all of his weakness but barely of any of his morals his compassion, duty to justice or vigilance.

Lady Rhona knew that she only had to stay with the man for a year and then she could enter that death like sleep from the white snow potion, falling into nearby oblivion from false-love's first kiss. She couldn't wait but tonight was the night she had to become pregnant with Hjalmar's child, The Bear of the Isles of Skye. The butcher of the sea tribes of Ullinarr.

Hjalmar finished feasting and drinking at midnight, he simply turned to Lady Rhona and said "it's time to breed like horses my love!" and laughed. "Ulfric, my washing basin!" he shouted and a tall nordic warrior snapped his fingers and a elderly woman came before him.

With a golden bowl, roughly decorated with warriors impaling boars with lances wrought through it's exterior. Within was a great amount of steaming water and Hjalmar quickly slammed the bowel down on the wooden long table and began to slurp the water into his mouth, swishing the water around and spiting it back out into the bowl. Chunks of food was flushed out each time he rinsed his mouth this way and gargled the hot, briny water. He then washed his beard in the water and finally blew his nose within.

As disgusting as that was he did cleanse himself somewhat. "Come woman" he said and easily picked her up in his arms and marched into the bed chambers in his royal tent. Bearskin furs were laid out in a great pile and he placed her down surprisingly gently. "Disrobe yerself" he ordered and she did immediately, her silky white skin almost shimmered from the fire-light of the hearthfire. His massive hands grabbed her breasts and he began to roughly suck on her teats, he was ruff but by the gods was he good, it hurt but also felt amazing at times. Her heavy hanging breasts were being sucked down his entire throat, she was coming close to climax just from him sucking. He roughly placed her hand on his crotch and she could feel his limp penis, barely erect from all the alcohol he consumed and flaccid, it would have been huge if he wasnt such a drunkard and a glutton but now it was rather shriveled and pathetic.

"Use your mouth woman!" he commanded and strangely enough, his rudeness kind of excited her. She pulled his woolen trousers down and she could see his massive, stinking balls and phallus. By gods did he stink! She quickly poured warm mead on his nethers and he laughed, this at least helped her to awaken that stinking man meat he wanted her to service. She swallowed him down and he groaned, she sucked and sucked and he was rather stubborn. Finally his flacid monster got erect and he got excited, he was almost as long as lord Arawann but much thicker.

"Ride me woman!" he laughed and she got a little scared but clambered up, faced away from him and slid him deep inside her. By the gods was he a stinky beast but he really had powerful hips and he was thick, almost as thick as her arms, he started to pump aggressively and she immediately climaxed, then he pulled out...he was somewhat limp and he stood up, he started furiously jerking his manhood. She was both disgusted at smelling his breath but impressed how strong, determined and angry he beat his meat until he was fully erect.

He spread her wide open and thrust deep inside her, *ouch*, he was rough but as he kept hitting his rhythm it started feeling amazing. She climaxed three more times from his monstrous pounding and suddenly he screamed in pleasure as he unleashed his mighty seed deep into her womb. He fell over and almost crushed her but she wriggled out of the way, he hiked himself up on one arm and gently pushed her away from under him, and when she was safe he crashed down into the bearskin blankets with a monstrous fart, it stank of rotten seal. Now his naked backside was exposed and he reeked of unwashed ass, Lady Rhona was about to puke but she grabbed a few of the animal pelts in the tent and placed it strategically over his backside. *Phew! Much better!* She thought.

What a beast, she thought, her legs were wobbly from being ravaged by such a bear of a man, he did know how to fuck but he was a lousy lover. She let him snore in the tent, got dress and walked into the night air to get a breath, she walked through the campsite of the Varangjar who were

165

sleeping, drinking or boasting of stories of slaying great sea beasts!.

Suddenly she found Bonnie, head of her Shelta tribe, sitting in the courtyard of the castle and listening to her bards play their fiddles, violins and antler flutes. Such a haunting tune to listen to. Bonnie turned to Lady Rhona and felt her belly. "Excellent deary, you now have two twins, the prophecy is coming to fruition. Jarl Hjalmar will get his son and Lord Duncan shall receive a grand daughter!" Bonnie smiled.

"Lord Hjalmar, his stench is most foul! Gods he smells like the bears he skinned to make his bed!" She laughed. "What do I do next time I wish to make love to him?" Lady Rhona inquired.

"Girly, take him back to the Cauldron of Dagda, wash his body they way we Shelta do." Bonnie insisted.

"Good Idea! When we move back to his castle in Gunnarholme, I will have them build a great hot bath, fueled by smoldering coals and ocean water so he might bathe his massive frame." Rhona replied.

As Bonnie and Rhona spoke suddenly three females approached them, one was a tanned woman who had wild, wavy auburn hair and she was the lover of Lachlann, Claidona the Green witch. There was a tall and regal woman with straight black hair and olive colored skin, Dierdre, the white witch. Finally the last woman was the blonde femboy lover of Finlay, Llewellyn, the red witch, with an extremely lovely and elfin face, plump pink lips and wavy blonde hair. They were frequently nicknamed green witches but this was somewhat inaccurate, the two sisters helped Claidona as she healed animals and so earned this moniker.
Lady Rhona looked at them quizzically "Oh what three lovely darlings have come to join us, I am the Lady Rhona, wife of the bearish Jarl Hjalmar and daughter of Lord Duncan. If I may ask what are your names?"

Bonnie smiled "let me introduce you to the sisters three, Llewellyn the Harlequin, Claidona the speaker of beasts and Deirdre the crystal Seer. They are a trio of witches, red, green and white in that order and they have formed a coven within our Wagon village. They shall offer you advice, entertainment and any services you need while you're pregnant with twins." Smiled Bonnie.

"Fascinating...." Lady Rhona looked left and right out of eyesight and ear shot and then she leaned into close to the sisters three "teach me some hedge magic" she whispered.

The all quietly laughed in unison and they all nodded in agreement. Suddenly Bonnie brought forth a wooden table of somewhat crude build and she pulled forth a set of cards. "Imperial Tarot my dears!" Bonnie smiled "let us predict the future with this set and see where our fates might take us in the upcoming years, my lasses." Smiled Bonnie.

And the night faded away, cards were read, some hands predicted sweet futures of find one's true love, but when it came to Lady Rhona only sorrow befell her hand, a collapsing tower, Balor the adversary, a dying lover, a shape-shifting Cusith, a monstrous dragon..Lady Rhona turned pale with fright. A Great calamity would befall her and possibly the lands she will come to inhabit then followed by a terrible metamorphosis.

Bonnie turned to Lady Rhona with a look of hesitation and said "Rhona my dear...listen, the cards are not always accurate or even misfortune sometimes might turn to fortune, sometimes those great Nordic stories told by the Gunnar have the hero themselves snatch victory from the vicious jaws of defeat..." Bonnie put her hand on Rhona's, who was shaking like a lamb. "Sometimes darling, a whole forest must burn to regenerate and regrow anew, saporlings springing from the ash." Bonnie looked Rhona in the eyes and they quietly nodded to each other.

Chapter 12: Voyage to Gunnarholme.

**"Who is that great one
who grasps the earth,
swallowing wood and water.
Bad weather he dreads,
wind, but no man,
and picks a fight with the sun.
King Heidrek,
guess my riddle?" ODIN**

(Hjalmar, Rhona, Connacht, his Kerns and all the Grai Shelta returned to
Clan Gunnar lands.)

After a week of celebrations and feasting for the glorious wedding
between Hjalmar and Rhona and their respective clans, peace negotiations
were made, trade deals were struck and both regions benefited greatly.
Fishermen, whalers and fur-trappers flooded into the southern provinces
selling their products on an extremely low tax and they made a small
fortune selling smoked salmon, whale jerky, ivory dice, walrus hide and
seal-fur clothes. On the flip side the Caledonian merchants brought fine
ciders, ales, meads and grain to the north. Food was so abundant and
profits so high even the lowest peasants grew fat!

The lowly Knox Clan territories, once protected by Clan Duncan were in
turn given to the Gunnar Clan. Lord Hjalmar and Lady Rhona rode by an
extravagant wagon across the midland farms of the Calhoun Lands, to the
Highland pastures of Clan Knox and then down into the pine covered
fjords of Clan Gunnar with a contingent of Hjalmar's personal honorguard,
the Huskarls, their heavy scale coats shimmered in the cold sunlight, they
rode by horse and the Shelta Wagon's trailed behind.

The first night they made camp, Connacht quickly dismounted his horse as
did Finlay and Lachlann. Connacht turned to his magical horse and

whispered in it's ears. "Dragga, Lukka and Zazu, you are free to go! I break this enchantment, you have served me well." and with that the horses started to shrink and change shape into the cat bodied humanoids that they originally were. Zazu turned to Connacht and said "By the way, my manhood is way bigger than thees!" laughing hysterically with Lukka and Zazu . Connacht snarled "Well yee are a fookin horse!" as he chuckeled at such audacity.

Lukka turns to Connacht and whispers in his ear "we still hate yee ya blood-drinking fabulous-bastard, but at least ye honored your geas and freed us. We swear we will not bring any harm nor trickery to yee, yer friends nay any of yer charges, animals and so forth. We leave in peace." Nodded Lukka and he turned to both Dragga and Zazu and waved them to follow. They quickly dropped to all fours and ran off deep into the pine forests nearby, possibly to never be seen again.

Llewellyn and Claidona, made their way out of their wagons and Llewellyn wrapped her arms around Finlay from behind as did Claidona. "darling" whispered Llewellyn "where hast thou horses gone to?" she implored.

"Sweet Lass, we have freed them from their bondage, they where no mere horses but Puca three, chained and bound to Connacht's Geas." He smiled.

"Goodness, I never knew that Connacht could harness magic!" she implored.

"My darling, his magic is only fueled by the drinking the blood of fae or consuming potent hallucinogenic herbs and mushrooms." Smiled Finlay.

"Even your people's magic is fueled by bloodlust? Such a strange people you Nords and Ostramann." She chortled.

"Connacht is a rare breed among us Nords, some say his own mother was a crone but that could be simple rumor to explain his strange form of magic." Finlay replied.

Claidona dipped in their conversation "Alas this is not a problem, our clan has horses we can lend you or possibly a wagon. Let me speak to these creatures and they should have no problem serving you faithfully." She beamed.

Lachlann smiled "my darling can speak to horses? Well at least isles of Samhain rarely grow dull!" He laughed, hell, they all laughed.

(Meanwhile on the sea-cliffs of the Orkney penisula facing north to the Ginnungagap Ocean)

Lord Arawann was furious and in a deep state of despair...he looked across the grey ocean of gingulgagap...the cold northern winds whipping his white hair, antlers and face...he grabbed the stump where his right arm once was, now black and burnt (by balefire which cauterized the wound), *how did he lose that battle to that bastard human? That Whoreson; Connacht Knox will never best him again!* He raged.

The sun was brilliant as it set in the east, the sunlight hewed across the islands that led the way to the Northern-most isle of Yule...known as the Giant's Causeway. These Islands were so strange, made of columns of basalt that rose in bizarre series of mostly hexagonal crystalline pillars that reached up from the sea. Throngs of gulls and puffins resides on these islands covering the tops of them in their white guano.
The sun set and as night settled in Lord Arawann spread his shimmering wings and flew across the dark void of the night sky, only the twinkling brilliance of the stars lit his way in the northern lands. Long did he fly with the wild hunt who accompanied him, swarms of hungry slaugh, Bane-sidhe whose powerful gossamer wings flickered in the night and handfuls of Bane-nighe hags who flew with bale-fire as they rocketed across the inky darkness of the night sky.

Days and nights did it take to cross past the cursed islands inhabited by by those filthy, pig-plowing Nords with the reek of slaughtered whales, seals and walruses bombarded his senses. He could see the fat bastards hacking the lardy sea creatures to bloody chunks and polluting the otherwise pristine azure sea waters with clouds of crimson blood. It must have been late fall, when many of those poor creatures migrated to warmer waters and exactly when the barbarous tribes of "sea wolves" mounted their longships with their harpoons, axes and javelins to butchers scores of these creatures. They then salted, smoke and dried the meats to sell into the markets of the other islands.

Lord Arawann's night vision was truly amazing as was most of the Unseelie fae, having lived in the subterranean regions below Samhain for centuries helped...especially with fighting off the savage denizens in those subterranean realms like the cursed spawn of Orcus, the Orcneas, Trow, Fachar and even the occasional Formorian-Giant.

Any abandoned carcass of these corpulent sea-beasts would immediately get swarmed by Arawann and his wild-hunt who fell upon their remains during the dark of night. Ripping! Tearing! Biting! Gnawing! To feast upon their flesh and fatty exteriors. The Wild Hunt was utterly ravenous from their nocturnal migrations.

The Unseelie had no hesitations when it came to devouring raw and bloody flesh, they learned to survive the hard way and thrived they did. After a week of hopping from island to island along the island-chain called the Giant's Causeway did they finally arrive before the homeland of Callieach. The Mother of Crones, Grandmother of Winter. One of the last goddesses from the mythic age still awake in this frigid wasteland.

Callieach was an ancient goddess of all the witches and crones and she in turn birthed several powerful daughters like the Nords; Urdr the guilt-ridden past, Verthandi the furious present and Skuld the anxiety-ridden future. One of her outcast daughters was Skathach; mother of Berserkers and powerful with Runic magic.

Yule was home to the mostly pure-blooded nordic clan known as the Volsungg. It was believed that the few Caledonian fishing villages that once dotted the shores of Yule were even before King Nithuadir and the Skjoldr tribes invaded. It was said a race of Dwarves once lived in the great islands mountainous central regions...were they all slain? Enslaved? Did they go deep into the heart of the mountain and merge with the stone there? Nobody knows.

What Lord Arawann knew was that prince Nuada was buried on this forlorn island after the first Samhain and that the winter goddess Callieach and her daughters have resided here as their homelands since the mythic

171

age.

It was time for his lordship to pay homage to the mother of all witches and the grandmother of all Unseelie. His ancestors swore a bloodpact to the Norns and Callieach in eons past to grant them victory against the Ostramann tribes long ago when they first invaded the islands of Yule and then Samhain. The Unseelie rose from the burial cairns or were utterly warped into monsterous forms and got their vengance on the Nordic armies which torched the palace of Dun Tara and destroyed the kingdom of An-Fhomar.

Long did he fly across the grass landscape, flocks of sheep and caribou gently walked across the emerald grasslands, feasting on the succulent plants below. Volsungg tribal people ran with their wolf-hounds hunting game across the violet heather and jade green pine forests.

A Careless shepherd with his sheep dog, slept in the pine forest while his flock was roaming along the pristine, alpine-meadows, devouring grass, blue mountain flowers and violet flowered heather...Lord Arawann nodded at his royal retinue of Bain-Sidhe and Slaugh and they dived down like a swarm of angry falcons from the sky...quickly abducting at least a two dozen bleating sheep... when the Shephered came too he roared in rage as the wild hunt made off with a majority of his flock into the twilight heavens. A rain of bloody wool and bones were left in their voyage to the central mountains of this frigid land.

Aunty Oona quickly flew up to his left flank, her blue skin almost revolting to look at, she smiled, her jagged and crooked fangs protruding from her thin lips. "Looks like we have more than enough to sacrifice to the mother of all hags, Callieach. We shall fly to her cairn and slaughter these victims there! Their blood should awaken her from death's slumber." Lord Arawann smiled in knowing that he shall have his dark revenge soon enough.

As the sun set and the full moon rose to it's zenith, the wild hunt flew up the mountains of Yule, they noticed various mighty ruins. "Must have been the Dwarven civilization before it fell to the Volsung and Ostramann invaders" lamented Arawann "They were fine smiths and jewelers, their king Wayland was captured by the King of the Skjodung tribe and forced to craft the finest arms, armor and jewels for the royal family but one day he got his revenge and slaughtered all the King's sons, some say even ravaging his daughter and burned the whole castle down...there is speculation that he either cursed the king or he himself was punished by the Gods, possibly turning into a horrid sea dragon of monsterous size." Whispered Arawann in dread.

"True, some say the accursed monster protects the island of Yule but alas he has only be encountered in the thickest of mists." acknowledged Oona. "Alas! The sleeping Cairn of the most ancient Crone is near!" Lord Arawann decried.

Before them in the snow-covered, pine-forested mountains they witnessed a sight of several great mountain tops. And at one of the tallest mountains they saw a massive, cyclopean cairn surrounded by monoliths. These stones were covered in an ancient text, written in the ancient Oghma language of the Tuatha De Denaan.

Primitive, massive, brutal, ancient, worn by the elements but relentless in it's stubbornness to endure. Four great monoliths surrounded what looked like a massive mound of stones, but there was a square like entrance which led the way within.

Lord Arawann, Aunty Oona and their hand picked guardians; the hags and Bain-Sidhe entered within the tomb, carrying several bleating sheep with them. The Slaugh had to hide behind stones and trees, they were too low in the ordering of fae to witness the tomb of an ancient first generation Tuatha De Denaan goddess.

The hallway almost looked like a cavern, with massive granite boulders and menhirs acting like the pillars to this stone Cairn, great flat and rectangular pieces of slate acted as the ceiling, while the walls where put together with various cut and square blocks of stone. The only mortar was clay that kept everything attached together. It was pitch black, even the night vision of the Unseelie could barely see through this unnatural darkness which seemed to undulate like a great inky cloud of smoke.

Aunty Oona sneered "Hags shadow! Let me conjure some Balefire to banish this magical darkness." She hissed.

Oona snapped her fingers and sickly green balefire erupted from her hands then danced in her palms, the darkness instantly crept back as she illuminated the stone hallways with her hellish flame.

They finally entered a large square room, with one massive stone sarcophagus surrounded by several, roughly hewed, stone pillars which lifted up the cavernous ceiling.

Lord Arawann gasped, for he was impressed. The burial Cairns he remembered seeing in Samhain were somewhat small and primitive for his Aos-Sidhe ancestors, nothing darkly majestic and monolithic like this. A circular engraving surrounded the Sarcophagus and from this engraving various channels led directly to the center, where the long dead goddess slept.

Arawann hefted up his glaive as did the other Bane-Sidhe warriors and they looked at each other... the Bane-Nighe Hags began to speak in their ancient Caledonian language, invoking balefire.

"A' Chiad Mhàiriche, Màthair na Geamhraidh a' crathadh fuar! Seana-mhàthar Crone Tha sinn, do chlann-nighean a' tabhann fuil nan neo-chiontach dhut gus am bi thu a' dùsgadh agus a' toirt taingealachd dhuinn anns an uair-uaire dùbhlanach againn!" they chanted in their raspy and tormented voices.

"What did they say Oona?" Arawann inquired and turned to the hag, she cleared her voice and translated "First Witch, Mother of Winter's cold bite! Grandmother Crone We, your grandchildren offer you the blood of the innocent so you might awaken and grant us a favor in our desperate hour!"

The Hags then beckoned to the Dark-Elven Prince, they nodded and looked at Arawann, he held his hand high and dropped it, this was the signal for the sacrifice of the victims. All of them simultaneously decapitated the sheep, their blood poured into the circular engraving which then pooled into the trenches and drained right into the Granite Sarcophagus with a soft, hissing sound.

Slowly the lid of the tomb was opened, a long-taloned hand gently peeled open the massive stone lid and elegantly pushed the top away, the grinding sound of granite was deep and foreboding, for the lid must have weighed several tons and it was brushed aside like it was an easy task.

Slowly she sat up from her colossal tomb. She was tall like a frost giant, her skin was ashen gray and she hefted one of her long, skeletal legs out of the tomb and placed her gnarled foot down on the freezing stone surface... the blood of the dying lambs easily levitated up the the sarcophagus and the etched lines onto her long dead skin and slowly strengthened her limbs.

Callieach was awakened, the mother of darkness, the queen of winter, vengeance incarnate for all fae kind. She stood erect and her head almost touched the ceiling of the great tomb. Her clawed hands hung down to her knees and each black claw was the size of a short sword. Arawann shuddered thinking about this horrific damage she could inflict on an army of fierce Bane-Sidhe guards or stalwart Ostramann Huskarls.

Arawann bowed down as did his honorgaurd followed by hags in deep respect. "Oh Great mother of hags and grandmother of the Unseelie, it is of utmost respect to witness your awakening from death's deep slumber." He said and Oona translated into the ancient tongue of Crones.

Callieach looked down at him, through her great hood wrapped around her head, it was supernaturally dark but he could see two glowing white pinpricks of white, icy light that followed him like as if eyes were made from the most frozen stars of deep winter.

She then spoke in a voice so deep, hollow but harmonizing with gasping creeks like the winter wind whipping across the frozen ravines. **"Tha thu air a thighinn a dhùsgadh an Blood Moon agus iompachadh a h-uile Fae seòrsa gu dorchadas mar sin dh'fhaodadh iad mu dheireadh a bhith air dìoghaltas air na treubhan de dhaoine? Feumaidh mi gun ìobair thu do phàiste atharrachadh dhomh gus am bi mi air ath-bheothachadh. Bheir mi seo dhut, togaidh mi thu às ùr, bidh mi a' sgaradh beinn a' phrionnsa Nuada ann an dà chuid agus gheibh thu air ais an t-slat agus a ghàirdean airgid. Bidh mi a 'dùsgadh an arm mallaichte de na marbh a chruthaich do sheòrsa mì-ghnàthach. A**

bheil thu ag aontachadh ris a' chùmhnant fala seo? Ma tha, òl mo fhuil ann an co-chomunn."

Oona looked mortified and Lord Arawann turned to her, "Speak, what did the goddess say?"

Oona hestiantly turned to Arawann and thus spoke. "You have come to Awaken the Blood Moon and turn all fae kind to darkness so they might finally have revenge on the tribes of men? I will need you to sacrifice your changeling child to me so I might be reborn anew. I shall grant you this, I shall build you anew, I will split the mountain of prince Nuada in twain and you retrieve his spear and silver arm. I shall awaken the cursed army of the Dead that created your misbegotten kind. Do you agree to this blood pact? If so, drink my blood in communion."

Arawann looked horrified... and he thought deeply, to sacrifice a child was a common form of geas with the truly powerful Crones that haunted the dark forests of the Unseelie lands. He just never imagined that they would ask such a powerful Arch-Fae lord such as himself for such a deal. He lowered his head in defeat, sobbing and nodded in agreement in silence. He knew he could always make more changeling children with human nobility but he had developed feelings for the vulnerable and foolish Lady Rhona, who laughed at his stories and danced naked with him under the full moon.

Aunty Oona whispered in his ear "It is no time to be soft, bring vengeance to mankind, slay the nordic invaders and enslave the rest of them so they would worship us as gods once again! You must be strong and relentless to bring about the age of the Blood Moon!" She exalted.

Lord Arawann nodded in agreement and looked at Callieach, the Giant Crone lifted her left arm out and slashed her wrist with her right hand's talons...black blood began to slowly pour out of her emaciated limbs, almost like the thickest of tar and she held it up to Lord Arawann's lips. He closed his eyes and bit into the exposed pierced veins...the thick black blood began to pour into his throat, it was freezing cold, he could feel his heart, throat and organs freeze up and almost stop moving within him...he could feel a strange vibrating sensation in his soul.

Suddenly he was out of his body and looking down from the ceiling, he could see his paralyzed form in agony. His face had a expression of sheer terror as he looked down at his comatose body. The Ancient Hag loomed over him like he was a small child, the hags and Bain-Sidhe themselves were frozen in terror as many looked up and pointed directly at him.

"I bind you to this Geas! I give you my power! Bring me your Changeling Child from Gunnarholme and all the fae kingdoms of the Caledonian Isles are yours!" Do you bind your soul to this service?" Aunty Oona screamed, her eyes glowing with green bale fire now.

Lord Arawann realized that she was possessed by the most Ancient Crone and he had no choice. He nodded his head to this unholy pact. Callieach turned to him and reached out with her massive clawed hand, green, sickly bale fire exploded from her palm and struck his soul on the ceiling! He screamed in agony as he felt pain even in his soul, the vile, green hellfire wrote oghamic letters across his glowing blue body, potent dark magic bindings...he was screaming the whole time...then suddenly everything went black.

He awoke in his body, stronger now, his muscles bulging in his purple skin...and glowing green glyphs etched all over his body, dancing green bale fire leapt around the edge of each arcane glyph.

The Crone mother materialized a staff in her hands, like obsidian but made from her own ebony blood. She hefted the Staff towards the ceilings and slammed it down on the rock hewed floor. In that moment a massive earthquake struck, the Bane-sidhe and hags could barely keep themselves from falling over, having to literally grab the walls or each other to keep each other upright. Dust and lose stones rained down from the ceiling but the Cairn was left relatively unharmed.

The Crone then swiftly jutted out her long right arm and pointed to the rough stone entrance of the tomb from where they entered. "There to the North, Nuada's Tomb has been split asunder! Go forth and claim your destiny" Said the possessed Oona.

Lord Arawann bowed his head and then swiftly left the tomb of Callieach, they flew north across the whipping cold winds and snow that heralded the rebirth of Callieach to this world. Suddenly the Wild Hunt found a mountain tomb split asunder with a massive cairn cracked wide open.

Alone one sarcophagus lay in the ruined tomb, a mighty silvered-spear and armored-arm lay elegantly upon the tomb. Here he lay, the first king of the Elves, father of the Tuatha De Denaan and he who liberated their kind from Balor and his armies. Prince Nuada the first high-king!

Arawann smiled and flew down, he grabbed the silver arm first and placed it on his dismembered stump, it quickly fused to that area! It began to twitch and flex like a brand new arm. He smiled and vicious grin, for not only was he remade but he was tenfold stronger than before! He could feel the power of the ancient gods coursing through his veins! Then he grabbed the shimmering spear, without the new silver arm, it would have been too heavy to wield but his new arm afforded him such power he hefted it with ease to the gray heavens and roared in victory! The wild hunt cheered for their remade lord, he would lead them to victory against all of Humanity!

Chapter 13: Arrival to Gunnarholme.

**"Would that I had now
what I had yesterday,
find out what that was;
mankind it mars,
speech it hinders,
yet speech it will inspire.
This riddle ponder,
O prince Heidrek!"
Odin**

The Mighty oaken gates were flung open as the Thanes played their ram horns to the high heavens and the marching Huskarls struck their spears against their shields.

Hjalmar has returned with the tall Lady Rhona. They rode on their royal wagon pulled by oxen and entered the great stronghold. Pyres were burning at this mighty castle to keep it warm for it was a brutally cold winter and freezing winds from the northern seas were billowing in to assault the land. Drums were struck in unison to celebrate the returning army of the Gunnar Clan. Connacht, Lachlann and Finlay rode besides the royal wagon of lord Hjalmar and lady Rhona keeping guard the entire time.

Jarl Hjalmar Gunnarson and Lady Rhona Calhoun dismounted their oxen wagon and walked towards the central keep, where the mighty doors were swung wide open by powerful Axe-bearing Berserker-guards to allow passage within. Both guards were giants among men, wearing the full coat of a bear on their heads, their fierce eyes piercing from underneath the fanged maw of their dead bear cloaks. The long-axes they wielded were massive and could easily hack an armored foe to shreds.

The Keep was a vast place with long-tables a plenty, the honorguard of Hjalmar, known as the Huskarls, dismounted and walked in single file lines to each table and sat down at their respective places.

Bread plates called trenchers were placed before them with an accompanying spoon and a thick, crimson-red stew was poured into each Trencher. The Stew was called Borscht and it was made of stewed red meats like beef or walrus, red-beets, onions, carrots, red-cabbage and flavored with bay leaves and dill. The color was an extremely dark, crimson red like blood itself. An accompanying bowl of musky sour-cream with it's own teaspoon was shared communally to pour a few spoonfuls into the soup. This cream when applied to the stew made it change colors to an almost playful and light pink. The flavor was rich and hearty with a gentle herbal aftertaste.

The Huskarls ate up not just one but two, three or sometimes four servings of stew and then would devour the now soggy trenchers afterwards. Large fireplaces filled with pine and oak logs burned continuously to keep the stone walls warm.

Connacht noticed the stone-walls were a mix of slate-stone with orange and green hints from rusted mineral veins in an otherwise grey and brown surface combined with dull granite. What caught his eye was that between the stones there was a concrete mortar, not just a primitive clay-mortar like most Caledonians...he must have paid Vyzantine builders to craft such a sturdy castle.

Hjalmar swept his hands wide open in a display of friendship and bombastically said "You are all my family our guests of honor for we shall feast upon the royal table!" this table was separate from the rest for it was finer, made from lacquered beach-wood with a fine red linen cloth that covered the top of it and comfortable, elegant padded chairs for each guest. Each Chair had various fantastical beasts carved into it's frame; sea serpents, dragons, griffons, tazzelwurms, lindnorms, whales, mammoths, sabertooths...all were whittled into fanciful designs of them battling one another like a somewhat gaudy yet impressive mural.

Excessive yet impressive for Connacht's tastes, of course rich Ostramann clans would go out of their way to craft such bombastic furniture to impress any guests to show off their newly acquired wealth and power in the world of late. Connacht smiled, for he knew being partially Nordic, the urge to brag and display one's position to your fellow piers but also being

180

partially Caledonian the urge to be humble and be at peace with the universe, not just perpetually compete against it. At times like this he enjoyed being of mixed heritage to both understand their perspective but also to remove oneself from petty displays of vanity.

Connacht laughed to himself between spoonfuls of soup, *Sea trade really must of been good of late*, he thought. *These Nordic and Ostraman shipping guilds must have coffers filled with silver coin*, he pondered.

As Connacht, Lachlann and Finlay tore into their meals so did their lovers Bonnie, Claidona and the Harlequinn Llewellyn and all of them drank heavily from their wooden flagons or rams-horns. Connacht did notice something though, Lady Rhona was in despair and barely ate her stew. Jarl Hjalmar seemed to notice this as well and gave her one stern look and slammed his meaty fist into the table with a face so fierce it would have given the largest of pale-bears a heart attack!

Lady Rhona quickly snapped out of whatever malaise claimed her soul seeing the sheer power of the fierce warlord, the whole table shook like an earthquake from that monstrous blow. She produced a fake smile and quickly started spooning mouthfuls of the blood-red gruel into her mouth. It was surprisingly good for Nordic cooking, this Borscht!

Hjalmar then smiled, knowing that his twin babies would grow strong from watching his new wife eat whether she wanted to or not. He thought to himself, *sometimes one must be cruel for the greater good of his people!* He nodded with this harsh yet sage teaching his ancestor's passed on to him and then continued devouring his crimson meal.

Suddenly the great oaken doors swung open and a massive woman stepped in, she was taller than all the brutish nordic warriors in the feasting hall, in some cases towering over them by even a foot and she was broad, thick and stout, making some of them look like starving children in comparison to her sheer bulk. She easily carried a mighty wooden maul in one of her hands, slung over her shoulder like a hard laboring ship wright. She casually placed the mighty wooden hammer down and lifted her hands out in an excited manner.

"Daddy! You stinking bear of a man!" she exclaimed.

"Oh ho ho! My goodness! Thruud my sweet, gargantuan apple of my eye! Come and give daddy a hug but don't break my bones yee Silly Shehemoth!" roared Hjalmar in happiness. He quickly stood up and the giant, beach-wood table almost flipped from his exuberance.

They ran towards each other like overjoyed giant children, the wooden planks of the feasting hall shook with every titanic footfall and they slammed into each other with familial love. Their fleshy bodies and powerful frames rippled from the impact as they slammed into each other with a mighty hug. Hjalmar was a huge man but Thruud picked him up in her hug and swung him around like he was a child. Connacht noticed her truly titanic thighs, though fatty, he could see the massive quadriceps flexing with each step she made.

Thruud was strange, truly a massive and powerful woman but she had a sweet, round, plump baby-face and her cheeks were delightfully rosy. She laughed in happiness at seeing her father again, her golden skin glinted in the light of the torches and fires that lit the great hall.

Even her arms and legs easily made the strongest berserkers look small in comparison. She truly looked like she was part giant but had the temperament of a charming farm girl from a local village. Her clothing was somewhat revealing but not excessively skinny, she wore a leather kilt, with great fur and leather boots, her chest was covered with a form-fitting leather chest piece. Her breasts were large but looked somewhat small for her size, for she was truly gigantic, possibly seven feet and a half. She had massive square-like buttocks, but very muscular and proportionate for such a giantess. Her eyes were lovely blue and her hair was woven down into several twisting braids like great golden chains of autumn hay.

Many warriors adored Thruud like a giant kid sister but very few ever had any sexual urges for the giantess. They still serviced her when she gently asked for a night of pleasure but comically enough she was the one that pursued, pressing them against walls and kissing them or bribing them with strong drinks.

Hjalmar looked at Lady Rhona and the rest of his guests, pointed to Thruud then exclaimed "This is my adopted daughter Thruud, a lovable behemoth who can shatter the skull of an orca with one blow!" They both laughed.

"Introduce thyself to my new wife, Lady Rhona!" Hjalmar beamed and introduced Thruud to Rhona who was still sitting at the table.

Thruud smiled and walked up to Lady Rhona, Lady Rhona stood from her seat and offered her hand to shake Thruud's massive paw of a hand. She laughed and wrapped her massive arms around Lady Rhona, giving her a warm, bear hug that lifted her easily off the ground.

Lady Rhona felt like a baby in those massive warm arms, so strong yet so soft. She felt a sudden urge of deep lust for this giantess, her nether regions got wet from the embrace. She wasnt the only one who suddenly felt intense sexual desire. Dierdre bit her lip looking at the hulking giantess, her massive ass and thigh muscles involuntarily flexing when she activated flexed her colossaly wide hips to effortlessly lift a large woman like Rhona into the air and gently rock her back and forth in the strong, warm and gentle embrace.

"Put her down already yee oversized bear-of-a-woman, lest she run away again but with yee!" Hjalmar roared in laughter as did Thruud. Thruud gently placed Lady Rhona down and the lady was quivering in the knees from such a embrace.

Thruud was an interesting character, men weren't attracted to her so much but many ladyfolk had a sudden urge of intense lust seeing such a mighty avatar of women kind. She was that masculine lady who made other women feel intensely queer for her. Lucky for them, Thruud herself actually enjoyed the taste of a woman's nethers betwixt her lips and tongue.

Thruud unceremoniously sat at the table of honor with the rest of the guests, right across from Connacht and by the gods she was a giantess. She towered over even the tall Connacht and she made him look slender, he sat literally in her shadow. Aside from her hulking body he could see

183

her big, fat, sweet baby face and he gently reached out with his gloved hand and playfully pinched her reddened cheeks. She smiled and scrunched her nose at him, like a massive, playful puppy.

"Look at you, so adorable in the face but so mighty in body. Like the baby of the Johtun's themselves!" Connacht smiled. "Maybe one day you can be a Gallowgalas yerself...or even a berserker!" Connacht laughed.

"Such a flatterer you handsome little man! Mind If steal him away for a night!" she laughed as she looked at Bonnie.

Bonnie laughed as well and said "sure, but please don't crush him!" she chortled. The entire feasting hall roared in laughter.

As the laughter died down Thruud suddenly began to look about and Hjalmar then interjected "Daughter what bothers yee?" he implored.

"Where did that silly bard go to?" She implored, craning her thick neck to the left and right scanning the feast hall as she spooned her borscht stew greedily.

Suddenly her walrus-hide backpack flew open and a handsome but petite man leapt out with an Oud!
It was none other than the good looking Finnigan! Singer, poet and bard from the isles of Beltaine!

Hjalmar stopped laughing and his face suddenly reddened with rage, Lady Rhona looked in both terror and confusion. Hjalmar kicked his thick, oaken table back with one blow and hefted his great axe with one hand. Hjalmar roared "Adulterer! Explain yerself!" he snarled.

Finnigan eyes went wide in terror and his face went white pale like a ghost. "Thruud, whats going on here?!? yee said yer father would love having a minstrel who both sings and dances!?!" Finnigan wailed. Thruud looked both shocked at terrified at her father's rage.

"You already ran off with my bride at castle Calhoun and now yee have the gual to come here to my stronghold and elope with my woman!" Hjalmar roared, his fist visibly shaking with rage that held the great axe, his face beet red, veins bulging on this temple. Quickly he hefted such a mighty cleaver into the air to slay Finnigan right at the spot, possibly splitting him in twain like a yule ham!

Connacht and Thruud quickly exchanged glances and intercepted the furious blow

Thruud smashed her hammer into the oncoming axe with such power it sent the weapon flying backwards and it struck the mounted head of a great elk, the taxidermy was split in half with a thunderous crack!. . "Daddy yee have drunken yerself into a rage! I will not let thee kill a guest! Don't make me beat yee senseless again!"

Connacht also spoke up, greatsword drawn to intercept and protect Finnigan. "Lord Hjalmar, control thineself! This was not the man who deflowered lady Rhona! There was an Unseelie fae-lord known as Lord Arawann, who somehow masqueraded about as Finnigan..."

"Enough of this pansexual elf-lord!" snarled Hjalmar, He started to realize his outburst and felt deep remorse. "Thruud my darling, thank you for bringing some sense into me. Connacht I thank yee for informing me of this imposter. Lady Rhona and Finnilay, my deepest apologies. The wine has addled my sense as did my rage and jealousy. I believe I shall retreat for the night and reflect on my outburst." he said in a depressed state.

Hjalmar hung his head low, and wiped the tears from his face. "Ah tragically I have let my rage take the better of me..." he mourned. Lachlann wiped his brow, sighed in relief and said "it's all-right Jarl, many men are insanely jealous of my monstrous cock!" Hjalmar's tear quickly dried up and he roared in laughter, a deep belly laugh and the rest of the terrified audience began to guffaw hysterically. Connacht and Finnlay winked at Lachlann and said "good call!" in unison.

(Several days passed)
A brutal, cold wind came sailing from the north, it would be a brutal winter from the looks of the monstrous snow storm that came whipping in with such howling ferocity. No Longer could the Ostramann use the port neart the great stronghold and had to rely on moving inland to hunt game such as Caribou and moose in the frigid wilderness of the Fjords.

Occasionally these fierce snow storms would abate and the whalers and fishermen could go to sea but many of them came back bloody and terrified...half mad and speaking of the drowned Varangjar-warriors from centuries long forgotten who would storm board their ships wielding ancient axes and shields that were still strong and slaughtering Ostramann sailors to then feast upon their flesh.

Others spoke of a monstrous giant, with one glowing amber eyes who haunted the misty seas, carrying only a massive horn on his side as he towered over the gray sea-waters. Others spoke of terrible accursed man-beasts who burrowed into cellars from deep below, they had no eyes, only pallid skin and gnashing, fanged maws wielding crude bone hatchets in both of their elongated yet strong arms.

Hjalmar sat upon his throne distressed, not only did this powerful snow storm stop all sea trade but strange monstrosities followed suit. He was Thankful for Connacht for raising a new generation of Gallowgalases and Kerns, many recruited from the Shelta and Caledonians who came to inhabit the highland province of Clan Knox.

This region known as Lennox was rugged; their farmland was not rich and there were frequent incursions upon their land from fierce Unseelie Warbands. The rugged environment bred many a fierce warrior and potent druids for The alpine highlands of Clan Knox was a place of constant strife, hardship and survival.

Connacht was outside in the courtyard with Lachlann and Finlay during a the Highland right of passage. He was now pormoted to the rank of "Master of Arms" and in turn he would bestow the position of Gallowgalas to a new generation of Kerns and warriors.

"Today I celebrate the fact that both of you fearless Kerns have now attained the title of Gallowgalas! We shall feast and drink but before that you must get a tattoo of blue woad placed upon your back and it must be your name written in Nordic Runes but then have Celtic knotwork as the border around such work. The Totemic animals of the Aesir gods or the Tuatha De Denaan should also be respected, Ravens for Wotan or the Morrigan, Bears for Thor or the Dagda, Eagles for Freya or Lugos, Elks for Freyr or Brigid, Wolves for Tyr or Nuada and so forth and so on.

Mountains, Forests, Seas, Valleys to represent the land and it's peoples. Honor your people, ancestors, lands and gods!" Connacht hefted his greatsword into the heavens yet it was still sheathed.

With that Connacht then grabbed two coats of Brigatine armor and two great weapons, one was the Dullahan's Lochaber-axe for Finlay and the other was an exotic Flamberge for Lachlann, it's wavy blade could inflict devastating cuts to flesh. Both of them were stronger, swifter and more cunning now, both had truly grown into fierce warriors and both of them truly earned this rank of Gallowgalas. Finlay and Lachlann winked at each other with a smile, they knew that this exchange of weapons felt most comfortable for both of them.

Other fearless warriors were then crowned as Gallowgalases and they in turn chose two willing youths to serve as kerns.

As the ceremony was finished the host of Gallowgalases and Kerns meet at the Keep's feasting halls and a whole roasted walrus was being served to them, it was stuffed with potatoes, cabbage and carrots and was gently spun over a bed of smoldering, red-hot coals.

One could hear the grease drip down onto the fire, the hiss of the boiling lard as it burst into flames.

The warriors gathered in lines from both sides with their trenchers, cutting of long pieces of fatty meat with their seax-knives or digging their two-pronged forks into the beasts exposed stomach to fork out steaming, soft potatoes and various other root-vegetables. They then returned to their tables to enjoy feasting while drinking a nice dark stout ale from their wooden flagons.

Suddenly Finnigan entered the rooms accompanied by a few other bards, the Boudhrain drums began to play in a upbeat and fast tempo, then entered the steel strings of the Dulcimers playing in rapid crescendos rising and falling several octaves. Finnigan began playing a Lute in a most joyous fashion and singing a quick paced sea shanty. It was time to celebrate the yule tide feast!

Boots were placed on the tables, tall leather boots, each warriors in fact removed his left leather boot and placed it on the long, driftwood tables. Beers of any color; whether they were golden weisebeirs, red marzens, nutty brown-porters or creamy black-stouts were poured into the boots right to the tall rim!

The Warriors in unison screamed "Zekke! Zakke! Zekke! Zakke! Oi! Oi! Oi!" and began the drinking competition drinking as swiftly as they could, streams of beer poured forth and dribbled on their beards and heavily armored coats as they drank as fast as they could.. What a Mess! But what a festive event!

The heavy snowfall died down and many villages from outside of the castle walked through the opened gates, festively decorated with mistletoe. They had a great bonfire built for them in the courtyard were they huddled near it. There was an unusual custom only Nords and Ostramann people celebrated, the burning of a yule-tide tree. This holiday was sacred to Wotan and his children and a great pine-tree was decorated with bells, ribbons, small copper and silver ornaments.

The peasants were also given a feast of roasted boars to eat and ale to drink with hearty bread to consume. A welcomed reprieve from simply eating oat porridge or greasy scorse-stew all winter long. The peasants were encouraged to take a few of the copper and silver decorations from the great winter tree but the golden stars on top had to be earned through a right of strength; such as arm wrestling or a right of cunning such as a game of chess.

Much fun was had by all and a few fist fights took place between drunken patrons which was quickly broken up or encouraged to take placed in the pit of honor. Finally as the Yule Tide tree was stripped of it's precious decorations it was pulled down right onto the courtyard bonfire and set aflame! Everyone cheered as night approached and the mighty pine burned hot, the greatest tree in the mountain highland was found each year, felled by the strongest warriors and then they heroically hauled the behemoth back to the Gunnarholme Stronghold.

The Crowd of Ostramann and Caledonians cheered and danced even if it was freezing outside. The generous amounts of cider, ale and even exotic bubbling wine warmed them as did the fatty flesh of oxen, boars, rams and seals roasted over the yule bonfire. Chestnuts, hazelnuts and various other nuts were roasted over flames whick popped open with loud pops! Children snagged these nuts with sticks and prongs then dipped them in honey, to devour afterwards with milk.

As the night wore on the festivities slowly died down and the cold weather just got even colder, to the point even boiling water would freeze over in minutes as midnight fell. Much of the smoldering coals and burning wood was scooped up and taken back to the peasants hearths to set their hearth fires to keep their humble homes warm.

The three Gallowgalases retreated to their warriors lodge and also carried many smoldering coals and still burning logs in cauldrons back to their great longhouse to warm the barrack's hearth fires.

They slept pleasantly that night, though the outside world was freezing the thick wooden walls and hot fireplaces protected them from the fierce cold.

The next day Connacht, Lachlann and Finlay awoke and looked out their windows, an extremely thick cloud hugged the ground. A mighty gray mist covered the land and obscured everything.

Many of the warriors were groggy, their eyes red from a hangover. Screaming could be heard from the mist followed by horrific groaning and whispering.

Connacht and the rest of his entourage could hear screaming from the village outside. "Men, Sally Forth! Fetch yer arms and armored coats, there is an enemy upon the common folk and we must vanquish them in battle!" He roared. He bolted up and ran with furious haste, he quickly donned his arms and armor as did his fellow warrior-brethren.

They flung open the heavy longhouse doors and a thick, milk-like mist covered everything before their eyes...the screaming grew more intense as was the groaning.

Connacht grabbed one of his last remaining potions of fae blood and chugged it down greedily. He quickly slid each runic ring onto his fingers but there was one he desperately needed in a situation like this, it was

Hagalaz, the rune of hail, storms and furious gales of wind!

He could feel the fae magic surge in his blood and he screamed Hagalaz then pointed his gloved finger in the direction of the courtyard. A furious gale blew forward, the mist was pushed aside easily but as was roofing tiles, hay and loose arrows on the castle walls. The Whole village could now be seen.
The nearby village was beset by a sizable army of walking dead...just like the damnable Draugr Connacht remembered fighting in the burial tombs of Ulster.

Tragically any peasants who were too slow or foolish enough to step outside were already dead or dyin, being hacked to blood pieces by the crude iron hatchets and cleavers of the walking dead. Those that survived were hiding in their cottages and longhouses, thankfully many of these homes had heavy walls of stone and or wood and the survivors made their ways to the tops of the houses. Men, womenfolk, children... and they savagely hurled large rocks, javelins, arrows and throwing axes at their besiegers. This makeshift volley killed handfuls of the advancing Draugr but there was just too many of them for the fierce villagers to fight off.

Suddenly Hjalmar came running out with his adopted-daughter, the Giantess Thruud. Two behemoths followed by a warband of fierce warriors. A Whole formation of shield-bearing Huskarls and Axe Bearing Berserkers swiftly followed. Connacht and Hjalmar looked at each other in grim determination, held their weapons high and charged into battle! They were quickly followed by Thruud, Lachlann, Finlay and the others. Their heavy footsteps sounded like a stampede enraged buffalo!

The Host of them smashed into the horde of walking dead. Hjalmar used his great axe to easily split open rotten shields, skulls and split torsos in half! With loud **Hacks and Crunches** did his Axe strike and split them asunder! The soaking-wet blue flesh of the draugr was viciously ripped apart from each titanic blow of their steel weapons.

Thruud caught a javelin in the shoulder, **Thwack!** She grit her teeth in pain, roared and ripped the bloody thing out and kept charging, she quickly arrived into battle and started swinging her mighty hammer in whistling circles. **Whoosh! Whoosh!** Went the hammer and as her hammer landed on her foes the massive weapon shattered iron armor, helmets cracked, axes split and bones were crushed with each loud **Crack! Crack! Crack!** Deftly she performed her whirling dance of death leaving a trail of shattered corpses in her wake.

Finlay came charging towards the mist, wielding the Dullahan's lochaber-axe, he pointed the weapon directly in front of him like a lance and he crashed right into a zombie warrior! Bam! Punching right through it's shield and impaling the spear tip through it's chest with a sickening **CRUNCH!** One could hear the ribs pop from the impact, Finlay then used the powerful muscles of his thighs, hips, core and lower back to hoist the writhing monstrosity over his head and sent it flying in an arc to crash back down on the frozen soil behind him with a **Thud!** He then quickly leapt in the air and brought the Polearm over his head with all his might and then brought the weapon crashing down with full force on the prone Draugr! **Thwack!** The pale blue horror's head was cracked wide open with a thickening crunch, much like a cleaver splits the carcass of a duck in half with minimal effort.

Lachlann used his wavy Flamberge with great skill, this cruelly, wavy-sword was driven into undead warriors and then quickly yanked out, sawing the foul bastards in twain like a massive band saw. **Zhrrrrrr! Zhrrrrr!** Went his Flamberge, his great sword struck swords and axes, **Tang! Tong!** deflecting them with his parrying hooks or crossguard which caused weird vibrations to reverberate down the weapons' poles. Many of the Draugr were quickly disarmed with such vibrations to then suffer the bite of the serrated-blade of the Flamberge, sawing them to bloody pieces!

Together did Lachlann and Finlay fight with frightening efficiency, where Finlay would use the back hook of his weapon to both impale and stop the monsters in their tracks and then Lachlann would plunge his wavy sword deep into their torsos and literally saw them in half like rotten chicken carcasses before a massive lumber saw. They killed scores of the rotten bastards together.

They fought furiously until no Draugr were left. Tragically some peasants were slain but the battle was won. Hjalmar order the local people and his warriors to reinforce the walls around the villages huts, they quickly used stones to construct a secondary series of makeshift walls around the farms to craft bastel houses. Hjalmar turned to Connacht and said "Sir, thou art a true warrior, yee truly are an exemplar, master-of-arms here at Castle Gunnarholme." Connacht beamed in pride.

Chapter 14: The Cursed Axe of Grom.

**"There is one father and twelve children; of these each
Has twice thirty daughters of different appearance:
Some are white to look at and the others black in turn;
They are immortal and yet they all fade away.
What am I?"**

Months passed, the winter still raged, colder than the beginning of the new year...the sea became icier and colder, glaciers began to form. Fishing and whaling became more difficult but that was not the worst of it.

The Army of the dead rose from the frozen seas of Ginnulgagap and the marched towards the great fortress of Gunnarholme. Hjalmar guided the surving villagers and cattle into his walls, the secondary outer walls that were built which defended the village outside of Gunnarhole was eventually overran. The Rest of the Villagers of the province of Skye with most of the Shelta Grai, were led by Finlay into the province of Lennox. Finlay and Llewellyn were good together, protective and very perceptive of any ambushes along the way. Finlay became an expert of his Pole-Arm able to Impale, Hack or Hook any Boggart, bandit or Draugr that got in his way.

Spring was setting in the mountainous lands of Clan Knox and food was being harvested there. Shelta wagons, full of food would return to Gunnarholme to feed the valiant defenders who kept vigilance of the lands of Skye and the adjacent northern regions. Connacht and Lachlann would lead their Gallowgalas warriors and kerns on Forays to hunt elk and moose or accompany the whalers to slay walrus and whales in the cold seas. These armed hunting forays fought many draugr and undead horsemen known as Nukalvee. There was word of the very rare encounters with undead giants that rose from the sea. Connacht knew that this wasn't just mere rumor, he remembered!

The Fimbulwinter had arrived, as the Nordic tribal people called it and it was a cursed winter, said to last for years and turn a land to deathly ice. Killing all the cattle, women, men, children and whatever survivors was left eventually turned to rabid cannibalism. Powerful dark magic could only bring about such a horrific winter which slowly froze the lands to death.

Hjalmar and Thruud would occasionally sally forth from the castle gates with their loyal warband; the Huskarls, they thundered across the icy terrain, their hobnailed boots crushing the ice and snow underfoot. Thruud would wielded her massive oaken hammer and pulverized the walking corpses of these dead warriors from eons past. Hjalmar would split them asunder with his two headed axe, inlaid with silver, gifted to him by Lord Duncan.

Lachlann and Connacht returned from a foray, they lost two whalers that day who fell into the frozen seas...but they claimed the corpses of four Walrus bulls. They hacked apart the walruses and stacked the bleeding carcasses onto their longships.

The Defenders of Clan Gunnar cheered, their meat supplies were running low. Scores of strong, burly Berserkers came running out, grabbing a large chunk of dead walrus, fins, torsos, tails and even their heads and pulled the still dripping hunks of meat back to the castle gates. They also held a funeral for the two dead whalers, their families wept bitter tears.

Tails were cooked first, the useful organs like heart, kidneys and pancreas were stored in barrels and covered with salt to prevent freezing. The intestines, stomach and lungs were chopped up and used as bait for fish for the next foray into the freezing Ginnulgagap ocean.

"Thankfully this amount of food should feed the castle for two or maybe three weeks." Connacht bemoaned.

Lachlann looked at him quizzically. "Why did yee send Finlay to lead the Shelta and peasant refugees to the Lennox province?"

Connacht sarcastically replied "Don't yee remember ya dunce? Ya went charging into battle against the Draugr Giant in the Ulster bogs basically a year ago. Let's say your good on the offensive but yer impatient on the defensive." Connacht smiled.

"Fancy way of saying I am stupid and only good for a fight but fine." Lachlann sneered.

Connacht chuckled "Lets admit things, you deserved that for what ya did."

Lachlann shook his head but smiled "aye, ya got me."

Bonnie was one of the few remaining Shelta people here, she swore to watch over Lady Rhona during her pregnancy.

One day a large, grey colored raven came flying towards castle Gunnarholme. It flew in circles before it saw Bonnie, now covered in seal hide and walking with a oaken Sheillaigh in the snow. The Raven gently flew down and landed atop her twisted staff and began whispering into her ear.

Bonnie whispered back "yes, I see, alright, a ocean dragon you say? The sea mother...her rival! I understand." Bonnie conversed.

Bonnie then quickly walked toward Connacht who was standing atop the castle walls, looking out in the ice covered sea and scanning the frozen fields.

Connacht looked mortified "It's already the fourth month of the new year, the ice should be thawing, grass should be growing, sheep and cattle should be nibbling on the new grass. But no, it's still the dead of Winter, colder than the twelfth month right before new-years. A great field of ice covers the oceans now...who knows what horrors can simply march onto our lands as we slowly starve." He lamented.

"Connacht, a messenger from the Goddess of death herself has come, the Morrigan, and she has relied a message to me. She has spoken in the ancient Oghamic script and she commands you thus." Bonnie paused for a moment and then continued.

195

"Go to the Fjords of the Northern Three,
Find the Axe of Grom you Shall See,
Bear the Curse of Orcus Faithfully,
Slay the Serpent Jokull Bravely,
Rip it's accursed heart Gleefully,
Flee from the horde most Menacingly,
Princess eats the heart most Tearfully.
Quoth the Raven"
Bonnie did say most Ominously.

Connacht sighed heavily. "Can ye stop speaking in riddles hastily and tell me what I need know
or I might fly into a rage quite..ahem...readily!" Connacht mocked sarcastically.
"My cheeky smile has turned into a frown...instantaneously!" She rebuttled.

Connacht shouted "Stop it, knock that shyt off! I am fooking tired of these riddles and rhymes!" he roared.

Bonnie jumped back as did this new raven friend of hers. "Alright, Connacht, Alright! Bones of the all-mother, calm yer flaming teats!" she chuckled.

"The Third Fjord and it's surrounding Islands is the region known as Orkney, a strange region said to have talking seals known as Selkies, pacts of boar-men the woads call Kork, said to be cursed by a mercurical fae lords into pig-men. Finally a tribe of Orcneas, the accursed children of Orcus, are said to dwell in the subterranean caverns in the nearby mountains."

"It is said the tribe was once loyal to the son of Orcus known as Grom, the God Slayer but they eventually turned on him and slayed him, devouring his flesh but leaving his mighty axe behind. I guess the god slayer was god-slayed? His kin murdered him but his cursed-axe is still said to be, buried deep in the subterranean realm below the Orkneys," she continued.

"The raven told me a terrible Ocean Dragon known as Jokullhaps has imprisoned a firbolg goddess known as the Sea Mother. She should bring spring to the Northern provinces of Samhain, Yule, the Giant's causeway and even Lughanasda but alas winter is still here. Her rival is a terrible son of Orcus known simply as Taran, father of the northern sea. He has imprisoned her in ice, crafted from his glacial breath!" She decried.

"Use the monstrous axe of Grom against this terrible Sea-Dragon known as Jokullhaps! Nothing else can pierce the scales of the beast! Be forewarned that one region of it's body has shed some of it's hardened scales and a well timed strike from the Grom's cursed axe might split the scaled armor open and reveal it's innards. Go within it's body and rip out it's magical heart. This should kill the Serpent and free the Sea Mother from her icy prison!" She said.

"Flee from the swarms of Orcneas and possibly even accursed Formorians awakening from their subterranean realm, use yer axe to collapse the tunnels behind yee to stop their swarms from ravaging the land."
"The final part to the prophecy is to feed the heart to a princess like lady Rhona. The still beating heart of the Dragon will grant her incredible power to break the Fimbulwinter and help the Sea Mother defeat Taran, freeing the land of this Fimbulwinter!"

"You must go alone on this quest, this is what the Raven has commanded!" Bonnie demanded.
"How do I even get there in this Fimbulwinter?" Connacht groaned.
"The Raven of the Goddess shall guide you there, follow her to the Fjord of the Orkneys".she bemoaned.

Connacht sneered "phhhhft! Easy for you to say" and he hefted his claymore from it's sheath from his shoulder and walked down the stairs as the snow and ice rained down in an aggressive blizzard outside...
Connacht reached into his satchel and found a Fire-whiskey bottle, smiled, popped the cork and drank it. *By the gods it still tasted like Shit and it burned horribly going down,* He agonized.

He gasped and coughed but whispered to himself, touching his stomach, "Kunan"...suddenly the killer cold abated, he could feel heat radiating in his bones and arteries across his body. The taste was still horrible , the aftertaste was horrific but the internal warmth kept the cold at bay...he could see the snow sizzling and steaming as it touched him. He could hear the sound of footfall from the keep's ceiling above him and a wooden window cracked open with a loud slam!

"Hold, Connacht, I now exactly where the Axe of Grom is buried! The dreamer gifted me this vision!" blurted Rhona, gasping, sticking her head out of a wooden window. Connacht turned his head up to see Rhona. "I had a vision of how Orcus died, Grom placed his axe near several hot springs before he died! I have drawn a map of the Maw of Orcus and exactly where the Axe is placed!" Rhona threw the map from her window and it gently bounced on the wooden deck below. Connacht walked up to the dried, leather scroll and by the gods! She hand drew an innate map of the subterranean realm!

Connacht Saluted her with great respect, Rhona waved to him and wished him well, Connacht then turned around and walked to the Oaken gates of Gunnarholme.
"Open the Gates! I shall crush this Fimbulwinter curse!" he roared and Hjalmar looked outside the Stronghold windows.
"What are yee mad? Yee shall freeze out there!" Shouted Hjalmar Gunnarson as he stormed out of the gatehouse.

"Shut that fat meat-pie hole of yers, I am out to break the Fimbulvinter! Order these northern oafs to open the gate!" roared Connacht.
Hjalmar was both furious but impressed with such bravery! He waved the Shield brethren to open the gates and the stalwart huskarls did as was ordered. The Oak Gates slammed open with a whine from the iron hinges. **BOOM!** Went the great wooden,

A Swarm of Draugr from outside came to life, the ice broke off their dormant bodies as they surged with dark magic and charged at Connacht! Connacht spat the burning whiskey onto his Claymore, flames erupted on his murderous blade and his weapons became an incinerating instrument of death. Connacht began to advanced by dancing in circles, twirling his blade with simple precision and each time the burning blade struck it literally caused the frozen draugr to explode violently! Their rotten flesh and ancient bones smoldered to ash from the magic fire. He ripped through twenty or more enraged draugr as he swung his sword in wild flaming arcs.

The battle finished as quickly as it started, Connacht ran past their ashen corpses. the blood of the fae still coursed through his veins and made his runic magic much more powerful. He also noticed that the Raven of Morrigan seemed to circle over him, watching with it's azure glowing eyes looking directly at him.

Connacht quickly ran past the ruined village outside of Gunnarholme Castle, a grim sight, the corpses of innocent villagers half-way gnarled into pieces...something was devouring them and it wasn't the draugr.

The Raven guided Connacht north, towards the shores and they headed east along the last remaining pine forests which clung to the shorelines cliffs. He jogged at a quick pace until her came to the carcass of a dead Elk, a red Elk of great size and a pack of wolves was feasting on it's body.

"Truly the king of the forest, now being torn to bloody shreds by a pack of starving sea-wolves, the end times were breathing heavily on the Northern coast of Samhain," Connacht despaired and shook his head.

Suddenly a massive wolf, much larger than the others walked up to him slowly and started snarling. Something was strange about this creature, it had azure blue eyes and a silver colored coat.

Connacht whispered "Algiz" the rune of Elks and animal ancestors. He could suddenly hear the giant wolf speaking very softly.

"Remember me! Yee bastard pig-fooker!" The Silver Wolf snarled in a harsh, growing and gravely voice.
Connacht gasped "Yer the mate of the Ebony Cu-sith!"
"Aye the name Airgid and my lover was Oidhche who you brutally slaughtered in cold Blood!" her fangs gnashed.

"Damned Nordic invaders! Yer kind brought this cursed winter upon us! We lived our lives simply enjoying the flesh of seals, whales and other sea-beasts that washed up on shores but this Fimbulwinter has driven all those creatures away! Bastard humans and their black-magicks!" growled Airgid.

Connacht growled "First, I am only partially Nordic and my ancestors that came here landed on Samhain centuries ago! Yee Damned Unseelie hold onto a grudge that has been long forgotten, yer kind has gone crazy thirsting for vengeance! It wasn't us that brought this terrible Fimbulvinter!”

“It was probably lord Arawann awakening some fooked up monstrosity simply to get his petty revenge or that's my guess at least!” He bemoaned.

The Cu-sith snarled “Liar! You are the ones who antagonized him with your ceaseless invasions!”
Connacht implored “Look, Airgid, It was Lord Arawann who stormed across the border and abducted one of our princesses, he did it specifically to start a Civil War between clans!”

The Giant Wolf snarled “How do I now yee speak the truth?”
Connacht pulled a bronze torc from his bag, gloriously entertwined with shimmering-green tourmaline gems. “This is a torc of truth, aye?”
“Yea, how did you get that from the Woad peoples?” she wondered aloud in amazement.
“They gave it to me when I ventured into the Twelve Duns, I shall place it on my neck and speak to thee. You know this relic makes lying impossible!” he said earnestly.

“Aye, its impossibly to lie with that torc on ye neck. Fine, wear it!” She commanded.
Connacht then placed the shimmering bronze Torc on his neck, Airgid sat on her haunches, impressed.
He then continued “I want to break this Fimbulwinter as much as you do, I will make a deal with yer wolf tribe, each week our Ostramann clan will offer you a generous portion of meat to your kin if I can ride you to the Caverns of Orcus!” He smiled and bowed his head.

She turned to her pack and howled high into the snowy heavens, they nodded and fled away into the forest to find shelter during this glacial snow-storm. Airgid then turned to Connacht.
“How humiliating! But I will do what must be done to help my wolf-children survive this time of endless winter!” snarled Airgid “Leap upon my shoulders and I shall take you to the unholy pits of Children of Orcus!”

200

the Cu-sith implored.

They rode up the frozen mountains and hillsides, the ice was slick and the giant silver wolf almost lost it's footing in the smooth ice several times but each time her black claws grew larger and fiercer to deal with the slick ice. She dug her large claws harder into the ice and ripped footings into it's surface with determined purpose.

They rode for several hours...Connacht could barely see through the relentless blizzard but the sun must have been around 2 in the afternoon. Connacht heard horrible horns in the distance, haunting and ghostly. "Damnation, it's the flayed riders!" snarled the Cu-Sith "The Nukalvee!" she groaned.
"What do we do?" Implored Connacht
"We run, but I am already tiring and they never tire!" snarled Airgid.

"Nay, I have a better idea, run to the top of the mountainside covered with snow! We will ride the Avalanche to victory!" The Cu-Sith and Connacht looked at each other and he rode to the top of the slope of a nearby mountain.

Suddenly the undead flayed riders could be seen riding around the bend of the mountain path, their bleeding hooves smashed against the snow. The Nukalvee riders were gaining on them.

Their appearance was utterly frightful, they looked like the fusion of a human upper body right were the torso merged with what would have been the horses neck. Below the neck was the galloping body of a horse, but they were completely flaycd with no skin, just raw, red flesh and blood dripping onto the snow.

Some described them as walking dead centaurs with no skin, an excellent description but they had no eyes yet could see and they had a perpetually screaming mouth, like they were suffering from the worst torture imaginable. The Nukalvee were truly terrifying to gaze upon and even more horrific to battle! They did not have hands, the hands were fused into long, barbed bone lances with vicious hooks that gave those weapons a serrated quality to horrifying to describe.

Connacht swiftly turned to Airgid in determination and fear. "Hear me now, Queen of the Sea Wolves! I shall scream to the heavens and shake the frozen mountainside asunder, it shall fall upon them, crushing them! Take whatever form pleases yee for we will fight them furiously and to the death!"

"Yee can fight them to the death if you wish fool human! I have several children I must raise! But I will assist you until I am too wounded to continue!" Snarled the Cu-Sith

"This I respect! Let us charge into battle and defeat them to the best of our abilities then!" Connacht then slammed his fist to his chest and bowed, a mutual sign of respect. The Wolf-humanoid also bowed it's silver manned-head in respect, it's glowing blue eyes shined through the white-out of the blizzard

Connacht held up his ringed fist into the heavens and screamed "Thurisaz!" as powerfully as he could! Suddenly a thunderbolt struck a nearby mountain and it unleashed a deafening boom! The echos rang across the mountains for they were intensely powerful. Connacht and the Airgid were almost deafened from such an incredible scream. It seemed like the gods of thunder responded with incredible effort.

Their ears were ringing, but suddenly an incredibly cracking and creaking could be heard across the mountains. **Ca-Kracka! Ca-Croom!** Connacht and Airgid could feel the ice and snow cracking under their feet, an avalanche began forming and started to drag them down the mountain-side. Connacht could see the Nukalvee surging up the mountain, screaming in unholy fury as the ice and snow crashed down upon them, sending these flayed centaurs flipping head over hooves as the furious onslaught of the avalanche struck them with the might of Thor's hammer itself.

The Nukalvee that were struck in the snow were pinned by the large chunks of Ice, Connacht fell upon them with fury, hacking their flayed flesh to pieces while the Cu-Sith changed her form to a two legged werebeast, tearing the flayed riders to shreds, biting their screaming heads right off and finally tearing their bodies in half with her dagger-like claws!

As they finished slaughtering the handful of flayed riders Airgid turned to Connacht "Hopefully that will keep them down for at least a few days...but more are on their way! We need to get to the Caverns of Orcus. Who ever yee offended have summoned some of the most terrifying fae to hunt yee down!"

More haunting horns could be heard in the distance.

"Oh gods above, in the lands of Tri-na-nog! I need to rest!" moaned the Cu-Sith.

"No time, Wolf queen! RAIDHO" Connacht screamed the Rune of the Chariot, the spoke-wheel of the gods! The exhaustion in both of them quickly vanished after each ragged breath. Suddenly they felt young and sprightly, full of vigor!

Connacht leapt on the She-wolf's back and continued his journey through the Orkney Peninsula... what was once a Nordic paradise of idealistic fjords covered with burbling spring was now completely white, frozen and unbearable during this endless winter.

The Cu-sith surged and ran at the fastest pace it ever has achieved in it's life, no matter how hard it pushed itself it kept charging onwards. Connacht showed her Rhona's map and she said "The Maw must be near by, but be warned I will not follow you in there!" she said with fear.

Connacht rode through several different mountain passes and trails until his destination suddenly appeared right before him.

A truly massive cavern with the walls of a gargantuan cliff-face...its stalagmites and stalagmites were jagged in appearance like a set of colossal fangs jutting outwards to devour anyone who ventured inside. It was at end of a great, snow and ice covered ravine and the moon rose above it in the sky. The Maw was truly titanic, like one raging, gargantuan mouth filled with icicles and rocky stalactites looked like a thousand fangs.

A foul moaning wind bellowed out of the gaping chasm, the stench of rot and death hung heavy upon the air...strange for such a frozen wasteland.

The Cu-Sith turned to Connacht "I made my end of the bargain, I will hold yee to yers! I shall leave this place now! I offer yee a simple prayer to our father, Frayr who was once called Cerunnos, father of the forest. Find your way to Grom's Axe and get the divine Vengeance that shall guide your hand!"
With that the Wulver gently pushed Connacht off her back and waited for him to enter the cavern before them.

Connacht entered past the Maw of Orcus and as he walked deeper into the cavern the light of the outside world slowly faded with each step. Connacht whispered "DAGAZ", the Solar Rune and suddenly his body glowed with a mighty solar aura of light, the light of the sun literally emanated from his body, illuminating vast regions of the tunnel and the frozen pools that formed on the floor. He could feel the blood of faeries extinguish in his blood stream as Sun run pulled his last reserves from his blood stream. As he slowly descended down the vast cavern, he suddenly felt something heavy smash right into him, he lost footing and was sent violently tumbling deep in the caves below where he crashed into megalithic stalactite in front of him.

He could hear a growling laughter behind "Fool of an Arsehole, yee think I would really forgive thee for slaughtering my mate? Hahaha!" Airgid laughed maniaclly and swiftly ran out of the cavern, Connacht felt enraged by her trickery.

I got not time for this Bull-Shyte, he vented and then picked himself up and walked deeper and deeper into the caverns below. As he crossed the winding lava tube tunnels, like great obsidian snakes that led him to massive subterranean caverns with high ceilings ...the walls were painted with strange surface paintings of humanoid beings hunting giant beasts from the mountains and forests.

The whole time the Raven of Morrigan led him deeper and deeper into this massive cavern complex, at times the ceiling actually split open to the outside air and snow would come wafting in on beams of cold, pale, gray daylight.

AS he ventured deeper he could suddenly see them;; pallid, strong, hunched over, devouring the carcass of a giant millipede, They had giant ears and a large nose like a vampire-bat but no eyes. Their faces were like men, horrifically warped men, their teeth though were rows of jagged, misshapen fangs of different lengths. Their arms were long yet muscular, but their legs short and powerful, they walked about on all fours while others ran around on longer legs like men. Their skin was so pale Connacht could see the blue veins running up and down their bodies. Their greasy black hair hanging over there face as they feasted on the putrid remains of this hulking invertebrate.

He was far enough away to see that they had no eyes and made clicking noises to effectively "see" their way around the subterranean realms. They did not notice the bright sunlight emanating from his body. Connacht quickly but quietly fetched a smooth river stone and flung it with his considerable might to the opposite side of the cavern. The stone smashed into the stone ceiling and shattered into several pieces, emitting a very loud crack.

The Orcneas lifted themselves up from their prey, they roared and with jackal-like yips and yaps as they charged towards the area that made the noise... many ran on their knuckles while others ran on their legs like men. All carried crude stone axe hatchets and bone clubs at this new threat.

The Raven then guided Connacht to another tunnel and they avoided the conflict altogether for there were too many there.

Finally Connacht came to an opening in the Tunnels that led to the outside world, Before him was a strangely peaceful hot springs areas, the water of this caldera released great plums of steam into the sky in white, steamy clouds and this small Valley was protected from the snow storm from all sides by tall and steppe hillsides. *This is the spot, Rhona's map led me here!* He Thought.

It was night time but the full moon was out, peering above the ravine walls on all sides of this valley opening. In the middle of the hot springs was an barren Island which was a mound of skulls and older candels. The candles were organized in a circle around a mighty Great Axe. The weapon was almost as tall as Connacht himself, with it's blade partially submerged in the rock outcropping.

The Raven landed on the handle of the axe, which was pointed to the sky and it began to peck at the Geat Weapon. Connacht understood what the avian messenger was saying and walked pulled the Axe of Grom from it's shrine.

"No!" quoth the Raven "make offering, light candles!" it cawed.

Connacht simply used a knife and flint to light all five candles on all five stars, organized as a pentagram around the mighty axe...the fire of each candle glowed green with sickly balefire as they came to light...Suddenly each ancient rune on the axe awoke with fel magic! The burning green bale was brilliant with eldritch light form magic runes.

These were very familiar to Connacht as Connacht gazed upon the Raven he simply whispered "Watch"

Suddenly these strange Orcish runes changed into the Dwarven Runes of his ancestors and he realized what they Said.

ᚷᚱᛟᛗ ᚷᛟᛞ ᛊᛚᚨᛁᛗᚱ

Geibo Raido Othala Mannaz – Geibo Othala Dagaz – Sowilo Laguz Ansuz Ehwaz Raido

"Grom God Slayer! He named his famous axe after himself, the rebellious son of Orcus, who committed the unspeakable act of slaying his own father in battle but freeing the world from his horrific tyranny. Grom, the God Slayer brother to Crom the Mountain God. This weapon must be powerful indeed!" Connacht whispered in amazement.

"Powerful but cursed!" crowed the Raven.

Connacht reached out to grab the handle of the axe but the Raven screamed
"Naked, you must be Naked!"

Connacht looked at her strangely, shrugged his shoulders and removed his heavily armor-plated coat, pants, wool shirt, fur boots and armored gauntlets. He also took off his Tall helmet. There he stood naked, noticeably thinner than when he first set foot on the worn roads to the Calhoun Stronghold several months ago.

Connacht reached out once more to the Axe of Grom and he stopped to look at the Raven
"You Take Axe...You leave your Sword!"
He then reached out and grabbed the axe, pulling it forth, he then placed the Claymore of CuChalainn within the in the hole, chiseled within the boulder at the shrine. The Sword surprisingly fit right in with a satisfying
schnickt!

At first nothing changed he felt normal but suddenly then, he felt the pain, agony crawled up his back and spread through his shoulders, it was like torture. He could feel his body become raging hot, like his flesh and organs were boiling in steaming acid. He doubled over and in horrific pain, he screamed and green balefire erupted from his mouth, eyes and nostrils. Connacht's muscles bulged, his bones snapped and reformed as he gained muscle. **Crack! Pop!** Went his tortured body.

His skin turned green and horrible; bale-fire danced along his body. His skin ripped open as monstrous, tumor like muscles bulged outwards, his teeth shattered as new, jagged fangs pushed out.

His jaw snapped in multiple places only to heal into a thicker and more powerful jaw. Finally horrible jagged horns ripped their way out of his skull and skin to grow into two massive curling crescent blades jutting from his forehead.

He was cursed yet he was reborn! He was an Orc, the bastard child of Orcus. Stronger, Taller, his skin harder and more durable, bone spikes erupted from his skin in many areas. The Axe of Grom burned, a raging green bale-fire all around the blade.

Connacht felt stronger, far stronger than he ever was, when he exhaled plums of jade fire erupted from his mouth and nose, like mist on a cold day.

The pain began to vanish and he admired his new body, he was wrath incarnate! Punisher of Oath Breakers!

As Connacht marveled at his new hellish, cursed body he could sense movement on his left side...he quickly turned on his feet and noticed a swift flying boulder flying at him at incredible speeds! Without even thinking, with lightning like reflexes, he hefted his axe in a defensive posture to block the incoming projectile and the stone struck his green, burning axe. The stone exploded into a swarm of green burning chunks that rained down all over the steaming hot springs like a rain of furious meteorites!

From the eastern side of the Ravine the brutish giant appeared, and he had a full swarm of Orcneas around him. The Behemoth had one eye, one large leg with a smaller one, as well as one massive arm and a smaller one. His mouth had powerful jaw muscles and large, blunted fangs. Connacht could see the whip markings across his back, this was a Fachan, a deformed cyclopean-giant and he was enslaved by the Orcneas!

He heard roaring, yipping and yowling from behind him, like a pack of wild jackals. It was the same swarm of Orcneas he bypassed earlier which had followed him to the hot-springs. Both packs charged through the hot springs at him, the Fachan being whipped with thorn covered whips by one particularly large Orcneas behind him.

As the two hordes surged toward him, the Giant furiously charged past them and leapt into the air, slamming his one massive fist on the mesa Island that Connacht stood upon. **Wham!** Connacht simply lifted his gnarled and taloned hand towards the rampaging abomination and spoke "Mannaz", the rune of Humanity.

The beast completely stopped it's assault and looked at Connacht. "Friend? Stop Orc torture.." It moaned sadly.

Connacht smiled with his tusk and fanged maw "Yes! We shall get Vengeance upon them!" Connacht smiled.

The Fachan smiled "Vengeance against Orcs!", he roared and then savagely turned around and slammed into the orcneas hordes that enslaved him.

He smashed them with his one mighty fist and crushing them with his one mighty foot. He even used the dark bale-fire in his eye to unleash a gout of fire, immolating several of the them in bright green hellfire. They screeched in horrific high pitched notes similar to enraged bats as their burning flesh sloughed off their bodies.

Connacht turned towards the orcs coming from behind him charged towards them, hefting his mighty greataxe in the air, he spun with his weapon, obsidian spears and Fanged axes struck him but it barely pierced his bulging muscular frame or he simply ripped the weapons out.

Green blood came spilling out from his wounds to then quickly regenerate as he hacked and dismembered these Orcs to bloody pieces with each sweeping strike from his mighty axe.

More and more of the cursed cannibals came pouring down the tunnels on both sides of the Ravine, the mud and water splashed in the hot springs as they constantly surged onward. Connacht's Axe struck, it was singing after bisecting and butchering each orcneas that attacked Connacht. The Gallowgalas could feel a burning rage in his stomach, welling up like boiling lava and he roared "Kuanan!" and spewed a mighty breath of fire like a hellish dragon, the cloud of furious green flames torched dozens of Orcs who surged towards him, sweeping his head back and forth while spitting out a massive cone of the sickly green doom.

Connacht ran out of the deadly fire and returned to swinging his deadly axe in wide arcs, chopping two, three or even four monsters to gory shreds with each vorporal strike.

He could see his new ally the Fachan, bloody and covered with spears and fang-axes, ripping apart, biting through and stomping orcneas to crimson ribbons on the other end of the hot-springs.

The battle slogged on until their were literal mounds of slaughtered Orcneas all along the hot springs, their foul green blood polluted the waters. The surviving Orcs fled, their numbers having been butchered in enormous numbers. Connacht smirked, he could hear their shrieks, wails

209

and howls echoing down the tunnels of this great cavern.

The Fachan collapsed in one of the hot springs, his wounds were fatal...his breath ragged.
"No!" Connacht screamed "You will not die like this!" he commanded.

His burning green hands touched the Fachan and it screamed in agony! "Berkano!" roared Connacht and the hellish fire covered the Fachan, it began cauterizing and healing his wounds but something was strange. The Giant began to grow, his muscles bulged, his weaker arms and legs quickly gained mass and strength, but the Fachan screamed in agony and suddenly a new arm ripped out of the center of his chest and a new leg from his lower back, both weak like the previous ones. A massive fanged maw split the giant's stomach wide open, snapping rapidly in voracious hunger... The Fachan picked himself up and started grabbing the corpses of the dead Orcneas.

The Fachan was stronger, more mutated, more fierce and utterly deadly.

Connacht smiled "Utterly amazing! You have changed into a even more deadly beast!"

"Wait for me here and I shall return with the Heart of this Dragon!" Connacht commanded.

The Fachan looked at him, his stomach maw biting the head off a Orcneas corpse and he simply said "yes" then he turned around and continued to devour the corpse.

The Raven circled once again and whispered "Follow, Jormagand close!"

Connacht nodded his head and followed, swiftly running on his long and powerful legs, each footfall thundered across the rocky ravine. The Ravine was strangely warmer than the surrounding lands of the Orkney Fjords.

These Volcanic hot-springs seemed to be a place that mostly kept the brutal winter at Bay. Connacht noticed that plants were actually blooming nearing the steaming waters but there were many scattered items left her by the Orcneas; human bones, cattle and sheep bones, shovels, scythes, boxes and bags of grain. *They were looting the nearby settlements here!* Connacht realized.

As Connacht finally cleared the Ravine he came upon a strange scene...a massive but frozen tree of unusual origin, a willow growing in what would have been sea water...surrounded by it's kindred, a whole forest of barren willows, their leaves died off from the horrible cold.

Sleeping around the tree was a great sea dragon, shaped like a massive eel or serpent, without legs or arms but one massive, fanged mouth and ridges and ridges of shimmering scales giving off a brilliant, mother of pearl iridescence.

The Raven flew directly towards the sleeping sea serpent, the child of Jormagundar himself. The bird landed on the massive willow tree and waited.

This was it, the Oceanic Dragon had to be slayed in battle or the Fimbulwinter would bear on, eventually extinguishing all life in the northern Domains! Connacht pondered in grim determination.

Connacht roared, such a mighty roar that it echoed all along the sea-cliffs that surrounded this frozen brackish delta. It was time for battle and Connacht didn't need any crafty artifice to fight this titan of the sea.

Jokullhaps lifted one eye, a brilliant azure blue eye that had one long slit like a cat. It lazily hefted itself up, guarding the Frozen Bile tree and it chuckled with a deep and sinister laugh.

"She is mine, forever, and you shall never have her...you cursed monstrosity!" Jokullhaps voice was deep and like gravel, it sounded like massive stone walls were grinding against each other in a slow moving earthquake. Each syllable was slow and forced as it gigantic jaws moved its lips, vocal chords and tongue requiring great power and incredible effort.

Connacht snarled "Nearly all dragons are also cursed by the Gods themselves! Face me in battle, beast! We shall fight for her honor! To the Death!" Roared Connacht.

Jokullhaps roared, his gills on his neck opened wide and the sound of air rushing into his lungs could be heard like a great swooshing sound. It then expelled the frozen air, a furious hail of ice directly at Connacht!

Chapter 15: The Heart of the Jokullhaps and the Sea Mother.

"I have no beginning, no end, and I'm in constant motion.
What am I?"

The furious tidal wave of freezing air and hailstones came raining down as a relentless avalanche of frozen death...But did Connacht flee? Did he seek cover? Did he dodge at the last minute?

Nay! He opened his fang-filled maw and vomited a storm of hellfire, a relentless cone of greenish-yellow death! The accursed flames smashed into the unrelenting tide of freezing doom.

Both streams of death smashed into each other and roiled into a phenomenal cosmic storm of opposing elements. So furious did the two breaths clashed that a fierce cyclone of green balefire, white hailstones, and foul black smoke roiled in furious revolutions before dissipating harmlessly in the winter skies.

Jokullhaps looked shocked and confused. Connacht, smirked then simply lifted Grom, the God Slayer into the cold, cloudy heavens. He suddenly howled in defiance, his long roar echoed across the vast bay. He then dropped his axe down, his eyes become alight with an unholy fire and he leapt off the shore and charged into battle, his heavy footsteps crushed ice underneath.

Jokullhaps could see Connachts determined advance, green burning flames erupted from his hulking, orcish body as Connacht flew into a furious, screaming rage. He Seemed to grow bigger and bigger! Burn hotter and hotter! Become more and more enraged as he stampeded across the frozen bay.

With a great effort the mighty dragon brought his heavily armored tail into the sky and struck down faster than lightning. **THOOM!!!** This time our

Gallowgalas leapt to the left at the very last moment. The Ice shattered, chunks of frost exploded into the chilly air all around his hulking form.

The hail of ice struck him, it hurt but it didn't even stop him as his massive footfalls crashed across the broken ice, leaping from large ice flow to ice flow as what was once a solid frozen battlefield was instantly shattered into various independent islands of ice.

Jokullhaps snarled and dragged it's massive tail across the frozen battlefield, performing a enormous sweep that pushed the frozen islands aside. **ZRAAAKKK!**

Connacht wasn't swift enough to dodge that blow and it sent him flying into the nearby sea cliffs where he unceremoniously crashed into a granite cliff. **WHOOM!** thankfully a cliff ledge caught him from falling into the nearby frozen sea water.

Jokullhaps roared in Victory and surged forward, his razor sharp maw wide open, ready to rip Connacht to shreds with his his saw-like fangs.

The Titanic monster bit down with incredible power, it's jaws snapping with such power it produced a thunderclap. **Whack!** But Connacht was no fool. He slammed The Axe of Grom down on the tongue of the beast and arched his back up, using his massive legs to pry the behemoths jaws slowly opened. His legs shaking with fury, the Jaws of mighty Jokullhaps were slowly being forced open, inch by inch.
Jokullhaps was utterly amazed at the sheer power in Connacht's orcish body!

Connacht then realized something, the inner lining of the Serpent's mouth was soft and not covered with this diamond hard scales. He opened his mouth and scream "Kuanan!" his favorite fire rune. His body became covered with more and more green fire. Jokullhaps thrashed back and forth in agony as his mouth burned hotter and hotter.

Jokullhaps whipped his colossal neck back and spewed his frozen breath out of his maw, just to spit out that accursed Gallowgalas-turned-hellfire-orc and his flaming body from it's soft inner mouth.

214

Connacht's was vomited into the high heavens, spinning in circles, covered in a prison of large icicles he could barely move. He felt so weak, his eyes drifting to a dying sleep, but no! He must awaken, the fury returned to him, the ice shattered, steaming and melted off his body and he could see the massive snake-like dragon coiled up, read to bite him. Connacht reached for his Axe....but there was no axe?

He looked around, whipping his head around like crazy and he could see his axe already plummeting, far away from his hands, falling into the sea in a great splash. **ZOOOSH!**

Jokullhaps, like a horrific god of eels rose up to an incredible height! As he lifted himself up from the waters the bay literally dropped in volume from his wake! The great Sea serpent rose up and up! Far above Connacht, who was still falling, plummeting, closer and closer to the freezing-cold, Grey waters below.

The Beast then slammed it's entire body down on Connacht with incredible power. **Ka-Dooom!** The tidal wave exploded in all directions from it's wake! Connacht was smashed into the sandy ground, the air knocked out of his lungs as cold, salty water flooded into his body!

Connacht's ribs popped, he could feel them shatter, his spine crushed..he couldn't move his legs... He never wanted to die like this...not now, not letting such a horrific evil slaughter his people and dominate the land! Even as he lie there dying his fury grew more and more at the thought of such an intensely evil being.

He could feel the life force leaving his raging body..but then, he could see them, a host of amazonian women, riding mighty eagles, a vision from the Gods themselves! Two mighty men stood next to these beautiful warrior-women. One was gigantic, fat of stomach but broad of chest, red of beard and furious in temper, a mighty hammer hung at his belt the other a tall warrior, one shield on his amputated limb the other arm holding a brilliant broadsword of excellent make.

"Pathetic, would I die in such a way? Call my name, Call my Rune you fool!" Said the red headed giant.

"Poseurs! Look at these Aesir fools trying to win over our boy!" suddenly another set of voices appeared on the opposite side of the heavens.

A Tall golden god with a spear, shining brilliant with sunlight and his friend, a massive, corpulent behemoth with a huge club appeared and sneered insults at the first two.

"Go back to Asgard or Johtunhiem ya tossers! This here is our lad!" said the fat god.
"Now, like the drunk-ginger said! Yer gonna die on us, humiliate us in front of these Nordic Wankers?" Said the Golden God.

Connacht spoke to this visionary deities "I feel honored, the gods of the Caledonians and Nords fighting over me! Ladies! Ladies! Y'all are beautiful even if yer a bunch of fat, drunkin, warlike, whore mongers! Thor, Tyr, Lugos and Dagda grant me yer powers so I might slay that Sodding Sea Serpent!" Connacht implored.

Suddenly Grom, massive, green, orcish and muscular flew up to him from out of nowhere, in this heavenly realm and said "What about me, yee arsehole! Yer using me fookin Axe! Now get back down there and beat that Dragon's arse!" With that Grom grabbed him in his massive hand and flung Connacht screaming, flying down to earth like a thunderbolt! His soul seeing his dead body and slamming into it!"

Connacht's mind exploded, a spark of white hot fury and willpower gave him purpose, he screamed "Thurisaz!" with such fury, in a great bubble it drifted to the surface and exploded...unleashing the mighty scream that echoed across the towering sea walls that surrounded the bay.

A great wind awoke, blowing across the entire bay, a furious, whistling sound heralded the rapidly spinning Godslayer and Bam! The fearsome Axe of Grom flew right into Connacht's hand with such force it was as if the Johtun slapped it into his meaty Palm! His eyes awoke! He could hear his bones regrowing! **Pop! Crack!**

Jokullhaps lifted himself off Connacht, sure that he was victorious but Connacht's bones re-knitted, his broken organs regenerated, his muscles grew back as he furiously snatched defeat from the jaws of death!

With righteous zeal and conviction, with vengeance and justice thundering in his heart, Connacht grabbed the dragon's diamond hard scales, thick like slabs of slate rock and shoved himself free with one mighty push. He skidded across the cold mud in the bottom of the freezing cold lagoon and swam upwards. His head bursting out of the frozen water's surface and looking about wildly, gasping for sweet air!

It was a riot of sights, shattered willow trees, large chunks of ice floating on the brackish cold water and the shimmering scales of Jokullhaups, adorning his mighty body like a scintillating coat of mail. Connacht violently struck the sea serpent's scales repeatedly, but even his furious Axe of Grom, The Godslayer, could not make even a dent on the adamantine coat of his colossal adversary!

The Raven of the Morrigan appeared before him once again, flying in circles around the titanic Jokullhaps, it looked at him and flew down to land on the underside of the coiled serpentine dragon. The bird landed on it's chest (for lack of a better word) and started pecking at a certain area, clear scales flecked off with each strike of it's beak.

Like a lighting bolt it dawned on the warlike Gallowgalas that this was the weak spot! He grabbed his mighty axe, Grom, flipped it around so the back spike could be used and leapt on the coiled up part of Jokullhaps and started to climb up the rock-like scales of the mighty beast. Using his open hand, the sharp axe spike and his feet would find footing and he would slowly ascend, climbing up the unsuspecting Jormagand.

Connacht climbed and climbed, up and up he went, faster and faster he moved like climbing up some extremely rugged yet scaly mountain side. He was so close, rounding from the dark blue back scales, to the more polished, smother, mother of pearl scales at the underside of the dragon.

But he was reckless, he slipped and started falling, the Axe was strangely still wedged deep into the monsters underside scales. It suddenly awakened in his mind to scream "Zasiruth!" which was Thor's run Thurisaz but backwards and by the gods! He flew to the Axe! Until his hand landed squarely on it's thick and stalwart handle.

Jokullhaps snapped to attention and began to thrash about, Connacht held tight with all of his effort not to be flung off this time. He was so incredibly close to the soft, pearly scales of the weak area of this dragon's armor. One handful, one axe pick, pushing two more footfalls and again and again...He was at the soft spot!

He could feel the force of Jokullhaps pushing him to the left and the right, like riding an enraged Bison! The Wind was literally whistling as it roared back and forth. Connacht brought the Axe quickly and turned the mighty Godslayer around and brought the massive hook crashing down on the soft area! **Bam! Crack!** The mother of pearl scales cracked loose! Gallons of Indigo blood poured forth! Chunks of dark purple flesh was ripped open, pouring out in chunks of visceral gore all around him and falling in the lagoon's water below.

Again and again he struck, furiously the dragon rocked back and forth, bucked, slammed into the sea's walls, roared in fury, spun in furious circles to kick him off and a couple of times the intense power of the dragon was even too powerful for him and sent him flying but to no avail! "Zasiruth!" he screamed as he was sent flying and it sent him returning to his Axe that was wedged in the dark violet viscera of the Colossal Jokullhaps!

With one sickening crack, Connacht split the beasts ribcage open and through the jagged opening he could see the monstrosities' massive heart and lungs inside, pulsating with it's purple blood. Jokullhaps screamed in agony, reared up and slammed it's entire body down in the lagoon's icy waters below! **Ba-DOOM!** The whole bay shook with fury like a apocalyptic earthquake!

Connacht knew the this sea-dragon, this serpentine horror was desperate and trying to crush him... again! But he learned from this monsters tactics and plunged into his cracked open, rib-cage. The beast struck the earth like a world-shattering meteorite which helped drive our Gallowgalas firmly in the chest cavity of the Jormungand with ease. The salt water flooded into the creatures organs and lungs and was freezing Connacht's skin, but he just grew more furious and the bale-fire boiled the water around him.

He turned Grom's Axe over to it's back spike and used the blade to cut each Aorta on this large, beating hart. Crimson red and dark-blue blood, colored the different Aortas and their blood came spilling out as he hacked and ripped each one free! The Heart itself, as large as his chest, was noticeably small for the sheer size of the beast...but while relatively small it practically radiated the most potent of magical energy, for it was dark violet but pulsating with azure electrical arcs and strange glowing runes of the most ancient Johtun writings.

He wrenched once, twice, thrice and a final forth time and ripped the heart free from it's chamber...this was in good order, for he could feel the air making his chest expand... he desperately needed air or he would drowned.

Jokullhaps screamed in agony, he had a multitude of vocal chords, similar to a whale and when it screamed in it's death throes the chords harmonized in horrific agony, like a symphony in various octaves all screaming with immense pain. The Dragon reared up to the high heavens, it's eyes rolled into it's head, titanic jaws going slack and it slammed onto the mud of the lagoon with it's back.

Connacht couldn't stand it, he ripped and hacked and kicked his way out of the purple viscera, the indigo blood and their pearlescent scales came exploding out of his wake, showering the frozen bay with their scintillating beauty.

The Raven flew to the mighty willow tree called the "Sea Mother" and it crocked, "offer her the blood of the dragon!" Connacht did as we was told, and swam with the still beating heart across the frozen waters and ice chunks to climb up the freezing mud and gently squeeze the heart of Jokullhaps near it's roots, the drops landed on the exposed, bark covered roots and the gray scaly coloration changed to a brilliant bronze, it began to slowly transform the roots in this way, small growing sprigs, grass and lichens started growing where the blood fell.

"Go speak the sacred Rune of the world tree, Yggdrasil!" Connacht knew exactly what she was speaking off; Eihwaz, the Yew Rune.

Connacht didn't shout but he sang, with incredible vibrato, in a shrill bass-

219

baritone, his voice warbling the Yew Rune
"Eeeeeeiiiiiiihhhwwwwwaaaaaazzzzzzz!" he sang.

The tree began to slowly go through metamorphosis, green leaves and white flowers budding from the hanging branches, green grass and rust lichen sprung around it's roots and even waves upon waves of humid, warm air washed over the area all around the massive willow tree...all it's bark turning from a saddened gray and ashy color to a lively, glowing, copper and bronze color as the Sea Mother began to awaken from her dormancy.

Connacht noticed that in large areas the Sea Mother had her bark stripped from her and the strange written language of the druids and the firbolgs could be seen...it was Ogham! The Sea mother must have been another of these mysterious bile trees.

Connacht could hear something from deep in his mind, it was like the voice of an ancient yet kind grandmother. *+Is he gone? Can I awaken now?+* She transcribed.

"Yes, awaken dear Sea Mother! Our lands are dying in the Fimbulwinter's icy jaws! If it gets any colder Fenris will snap his chains and bring his children, the Vukodvlaks! To rend humanity to bloody shreds! We beseech thee in this hour mother of spring, mother of warm seas!" Cried Connacht.

+Thank you darling, my strong lad, for saving me from that horrible serpentine dragon, Jokullhaps! I shall summon my Seelie children to aid you on your quest!+ She transmitted.

+Help me summon the mighty spring storm! Use your magic with mine to call a epic cyclone from the Solstice Sea to bring warm rain to melt this ice prison that strangles the land!+ She messaged.

Connacht lifted his ring-covered fists to the skies and screamed in Runic "Halgaz".

The Sea Mother began to change, her mighty trunk split and grew massive legs, her thick boughs turned to bark covered arms and from her upper torso sprouted the wooden face of an ancient yet kind crone. She pointed her multiple bough-arms to the heavens and pointed her branch fingers to the gray skies and screamed in Oghamic "**Doindeann!**" as she sketched the long script from in the sky.

Powerful winds began to kick from the west, blowing away the blizzard and Connacht could see a massive thunderhead... lightning and great gray streaks of torrential rain drizzling down over the frozen, glacier covered sea. The storm was moving so fast that it would soon arrive on the shoreline in a few hours, by his estimation.

The other trees began to awaken from the waves of warm, moist air emanating from her body and moving out in lazy novas across the surrounding lagoon...the chunks of ice quickly melted, the shattered willow trees began to spring budding leaves and flowers. Fish, birds and frogs began teeming around the mighty Sea Mother.

The Sea mother pointed at the earth and shouted "**Paisde!**" which means "children" in Oghamic. A great Conch shell came bubbling up from the muddy waters of the bay, she gently lifted the gargantuan mollusk-shell with two of her bough-arms and hefted the spiraling horn to her lips, sucking in one great gulp of air she placed the conch to her barked-covered lips and blew a magnificent clarion call, which was the most clean baritone note that echoed across the land for miles.

After a long note she finally stopped, she waited for a few moments and suddenly the chorus of several other horns and conchs could be heard from every direction, their clarion call could be heard in return.
She finally spoke from her cracked, dried lips and said "They heard my call, noble warrior, go back to your castle... they will guide you there."

"I will take the fight to Taran but if you hear my Conch from the sea, bring help, for I have been weakened by being frozen for so very long by that Dragon's freezing breath." she said.

Connacht saluted the titanic Sea Mother, even for such a horrific cursed orcish form, she could see his eyes shines with a nobility beyond many of the inhabitants of the island. He Saluted her and she nodded and bade for-well.

Connacht ran from the awakening bay, the lagoon was coming to life, the grasses and kelp growing, crabs, gulls and various sea life returned to the Sea Mother's hidden alcove. Strangely enough a entire pod of seal arrived into the warm brackish bay... they saw around the sea mother and she gently caressed them with her bough-arms.

These strange seals were singing and whistling in Nordic of all things, Connacht realized that these were no ordinary seals, they must have been the singing Selkies of sea shanties.

Connacht turned around and surged up the trail back to the ravine with the hot springs. As he kept running eventually he came to the ominous skull shrine and he noticed his Sword was still plunged in the central altar. The Fachan was there still devouring the corpses of the orcneas but it was mostly bones and patches of leathery skin "Finally you have Come!" he shouted.

The Raven landed on his famous claymore, but the sword was changed, the blade had a wavy pattern, that screamed it was lethal, like the Saxon Flamberge of the mainland. Nordic Runes were written across it.

Quote the Raven "You must exchanged the weapons to have your Sword! If you take the Axe instead you shall be permanently cursed!"

Connacht thought good and hard, the Axe was powerful and it replenished his magic quickly enough but it was a dangerous sacrifice, *to be seen as a demon by my own people, to attract Orcneas to where I live, to fly into bloodthirsty rages with such incredible might*. He pondered.

"I return thee, Axe of Vengeance, Godslayer! I take my sword to it's rightful place, Blade of CuChalainn, I name thee "Slaughtersong!". " Connacht shouted as he ceremoniously returned the mighty axe to it's skull shrine and pulled his greatsword, now blessed with Runic magic from the shrine.

He could feel the power of the awakened sword, the powerful soul of

CuChalainn seemed at peace now, no longer enraged and the weapon still teemed with his magical essence. *You are free of your cruse CuChalainn? Your soul is finally calm.* He thought.

Already the vanguard clouds from the ocean broke over the land, raining down globs of cool rain that battled with the furious snow of the blizzard...hail, slush and slurry covered the hot springs.

Connacht turned to the Fachan and said "Honorable giant, what is your Name?"

"Me name Bolg!" he bellowed into the heavens.

"Come then, most noble and heroic Bolg! We shall fight our way past the maw of Orcus and return to Clan Gunnar's besieged castle!" Roared Connacht

Connacht leapt on Bolg's back and rode on his mighty shoulders into the darkness of the great cavern, he strapped the gigantic beating heart to his back. While wielding his wavy claymore on one hand, while holding onto a greasy black tuft of hair on his other.

The Behemoth thundered on all fours, his knuckles and hooves struck the cavern floors like loud wardrums, booming echoes across the caves. The Orcneas returned in swarms but the Fachan simply plowed through them, crushing their bones under each massive footfall.

Faster and Faster Bolg surged, through the open caverns with their impossibly high ceilings and tight cliffs into the winding lava tubes themselves... He followed the gray raven as it guided them through these labyrinthine tunnels.

Finally Bolg charged to a vast opening near the entrance of the aptly named maw of Orcus. Connacht leapt off the misshapen giant and shouted "Are yee not coming with me?"

"No lad!" Bolg cried aloud. "Me shatter stone pillar! Me bring whole mountain down on whoreson Orcs!" he roared in glee.

Connacht respected that request, they must have enslaved and tortured the mutant beast for years.

"Bolg I shall see thee on the other side, noble giant!" and Connacht turned and ran out the Cavern's entrance. Bolg Saluted him, turned around and charged as swiftly and powerfully as he can, slamming into a natural stone pillar at the center of the opening, it cracked but still stood strong. Bolg slammed his fists over and over again into the thick stone pillar. **Whoom! Whoom!** His massive fists struck while more and more cracks formed on it. Chips of stone and clouds of dust burst outwards from each colossal strike.

The Orcneas hurled a storm of barbed javelins at him, many pierced his hide with spears and lacerated him with sawtooth clubs. It did not matter to him. His fists thundered over and over again, the stone chipped, cracked and finally a massive **Crack!** Which echoed across the cavern walls. More and more sickening cracks formed on the stone pillar until it exploded from all the weight of the mountain.

The ceiling slowly started falling at first and Bolg laughed maniacally as the orcneas furiously, hacked, slashed, stabbed and bludgeoned his warped body. The pain would kill a lesser being but Bolg cared nothing for it!.He just laughed manically at the top of his lungs as they dog-piled him. The last thing he saw was the ceiling moving faster and faster at him and then **Tha-Doom!** Darkness...

Connacht was running through the slush covered mountain trails, grass and mud began to spring forth from the wet, slick snow. Connacht could hear the mountains quickly crumbling and snapping behind him and he looked directly back to where he came from. The whole mountain side imploded, cracked and collapsed... the maw of Orcus collapsed in on itself with great plums of granite dust kicking up from where it was. Just a huge piled of shattered stalagmites and boulders was left.

"See Thee in Valhalla Bolg! Or maybe Tri Na Nog? You were more more honorable than the majority of my fellow clansmen!" Connacht saluted by slamming his fist into his chest.

Connacht turned once again and made his way down the mountain trails, "From the horrors of the maw of orcus to the wonders to the Bay of the Sea Mother!" decried Connacht.

As Connacht ran past the mountains, highlands and valleys on the trail, it looked like life was waging war on frozen death! Some areas were cursed with the the dead of winter and the other areas blessed with the dawn of spring. The contrast was both intense and unnecessary!

Connacht beamed with pride, grabbing the "Slaughtersong" in his right arm. He surged forwards with renewed vigor to crush his enemies, the armies of orcneas, the army of the dead, the walking dead giants and even the Unseelie fae.

As Connacht began his journey from the fjords to the sea cliffs he came upon a sight, a whole battlefield of dead skinned terrors, the Nukalvee battalion was shot to ribbons by a hail of arrows.

As he walked up to gaze upon the sight, arrows piercing these horrors, he noticed that they were crumbiling to ash. The arrows were not humble crossbows bolts of the clans. Nay. These were finely crafted arrows from Yew, the tips were bronze colored arrowheads. This must have been the work of the elusive Aos-Sidhe Elves.

Connacht could hear howling from the forest and he recognized the mournful note on the calls of these creatures.

From the pine forests nearby several of the sea wolves led by their mother, Airgid, could be seen running out onto the grass shores of the coast. Behind them a full battalion of humanoids, tall, fair of skin and covered in scintillating bronze armor. Their longbows were made of the finest alablaster colored wood and each of them bore twin sabers attached to their thighs, also made of bronze.

"Well, Cusith, wolf mother! You have brought yer kin and several guests with yee.. these must be the Aos Sidhe? The elusive elves of the mythic age, said to serve under the very gods of our island homes!"
Smiled Connacht.

The large lupine-humanoid looked at him with knowing, azure eyes and spoke "Yes, apparently our forest friends have dwelt in the deep pine forests for centuries but we never even found them, they only revealed themselves at this time." She snarled.

"We were summoned here by the Sea Mother's clarion call, more of our kind will soon arrive riding atop the great Vixens of the forest lands." Said a particularly eloquent lord of the fae riding atop a large red fox the size of a horse.

'Well lets not be waiting shall we?" said the Sidhe lord "to battle!"

The Cusith bowed it's head to Connacht, he leapt upon the beasts back and together they rode onwards to the Castle of Gunnarhiem as the strange and wild weather just grew even more chaotic and aggressive.
Many of the Aos Sidhe archers gently brushed and beckoned the sea wolves to approach them with gifts of dried meat and scratches around the ears and chin. The large wolves also allowed these fae archers to ride them and they quickly rode behind Connacht and their Elven lord. The other archers, broke formation and simply sprinted behind them.

As they rode further westwards on the well worn path, the Elk-cavalry of the elves appeared in the forests and rode upon their flanks, apparently Vanguards and Sternguards awaiting their approach. Tiny flying fairies known as sprites came flying in from the trees, they bore miniature bows and arrows or even small lances the size of sharp knives upon themselves.

Connacht could still feel the heart on his back, the massive, beating heart of the dragon still drumming upon his back. Some potent magic kept the strange organ alive and beating, even thought it's master was long dead.

Suddenly before them appeared to brutal formations of stout yet short warriors...Connacht remembered these bastards well. These warmongers were called Redcaps and they formed into two dense, circular phalanxes, shields overlapping with their crude, barbed iron spears arrayed in ranks.

Connacht snarled "Move ye damn bastards unless I hack my way through your misbegotten kind!" He roared.

Their Sarjeant marched before the defensive formations "Nay! Blood Drinker! We came to give yee protection on Lord Arawann's command. A large horde of draugr blocks the road before and bastard Nukalvee raid the road behind us! But you must accept the Bain-Sidhe lords offer!" snarled the fanged dwarf, his spiked mace covered in long and vicious spikes ready to rip armor asunder and shatter skulls like overripe melons. "Aye, I'll hear the bastard out! Summon the whoreson!" Connacht growled, the Redcap Sarjeant smiled.

The Sarjeant, Yarg, reached for a ram's horn on his side, pulled it free from a hoop and played a long, haunting note from it.

Connacht could hear the all too familiar sound of the furiously-buzzing dragonfly wings of the Bane-Sidhes. These elites dark elves grew powerful wings to propel them into battle and allow them to descend upon their quarry impaling them on their silvered glaives with incredible force.

Connacht turned around and noticed the bastard himself, lord Arawann flying down with his honorguard, smiling the whole time.

"Yee must be pleased with yourself, bastard adulterer!" Connacht snarled. Lord Arawann, smiling gleefully replied "of course, oaf!"

Lord Arawann's expression turned serious "I can reach Gunnarholme faster than any of you, past the swarms of draugrs who are now accompanied by those flayed Nukalvee and corpse-giants from the frozen seas. Squeeze the heart of Jokullhaps into the golden Cornocopia that I have brought and I will deliver the sanguine gift to the princess herself." He claimed.

"Bastard! Alright, don't you hurt her, she is pregnant with your child and lord Hjalmar's!" snarled Connacht.

"You know I love that full figured, elegant, Auburn haired, lusty and curvaceous lady more than anything else in this world. On my honor I promise I would never hurt her nor my unborn babe." Lord Arawann earnestly took a knee, planting his mighty glaive in the earth and bowing his head with great respect. Connacht noticed the amazing silver arm that replaced his former limb, it looked like full plate but it was so elegant and moved with such dexterity, it was also covered in the strange oghamic text of the past.

"Fine! I believe yee loves her but yer vows aren't worth Shyte in my mind. I know yee loves her with all your heart and yee deeply yearn for that baby to be born." Connacht then walked over to the Violet skinned lord, grabbed the beating dragon heart from his back, took out a dagger and stabbed the bottom of it..

The Indigo blood poured rapidly into the large, ornately decorated cornucopia, it's opening represented a fierce, roaring boar's mouth and the knot-work was exquisite around it. As the blood approached the top, Arawann looked up with a coy smile. "That's enough for now. Let's not shed tears for spilt dragon blood, shall we!" he laughed coyly.

Connacht lifted the heart to his lips and drank from the pumping wound, the rich, heady, intoxicating indigo blood poured into his mouth... it tasted like iron, obviously, but also strong like a potent spirit like absinthe or vodka.

There were other strange notes, like the minerals of the deep sea, fish oils and a strange electric tang that danced upon his tongue and nerves. This was quite possibly the most powerful of magical blood he ever consumed.

"Yes! Yes! Barbarian, consume the rich blood and fuel your crude, savage magicks from the northern realms!" Snarled Arawann.

"Tasted better than the piss for blood that I took from that pathetic stump, yee fool bastard!" Connacht chuckled viciously.

Lord Arawann frowned "I shall forgive you for this time only! Much more important things and events must take place before I have the pleasure to impale you in a future battlefield." Lord Arawann then smiled, having a sensation of pride, fantasizing about impaling the Gallowgalas in the foreseeable future.

"I bid thee ado." Lord Arawann said, sarcastically bowing and then spitting directly between Connacht's boots.

Arawann's wings rapidly began beating, blowing flecks of ice and mud everywhere as he hovered several feet over the ground and quickly flew westward towards Castle Gunnarholme, his Honorguard of Bain-Sidhe followed him swiftly, shimmering across the skies with their iridescent wings.

The Bain-Sidhe bastards always knew how to make a scene in style! Connacht thought.

Connacht then turned to Yarg and his red cap formations and barked "allright redcaps, yer mine now yee bastards! Quick time to castle Gunnarholme!"

Yarg smiled, nodded his head in respect, his red-head and braided beard bouncing wildly. Yarg then lifted his spiked morning-star in the air, barked a command in his tongue and the cruel, dwarven warriors broke formation and started quickly jogging in place behind the host of elven riders. They ran directly on the flanks of the Aos Sidhe archers, surprisingly fast for such heavily armored warriors.

Suddenly a loud clash of thundering hooves could be heart accompanied by hellish screaming. Connacht and his allies turned around to witness a formation of Nukalvee riders descending on their flanks. Connacht barked orders "Redcaps! Form a shield wall!" and they swiftly formed a dense wall of shields and spears. "Archers, use the shields as cover!" and the Aos Sidhe quickly ran directly behind the Redcap shield-wall.

"Fire!" He screamed and swarms of arrows set loose, flying across the sky and hit their marks! Killing scores of them but more kept coming, running over their fallen comrades, crushing their bodies with their flayed hooves.

The Archers kept firing and Nukalvee were struck down but more and more kept surging out of the seas or mountain pass behind them.

"Ba-Rooooom! Ba-Rooom!" A loud, sinister horn could be heard. From the pine forests a handful of heavily armored Dullahan Knights came crashing down, right in front of the road between the allies and the charging Nukalvee! The Dullahan knights smashed right into the charging, flayed-horsemen with ferocity. Their mighty battle-axes and morning-stars hacking the terrors to shreds while serrated bone sabers struck back at their heavily armored bodies but were easily deflected with sparks ricocheting everywhere!

Such a furious melee, the Dullahan were superior warriors but were badly outnumbered. Never-the-less the Dark Knights held their own and began to savagely grind their enemies down in melee.

"Yee can thank Lord Arawann for pulling such fierce allies in a time like that!" Yarg smiled sarcastically at Connacht.
Connacht looked down at Yarg and sneered "Shut it ye wee bastard!"

Chapter 16: The Awakening of the Dragon at the battle of Gunnarhiem.

**"Who is the lone one
that lurks in the hearth
and stems from stone.
No father or mother
has Eager-to-Shine,
there will he spend his life.
King Heidrek,
guess my riddle?"
ODIN**

Connacht leapt on Airgid's back and hefted his mighty claymore into the air, the Slaughtersong. It shined brilliantly in the daylight and he pointed it forwards and roared "Onwards to Gunnarhiem lads!" and the host of them charged forwards.

The Aos Sidhe riders surrounded him with his red-caps spearmen and elven archers running behind him. Just a few more wiles of the windy and winding coastal path and they would arrive to the sweeping fields outside the Gunnarholme Stronghold.

Large bodies of draugr blocked their way. Connacht was wise and didn't waste men, the Aos Sidhe would fire swarms of arrows at them and inflict several casualties. They would then retreat as the hordes of walking dead would close in with their shambling charge, in turn the redcaps formed their circular shield wall formations, known as schiltrom... and the damned horrors would be impaled and hacked to pieces with spears, axes and cleavers. As the hordes of walking dead bored down on the Redcap phalanxes suddenly Connacht and his men would come swooping in with the Vixen lancers, impaling or hacking the dead to pieces with bronze glaives, his claymore would hack them to shreds. The Cusith and her wolves would rip them asunder with fangs and claws, running them over in scores. The elven cavalry moved so swiftly and with expert care they would simply carve swathes of destruction through their enemies to then retreated swiftly behind the safety of enemy lines.

Large swarms of these long dead warriors were slaughtered in scores using these well timed and executed tactics. Connacht noticed how surprisingly well these Seelie and Unseelie forces fought together. They suffered very few casualties in comparison to the hordes of undead they butchered.

After much furious fighting Connacht finally arrived before the colossal and stalwart walls of Gunnarholme.

The land was still frozen over, but the ice was melting from the furious winds from the Orkney Fjords. The Sea mother was using her powers to fight back Taran's dark magic. Connacht was shocked as to what he witnessed, an near infinite horde of the sea draugr pouring in from the icy seas, now with broken ice flow on the shores and rocky sea cliffs...they were like a innumerable horde of pallid ants, their horned helmets, segmented plate and chainmail armor creaking, their lithe yet muscular frames dragging their crooked feet and wooden shields into battle, armed with ancient iron axes and maces they marched ever onwards.

Even Undead giants, either frost or sea giant, followed them, they picked up boulders and flung them at towers and walls of catle Gunnarholme, though they were clumsy and frequently crushed many of their own when the flying stones went in awkward directions crushing their victims beneath.

That Bastard, Lord Arawann was correct... it would be impossible for them to reach the castle on time. This army was coming very close to smashing the walls in and shattering the great oaken gates of the castle. Two massive, dead giants both hefted a great battering ram, made from the largest pine tree of the forest and they slowly but methodically slammed the makeshift ram in the gates, over and over again. Each massive blow sent wooden splinters and shards flying everywhere.

Suddenly a large contingent of the undead noticed Connacht and his rag tag army of Seelie and Unseelie fae and broke from the rest and surged forward. They where led by one massive zombified giant who was wielding the great, iron chain of a long forgotten Drakkar longship, the anchor still connected to it.

"Get Ready men!" Connacht roared as the Aos Sidhe archers spread their formations wide and began firing swarms of arrows at the oncoming draugr horde.

(Meanwhile at the Castle Gunnarholme)

Thruud was running around the great defensive stone-walls of Gunnarholme, she helped pick up wounded berserkers and shield-brethren in her strong arms, taking them into the longhouse barracks to be healed by Shelta witches and druids. She would grab massive ballista-bolts, gargantuan arrows that were the size of proper spears, and she placed them in the large wooden bows stationed on the walls, she would quickly wind-up the devices, using her great strength, arm a large bolit into the ballista and then aim the bow directly at some draugr-giant and fire the arrow right through their rotten eyes to impale their brains behind with a massive **Thwak!**. Each Ballista when fired released a large **Thunk!** as the steel strings snapped into place from great tension, striking the large bolts with incredible force. Thruud killed a dozen or so of these necrotic Johtuns but that still wasn't enough, for every giant slain two simply had large bolts driven through the dead parts of their body, simply inconveniencing them.

The two giants using the giant-ram already smashed in the first gate and were battering in the gate to the inner courtyard.

The twin Johtuns hammering the gates were even bigger and tougher than the rest, ballista bolts didn't even seem to pierce their horn-crested heads so Thruud had to rely on the final strategy of boiling hot oil in cauldrons, going to the gatehouse and pouring the smoldering oil down the siphon-gutters to assault the behemoths-zombies below with burning death.

"Now! Burn the bastards!" she screamed and a hail of burning arrows rained down on the pale blue skinned monsters... columns of fire crept up their bloated, pale fleshy torso. The sound of fat and skin sizzling and popping was strangely delicious like a suckling pig. This fire seemed to only annoy them and Thruud could see more boiling cauldron's of oil nearby, she grabbed two at a time and poured them down the oil siphons, raining the black, boiling tar on them and causing them to burn hotter and hotter, the fire growing larger and more massive with each cauldron.

The Giant's though undead, could feel the fire raging all over their bodies and they began swiping their large bodies with their fists while screaming and bellowing in agony. Their deep, gravely voices shook the very walls of Gunnarholme as they roared in torturous pain!

Thruud could see an opportunity, as the Johtuns dropped the battering Ram they were not focused, and she was directly above them. Thruud hefted her mighty wooden hammer, roared in fury and she leapt down, hammer pulled back way over her head, her golden braids flapping in the artic wind.

She fell like a thunderbolt and she crashed onto the the first Giant, Her mighty wooden hammer came crashing down with full force **Thwak! Krak!** Using all the muscles in her body, like a great muscular tiger pouncing on it's prey. The Hammer struck with such incredibly force,**Wham!** When it struck it cracked off the Zombie giant's left horn completely and the bony ridge was cracked wide open!

Again and again she hefted her wooden hammer with relentless ferocity and almost suicidal determination to break these hulking bastards. Finally the entire ridge of the skull was cracked open. She reached into the beasts shattered skull while it was waving it's arms around and grabbed the brain, ripping chunk by bloody chunk. The Frost giant draugr kept trying to crush her with his open hand strikes right to the fracture in the skull. Thruud simply kicked the hand with her tree trunk legs, kicking the hand back with each donkey kick she delivered.

She could see the brain stem inside the skull and she moved as swiftly as she could, the giant now reached into it;s own skull trying to crush her between it's jagged finger nails. Grabbing a brutish seax dagger she leapt to the brain stem, reached in with her dagger and cut it in directly in half. Black gore showered all over!

The Johtun groaned, she killed the bastard. She quickly ran out of the bastards skull, grabbing the limp hand and pushing it out, she grabbed her massive hammer and leapt out of the giant as it began to fall.

The dying Draugr Johtun slammed into the other one, pushing it right into the last Oaken gates and the gates simply buckled from the collapsing dead behemoths. Oak splinters, beams, shards came raining down everywhere as the two zombie colossai smashed through the gate and struck the earth, causing a local tremor which shook the walls, rattled the doors and left a rampart of dead flesh.

Hjalmar could see that the second giant was pinned to the ground by the first one and he started to pick himself up. "Take that ya foul bastard!" roared Hjalmar and flung his heavy war axe directly at the fallen brute...it struck his skull with incredible force and buried itself into his skull...Thruud came running up the back of the second giant, now dead, leapt off to land on the back of the first giant, hefting her huge hammer high in the sky, she then smashed the hammer into the blunt back end of the Axe with a booming **Crack!**...She Drove the Axe much deeper into the skull of the giant.

The Draugr Johtun was convulsing in it's second death and Thruud kept hammering the back of Hjalmar's axe! **Whack! Whack! Whack!** Went her Maul and each strike with her great weapon drove Hjalmar's axe ever deeper until it split the monsters brain entirely in half...killing it fully!

She breathed heavily, gasping. Hjalmar ran up and grabbed the fractured skull with his hands, pulling as hard as he can to get his axe. Thruud could see that even her mighty adoptive father couldn't crack the skull open so she used her large booted foot to slam her heel into the back of the fracture and pushing with all her effort... the thick skull cracked open and Connacht grabbed his axe from the ruined brain matter and wrenched it out with much force, showering everything with black blood and rotten gore!

Thruud was exhausted as was Hjalmar, she walked up to him and hugged him, he hugged her, they didn't care with they were covered in the black gore of the slain zombie giants... it was good to hold their beloved family members once again. The end was coming for them but at least whatever acts of glory could grant them respite in the gold feasting halls of the gods in Asgard and Valhalla.

(Meanwhile in the Stronghold's Keep)

Lady Rhona could look outside her window, the battlefield was intense, two giants shattered their way past the first gates of the walls of Gunnarholme and were battering their way into the second gates, until Thruud heroically slaughtered both the using burning oil, her hammer and the help of Hjalmar.
During the furious battle outside she did witness the walls shudder from the rampaging giants and even dust get knocked from the walls, it was like suffering a constant earthquake which would not relent.

She stat in her bedroom at the top of the central stronghold, the massive tower called a keep, the most important part of the castle. Bonnie had attended to her, feeding her porridge with butter and blue berries, it was delicious and easy to eat but bonnie left Rhona to give her some sleep.

Lady Rhona heard the gentle rapping on her windows facing the ocean, she turned and she could could see the handsome face of her dark elf lover smiling down on her. His glowing eyes had a mischievous look to them as his coy smile. She quietly sneaked over and opened the windows for Lord Arawann and he spoke.

"Oh, handsome lord, my true love, alas I am pregnant with twins, I am married now but oh how I desire to find a way to run away into your loving arms and we can make passionate love under the full moon again in a steamy hot-spring somewhere high up in the Twelve Duns mountains." She smiled with her forlorn eyes.

"My love, fear not, one day I will find a way to whisk you away from here but maybe after you have given birth to your beautiful twins. I have heard that one of them is my very own little changeling youth, how excited am I too see such a mysterious baby of bouncing joy." Smiled Arawann.

"Oh my Lord, how I desire you so much, how I bare the suffering of being wed to this Drunkard, this Brute Hjalmar! I just don't want another Clan War, so many peasants, gypsies and even fae people were slaughtered in that last war due to blood thirsty and hot headed clan-lords fighting for power and supposed honor." decried Rhona.

"I understand my love, you will one day, soon enough get your freedom from a false death, maybe we can sneak away for a few hours of passion while your pungent yet heroic husband fights off a massive horde of the cursed dead and if they are overwhelmed we can at least abscond with you to the dark side of the island so you might give birth to these precious children of ours." Lord Arawann smiled and Rhona smiled back at him.

"Ok my love, grab some warm coats of the thickest wool. Seal-hide, fur boots and so forth for I need you very warm for where we shall go. We need to sequester you and those magical little babies inside your womb to a place of mist, where a certain crone awaits you so we might complete a important prophecy my love. Quickly now your ladyship." Lord Arawann smiled but gestured her to move quickly.

She quickly began donning her wool and seal leather coats, her fur boots, he wolfcoat hat, all to quickly warm herself. She became bundled up and was almost smoldering, sweating inside so much heavy clothes and coating.

"Am I ready?" she said. Arawann smiled but then suddenly the chamber door was kicked in wildly with a deafening **Whack!**...In stepped the massive brute that was lord Hjalmar, breathing heavy, snarling, his face beet red and then in walked his hulking daughter, her face sickened at what she saw.

Covered in the black blood of draugr giants, cold snow misting on their raging hot bodies after a major battle. They marched into the warm bedchambers of Lady Rhona. When they both witnessed Lord Arawann they griped their weapons tightly in their meaty hands.

"Well well, looks like the guards ratted on us my love!" snarled Arawann.

"No please, no more violence! I might not love Hjalmar but I don't want him to die, for all his weaknesses he still has fought valiantly to keep me safe!" Lady Rhona screamed.

Lord Arawann smiled "Oh I wont kill him nor his daughter and I will keep you safe." He smiled.

237

"But I will have a bit of fun with them!" like a devilish cat he smiled a wicked grin.

"Fooking pig! Fooking whoreson!" roared Thruud and she flung her gargantuan wooden hammer directly at Lord Arawann.

Lord Arawann used his magnificent silver arm and punched the incoming oaken chair, it exploded into a million chunks of wood, showering splinters everywhere. He looked at the knuckles of his glorious silver arm, smoke literally rising from such an impact, the knuckles themselves glowing an amber-orange color. "Truly, Magnificent of make!" smiled Arawann, admiring the quality of Prince Nuada's arm.

Lord Hjalmar charged at Arawann! His axe raised high to the sky, his footsteps thundering with fury, each footfall shuddering the stronghold falls with Hjalmar's immensely heavy footfalls. Hjalmar closed the distance much faster than people would expect for a man of such incredibly bulk, swiftly bringing the great axe down with such incredibly force it would have decapitated a moose or a full grown bear... But Arawann easily caught the furious axe with his silver arm once again and with one move yanked the great axe free from his mighty hands and then punched him right in his sternum with his other arm.

The Punch was so powerful that it knocked all the air out of Hjalmar's lungs and stopped his onslaught with one blow. Arawann quickly spun the great axe around with a flick of his wrist using his godlike silver arm and brought the blunt end down, crashing down hard on Hjalmar's kneecap! **Crack!** The bones in the kneecap shattered with such a violent force, the shattered bones stuck out of his leg.

Hjalmar screamed in agony. Lord Arawann smiled and laughed, he then slapped the giant nordic lord right in the face with his good arm and sent him hurtling across the room directly into Thruud. They both tumbled, legs over head and smashed into a large long table **Boom!** bowling the thing over.

Lord Arawann was impressed, he never thought he could survive the combined might of both Hjalmar and Thruud in combat. This Silver Arm of Prince Nuada gave him incredible strength!

Lady Rhona looked shocked "ye didn't have to do all that!" she gasped. "Oh come now Rhona my love, they could have murdered me with their blood thirsty rage, better to show them my power so they may respect me and my kindred next time we meet." he smiled.

"Come my love" Lord Arawann replied and Lady Rhona leapt into his open arms, he grabbed her plump hips with his soft, natural hand and picked her up into the air athen he flew away with her through the open window and into the gray heavens beyond.

They flew and flew, she could hear and feel the aggressive vibrations of his iridescent wings, aggressively thrumming through the freezing cold mist that settled over the seas of the north.

The trip lasted for something like half a hour, her face was stinging from the cold but she was otherwise quite warm.

She pondered how they all arrived to such an event, lords know what fates transpired to lead to such a massive battle at the castle, that lord Arawann defeated in battle returned far stronger than ever before to easily dispatch one of the greatest warlords and his giantess of a daughter so easily. What was in store for them? She wondered.

Lord Arawann hovered in the dark gray, swirling mist and then suddenly hovered downwards with the rest of the dark elven honorguard. He gently rested with lady Rhona by his side, their feet almost effortlessly touching the sand stone islet in the northern sea... mist, so cooling to the touch was slowly being pushed by the winds in gentle spiraling miniature vortexes about them.

There she was, towering nearly eight feet tall, skin pallid blue like a drowned corpse, long obsidian claws cut into the soft sand stone cliffs near her as she wrote oghamic script into the islands bedrock.

"Aunt Oona, we have arrived." Lord Arawann spoke with respect and he bowed before her with the rest of his bane-sidhe guards. Lady Rhona quickly followed suit.

This Bain-Nighe Hag known as Oona, the loveable aunty Oona as she was called before, changed forms into her true, cursed self was a formidable sight. Taller than Thruud and almost as strong, with claws that were long like a Wulver or Vukodvlak, she could disembowel a fierce Huskarl-warrior with one swift slash of her giant claws and it has been said that she has done so before.

"Good, you have brought you true love" Oona smiled "Bring her forward so I might smell her and sense her twins." Said the monstrous Oona.

Lady Rhona was scared and looked back at Arawann who simply nodded her head, she then turned to the towering Oona and walked forwards. Besides her stood a humble white lamb, bleeting for it's mother, but alas it mother was not there to comfort the lost soul.

"Lord Arawann please give me the Golden Cornucopia." said Oona in a creaking voice.

Lord Arawann simply did as he was commanded.

She took the shimmering, golden, finely inscribed Cornucopia, filled with the indigo blood of the Jokullhaps, the serpentine dragon of the great ocean, and she poured the blood into a large ram's horn sitting atop a flat, stone shrine...

She gently mixed the blood of the sea serpent with the rich sangria within the horn as she mixed the red elixir she began chanting in Ogham.

Suddenly a longship was rowed towards the island, three other women where on the longship. Rhona looked and she instantly recognized them. It was Llewellyn, Deidre and Claidogna and each of them held a potion; Black, White and finally Yellow potion in Llewellyn's hands. As the longship moored on the island they gently boarded the shore and walked towards the circle that Oona had crafted. Oona procured a final potion from the dragon's blood and wine, it was all red and emitted an aura of crimson light!

"Nigredo, Albedo, Citrinitas, and Rubedo!" spoke Oona. "These are the four great potions of Alchemical metamorphosis! They represent the four powerful elements of antiquity when mortals discovered magic across these strange lands." She croaked.

"Consuming them in order shall give birth to a state known as the "Philosopher's Stone" where you a granted one wish along these lines; Metamorphosis, Immortality or Transmutation."

Lady Rhona and Llewellyn looked at each other in sudden terror. "Is there only enough for one transformation?" Llewellyn implored.

"No, there is more than enough but we need a sacrifical victim to give it's life to empower this high magick!" Oona demanded.

Llewellyn looked downwards and she sighed "Allright sweet Rhona, you were destined for this.." a tear dripped down her eye. Lady Rhona hugged her and placed her forehead on Llewellyn's "Hey, lovely, one day I will pay you back in kind!" they smiled and then kissed passionately.

Everyone else was surprised but Llewellyn smiled. "Another day, but these potions were both difficult to concoct and made from the rarest materials. You need to save this land, we will focus on my transmutation afterwards." Lady Rhona nodded and then, gather a strong breath, thought for a moment and walked into the center of the ceremonial circle. She could smell the sea-brine on the winds that whipped by.

First she walked to Claidogna, who held the black potion **Nigredo**, the elixir that represented earth and putrefaction. She held up the tall vial and drank it...by the gods it stank of shyte and the flavour was incredibly bitter, she wanted to vomit, her eyes watering but she swallowed it down, willing herself to swallow the vile liquid. "By the gods that was the most disgusting and rotten thing I have ever drank, what is in that horrid drink!" she exclaimed. Oona smiled, her jagged fangs poking out from her lips "charcoal and horseshit!" Lady Rhona look mortified. Memories of her alcoholic father beating her mother flooded her mind, memories of her own mother fleeing from Dun Calhoun and abandoning her stormed her heart...absolute despair.

Rhona walked up to Deidre and she noticed the white potion, **Albedo, ,** in her hands and she drank it...it was bland, almost flavourless but it seemed to wash away the horrible flavour of **Nigredo**. The drink was like water but had a milk like after taste. This potion represented water and birth, ignorance and awakening. She had memories of reading various books and studying music several years after her mother abandoned her. Long periods of reading tablets left by the druids, written in Oghamic.

She turned to lovely Llewellyn and she could see the sweet smile on her face, there was the golden potion, **Citrinitas,** and she drank it. This one was both rich and sweet, like it was made from the most sun ripened fruit or even honey. This potion represented the sky, growth, mastery and intellect. She then was awash of memories playing the hammer dulcimer at court before a great audience, they cheered hearing her lovely tunes, even her father wept to such an amazing melody.

Finally she walked to the hulking, hunched over Oona. Oona held the crimson **Rubedo** in her hands. Rhona drank this potion and by the gods it tasted strange, but she could feel a potent burning sensation on her tongue and her muscles twitched aggresively. As foul as it tasted Lady Rhona desired freedom from bondage and vengance upon the wicked.

Lady Rhona could sense this feelings inside her, she could see the rings of energy emanating from her body using her auramancy. She had visions... of a dragon with iron scales, breathing fire upon the wicked, destroying the army of the dead with it's razor sharp talons and fangs! Rubedo was the final potion, it repersented fire, change, justice and sheer willpower!

"Atharraich am bòidhchead gu bhith na bhiast " croaked Oona, she then picked up the lamb and with one swift slash of her claws slit it's throat open.

Lord Arawann quickly grabbed Lady Rhona, he began disrobing her and covered her mouth from screaming "Shhhh my love, soon you will be granted your dark wish, be calm." Lady Rhona was still terrified but she understood that Arawann wanted to give her a powerful gift, she calmed herself.

"I must shower you with the blood of the innocent." Said Oona with her gravely voice "And I must shower your unborn children with the blood of the innocent."

She lifted the dying lamb into the sky with her long, cruel clawed hand and poured the blood all over Lady Rhona...She was only wearing her sleeping gown now and the lamb's sanguine essence poured all over her fair white skin, covering her breasts, legs, navel and face with the lifeblood.

Lord Arawann let her go and she grabbed herself for it was cold, the fresh air billowing from her lips, the warm blood stank of iron and filled her senses with it's carnality.

"What did Oona say?" implored Rhona meakly.

"She said "Transform a Beauty into a Beast"." Arawann said, tears running down his face.

"What? What are yee sayin......?" before she could finish her sentence the magic kicked in and she roared a monstrous roar of agony.

Arawann grabbed her as she underwent the horrific transformation and threw her violently into the sea water outside that was surrounding the island. She splashed into the water, writhing and screaming monstrously.

She screamed in pain, her flesh began to rot and turn black from putrescence. She died, maggots began to crawl around her floating corpse. Suddenly she rose from the sea water, groaning in undeath. As she started walking with her hand out, her body convulsed and she keeled over in the water, clutching herself in the fetal position. Her rotting flesh fused and she formed into something like an egg...the flesh sloughed away into the sea water.

Instantaneously the white egg emerged from her putrid remains, very large, like an ostrich. Screaming could be heard in the egg. A tiny fist cracked open the shell and she emerged from the egg, a miniature version of herself. Her new, albino body started to grow and grow, the sea water boiling around her.

As she grew taller and stronger her body changed, she grew golden scales and began to laugh hysterically. Small vestigial wings like that of a duckling sprouted from her body. Her fingers grew longer, sharp white nails sprouted from her hands.

Suddenly she was tall like a giant but she knelt over, placing her clawed hands on the ground. Iron like scales sprouted from her new skin, her fingers cracked, snapped and suddenly grew even larger, massive claws ripped out her finger nails in showers of blood. Another set of iron scaled arms ripped out of her back but with only two fingers on there ends, the secondary arms quickly elongated and a gigantic, blood red membrane grew from it and formed into wings. She kept growing, her muscles bulged, her legs and arms grew massive, she grew taller and stronger than even Oona and Arawann combined.

She Roared again in pain and rage "What have you done to me?!?!" as she roared in her monstrous fanged maw.
Lord Arawann "You are truly perfect, for now you have turned into a mighty Dragon! Bring burning death and razor sharp vengeance upon the army of the Dead! Seek out the Frost Giant Taran and help the Sea mother crush him in battle! My love you will soon be free of Hjalmar, no longer needing to keep up the facade as a queen to a violent drunkard!" cheered Arawann.

Oona creeked "Only a pure and loving soul such as yourself could fully manifest the sheer power of the Dragon's curse! Crush your enemies and demand respect from the Ostramann clans! Seize your destiny!"

Slowly it dawned on Rhona, She could now do as she wished, no guilt trips of ceaseless clan warfare, no forced womanhood and acting honorable and ladylike before the court!.

"My Love! Awaken! Your armor is like adamantium plates, your claws are like Sabers your fangs are like pikes and your breath shall be their Doom!" Roared Arawann.

Rhona now transformed into dragon, roared into the heavens as a massive column of hellfire exploded from her maw to surge into thick clouds above. Lord Arawann flew to her back, grabbed the thick, iron scales and said "To battle my love!"

Rhona the Dragon, flew into the sky and Lord Arawann cried "lets us free the castle of Gunnarholme from the army of the dead!" he then pointed his silvered glaive in the general direction from where they came from. Her titanic, blood red wings flapped against the cold air with great force, pushing them forwards with each mighty stroke.

Her mighty wings beat furiously with purpose, the mist and clouds were blown aside from her rampaging advance and she sailed right over the walls of the gargantuan fortress...already the great army of draugr came pouring in through the breach!, she opened her razor sharp maw and unleashed a storm of hatred and hellfire upon the invading army of draugr! **Zhruuush**! They were set alight and they screamed in agonizing fire as she left a trail of destruction.

The defenders of the castle cheered, Hjalmar and Thruud roared, even though he hobbled about on a makeshift cast for his broken leg.

Connacht was in the thick of combat, fighting side by side with Yarg the redcap sarjeant. Scores and scores of sea draugr flung themselves at the brutal shield walls of the redcaps, only to be hacked to shreds by battle axes and spears. A furious hail of Arrows struck the clambering draugr as they climbed over the mounds of their own dead, scores were slain but the stubborn bastards had to be hacked to ribbons or burned to ash to fully die.

Many of the redcaps were eventually overwhelmed and hacked to pieces by crude cleavers, hatchets and spiked maces of Draugr the horde.

Tragically Connacht noticed that many of the Vixen riding Fiannu were slain to a man. Those gallant charges were heroic and killed many enemies but they were risky and a toll was taken on the giant foxes and their riders.

Connacht looked up and a magnificent irust, red-dragon was soaring over the battle field, it had a fierce red mane of hair. Tragically the colossal asshole, Lord Arawann was riding atop this Dragon directly into battle. "Of course the vain son of a bitch had to steal all the glory!" Connacht quietly growled to himself.

The rampaging giant was charging directly at Connacht, this was the one that had a massive anchor and chain yet it wielded with both hands. It twirled the mighty weapon in circles and then brought it high to the sky and slammed the weapon down with incredible force! **Whoom**! Connacht quickly screamed "Dodge!" and most of the redcaps did but a handful of them were completely crushed from the impact of such a titanic chain and anchor...everyone around them, the Aos Sidhe archers, the redcap shield-bearers and the endless swarms of draugr thrall, all fell to the ground from the local quake which struck the earth with immense force. **KaDoom**!

The Draconic Rhona could not tolerate that and flew with rage directly at the giant, she landed atop him, using her massive clawed arms, she ripped his rotten maw open and sucked in a massive breath! Boom! She vomited burning death deep into his mouth and gullet below, the zombie giant thrashed but in sheer pain as he was was quickly burned from the inside out... it's stomach, belly and lower back where the first to get completely incinerated to char.

She flew around the battle field leaving trails of destruction and fiery wakes from her furious flight...Draugr giants and formations where annihilated. She made sure to kill a majority of the Giants and then she swiftly flew off into the approaching storm clouds heading north,

Connacht smiled "crazy son of a bitch Arawann, crushed damn near half of the army of the dead and butchered all their giants! And now they fly over to simply disappear and not finish the job? Capricious milk-drinkers!" Connacht chortled.

The survivors of the castle surged out with Hjalmar, Lachlann and Thruud leading the charge, their furious berserkers hacked the draugr to pieces with their battle axes and great swords. The shield brethren impaled the undead on spears or cut them to ribbons with broadswords and hand axes. Archers surged up the walls of the castle and hit their targets with fury and accuracy.

Connacht heard horns once again, the antler flutes and mastodon tusk horn of the Spriggans. They came surging up the hillsides from the south led by the fierce Finlay and followed by a host of Shelta crossbowmen and Woad warriors, completely naked, wielding their backwards facing Falx-sabers and long shields.

The Army of the dead was getting hammered from the front, the north and the south and they were being slaughtered wholesale. Connacht lifted his sword, leapt on Airgid's back and charged into battle with the resit of the Aos Sidhe cavalry.

(Elsewhere in the Frozen Ocean of Ginnulgagap)

The Dragon Rhona roared in rage "Where is that frost giant bastard?!" she was flying through the storm furiously, spinning vertices circled the oceanic cyclone, where the warm rains of the Sea-mother fought against the freezing winds of Taran.

She cut through the mist and came to an Island where she witnessed them battling, they where literally striking each other with their titanic fists on a barren island. Taran towered over her but she held her own, punch for punch, blow for blow! **Whoom! Wham!** They exchanged blows and battled furiously.

"Come my love, let us defeat Taran but we cannot slay him! As evil as he maybe is, he is still necessary for he brings the rain, snow and cold of winter to the Solstice Isles!" shouted Arawann.

"Who gave this god such powers? What idiot assigned him a profile over something so necessary?" The Dragon Rhona snarled.

"Alas it was the trusting sun god, Lugos, who as a peace offering gave the last few remaining Formorians a few roles in the divine order of things." he explained.

"Let us hurry, he is empowered by the Fimbulwinter!" Arawann exclaimed.

She nodded her massive head in agreement and darted forwards, she slammed her wings shut and plummeted with such incredible force, she looked like a dragon impersonating a sea eagle ready to kill it's prey with one swift strike.

Kazoosh! She struck with great force and slammed directly into his back! Taran screamed with fury, even for being one of the greatest Formorian sea giants this blow struck him hard enough to knock the wind from his colossal lungs.

Taran now tried to reach for her behind his back but the Sea Mother leapt into the heavens and delivered a flying right-punch directly into his jaws, **Boom**! shattering his teeth and knocking him down.

Draconic Rhona dodged hitting the ground at the right time and flew up into the sky, breathed in a mighty gale of air and then vomited furious fire all over Taran's face. The king of sea giants struck his burning, monstrous, tusked face with his hands, screaming in agony

The battle was furious, the ice was already breaking as Taran began to loose his magical powers over winter. The Sea Mother crawled over him and began to repeatedly smash her massive fists on his face.

Taran was defeated and gasping for air, his rock-like teeth were shattered. His limbs where broken and twisted.

Victory was theirs, The Sea Mother lifted up her colossal arms and screamed in victory. Taran lay gasping, the titan was defeated and dragged himself off the geometric island in the giant's causeway... he pulled himself into the deep sea and swam away to retreat in the giant's kingdom deep in the abyssal realms of the Ginnulgagap ocean.

Lord Arawann and Rhona the dragon roared in triumph

"My love we have saved the day! Let us return to Oona so you can be changed back!"

They flew and flew as the cyclone moved closer and closer, the cool rain and humid air cracked the frozen glaciers and melted the ice that covered the land. Grass bloomed and leaves budded with the defeat of Taran. Life returned to the land.

Finally they arrived before Oona on her islet along the giant's causeway chain. Rhona landed in the sea water for she was too massive for the island. Suddenly the Dragon Rhona began to decay and fall apart.

"Too bad, I was starting to love this form!" she smiled, Arawann smiled as well "you truly have become powerful and free. Let's us return you to Gunnarholme so you might give birth peacefully to those enchanting twins sleeping deep within your womb!" Arawann smiled

The Draconic form started to fall apart, it flesh and scales sloughing off into a great pool of decaying tar...from the tar emerged a very large egg, human sized to describe it in the common parlance.
Lord Arawann flew over the egg and gently struck it with his Silvered Glaive...this gently cracked the egg open and Rhona appeared in all her voluptuous human goodness.

"Turning into a blood thirsty dragon has gotten me mighty hot and ready my love" she looked lustfully.

"Yee Know, we won that battle...maybe we can spend an hour here having a moment of passion before I go back to the mundane humdrum existence of the castle!"

He quietly pulled her close and they kissed passionately, she disrobed once again but now the air wasn't freezing cold... it had pleasant drops of rain and cool winds. Her hands traveled down Lord Arawann's violent waist and he felt massive, throbbing and excited. She grabbed the back of his head and gently led his long black locks down to her nether regions where he gently kissed and licked her womanhood with passion. She moaned and groaned wildly and had one incredibly hour of animalistic and passionate sex.

Llewellyn looked amazed and saddened at the fantastic, draconic and wild sex goddess that Rhona had become. She felt a small finger tapping her shoulder and she turned around. A Small blue fairy appeared before her.
"Good day darling, I heard yee want to also go the ritual of metamorphosis?"

"Yes, that would be delightful." She said with yearning in her eyes.

"My name is Mog my lovely and I am slowly dying, I was Lord Arawann's servant but he discarded me after he discovered his mistress Rhona, as a Slaugh my life is rather short. I shall offer my life to thee but do me a favor...return me as a homunculus!" Mog implored.
"I promise this!" they nodded at each and approached Oona with a final request and Oona smiled.

The Four potions were still there, Llewellyn drank each one in turn, no matter how terrible they where.
She first drank the fecal Nigredo, then the milky Albredo, the golden Cinatras and finally the crimson Rubedo! By the gods the tastes were horrible, foul, sweet, electrical, plain and everything in between.

"Goodbye sweet mog!" She said and he looked at her "goodbye sweet Llewellyn!" she lifted him into the air, grabbed her Seax-dagger and slit his throat...his azure blue blood poured into her mouth...the ritual was complete.

She felt the pain and the agony as she screamed in suffering, then flung herself into the briny tidal-pools near the island. Her flesh began to decay and rot, she made one last wish in her mind "I wish to be reborn as a woman who can bear children!" and then she closed her eyes...fading into the darkness.

Chapter 17: The Birth of the Changeling Twins.

"I look at you whene'er you look at me;
You see but I see not; no sight have I;
I speak but have no voice; your voice is heard;

My lips can only open uselessly.
What am I?"

(Nine months pass.)

It is Autumn once again and Feast of Samhain was once again being celebrated at Castle Gunnarholme at the magnificent fjords of Skye. Hjalmar was in a joyous mood, he was singing and dancing with his beloved step daughter Thruud. Lady Rhona happily watched them celebrate in the courtyard. Any day now, Lady Rhona thought, she can feel her stomach, swollen with twins. She can feel them kicking, ready to be born into existence.

They guests have arrived, the fierce highlanders from the lands of Ulster, Lennox and Calhoun have arrived. The Elderly lord Duncan, tall and regal, his red and white hair billowing wildly from the northern winds soaring through the craggy fjords.

The feast was ready! A great sea Elephant was slain, gutted, skinned and roasting over a bonfire and in turn several lambs were butchered and placed inside this mighty sea beast. Thruud and Contacht together slayed this beast as they went sailing through the giant's causeway near the isles of Yule.

The Highlanders brought flagons of ale, mead, wines potatoes for roasting and loaves of barley bread, blood-cakes and a cornucopia of apples, figs, pumpkins, grapes with various berries plucked from the forests.

Lugos the sun god of the Caledonians and Freyr the horned god of the Ostramann tribes was worshiped on this day, great wicker-men were constructed in their honor. Little straw dollies of the gods were constructed and given to children during this time. This great feast was in celebration of the years great harvest, gathered as the cold winds began to fly in from the north during the nights. This full moon illuminated the azure blue night landscape around the Gunnar stronghold.

Finlay was seen dancing with Llewellyn but something was different with Llewellyn, she gained weight, she was voluptuous and curvaceous. People still thought Llewellyn was a femboy but very few people witnessed her transformation into a woman who could give birth. She wasn't pregnant yet but who knows how long she had with Finlay lusting after her constantly.

Soon the three witches arrived and began their stellar performances. Llewellyn, the red, Cloidnah the Green and Deidre the Ivory Seer. The combined audience of Ostramann warriors and Caledonian highlanders cheered and danced in celebration.

(Later on as evening approached)
Lady Rhona groaned in agony. She could feel her water break, the sheer agony of it all. Her already heavy breasts swelled to massive size, hanging down to her hips and fat with milk. She began to sweat and scream, Hjalmar and Thruud looked at each-other alarmed for it was happening! Bonnie looked deep into Lady Rhona's eyes and pulled forth the deadly "White Snow" potion from her pouch but Lady Rhona shook her head, "not today!" she whispered. Bonnie nodded her head and placed the potion back in her pouch.
They easily picked her up, Thruud grabbing her left leg and Hjalmar grabbing her right leg, placing her on the great beechwood table. Thankfully Rhona was wide of hips and the first baby's head was already crowning from her birth canal.
Thruud quickly placed her hands on lady Rhona's labia and gently pulled the baby out from Rhona's spread legs. A Miracle, the first baby was a strong and healthy boy! Thruud gently gave the baby to Lord Hjalmar and he was giddy in happiness "A baby boy!" he exclaimed in victory.

Suddenly the second baby started to crown, but something was wrong...the legs were coming out first!
Thruud looked at Hjalmar in terror but Hjalmar was far more focused on the the firstborn boy in his arms.

Thruud was alarmed when suddenly Bonnie, the Shelta chieftain quickly came to her aid and forcefully but gently tugged the babies feet forward. The second baby, a girl, was pulled out with success but again, the umbilical chord was wrapped tightly around her neck! And the baby was blue, like she was asphyxiated, having no air and near death!

Bonnie swiftly grabbed a knife in her dress and slit the umbilical chord but to no luck, the baby was still blue. The child was a stillborn!

Thruud looked in terror at lord Hjalmar and he looked at them with no emotions "meh, still births happen, I got the son I always wanted!" he casually said.

Thruud was shocked, a mixture of rage and fear streaked across her round face

"Shhhh, shhhh, I know the problem." Said Bonnie and she lifted the blue baby by the leg and began to slap the child with her hand. The baby didn't move and she looked at Connacht at the other side of the room.
Their eyes transfixed with utmost seriousness and he whispered a word, (BERKANO) suddenly his eyes glowed golden in determination...and Bonnies eyes also glowed amber, catching his intense focus.

Suddenly Bonnie whispered into the stillborn's ear, (BERKANO) snapped her fingers in front of it's face and made the runic symbol for BERKANO, the rune of the tree of life.
The blue baby opened it's eyes....

253

Glossary:
Alchemy: Most of the potions mentioned in the book

Antivenom: made from bee and snake venom, fungal molds and possibly bitter melon. Used to kill diseases, poisons and even curses in someone's body.

Blood-Elixir: potions made from Fly Amanita, Psiocobilin, Worm-Wood and sometimes even the azure-blue blood of Fae-folk. Replenishes ones magical power and can allow someone to see illusions.

Cold Iron Bombs: Bombs that explode and hurl clouds of cold iron powder...generally used for killing low fae or crippiling them.

Fire-Whiskey: Are bombs made of sulfur, strong whiskey (or other alcoholic spirits), red peppers and blessed with the fire rune of Kuanan. Used as explosive bombs and excellent against undead.

Glowing Algae: a type of potion made from glowing algae from the sea, illuminates darkness and the invisible.

Mercurical Poison: a deadly and potent poison made from mercury and lead. It is said to cripple some of the most powerful opponents.

Silvered Bombs: Bombs which release clouds of silvered powder, generally excellent at negating magic and crippling more powerful fae folk and lycanthropes.

Panacea: a Potent healing potion made from tea-tree honey, aloe-vera and bone broth. Excellent for healing wounds and stopping bleeding.

Ritual of Metamorphosis: Known as the great work or Magnum opus, it is famous for being able to turn lead to gold, grant immortality or at least long life, metamorphosis into a new form and creating the intelligent homonculus or the powerful golem.

Nigredo: The black potion of putrescence said to be made from horse manure and or rotting flesh. This potion brings about despair, loss of hope, self loathing and even undeath. It kills the ego but is a fertile environment for rebirth.

Albredo: The white potion of birth and rebirth. It awakes ones mind and even body, it is said this potion makes one aware of how ignorant they are of the vast universe. Said to be made from milk and eggs.

Cinatras: The Golden potion of learning. Said to be made of saffron, mangoes and turmeric. This potion is a potion of amazement and wonder, learning the vast secrets of the cosmos and the inner mind.

Rubedo: The Final potion, the potion of power and of reaching one's Zenith. Might, fury, vengance, passion and determination are the emotions that drive this potion. Said to be made from the blood of a powerful beast.

Fae, Cursed and Undead:

Aos Sidhe: Known as Elves on the continent of Hravenholme and Johtunhiem. The tall eared tribes of fae who side with the gods of nature like the Tautha and Vanir. Seelie.

Bane Sidhe: The winged aristocrats of the Leanan Sidhe or dark-elves. Known for having dark purple and blue skin and dragonfly wings. Their screams can stun a foe in battle. Unseelie.

Bane Nighe: Powerful Hags of the Unseelie, they can place potent geas or curses. Tall, blue skin with long black claws.

Basket Weaver: A rare, serpent or eel like fae of massive size that can use illusions and is cunning enough to trick prey into their maws. Hearth Fae

Bog-Leapers: Fae beasts who are a mix of Bullfrog, Bulldog, Fox-bat and even a scorpion fish. Most of them are ravenous and animalistic but it is rumored some of them can speak. Unseelie.

Boggarts: Fat, burly goblins with powerful fanged maws like bull-dogs, they fight with crude halberds known as Billhooks. Unseelie. Also known to forge tools for farmers.

Brownies: Plump, wholesome hearth fae who gather root vegetables like raddishes, sun-chokes and potatoes. They generally help and live with poor villagers. Humble relatives of dwarves who prefer farming. Seelie.

Centaurs: A race of horse and stag fae who mostly dwell in Hravenholme. Seelie.

Clurican: Relatives of the Leperachauns. They prefer wearing red and drinking but they also horde wealth to some extent. Hearth fae.

Cu-Sith: Fierce wolf-humanoids of the Unseelie.

Draugr: Undead Nords who were cursed with undeath after the destruction of the An-Fhomar elven kingdoms. Cursed Undead.

Dwarves: a group of squat but strong and hearty fae, known for forging weapons and armor. Related to the Brownies, Knockers and Redcaps of the Caledonian and Solstice Isles. Seelie.

Dullahan: Heavily armored dark knights of the Unseelie armies. Cursed Undead Unseelie.

Dyrad: Deer folk who have bodies similar to Centaurs. Seelie.

Fachan: a race of deformed giants, possibly related to Formorians.

Firbolg: Humble mountain giants said to have been metamorphosed into giant trees. Seelie.

Formorian: Possibly extinct and monstrous giants who are said to sleep deep under the earth. Related to Orcneas. Cursed.

Green-Lady: plump, elderly female fairies known to use healing magic and able to break curses. Seelie.

Hamadyrad: Deerfolk who run on two legs and play magical instruments, related to satyrs, centaurs and hamadyrads. Seelie.

Knockers: Relatives of dwarves, known for living deep in the earth and mining gems. Hearth Fae.

Leanan Sidhe: Vampiric dark elves and servants of the Bane-Sidhe.

Johtun: Once living frost giants now undead and leading great armies of Draugr. Cursed Undead.

Leprechaun: relatives of Cluricans, more sober and greedy than their cousins. Hearth Fae.

Nukalvee: Undead relatives to centaurs. Cursed Undead.

Orcneas: savage warlike, blind and cursed humanoids with chiropteran features and they dwell deep under the earth. Cursed.

Pucas: A species of cat-humanoids distantly related to Cu-sith but far less vicious and much more focused on being tricksters and playing pranks. They can shapeshift quite easily and prefer taking the forms of horses. Hearth Fae.

Pixies: a minature type of winged fae that can use low level illusions and is quite talkative. Also known for playing pranks. Seelie.

Red-Caps: Cursed Dwarves, larger and stronger than dwarves and formidable fighters. They are obsessed with warfare. Unseelie.

Selkie: Fae who can transform from lovely young men and women or into playful, talking seals. Seelie.

Slaugh: Swarms and swarms of sadistic, miniature fae with mouths filled with razor sharp fangs. Known to swarms over and abduct sheep or people and sometimes eat them alive while in the air. Unseelie.

Satyrs: Mountain goat relatives of Hamadyrads known to play their flutes in the mountains. Seelie.

Trow: deformed giants, relatives of Trolls from Johtunhiem, with armored and rocky skin, massive claws for tearing through stone and a nasty dispostion when violently awakened. Generally prefer sleeping deeply. Hearth fae.

GODS:

Angus: Pansexual male god of love

Anu: Another name for Danu. Ancient.

Balor: Father god of the formorian enemies, the sea demons. Also some gods are related to this terrible titan. He was slain by Lugh in battle.

Bres: Son of Balor, Also Half Formorian and was the second king of the Tuatha De Denaan before being slain in battle by Lugh.

Brigid: Goddess of Healing, birth, life party of the trinity of goddesses and or crones. Healing, poetry, and wisdom.

Cailleach: Ancient Crone goddess of Winter and Ice. Ancient.

Cerunnos: Horned god of male verility and creator of the hamadyrads and satyrs. God of forests and nature. Ancient.

Crom: Son of Orcus, God of the mountains and one of the fathers to the ancient orcish race Ancient Danaan God who slayed Orcus. Since Crom broke his oath to Orcus he was cursed and turned into a mountain.

The Dagda: Giant, half firbolg god of strength, verility, gluttony and fertility. Part of the male trinity.

Danu: Mother of the Tuatha De Denaan Gods, mother of earth, harvests and springtime.

Ancient.

Grom: Brother to Crom who helped slay Orcus, he was cursed because he broke his oath to Orcus and his soul became traped in his enchanted greatsword. Another father to ancient orcish race and the cursed offshoots known as Kork.

Epona: mother goddess of the horses and centaurs.

Ith: Danaan was god of agriculture, grain and harvests. When slain by three Tautha De Danaan Sidhe lords it was his death that brought about the great Ostramann invasions from Johtunhiem, Hravenholme, Thurgundia and beyond.

Lugos: aka Lugh the sun god and known as the king of gods and god of many skills. He is skilled in combat with a spear. His father is Cian (a god) and his mother is Ethniu (formorian daughter of Balor, therefore Lugh is the grandson of his arch nemesis Balor).

Macha: Modern Goddess of Horses and fertile farm land.

Mannan mac Lear: The great sea god. Son of the ancient sea god known only as Lear. Said to be the guardian of the isles of Mann and having given gifts to a local ruler named Cormac in the ancient wind age.

Morrigan: Goddess of War, Fate, Soverinigty and Death. Consort to The Dagda. Trinity

Nuada Airgetlám: First King of the Gods. He had his arm torn off by a Firbolg Champion known as Sreng at the first battle of Maig Tuired. A Silver arm was forged for him by Goibniu, the black smith and magically attached by Dian Cecht the healer. He was slain by Balor who in turn was slain by Lugh at the second battle of Maig Tuired. Now kindly god of the afterlife.

Orcus: Foreign Titan, psychopomp and cannibal god of the underworld.

The first father of both Orcs and the Formorians. Balor is actually one of his most loyal sons. Vowed to slay the Aesir and the Vanir (Tautha De Denaan) for slaying his father Ymir in the Dawn Age.

Ogma: aka Ogmios is a good of writing, bards, education and learning. He is part of the male Trinity with the Dagda.

Rhiannon: Goddess of Rebirth, the fae, spiritworld, dreams, mystery and inspiration. Also Trinity.

Sea Mother: Goddess of kelp forests and worshiped by Selkies she wars with a terrible frost giant known as Taran who comes from the northern Oceans.

Sreng: Champion of the Firbolg who ripped off Prince Nuada's arm at the first battle of maig Tuired. He was given a region of Caledonia/Samhain known as Hibernia to rule over after being defeated by Nuada...it is said the fierce-some Fachan giants are his descendants.

Taran: a terrible sea giant who controls freezing storms and icy waters, he can also summon armies of drowned dead and draugr from the freezing depths.

Taranis: A God of Thunder, Lightning and Storms who flies across the sky in a chariot. Ancient.

Runes:

The Runic language is used by Wyrds and Shamans in Johtunhiem, the Issenvald, Gunnarholme, Hravenholme, the Yule Isles and finally the Isles of Samhain. Connacht, being a Galeo-Nordic/Ostramann Gallowgalas has learned how to harness both the Dwarven Runic language and Vyzantine Alchemy, he can especially harmonize both disciplines.

(Eldar Runic Alphabet)

ᚠᚢᚦᚨᚱᚲᚷᚹᚺᚾᛁᛃᛇᛈᛉᛋᛏᛒᛖᛗᛚᛜᛟᛞ

1.) FEHU: Rune of Cattle, Rune of Prattle, Word of Wealth and Sexual Health. When activated this rune can help Connacht find a treasure stash or vein in the mountains. It can also determine if something is an actually valuable gem or precious metal.

2)   URUZ: Rune of Strength, Rune of Length, Symbol of Bulls; Crusher of Skulls. represents a Bull. It symbolizes Strength, Tenacity, Courage, Untamed Potential, Freedom. Connacht can activate this run and it gives him on incredible feat of strength.

3)   THURISAZ: Rune of Thor, Rider of Boars, Lord of Storms, his Hammer Transforms. Holy Rune of Thor or Thunnar. This rune can infuse Connacht's weapon with electricity, unleash a deafening thunderbolt or scream and even make a weapon fly and return to his hands.

4.)ANSUZ: Rune of the River, Rune of the Giver, Rune of the Speaker, Rune of the Seeker. Connacht can use it to read a forgotten language or even speak an unknown language or learn a new language rapidly.

5.) RAIDHO: Rune of the Wagon, sip upon the Flagon, Rune of Travel, Watch time unravel. When this rune is activated by Connacht horses can become tireless and it even allows him and allies to run uphill for hours.

6.) KUANAN: Rune of Fire, Rune of Desire, Rune of Passion, Rune of Action. It represents a Torch. When this rune is activated it can allow Connacht to warm his body in freezing conditions, fly into a litteral burning rage and spew fire from his breath. His weapon can also be sheated in flames burning through swarms of enemies.

7)   **GEBO: Rune of Gifts, for joy to uplift, Rune of Generosity and of False Modesty.** Represents a Gift. When Connacht activates this rune he can then give a gift of some kind and the gift bearer would be hard pressed to betray him or and vice versa.

8)   **WUNJO: Rune of Merriment, Rune of Accomplishment, Rune of Harmony, Rune of Honesty.** represents Joy. Connacht can place this upon a musical instrument and it can instantly lift the spirits of humans or fae.

9)   **HAGALAZ: Rune of Hail, Rune of Gale, Rune of Wind that leaves one Skinned.** represents Hail. When this rune is activated it can unleashed a vicious cyclone of wind that blows arrows and javelins aside as well as obscures Connacht.

10)   **NAUTHIZ: Rune of Hardship, Rune of Guardship, Rune of Determination and who finds Salvation.** represents Need. Connacht can use this rune to help his allies overcome fear and despair or when cast reversed can weaken enemy moral.

11)   **ISA: Rune of Frost, Rune of Ice, Cold Winds Lost who pays the Price.** represents Ice. Connacht can use this rune to freeze fires, armor and even weapons in place, stopping or slowing armored foes.

12)   **JERA: Rune of Years, Rune of Time, Traverse the Spheres in icy Rime.**   represents the Year. I Connacht can use this rune to determine how long till a harvest is ready or what is assailing a harvest. He can also easily determine both the time of day and night using this Rune even underground.

13) **EIHWAZ: Rune of Yew, Rune of Trees, See the Dew with utmost Ease.** represents a Yew Tree. Connacht can use this to psychically communicate with trees, plants or the dead themselves especially of past events.

14) **PERTHRO: Rune of Dice, Rune of Fate, Some rolled Twice while others come Late.** represents a Dice Cup. It symbolizes Fate, Chance, Mystery, Destiny, Secrets. This rune can be activated to make dice rolls extremely lucky or unlucky based on who the spell is cast upon and if the rune is cast right side up or upside down.

15.)**ALGIZ: Rune of Elk, Rune of Herd; From same Yelk their forces Spurred:** represents an Elk. This rune can be used to find problems with animals and feel their feelings or have psychic visions of their thoughts. It can also summon herd animals to fight on the users behalf.

16) **SOWILO: Rune of Sun, Rune of Purity, Darkness it Shuns and grants Security.** represents the Sun. Connacht can use this rune to purge disease and poison and illuminate darkness.

17) **TIWAZ: Rune of Tyr, lord of War, Who knows not Fear, Justice settles the Score.** represents the god Tyr. This run can activate a potent but short lived rune that makes armor and shield nigh impervious. It can also make one equal to their opponent in a duel for a short time.

18.) **BERKANA: Rune of Birch, where the doves Perch, Rune of Fertility and loving Civility.** represents a Birch Tree. Connacht uses this wound to heal grievous wounds and possibly even regenerate missing limbs. Some say this Rune can even bring stillborn infants back to life.

19.) **EHWAZ: Rune of Horse, Rune of Force, move through the Course back to the Source.** represents a Horse. This rune can allow Connacht to leap very high or long distances. This rune can also help one find the right route to a location or know the direction of lost destination.

20)	**MANNAZ: Rune of Man, Rune of Friend, together on Sedan with coin to Lend.** Represents Humanity.. Using this rune makes it very hard for others to hide the truth from Connacht and it can help him persuade hostile people at least to help with something trivial.

21)	**LAGUZ: Rune of Waves, Rune of Hope, Dreams that Crave and Dreams that Cope.** represents Water. Connacht can use this rune to cleanse filthy water or make ships and boats more stable in rough waters. Connacht can also swim in very cold water and hold his breath for a long time using this Rune.

22)	**INGUZ: Rune of Seed and Rune of Growth, Do take heed and keep thy Oath.** represents a Seed. It symbolizes Goals, Growth, Change, Common Sense, The Hearth (Home). When this rune is activated it allow Connacht to read minds especially of allies but more difficult among enemies.

23)	**OTHALA: Rune of Heritage, Rune of Ancestors, Honor thy Parentage less they become Monsters.** represents Inheritance. Connacht can place this rune in a home and the hearth spirits can psychically alert him to invaders robbing his facility. Placing this rune on crops or gardens also makes them very fertile but it can only last for a year.

24.) **DAGAZ: Rune of Dawn, Rune of Awakening, So Awakens the Fawn to find what is Happening:** represents Dawn. When Connacht activates this rune his weapon can unleash a great aura of sunlight in darkness. This Rune is also said to awaken powerful giants and trolls sleeping in statues and trees from their eternal slumber.

VI Longsword, Greatsword and Weapon Techniques:....

Offensive stances: The Stances are used to deliver powerful area of effect and singular attacks....

Roof Stance (Vom Tag): The most offensive Stance.... The sword is lifted over the head with the blade pointed behind the swordsmen and the pommel facing the adversary.... It can easily deliver a devastating strike of wrath from over head splitting an enemies skull, chopping their spear in half or slitting their throat with one mighty blow.... This stance can perform sword twirling, Zwerchau strikes to the temple or devastating Strikes of Wrath....

Ox Stance (Ochs): The sword tip is now facing the enemy and the pommel is facing the swordsmen, held directly horizontal from the swordsmen's face and pointing like an impaling spear, great for countering attacks and then impaling one's enemy through the neck and or eye....

Fool Stance (Alber): Where the swordsmen blade is facing down to the ground in a downward and vertical position, its a deceptive stance generally to coax defensive fighters into striking vulnerable areas but not seeing the deadly counter attack that is incoming....

The Plow (Pflug): Can be used offensively or defensively.... The sword is facing vertically in front of the swordsmen and leaning forwards at a 45 degree angle.... The Swordsmen is holding the handle down near his navel.... This stance can attack the hands, arms and face with counterattacks....

Defensive Stances: These techniques are used to deflect, counter and stun armored foes....

Half-Swording: Where the swordsmen, grabs the secondary handle of the sword known as a Ricasso and uses the sword like a quarter staff to block, stab, bludgeon with the tip and pommel.... Its is probably the most defensive of stances.... The tip of the sword is used like a spear to poke eyes behind visors.... This is also a defensive stance used primarily against enemies with superior armor and the swordsmen can easily switch in the Mordenhau stance....

Mordenhau: The murder stroke, where the sword is held completely ass backwards from the plow, where the blade is held by the hands and the pommel and crossguard are used as blunt, bludgeoning weapons to deliver concussions to armored opponents....

Near-Ward Stance: a powerful defensive stance where the sword faces behind the swordsmen horizontally and facing down like a tail and it generally is used to deliver a powerful rising counterattack to strike the enemies downward blow and deflect with a side step and then deliver a devastating counter attack....

Zornhut: Similar to the Near Ward Stance but it looks like an upside down and backwards plow stance with the sword held directly behind the swordsmen and facing down vertically, it functions similar to the Near ward in delivering a powerful counterattack with footwork, followed by a lethal secondary attack....

Special Thanks:....
To these authors and creators for they are the Giants that I have stood upon their shoulders and learned to craft my artwork, research, inspiration and lore to help me write this fantasy book and future series.... Inspiration from and special thanks to....
WIKIPEDIA....
Grim's Fairy Tales by the Brother's Grim
Tales of North Mythology by H....A.... Guerber
Faeries by Biran Froud and Alan Lee
Irish Fairy and Folk Tales by Fall River Press
The Prose Edda by Snorri Sturluson
The Book of Celtic Myths by Jennifer Emick
The Hobbit by J.R. Tolkien
A Game of Thrones by George R.R.Martin
The Witcher; The Last Wish by Andrzej Sapkowski
(5) Story Crow - YouTube
(5) Irish Myths - YouTube
Medievalists....net - Where the Middle Ages Begin (For the riddles)
Greek riddles - Wikipedia (more riddles)
DARKFOOL
OX
PIG
GWAR
BABY METAL
KMFDM
THE HU
NINI MUSIC
MINISTRY
3 TEETH
WHITE ZOMBIE
MASTODON
DETHKLOK
3 INCHES OF BLOOD
MADELYN MONAGHAN
LEO ROJAS
JONNA JINTON
ARYUN-GOA
OTYKEN
EVAN PLAYS DULCIMER

AFRO CELT SOUND SYSTEM
WHITE ZOMBIE

ROB ZOMBIE
SKYRIM
GOD OF WAR
BALDUR'S GATE 3
DUNGEONS AND DRAGONS
NUMENERA
VAMPIRE THE MASQUERADE
THE GUYS AND GALS AT PRISTINE TOWER!!!!
VALHYR.COM....
.... **Notes from the Author:....**

A Note from the Author, Azhorg.

The Lunar Saga of Samhain was written to actually be a place to give voices to ethnic and sexual minorities a voice.... Lady Rhona is an expression of the hardships women faced and still face due to arranged marriages and societal pressures.

The Unseelie fae are an expression of people oppressed by colonization but also of people living in the past and making their trauma their entire personalities, they represent the unhealthy obsession of revenge and living in the past.... The Draugr are the sins of one's ancestors constantly plaguing, an eternal guilt trip of genocide, conquest and toxic masculinity to the main characters and are examples of what not to emulate especially for Ostromann and Nordic characters.

Yes there are lovable queer characters and hot consensual sex but this is to illustrate the real world urges of human beings and not have them live up to impossible, narcissistic standards.... Nobody is perfect in this world and there is a lot of moral gray but there is also a clear black and white as well.... I wanted to give a commercial voice to Celtic and Germanic lore that was actually badly plagiarized and demonized almost a hundred years ago.

I want "The Lunar Saga of Samhain" to be a place where rare and endangered cultures and languages to be expressed once again.... I honestly hope no one takes offense to my story it was meant to be thrilling, dark, emotional, filled with love and sex and adventure.... Humanity and the fae's worst enemy is basically itself expressed with monstrous curses, bigotry, revenge and never forgiving.